THE TRUMPET
AT TWISP

HERE'S WHAT PEOPLE ARE SAYING ABOUT THIS BOOK!

"A compelling and timely read! A contemporary war story that will engage readers while reminding them of battles fought beyond our normal lives. I so enjoyed The Trumpet at Twisp—the great characters and engaging story. I gained such an experience of the Middle East conflict."

CINDY MARTINUSEN—Author, *The Salt Garden*

"Doris Elaine Fell has always been a force to be reckoned with, but Trumpet at Twisp strikes the reader right between the eyes. With up-to-the-minute insights into realistic characters caught up in the twists of fate in our present war, this author makes the battle personal for each of us. An award winner for sure."

HANNAH ALEXANDER—Author, *Hideaway* and *Safe Haven*

"Readers who relish a taut, fast-paced story torn from today's headlines will adore Doris Elaine Fell's dazzling new novel, Trumpet at Twisp. Fell spins a spellbinding tale brimming with international intrigue, romance, exotic, far-flung locales, compelling characters, and a multilayered plot with enough twists and turns to leave you breathless."

CAROLE GIFT PAGE—Author, *Becoming a Woman of Passion*

"A generational story that will captivate you from page one and make you long for more as you read the final line. You'll be drawn to these true to life characters that have lived and loved their country. Give yourself the pleasure of following their journeys as they work to balance life between home and the battlefront."

JUDITH MILLER—Coauthor, Bells of Lowell and Lights of Lowell series.

"Trumpet at Twisp seeps into your soul. A modern-day saga of tragedy and triumph, grit and grace."

KATHY HERMAN—Author, The Baxter Series and Poor Mrs. Rigsby; www.kathyherman.com

THE TRUMPET AT TWISP

Doris Elaine Fell

HOWARD
Fiction

Our purpose at Howard Publishing is to:

• *Increase faith* in the hearts of growing Christians

• *Inspire holiness* in the lives of believers

• *Instill hope* in the hearts of struggling people everywhere

Because He's coming again!

THE TRUMPET AT TWISP © 2004 by Doris Elaine Fell
All rights reserved. Printed in the United States of America
Published by Howard Publishing Co., Inc.
3117 North 7th Street, West Monroe, LA 71291-2227
www.howardpublishing.com
In association with the literary agency of Alive Communications, Inc.
7680 Goddard Street, Suite 200, Colorado Springs, CO 80920.

04 05 06 07 08 09 10 11 12 13   10 9 8 7 6 5 4 3 2 1

Edited by Ramona Cramer Tucker
Interior design by Gabe Cardinale
Cover design by Chris Gilbert, UDG | DesignWorks

Library of Congress Cataloging-in-Publication Data

Fell, Doris Elaine.
    The Trumpet at Twisp / Doris Elaine Fell.
      p. cm.
    ISBN 1-58229-391-0
    1. Persian Gulf War, 1991—Casualties—Fiction. 2. September 11 Terrorist Attacks,
2001—Fiction. 3. Persian Gulf War, 1991—Veterans—Fiction. 4. Friendly fire (Military
science)—Fiction. 5. Washington (State)—Fiction. 6. Mothers and sons—Fiction. 7. War
widows—Fiction. I. Title.

PS3556.E4716T78 2004
813'.54—dc22

                                                                    2004052360

To Ryan, my first great-nephew,
and to his siblings, Jesse and Hannah Marie,
with deep affection.
We may drift apart as you grow older
(even as I grow older),
but I will always love you and pray for you.

With thanks to Scott, Jim and Judith, Nancy and
Deborah for military, technical,
and historical advice.

To Jim S., who survived the Anzio Beachhead,
and in memory of the men and women
who gave the last full measure of devotion
on the desert sands of Iraq and Kuwait—
and for those who loved them and mourn them.

PRAISE HIM WITH THE SOUND OF THE TRUMPET!

—Psalm 150:3

PROLOGUE

SPRING 2003

Boom! Boom! Boom!

The night erupted into a ball of fire.

Then an eerie stillness. Darkness hovering. Dawn not quite cracking the horizon.

Seconds later another thundering blast ripped through the sky—explosion after explosion.

Robinson Gilbert stood on the rooftop of the Palestine Meridian Hotel, his heart thumping erratically as the bombs exploded over Baghdad. The high-rise swayed, rocking with increasing intensity. He expected the twenty-story hotel to crumble and turn to rubble. He waited, palms sweaty.

His spine tingled, his back so rigid that he felt taller than his six-feet-four. Standing there, staring at a world gone mad, Robinson was disillusioned, weighed down by the fog of a war he didn't want. The sky glowed a fiery crimson, silhouetted against the predawn. Mushrooms of yellow and orange fire clouds reflected in the shimmering water of the Tigris River. In the distance funnels of black smoke rose eerily above the center of this city of five million.

Other journalists scrambled to the rooftop to join him—one of them still struggling into his pants, another tucking his polo shirt in place. The reporter from Munich shouldered his video camera. The young Italian photographer, Ricardo de Nuccio, shoved his big, crooked toe into his Gucci loafers.

De Nuccio swore as he dropped his camera bag and pawed inside for his gas mask. His handsome face distorted, his voice

1

mocking, he glowered up at Gilbert. "So you got your war?"

"Not my war." Robinson's retort was muted by another blast.

Peter, the Brit who often shared coffee with Robinson, wedged his way in-between them. "I find this bombs-away a right nasty way to awaken. What about you, Gilbert?"

"Couldn't sleep."

"You and your sixth sense."

Words burst past Robinson's dry lips. "I'm thinking about my son."

"Sorry. He's one of the embeds, right?"

Robinson glanced at de Nuccio and lowered his voice. "I'm the fool who got Robbie the job. I should have encouraged him to stay home."

"Reporters have always covered wars. It's a journalist's high." Peter winced. "As sick as that sounds to the general public . . . Don't worry, Gilbert. That kid of yours will have to kick the sand for days just to get here. But we've got a front seat for the showdown."

On the streets below came the wail of emergency sirens. Shouts of protest in Arabic. The pop and crackle of burning buildings. The acrid smell of smoke. Of death.

Robinson's chest heaved, his breathing spasmodic. For the first time in his long career as a correspondent, he wondered whether this was the war—the one more byline—that would take him out in a blaze of glory. If so, he would die fulfilling his dream of being on hand for the downfall of Saddam Hussein.

But glory? What kind of a fool was he? Some—even some at the Pentagon—viewed the unilateral journalist as little more than a mercenary, a soldier of fortune independently roaming the streets of Baghdad. Call him what they would. He had his eye on the story—and the commitment and passion to tell it.

He'd spent his career taking the risks that put him in the line of fire. But hadn't the past thirty years been enough? Wasn't it time to unplug his computer, give up jetlag, and step back from the limelight far away from the famed Gilbert headlines and public recognition?

He was close to burnout after spending a lifetime covering wars and dangerous overseas assignments from Vietnam to the Persian Gulf War. He'd covered the home front too—from the 9/11 terrorism attack to the Columbia shuttle fragmenting in the sky in February. Then he'd nosed around on his own, doing an independent probe as NASA investigated the disaster. Even now he'd chosen to go it alone to cover the war from the heart of Baghdad.

"Did you report on the first Gulf War, Gilbert?"

"Yeah."

"I missed that one."

And be glad you did, Robinson wanted to say. He'd covered both wars—a fight for the same territory but with different excuses. One war for the liberation of Kuwait. This one for the freedom of the Iraqis in a war against terrorism. This war was different. For the first time in his career, he would appear on a television news report as a guest. He preferred straight journalism. But he wanted the public at home to know what was happening. Robinson seldom made his political leanings public, but inside he struggled against the bureaucratic mumbling that protecting oil wells was a calling card to war.

Now, as the hotel shook again, he turned to the man beside him. "We never finished the job the first time."

Robinson wondered whether Peter supported Prime Minister Blair or had any political affirmations at all. Peter, an amicable sort, seemed almost blind without his glasses.

Peter squinted as he gazed at the fireworks. "That kid of yours . . . is he married?"

"Engaged—this Middle East crisis delayed the wedding."

Another guided missile slammed into its target. Another bomb shattered Saddam's city. The explosions pricked at Robinson's nerves as more blasts shook the foundation. He couldn't see them or hear them in the night sky, but he imagined that the pilots in the F-117 Stealth fighters were running on sheer adrenaline as they dropped their bunker busters. And, somewhere out in the Gulf, American warships were firing their cruise missiles. He shivered, excusing it as excitement, as pride in his country. In a way he felt distant, detached, but it still bothered him. Did he have any right to exhilaration at the death of this city?

His dry mouth tasted bile. Would he even be alive when his son reached Baghdad?

"Why don't you try to reach your son by satellite?" the Brit suggested.

"I've tried to reach Robbie for days just to hear his voice. But all this high-tech equipment is useless." Robinson's words faltered. "I just wanted to tell my son to keep his head down."

He knew from the Al Jazeera television coverage that the coalition ground forces had crossed the Kuwaiti border, heading northward. Thousands of British and American troops were mapping out roads of their own, picking their way through minefields, fighting off the bursts of fire from enemy troops, and battling for every inch of the 350 miles of desert sand. His son was in the middle of it.

"He'll be okay, Gilbert. Just pray for him."

As the plumes of smoke rose, Robinson gave a brusque nod and braced for the next tremor before inching away from the others.

As he watched the city burn, he thought of hell. Thought of God and wondered whether he had waited too long. His son, Robbie, was the praying man in the family. Robinson knew there were no guarantees in this war . . . or in any war, but he had long held God at bay. Now that life seemed closer to hell than heaven, he longed to speak to his son. Longed to commune with the God he did not know.

Instead, he gripped his satellite videophone and spoke in a booming voice to the nation back home: "This is Robinson Gilbert, once again reporting live from Baghdad . . ."

In a few hours the early morning sunlight would stream through Meagan Juddman's living room windows, unveiling the craggy Cascade Peaks and the Methow Valley she loved. March hovered between seasons, with spring's bouquets of wildflowers budding on the hillsides and the melting snows of winter rushing down the Twisp River.

But for now the mountains were silhouettes of darkness, and the news only added to her despair.

Meagan's legs went numb as she stared at the television screen. Last week the news had focused on war protestors on the streets of California and in Paris. On unsettled resolutions at the UN. On the president and his war team setting deadlines—a leadership determined to go it alone into the Iraqi desert.

Yesterday the airwaves crackled with reports on the convoy of young soldiers waiting to cross the Kuwaiti border into Iraq. Of men checking their weapons. Touching pictures of soldiers being baptized in makeshift baptisteries in the sand. Of men—boys really—kneeling on one knee, eyes closed in prayer, their M-16s and gas masks clutched in their hands.

Now every channel had turned to the city of Baghdad. Meagan watched the blurred image of war unfolding and shuddered at the sound of explosions, the color of the fiery sky. Her knees buckled at the thought of innocent people dying. She eased back toward the sofa and sank into its soft cushions.

The knots in her stomach tightened. Casualties were inevitable. She knew that some of these men and women would not come home again. For them the war would be over. But for their loved ones the war would never end. Meagan's eyes filled with tears, the bitter tears she thought were long behind her. *Déjà vu!* History reinventing itself. The battle for Baghdad had come full circle, once again threatening the lives of those she loved.

As the television transmission cleared, the war correspondent's face came into focus. Meagan recognized him and remembered the last time she saw him. Robinson Gilbert was still a handsome man. Tall. Straight as an arrow. Thick hair, windblown at the moment. He stood on the edge of the hotel rooftop, looking much younger than his years with his shirt sleeves rolled up, his collar unbuttoned, and a camera slung over his shoulder. He was twenty years her senior, yet she remembered him as incredibly charming, his voice deep and seductive. But today his normally flirtatious gaze was solemn.

Once—in the darkest time in her life—he had tried to help her battle the Washington bureaucracy. Would he—could he— help her again? Her hand shook as she reached for the telephone. She'd place a call to his editor in Washington DC and beg to be put in touch with Gilbert. But her timing was off. The switchboard was down.

The Pentagon was too busy with its war to consider Meagan's needs. The army too distant. The news broadcasters too busy gathering news to think of consoling widows or comforting children without fathers, parents without sons. A long time ago Robinson Gilbert had told her if she ever needed him, to let him know. She had sought him out twice before. He had failed her once. But if she could contact him, maybe he could track down the whereabouts of Ryan and Tharon in the desert of Iraq.

She forced herself to look away from the television. Her eyes settled on the photos on her credenza—the familiar faces of the men she loved. Cameron in the center. Ryan to his left. Tharon on his right. Meagan disliked commercial photography. For her, candid snapshots were more realistic, and always filled with memories. Her lip trembled as she stared at the picture of Cameron the last time she saw him, trumpet in hand.

And then there was Ryan—more boy than man—glancing back over his shoulder with a quick wave and quicker smile. At last she focused on Tharon—dear Tharon in his work jeans, his bare back to the sun, tearing down the FOR SALE sign on his property in the mountains.

Her foreboding deepened. *Keep looking at them, Meagan. You may never see any of them again.*

PART 1

Spring 2003

Even though I walk
Through the valley of the shadow of death,
I will fear no evil, for you are with me . . .
In the presence of my enemies.

—Psalm 23:4–5

CHAPTER 1

Sandstorm!

For days the greatest fighting force in the world had wilted under the sweltering heat, waiting for the convoy of tanks and armored vehicles to move out across the Kuwaiti border into the unknown. Into war. Into sand dunes. Into yesterday's drenching rains.

They were an invincible marching army, moving on command. Bravado and the confidence of youth abounded. Whoops of delight that the wait was over. Eagerness to get the job done—to go home again.

Everything—even the soldiers—looked the color of sand. Except for their facial expressions and voices, the soldiers in desert-camouflage uniforms appeared identical.

Robbie Gilbert, an embedded journalist, kept a frayed photo of Adrienne Winters in the liner of his helmet. Beguiling Adrienne had spun magic on his heart the day he met her in Paris. They'd been just a couple of kids then, attending the American Academy near the River Seine. He thought her beautiful. She thought him ridiculous, amusing. But she had always been his girl. Today was supposed to be his wedding day. Instead, he was 350 miles from Baghdad, a world away from his fiancée.

Clutching his laptop, he wrote in his journal: *Adrienne, I miss you, but I'm proud to be riding with these men and women.*

Day two brought more sweat and sand. Another twenty-four hours packed like sardines in the Bradley, their cheeks pressed against the muzzle of their M-16s, their bodies sleep deprived and covered with dust. Robbie rode with them, but they didn't accept him. He carried a computer and a tape recorder, not an M-16 and extra ammunition. How could he shoulder his share of the battle?

But in the weeks back in Kuwait, he'd slept where they slept—in the belly of an armored vehicle or bedded down by the wheels of an Abrams. He'd showered with his clothes on—just like they did—accomplishing both bath and laundry with the same bar of soap. He'd used the same latrine. Heard the same jokes. Kicked the same soccer ball out over the desert sands where the men, with reluctance, acknowledged his skills.

At dusk Robbie kept his eyes cocked for foot-long desert snakes. At dawn he waited eagerly for mail call. With gut determination he rode the strenuous midnight maneuvers with them. But out here on the long push toward Baghdad, he felt isolated, estranged from these soldiers who cleaned their weapons as he sat with a laptop balanced on his knees. These last few days he felt less of a man for being a noncombatant and twice had been forced to defend his position as war correspondent with those in command. But didn't he swat the same bugs as these men? Eat the same MREs? Wasn't his back also rubbed raw as they rode along with their bodies braced against the metal of the armored vehicle?

His only comfort came with thoughts of Adrienne: her soft mauve lips against his. Her warm body in his arms, embracing him. Her large mahogany eyes misting when he said good-bye.

He glanced at the faces of the men across from him. Somber. Their thoughts, like his, no doubt on their own loved ones. *Oh, God, I want to be up to this job. I want to drive into Baghdad as their friend.*

With the battle ahead, how could his prayer waft its way to heaven? It struggled to slip past his cracked lips. His body clock was out of kilter, with days and nights turned inside out. He and the soldiers weren't riding midnight maneuvers any longer. Their drive northward was the real thing. Relentless, miserable days with the glare of the sun on sand and the fear of the enemy appearing from nowhere. And miserable nights of pain—riding over the sand dunes, sitting upright in the armored vehicle with their heads swaying and their spines merging with metal.

And then day four. All day as the convoy roared toward Baghdad a wind stirred over the sand, whistling through the sagebrush. Swirling with increasing intensity. The men lowered their night-vision goggles, but a fine coating of sand fogged their vision, obliterating the path ahead of them.

They kept to their grueling pace for another half-hour, advancing under a full moon until they were left scanning a horizon they could no longer see and staring into the blackness on either side of them. The convoy came to an abrupt halt with the *shamal* gusting at sixty miles an hour, creating undulating waves in the desert sand. Blinding the soldiers to their surroundings and to the threat of the enemy lurking there. Choking them. Coating their nostrils with sand. Making sandpaper of their throats. Pelting their skin with grit.

Robbie scrambled down from the back of the Bradley and hunkered down by one of the Abrams tanks. As he landed hard on his rump, his Kevlar helmet pushed forward; it rimmed his thick brows, its strap rubbing his bristled chin raw.

A soldier dropped down beside him and slapped his ammo box into the sand. "That you, Gilbert?"

"Yeah."

He recognized Sergeant Danston's voice. Danston was a ten-year army man. Confident. Purposeful. One of those sticklers for military rules and regulations. When his men complained, he ordered them to clean their guns again. Yesterday, when the convoy slowed its thundering drive, he'd shoved two of the men out the rear end of the Bradley and made them run a pace or two in the desert heat. They kicked sand for several yards before Danston extended his hand and pulled them back on board.

Right now Danston's rugged face looked weather-beaten, the whites of his eyes blood-red. He bragged about taking all of his men home again, bragged about keeping out of the line of fire, but he wore his blood type in bold print on his flak jacket.

This time the sergeant grumbled. "Just my luck. I'm opposed to outsiders riding with us. And here I am, sitting out this storm with a journalist."

"Better than waiting it out with Saddam," Robbie threw in.

Struggling to his feet again, Danston braced against the wind as he shook out his canvas bedroll and tucked it over the wheel of the Abrams. For ten minutes the two of them huddled beneath the smothering makeshift shelter with the stench of human sweat between them and the wind snapping at the canvas. Then the *shamal* whipped into a frenzy that swept their Tinkertoy refuge away.

"Sorry, Gilbert. I'm not an engineer—that's why I went infantry." Danston cocked his ear. "I don't like it."

"Sitting out a storm with me?"

"That too. But this weather has brought our whole convoy to a standstill. We're sitting targets. The enemy could attack from any direction while we wait out this storm."

Robbie held up five fuzzy fingers. "But how can they see us?"

"They grew up in sandstorms," Danston shot back. Then, more amicable, he added, "You got any family, Gilbert?"

Robbie crooked his neck, sending unwanted twitches along his spine.

Sergeant Danston leaned closer. "You know, those folks we left back home. The ones who know more about this bloody war than we know, thanks to CNN . . . Do you work for CNN?"

You know I don't. "No, for a syndicate in Virginia."

Danston spit into the sand. "Haven't read your reports. Don't know whether you are any good or not."

Robbie bristled. "My editor is satisfied. That's what counts."

"They're not apt to pass muster with me. I don't think there's any place in this man's army for a noncombatant."

"Look, I'll do my job. You do yours," Robbie fired back. "You're good at what you do, Sergeant, and I'm good at my assignment. We've been locking horns ever since we met in Kuwait. Whether you like it or not, I was assigned to this unit, and I'm going all the way to Baghdad with you."

The sergeant stiffened. "You know, I could have you sent back for insubordination."

"Fat chance. You wouldn't like the headline: *Sergeant Danston Sends Journalist Home*. Besides, I think they've canceled all public transportation from here back to Kuwait . . ."

Robbie was exhausted from fighting the desert heat and trying to stave off the fine particles of sand that bombarded them. He didn't want to fight the sandstorm and the sergeant's contempt any longer. He lowered his head, agitated that Danston had gotten the best of him. Robbie's breathing grew more labored as the sand clogged his nostrils. He wanted this man as his friend. His life depended on it.

"Look, Sergeant, I was out of line," Robbie apologized. "You have a lot on your mind, taking raw recruits into battle."

Danston growled back, "You're a greenhorn too. But I've promised my men I'm going to take them all home again."

"That's a heavy burden."

The sergeant's eyes darkened. He leaned over and thumped the laptop sheltered in Robbie's Kevlar vest. "Gilbert, when the time comes, stay out of our way."

"All roads lead north, Sergeant. Yours and mine. We have the same goal. Get this war over with and get back home."

"That's settled then . . . So do you have a family?"

"Yeah, I have a family." Robbie thought about his girl back at the Winterfest Estates. He didn't want to talk about Adrienne to this stranger—nor awaken his longing for her.

There was little to say, either, of the mother who had walked out when he was a boy. But he could speak with pride of his dad, his best friend. "I have a dad."

"Sitting in some office with his feet on the desktop?"

"That doesn't describe him." An unwanted ache formed in Robbie's parched throat at the image of his dad: tall, silver-haired, deep bass chuckle. Cocky and arrogant, but with a heart of gold for those who were hurting. "He's another noncombatant—a journalist, always on the run for a news story. Right now he's covering the war from Baghdad."

"Holed up in the Palestine Hotel?"

"Yeah."

"Is he some kind of nut?"

Robbie ignored the barb. "Dad likes being in the thick of things."

He saw momentary envy in Danston's eyes. Or were more flecks of sand burrowing beneath his eyelids?

"Maybe your dad will meet up with Saddam before we do."

"Maybe."

Danston spit out more particles of sand and darkened phlegm. "I go where the army sends me. But you could be home eating a chocolate sundae. Is covering a war worth this misery?"

"It's our job."

"Then you must be in it for the glory ride."

Another soldier crawled over to the spot beside them. "Hey, Sarge, give our modern-day Ernie Pyle a chance."

"Why should I, Mitchell?" Danston frowned. "How'd you know about Pyle? He was a journalist in World War II. Long before your time."

"Before your time, too, Sarge, but my grandpa told me about him." The kid pushed the strap of his helmet away from his chafed chin and secured a scarf over his face. It muffled his words, making his wide, dark eyes more prominent. "Gilbert here carries that little Book of his. Maybe he has God on his team. So I crawled over to join you . . . I hate this storm. I hate this war."

Danston shrugged. "I'm not a religious man."

14

Robbie licked a dab of saliva over his lips. "And I'm just a prodigal who made peace with God." He looked at the teenage soldier. "Give God a chance, Jared. I did."

The sergeant scowled at them both. "And all it got you, Gilbert, was a place in the desert."

Robbie stretched his legs, and more sand flowed into his boots. "Not a bad place when you consider that God met Moses in the desert."

They were trapped in a powdery brownout. The sergeant swallowed some water from his canteen. He took another swallow, rinsed the grit from his teeth, and spit with a vengeance. The winds picked it up and blew it back. "Mountain spring water never tasted like this."

"Sergeant, I wonder if they have an ophthalmologist in the next village."

"Looking for a pair of glasses, Gilbert?"

"I'd like to get the gravel washed from my eyes." Robbie faced Jared. "What about you? Where's your family?"

"Scattered. All seven of us." Jared jabbed at his eyes with his knuckles. "I'd give anythin' for some of my mom's chicken and dumplin's. And I've got me a pregnant wife waiting for me back in West Virginia."

Robbie hunched forward. "Then you'll be glad to go home again."

Jared picked at the dirt beneath his nails. "If I ever get there."

Robbie felt certain Jared was running scared. They all were. "When the storm ends, I'll loan you that little Book of mine."

"I'm not a good reader." Jared stumbled to his feet and bent into the wind, his boots kicking up sand.

"Just like a kid," Danston put in. "Off to relieve himself right in the middle of a storm. He'll get himself lost, and we'll have to send out a search party."

"He's just scared, Sergeant. Homesick."

"Who isn't? I'm out here priming my men for battle, and you're out here spouting from the Good Book. We're in war, man, not some fancy cathedral. We're not up to a sermon." The sergeant patted his ammo box. "Most of us are pumped up. Ready for war. Ready to get this job done and get home again. There's just a handful who have written themselves off. But, Gilbert, when you send your news articles in, none of us wants to be recorded as a coward. Not even Mitchell."

"I'll do my best."

Danston turned and faced the Abrams, curled into an embryo state around his ammo box, and slept.

As the hours rolled by, Robbie braced himself against the Abrams. The sand caught between his teeth. Gravel scratched his eyes and scraped his cheeks raw. Sleep-deprived, he grew angry at Danston, who snored beside him. Robbie didn't dare open his Book, lest the tissue-thin pages be shredded by the gusting winds. He groped for his water canteen, took a swig, and was rewarded with a mouthful of grit.

CHAPTER 2

When the sandstorm abated, the desert filled with the grinding roar of hundreds of vehicles warming up and moving out again. The men grumbled as they boarded the Bradleys and armored vehicles.

A sooty-faced New Englander turned to the man behind him. "I think I'd rather be out there on the *Abraham Lincoln* or the *Kitty Hawk*."

"Not me. I get seasick. Hey, Sarge, are you sure the storm is over? Look at that pea-soup haze on the horizon."

"Knock it off. And get on board. We've got a war to win."

The sergeant turned and squared off in front of Robbie. "Come on, Gilbert, you can ride with us this time."

Robbie tossed his rucksack in the back of the vehicle and, with a running start, hoisted himself on board and eased his body onto the miserable metal bench.

"Hi, Gilbert."

Robbie found himself sitting across from Jared Mitchell. He guessed the kid to be eighteen, nineteen at most. His youthful face was narrow with a gritty fuzz for a beard; his crooked nose was dry and peeling. He wore a bandoleer over his shoulder and across his chest; the pockets of the bandoleer bulged with bullets.

The kid concentrated on emptying sand from his boot. "I hate this sand. Hate this war."

A familiar refrain, Robbie thought.

"I told you, knock it off." Danston's voice sharpened. "Get your gun cleaned up. The sand didn't do it any good."

17

Robbie had kept his eye on Jared through the three-day sand-storm. Now he was alarmed by the twitch along Jared's jaw and his furtive glances. "When's that baby due, Jared?"

The thick lips twisted into a smile. "In June."

"Then, like the sergeant said, let's get this job done so you can get home again."

Jared was crammed in the Bradley, shoulder to shoulder with the rest of the men. But he seemed the youngest of the lot, boyish and so out of place, as though he should be back home going to the school prom. These soldiers were all twenty or under, all depending on the sergeant to get them back home again. They rallied each other with a "get Saddam" battle cry.

All except Jared. "I don't like it. We don't know what's happenin' with the other units. We don't know whether the Turks have crossed over into Kurd territory. We don't know whether an Iraqi unit will ambush us on the next turn."

The sergeant's knuckles clamped. "Can it, Mitchell. We don't need to know. Just concern yourself with this patch of desert we're riding in."

Jared's twitch pulsated. "We don't know if we've got Saddam yet or not. How do we know what to expect when we get there?"

"Expect trouble. You were trained for this job, soldier."

Thanks to his communication with his publisher, Robbie knew there were three main thrusts moving toward Baghdad. The Brits were holding their own in Basra; the Americans were advancing on two routes with skirmishes along the way. Casualties were still minimal, but any loss would be demoralizing for the troops.

The sergeant's warning had been clear from the beginning. "Gilbert, keep news on losses, gains, or movements of other units to yourself. This is our patch of land right here. That's all we need to defend."

Right now Robbie wanted to argue that it would encourage the men to know that the Screaming Eagles of the 101st Airborne were already destroying Republican Guard units along the way. That the 1st Marines from Camp Pendleton were softening the way for the advancing troops. No weapons of mass destruction had been found. Shouldn't the men know that?

But one look at the tough, cocksure sergeant silenced him. Robbie prayed that the sergeant would take notice of Jared Mitchell withdrawing into himself, his fingers in constant motion. Robbie leaned closer. "You know, Jared, that Book of mine says, 'Let not your heart be troubled.'"

"You think mine is?"

"I'll let you be the judge."

Jared kept kneading the corner of his camouflage vest.

How could he talk to Jared about eternity and mansions in glory? It would be confirmation to Jared's fears that he was facing a body bag. Robbie decided he'd talk to Jared later when they were alone. Or maybe he could put in a word to the chaplain.

"This your first battle, Jared?"

"Yeah."

"Mine too," Robbie admitted.

"You scared, sir?"

"Yes. You?"

More than the dust seemed to choke Jared. "I have this gut feelin' I'm not goin' to make it."

"Stick with me. You'll get home again."

Jared's hollow eyes met Robbie's. "You gonna protect me with your pen and paper? No thanks. The sergeant told me to stick with my platoon. At least we're carryin' ammunition."

The boy was still showing some spunk. Robbie chuckled and took a gulp of dust.

"I'm sorry, sir. I just don't want to get killed out here. The last thing my mother told me before I left was to dive for the nearest ditch when I saw the Iraqi soldiers comin'."

"When the time comes, you'll do okay. My dad tells me all the time to keep my head down, yet he's always in the thick of a battle . . . I told you about my father, didn't I? . . . He's a foreign correspondent. He was never the conventional nine-to-five dad with a lunchbox. I grew up overseas for the most part. Italy. London. A year in Tokyo. And spent the best part of my boyhood in Paris. That's where I met my girl."

"She French?"

"No, the daughter of an American diplomat. What about your family, Jared?"

"My old man worked the coal mines of West Virginia. Never even crossed the state border, not once in his fifty-four years. The black lung took him out. But if we do many of these sandstorms, my lungs won't do much better."

The sergeant glowered. "So why did you join the army?"

"To escape the coal mines," Jared answered. "I told you I liked my mom's chicken and dumplin's, but there wasn't much about my dad to like. He was never home. Always workin'. And when he was around he yelled a lot. When he died, I didn't even cry. I want to be a better dad than that. I want my boy to miss me when I'm gone."

Robbie stretched his cramped leg. "I guess I lucked out, Jared. My dad's got a big heart." Nostalgia merged with his words. "He's a good-natured giant of a man. Got a hearty chuckle. A booming voice because he had to shout above the noise in the newsrooms. Might be big enough to scare Saddam into surrendering."

"Not a chance," the sergeant mumbled.

"Dad worked long hours, but he was always there for me. If he had to work late, he'd take me with him—let me sleep on a cot in the men's room or in a sleeping bag by his desk."

The sergeant's lip curled. "Well, I grew up on army bases. My dad was a drill sergeant."

"Always marching?" Robbie asked.

"It wasn't a bad life. I learned to adjust moving from one school to another. It was the one life I knew, so I joined up the day I turned eighteen. My mother had fits. Dad was as proud as a peacock." Danston stifled a coughing spasm. "I considered getting out, but after 9/11, I re-enlisted."

Robbie went on bragging about his namesake. "My dad has always been my best friend. Still is. My fiancée and I delayed our wedding a few months back because Dad couldn't get back in time.

He was weathered in Bermuda, chasing a story. I couldn't think of marrying without my dad standing up for me."

"You could have flown to Bermuda," Danston suggested.

Robbie squirmed. "You don't know my girl. Adrienne has her heart set on a garden wedding at the Winterfest Estates in Virginia. She called off the ceremony until I get back from Iraq. She told me when we get married she doesn't want a war separating us."

As Jared wiped the soot from his face, a slight flush crept in. "When we knew I was goin' overseas, my girl and me headed to the justice of peace and cinched the deal." He tapped his helmet. "She's pregnant. Got a picture of the baby right here." He loosened the strap and whipped the helmet off to free the sonogram image. "See. That's my son."

Robbie saw nothing but a blur as the Bradley bounced along. "How do you know it's a boy?"

"Has to be. If I don't get out of this bloody mess, I need a name-sake. This goin' to be a father is somethin' else. I up and quit drinkin'. And if I live long enough, I think I'll leave the army. Get a job. I want to be a good father."

Robbie leaned forward. "You will be."

Jared kept digging at his fingernails. "Only thing that comes close to this war in my whole life was huntin' down rabbits with my big brother. Sometimes we let them go."

The sergeant scowled. "These aren't rabbits, Mitchell. They're the enemy. You get them before they get you."

As they pushed on toward Baghdad, Robbie longed for a toothbrush and a shower. Longed to be back in Virginia with Adrienne. Longed for the right words for Jared Mitchell.

Three days later the alarm spread down through the convoy. *Incoming missiles.*

Within seconds they donned their gas masks and biochemical suits. They radioed ahead for air power.

Three Bradley fighting vehicles and a lone Humvee were sent ahead on a scouting patrol. Danston and his men drove their vehicle in the tracks of the vehicle ahead of them, avoiding the threat of land mines and the deep crevices to the side.

Robbie pushed the On button on his tape recorder: "We are thirty minutes ahead of the main convoy. Our scouting vehicles look like dots on the desert sand as we creep forward, searching for the enemy. The men traveling with me are alert. Fingers trigger-ready. Fear grips us. Gut-wrenching fear. Mine and the soldiers who ride with me."

He peered out of the rear of the vehicle and scanned the sky. Nothing. As their patrol turned to the right, he saw the gunner in the lead Bradley riding with his head and shoulders poked out of the turret. Suddenly bullets pelted their vehicles.

In that second before the men dove from the Bradley, Jared tossed off his gas mask. Robbie saw rage on Jared's face, a madness as he shouted, "Nothing but rabbits."

Jared leaped from their vehicle and belly-crawled through the sand as the rest of the men took position behind sand berms.

More shots pinged off the front of their vehicle. "Where did those shots come from, Sergeant?" Robbie asked. "I didn't see any Iraqis."

"Keep down, Gilbert." Danston scanned the desert. "I hope that wasn't our own artillery. The Iraqis could be anywhere. Hiding in the reeds along the river. Behind those sand dunes. Just keep down."

"I've lost sight of Jared. He was crawling forward. Going it alone."

"The poor fool. Maybe his instinct will kick in. He's fighting mad. Maybe he snapped. I can't risk sending anyone after him."

"There. Over there," the gunner shouted. He raised his hand from the turret and signaled *Hold your fire*.

From over a sand dune, a half-dozen Iraqi civilians approached the patrol, their hands held high in surrender. A woman and two children led the group. Several yards ahead of Robbie, Jared stood

THE TRUMPET AT TWISP

up. Calm. Rifle steady. He reached into his pocket and tossed some candy to the children.

Robbie screamed as he spotted the Iraqi truck bouncing over the dunes. "Get down, Jared!"

But Jared was still smiling at the children when the Iraqis pulled out weapons and began to fire. Shells exploded from behind Jared too. Above him a fighter jet swooped low and strafed the ground. Jared reeled, caught his balance, and began firing his M-16. Watching him, Robbie was convinced he saw Jared's lips form the word *rabbits*.

Three more Iraqi trucks rolled over the sand berm; their fifty-caliber machine guns sprayed the sand and peppered the Bradleys. The plane was coming back, but the Iraqis advanced without stopping. Launching their rocket-propelled grenades. Setting off their homemade bombs. The Humvee blew into the air and came down in flames, the crew commingled in their earthly descent.

From above came more strafing.

"You idiots," the sergeant called. "We're not the enemy."

Robbie lay flat on the ground, his face in the sand. He risked looking up. *If only he had a gun. If only he could be a soldier.* Ahead of them Jared was still firing his weapon.

Sergeant Danston's lips tightened. "The poor fool thinks he's killing rabbits."

Another soldier moved forward and fell beside Jared. Jared snatched the grenade from the wounded soldier and tossed it, then fell facedown in the desert sand, his body motionless.

The sand was splattered with the blood of American soldiers and Iraqis. The wounded crawled to the protection of the vehicles.

It was hours before the battle ended and they could make their way to Jared Mitchell's body. The sooty-faced kid who had talked about his pregnant wife and unborn child was dead.

The sergeant unlaced Jared's boots and placed them on the sand in a makeshift memorial. He positioned Jared's M-16 rifle upright between his boots. "I promised the kid I'd get him home. The fool kid. He didn't have a chance."

Robbie wiped his mouth with the back of his hand. "I never watched a friend die like that before. But did you see him grab that grenade and toss it back at the enemy? That's worth a medal for valor, right?"

"He defied orders crawling out there ahead of the rest of us. He must have been gunning for rabbits." Danston jammed Jared's M-16 deeper into the sand, balanced his helmet on top, and dangled his dog tags over it. "It will have to do for now. The mortuary team will be along. We have to keep moving." The sergeant paused, then turned sarcastic. "Or do you want me to wait a minute so you can send in your news report? That way you can announce to the world that we lost some of our men. That we were pinned down by the enemy."

"I'd rather say a prayer."

Danston wiped his brow. "I think Mitchell would like that, Reverend."

Robbie began a brief prayer, but seconds later the sergeant clamped his shoulder. "Forget the still waters. I don't see any out here. We have to keep moving."

"I know. All roads lead north to Baghdad."

They swung up and took their places in the back of the Bradley. Jared's space was empty. The forlorn expressions of the other men wrote themselves indelibly on Robbie's mind. He would remember those expressions when he spoke to the nation: fatigue, fear, rage. Battle-scarred warriors.

As they drove off, a desert breeze caught the strap on Jared's helmet. Robbie chortled, an odd, convulsive chuckle. "Sergeant, I was just thinking how much Jared hated that strap under his chin."

"Don't we all?"

An hour later Robbie removed his own helmet, took his satellite phone in his hand, and in a surprisingly strong voice reported live to the nation back home: "This is Robbie Gilbert, embedded with an army unit south of Baghdad. Today we were pinned down by enemy fire for five hours. We took our first casualties. One of them was my personal friend, a man who rode out a sandstorm with me. A man who would have made a wonderful father."

They spotted a bright green road sign to Baghdad one hundred miles from the city. Then one at fifty miles. Another at ten. With adrenaline pumping, they rode on through the dunes and scrub grass with the rumble of U.S. artillery pounding the city ahead of them. Now they were a mile from Baghdad. Ahead of them came the thundering roar of the big guns. The whistling sound of precision-guided bombs.

At dawn they moved into Baghdad. Down streets lined with palm trees. Past bomb-riddled buildings. Frightened refugees stood on the streets watching the soldiers and tanks roll into their city. A few waved, but Robbie knew pockets of resistance lurked around every bend. Saddam loyalists. A few threadbare soldiers from the Republican Guard. Frightened Iraqis taught to defend the city to the last man. Foreign mercenaries. Smoke billowed from the west corner of one of Saddam's main palaces. The city smelled of ash and destruction. Army medics carried the wounded soldiers and civilians toward the battalion aid station.

Danston and his men leapt from their Bradley, rifles ready. Robbie kept on the heels of his unit as the sergeant and his men kicked down gates and began their house-to-house sweep.

Hours later they entered Saddam's main palace. What had once been splendor lay in ruins.

Robbie rounded one crumbled wall and stared in disbelief at three American soldiers huddled there. The tallest man lay face-down, motionless. The other two were backed against the broken wall, bleeding but alert, their faces etched with fear. Behind them were shattered stained-glass windows. Above them ornate, painted ceilings.

"It's okay. You're safe. I'm Robbie Gilbert. An American journalist."

"I'm glad you're here. I'm Brad Swensen. PFC. Third Infantry. This here is Julio. Julio Hernandez. He's hurt, sir."

As Robbie turned the soldier's chin toward him, Hernandez's eyes hardened. Dried blood covered his cheek and chin. The strap of his helmet and uniform were drenched with sweat and blood. His M-16 lay across his legs, a limp hand on top of it.

"Over here, Sergeant Danston," Robbie called. "There's some wounded."

Danston came on the run, his M-16 steady in his hands. It was the way Robbie wanted to remember the sergeant when he went home. Cautious. Confident. A leader of men. The knuckles of his right hand were scraped raw. His night goggles were braced against his Kevlar helmet. His face was solemn, his eyes alert.

Danston swung his M-16 side-to-side, keeping his back protected as he nudged the soldier lying facedown. "What happened?" he demanded as he radioed for the medics.

Swensen shook his head. "Friendlies, I think. We tried to tell them we were Americans. They wouldn't listen."

Danston nodded. "They were frightened, soldier."

"Yeah, so were we, sir."

Danston turned and glared at Robbie. "If this is another friendly incident, I don't want a journalist nosing around. There will be an official investigation. So this doesn't go in any written report of yours. And you'll be accountable to me if you blare it over the television. We're not a news story. Got it?"

Not yet. Someday.

Robbie's brows knit together. There was no need to explain to Danston that he was merely a guest on the television station. Once the war was over, he'd go back to being an investigative reporter. Nothing more. Nothing less.

Again Danston nudged the limp soldier. "And your friend?"

Swensen's voice cracked. "I think he's dead, sir."

"Are you sure our own troops fired on you?"

"Yeah, Sarge. I thought they were going to kill all three of us."

Danston stared at Swensen, ignoring Hernandez's listless eyes. "What happened, soldier?"

"We were rounding that corner of the room. Some Iraqis came at us from one direction, and some of our own men came from the other hall, weapons firing. This guy took a flying leap and knocked me to the ground. If he hadn't, I'd be dead."

"Go on."

"Then he stood up. Yelled that we were Americans. But they kept firing. They caught the guy in the back and legs. He just stood there for a minute, then they misfired and a piece of the chandelier fell and knocked his helmet off. He had this funny look and then he pitched forward."

"Where are those medics?" Danston barked. "Stay with the wounded, Gilbert."

"Yes, sir."

As Danston disappeared, Robbie knelt down by the inert soldier and saw a slight rise of the rib cage. "Hey, he's not dead."

Clear the man's airway. That's what they had told him at the reporters' boot camp in Quantico, Virginia. *Never move a patient.* Another Quantico rule. He'd already broken some rules along the desert road, so why not one more? Robbie rolled the injured soldier over and positioned him on his back. He shuddered at the gurgling sound in the man's throat. Cringed as blood spurted from his chest.

At boot camp they had told Robbie to stay out of harm's way, and yet here he was, kneeling in the midst of a war, his hands bloody with another man's wounds.

"Come on, soldier, don't die on us . . . What's his name, Swenson?"

"We never saw him before, sir. But he saved our lives."

Robbie turned the dog tags over and read the name. *Juddman.* For a moment his gut knotted. He thought he would vomit.

"You okay, sir?" Swensen asked.

"I think I know this man."

But before Robbie could explain, the medics were there, loading the wounded soldier on a makeshift stretcher. One of them turned to Robbie. "You with this man's unit?"

"No, I'm one of the journalists."

"Looks like you can write yourself quite a story."

"I already know his story." Robbie touched Juddman's shoulder. There was no response. "Take good care of him for me."

Six days after reaching Baghdad, Robbie stood within the palace ruins bemoaning his marching orders to return to the States. He hadn't even searched for his father. A man didn't leave his unit or the men he served with for a family reunion. Robbie wanted to swim in Saddam's pool, sleep in one of his luxurious bedroom suites, and shower in one of his marbled bathrooms, but it was too risky. He had to stay alert. To stay on guard.

"You're looking glum this morning, Gilbert."

He looked up and saw Sergeant Danston standing there, his craggy face quizzical.

"I've had a call from my newspaper. I'm to pack it in and go home. They think my assignment here is over."

"I hoped you'd stay on with us. The men like you." There was a camaraderie in the crusty voice that hadn't been there before. Somehow, during the long hours and days together, Robbie sensed that he'd gained a measure of the sergeant's respect.

Danston shrugged his broad shoulders. "I guess this is it, Gilbert. We've come a long way together."

"Yeah. In a short span of time."

"What are your plans?"

"Getting married is number one on my agenda, Sarge."

"Getting home is mine." Robbie sensed the weight and longing in Danston's curt words.

"If you get back to the States in time, come to my wedding. What about you, Sergeant? Do you have to stay on in Baghdad?"

"There's a rumor our unit will be sent home soon."

"That's good, Danston."

His jaw locked. "Except I promised to take all my men home with me. And that included Jared Mitchell."

Robbie winced. There was nothing he could say to ease the sergeant's pain. But he replied, "At least they told me at the aid station that Private Juddman was flown to Germany for treatment."

"He'll make it, then?"

"I don't know. But I plan to go home by way of there to check up on him."

"The reporter gets his story, is that it?"

"No, it's more personal than that."

Flecks of gray shadowed the sergeant's eyes. "This Juddman case got to you, didn't it? Whatever you're looking for, Gilbert, I hope you find it. I didn't know Juddman well. Not in my platoon. But he's part of the Third Infantry." The sergeant thumbed his helmet back on his forehead. "Don't forget that wedding invitation, Gilbert."

"I'll have Adrienne put you on the list."

Robbie and the sergeant shook hands, and then Danston made his way through the palace rubble, his boots kicking against the chunks of concrete strewn across the parquet floor. Without looking back, he turned east and walked with confidence across the palatial no man's land, then slipped through a jagged hole in the garden wall.

Robbie watched him go, then turned to face another man strolling toward him. As he squinted, relief exploded inside him. He ran through the debris and thrust himself, like a prodigal son, into his father's outstretched arms.

CHAPTER 3

Robinson Gilbert stood in the bombed-out ruins, gripping his son's shoulders. He gulped down his emotions and forced the reporter in him to kick in. The sun streamed through the shattered stained-glass windows, casting its shadows in multicolor on his son's somber face. In the window he saw shards of a once majestic palace. In his son he saw new strength; in himself he felt deep pride for his only son.

Hang tight, Robinson, he told himself. *Give your son space. He's just come through twenty-one days in the desert. Tasted the baptism of war. It's too soon for backslapping. Talks of home.*

They did not agree on this war. Robbie had left Virginia all gung-ho, patriotic. Even willing to put a hold on his wedding day in order to be part of the downfall of a dictator. But Robinson hated each new war with intensity, this one more than others. Over the years he'd been captivated with the strange beauty of the desert. The mindset of the Arabs. The Bedouins' nomadic way of life. Islamic women intrigued him with their mysterious beauty. The unyielding land fascinated him. His wanderlust kept bringing him back.

But today it was not his love of the land or his hatred of war that consumed him. Everything inside him thrilled with the glad safe return of his son. An ornate chandelier dangled precariously from the mosaic dome above them. To their right, a wide hardwood door had been torn from its hinges. Through that doorway lay Saddam's massive swimming pool with an elaborate waterfall in

Italian marble. And not twenty feet away Ricardo de Nuccio snapped pictures of a tyrant's downfall.

As Robinson struggled to find the right words, Robbie broke their silence. "Welcome to the palace, Dad."

Robinson's gaze went back to Robbie. He squared his jaw. He'd never cried in front of his son. He wouldn't now. What was there to cry about? Robbie stood in front of him, alive.

But in twenty-one days Robbie had turned war-weary. His Kevlar vest was sprinkled with someone else's blood. The sparkle in his smoky blue eyes had glazed over, leaving those expressive eyes speckled with shades of gray. The stubble on his chin was more than a five o'clock shadow. His clothes—half-military, half-civilian—smelled like a fish market.

Robbie, you are no longer a boy. You haven't been for years. But what happened to your lighthearted, jovial way? You crossed the desert and lost your easy smile along the way.

Robinson gripped his son's shoulders again. "You made it."

"Had to. I promised to meet you here in Baghdad."

The voice was Robbie's, the touch of humor definitely Robbie. But the battle-scarred man was someone new. Robinson hugged his son, absorbing some of the stench on his own clothes. "Why didn't you contact me at the hotel?"

"I couldn't leave my post."

"You look like you haven't slept for days."

"We were out on patrol today on one of those house-to-house sweeps. The men were in full uniform, sweating bullets. One of them was wounded. Another was a heat casualty. I never dreamed it could get so hot." Robbie's voice trailed off.

"You're drinking enough water?"

"Liters of it."

"Have you thought about using some of the water on you?" Robinson wrinkled his nose.

Robbie grinned. "That bad? They promised us a new staging area with portable showers. We're still waiting." He glanced toward the massive swimming pool. "I'd like to plunge in there and then doze for an hour in one of the luxurious guest rooms."

"I have a pad over at the Palestine."

"As opulent as this once was?"

"Nothing in the city is the same. Water is at a premium. Electricity is out in much of the city. But you can go back to the hotel with me for a shower and shave," Robinson offered.

"I smell that bad, Dad?"

"Like rotten fish."

"We didn't travel with portable showers or latrines. But I look at the people in this city, and I've got it good. Clothes on my back. MRE rations in my belly." Robbie shrugged. "I'm afraid the people blame us for their problems, but it was Saddam who squandered the wealth of the nation on himself while his people starved to death."

"It doesn't seem like the cradle of civilization, does it?"

"My sergeant scoffs at this being a land of biblical history. He said he couldn't see God in its bombed-out ruins."

"I don't know much about this God of yours, Robbie."

"Then let me tell you about Him."

"Some other time, Son."

"Don't wait too long. I thought about you—worried about you. I knew they were bombing the city."

"But I'm glad I'm here. I like reporting live from this city. Why, the other day I stood on the shores of the Tigris and told America that I was reporting history in the making as a convoy of American troops roared into downtown Baghdad."

"Were you looking for me?" Robbie asked.

"In every face. I'm just sorry you didn't get one of those hero welcomes like they did back in Paris in World War II."

"They still see us as the enemy, Dad. Getting here was half the battle." Robbie rubbed his sandpaper jaw. "Now we have to help these people break free from a dictatorship."

Robinson agreed. "We've a long journey ahead . . . Will you be going home, Son?"

"Will you?"

"Not yet. A couple of the journalists are leaving—de Nuccio for one, that photographer over there. But I want to see this city back on its feet again."

"Dad, it looks like my unit will be one of the first ones rotated home. And I had word from Virginia that it was time for me to head back. But I have no permanent commitment to the newspaper. I covered the assignment when I crossed the desert, so if you want, I could stay on with you."

"And Adrienne—would she wait for you?"

"She'd understand, especially if I told her my job wasn't finished yet. I just spent the last few weeks with the backbone of America. They're just kids, Dad. I'm ten years older than most of them. I feel like an old man."

"War does that, Son."

"We lost some of our men coming across the desert."

"I'm sorry, Robbie."

"Sorry that I had to see it? Or sorry that they died?"

"Both."

"There was a young man named Jared Mitchell, our first casualty. He was excited about being a father—carried the sonogram of the baby in his helmet . . . I'm going to look up his wife when I get home."

"Don't get involved, Robbie."

"You did."

Robinson did some mental gymnastics, his thoughts racing back to the ambush in Vietnam and the loss of marines in Granada. He'd done stories on them, but from the war zones, not from their homes. And the soldiers killed on war maneuvers at Fort Campbell—he'd covered that one too. He pressed his fists against his thighs. "Yes, I wrote articles on soldiers who lost their lives, but I never looked up those families. Don't get involved, Robbie."

"Don't get involved?" Robbie's eyes burned with conviction. "You set the example by caring about the people you wrote about. When I get home, I'm going to track down the stories of these men and women who crossed the desert."

"Is Adrienne to support you in this new venture?"

"Never. I'll keep my job at the paper and write at night."

Robinson studied his son's dirt-smudged face. "How many bride-grooms do you know who spend their nights writing about war?"

"Then I'll get up at dawn and write."

"This Jared Mitchell—how was he killed?"

"It's already under investigation for friendly fire. He took hostile fire as well. A long time ago, Dad, you told me we try to comfort families with 'Taps' and a folded flag. You were always going to do a story on that. You never finished it. I intend to."

Robinson hated the sound of "Taps." Still did.

"There's another soldier I'm concerned about. Do you remember the Juddmans? We met them on the Italian Riviera. Saw them again at Fort Riley."

Do I remember the Juddmans? Robinson didn't need his memory jostled. He looked away. When he faced his son again, they were eyeball to eyeball. Tall men. Determined. Men of integrity. Men avoiding what was tearing them apart.

"I remember the pretty Rosalie who checked us in at the villa."

"Not her, Dad."

With effort Robinson turned his thoughts from the gorgeous Italian girl—one of those young women who still found a silver-haired man attractive. He allowed Meagan Juddman's face to come back. A face that was never far away. "You mean the American soldier and his pregnant wife? What made you think of them?"

"I found a wounded soldier by that name."

"Coincidental."

"I don't think so. The kid could be old enough. That soldier's wife? What was her name?"

Meagan. Her name was Meagan. "Meagan Juddman?"

"That's it. Meagan Juddman went through hell during the Gulf War. Now she may be facing it all over again." Robbie glanced at his watch, noting the time and date. "By now someone may be knocking on her door, telling her what happened."

"Was it bad?"

"Yeah. He wasn't responding when we found him. Head injury. Multiple wounds. They weren't certain he'd even make it to the hospital in Germany."

"If he doesn't make it, they'll ship him home from Ramstein, back to Dover Air Force Base in Delaware."

"And if they do stabilize him, Dad? Where then?" Robbie asked.

"Likely Landstuhl, five or eight kilometers from Ramstein. That's where most of our wounded are going."

"I'll start there. So you do remember them?"

Robinson squirmed, not wanting to recall how he had failed Meagan Juddman. She wanted to know what happened to her husband on that small strip of desert in the Middle East. There were those in Washington who chose to silence her. Robinson had backed off to protect them both.

Robinson winced. He knew in the past that he'd made a lousy husband, and in Meagan Juddman's case, an untrustworthy friend. But as he looked at Robbie now, he knew he'd been a good father.

"Forget the Juddmans. We don't want to stir those flames again." Robinson did an about-face and headed toward the toppled hardwood door. He plowed his way through the rubble to the pool.

Robbie followed. "Why do you want me to forget it? Because you found Meagan Juddman attractive—and knew she was too young for you?"

"That's not fair, Son."

"I wasn't blind."

"You were just a snub-nosed eleven-year-old back then."

"The first time. But I was almost eighteen when I saw her last. And that time she was crying on your shoulder, begging for your help."

"And I let her down."

"Not your fault, Dad. The Washington investigation said she was wrong. That there had been no mistakes on the government's side. And did you believe that?"

"Not for a minute." Robinson kicked off his shoes and socks and rolled up his pant legs. He eased down on the edge of the pool and dangled his feet. He exhaled through pursed lips as he thought of Meagan Juddman's exceptional beauty, her independence.

"Meagan insisted there was a military cover-up. But I couldn't prove it until I met Major . . . what did I tell you his name was?"

"Martin or Marsh? Something like that."

Robbie dropped his rucksack beside his father's shoes. "I was just a kid, but Mrs. Juddman treated me like an adult."

Robinson laughed. "She wasn't much more than a kid herself when we met her. Eighteen or nineteen, I think."

The first time he had seen Meagan Juddman she was sitting on the patio terrace in the Italian Riviera, with a backdrop of orange lilies and apricot trees on the hillsides behind her. Her tawny hair looked like burnished gold in the blistering Mediterranean sun. At the sound of his footsteps, she had turned from watching her husband hike down toward the beach and faced Robinson. It had been a quick tilt of her head, but enough for him to know that her eyes were dark and alluring. And in that split second he envied the man who had her attention, her love.

"You're right, Son, I was taken by her—more so because she was out of reach. Charming. Married."

"Because she was young?"

"More than that. She had a mind of her own. A husband who adored her. She reminded me of Katy-did."

"Katy-did?"

"Your mother."

"You called my mother that?"

"Only in the privacy of our boudoir."

"You never talk about her."

"There's not much to say. But your talking about Meagan

Juddman reminds me of Catherine. In some ways they were much alike. Beautiful. Vulnerable. Independent. When I first met your mother, she was like Mrs. Juddman. Aloof and captivating. Catherine never needed me. But I had trouble taking my eyes off her—off either one of them." Robinson turned, avoiding the glare of the sun on the water, and studied Robbie's profile. The set of his jaw was strong like his mother's, his mouth sensitive like hers.

"What a strange place for us to be talking about my mother. I never understood why she didn't want me—why she never tried to get in touch with us."

"She did want you, Robbie. But I told you before. I wouldn't leave town without you. We split everything else down the middle. The bank accounts. The stock portfolio. The property. I told Katydid she could keep her conglomerate for a bedfellow; she could have her career twenty-four hours a day, but I wanted my son."

"Was I a hindrance to her?"

"No, she was sick around then. Violently ill. I worried that it was something serious. Vomiting. She was hospitalized for dehydration. That was the deciding factor. She argued, but at last agreed to my terms. Full custody of you was the best part of my breakup."

Robbie toed his rucksack. "When she walked away, she really walked away."

"We both did the walking, Robbie. We argued so much. Couldn't agree on our careers or schedules. Made appointments and broke them. Made promises we couldn't keep. Mothering didn't come easy for her, but she loved you. We thought it best to split up while you were young so it wouldn't hurt so much. We just ended up walking away in different directions."

"She wouldn't know me if she ran into me on the Baltimore Turnpike."

"She does drive fast." *But she'd know you. I've sent pictures of you over the years. Always by Express Mail to make certain she got them. I have no doubt she's watching you on the nightly news. She knows your voice by videophone . . . If it weren't for Catherine, you wouldn't even be here, Son. She gave you your big chance in journalism—embedded with the troops. And I'm sworn to secrecy.*

"She probably doesn't know my birthday."

"A mother remembers things like that. When we called it quits, we agreed. No looking back. No bashing each other or keeping in touch. No nasty phone calls . . . But we were talking about Meagan Juddman, weren't we? The last time I talked to Meagan, she slammed the phone down." Robinson adjusted his hearing aid and grinned. "Wouldn't be surprised if that caused my hearing problem."

"You can't fool me. That explosion in Kosovo dulled your hearing."

"I've always hated that old gadget. Makes me look like a weakling—Maybe that's how Meagan Juddman saw it—how she saw me."

"I don't see it that way. That little gadget, as you call it, can never change the man you are. Never." Robbie cleared his throat. "Out of sheer curiosity, have you heard from Mrs. Juddman since the last time you talked?"

"No. Even after we lost touch, I wrote that article on THE FRIENDLY FIRE COVER-UP for the *Post*. I sent Meagan a copy of it, but she never answered."

"Maybe it was too late by then. Maybe she no longer cared."

"Oh, she cared all right. She wasn't the type to give up. I think that's what I liked about her . . . Sit down, Son."

Robbie leaned down and unlaced his boots. He groaned as he eased them off his blistered feet and, with a grateful sigh, allowed the water to wash over them.

"Your socks look like they could walk on their own." Robinson pointed to the pool. "Give them to me—I'll wash them for you."

"Don't think Saddam would like my filthy socks defiling his pool, Dad."

"Don't think he cares, wherever he is. If you go back to the hotel with me, I'll lend you a pair of my socks."

"I still have a spare in my rucksack. I just wish I had the Juddmans' address there as well. You never let someone's whereabouts stop you when you're after a story. You know every trick on the Internet . . . so help me, Dad. How do I find Meagan Juddman? I have a gut feeling that this is the same family. Her husband, Cameron, was a twenty-year army man, right? Military straight through."

"He didn't get the twenty-year career he'd planned."

"I know. But how can I get in touch with Meagan?"

"How would I know?" Robinson felt a twitch at the corner of his mouth. He'd lied to his son. Something he never tolerated in Robbie. He knew where she lived. He'd seen Meagan Juddman in recent years. Just before September 11.

With reluctance, he murmured, "Meagan grew up in Eastern Washington—a couple of hours from Spokane. She went back there with her son to live."

Robbie wiggled his toes in the pool. "Can you be more specific? Check your address file. Go there with me."

"Not this time. Just take the North Cascades Highway. But don't make my cowardly mistake. When I drove past her house, I kept driving." Robinson paused. "Well, that's not altogether true. I parked across the street and watched her. She was wearing shorts and a tank top, her hair as golden as it had been that first time we saw her on the Riviera. She was cutting back a rosebush and seemed at peace with herself. So I drove away."

"I didn't realize how much she meant to you."

"I think I wanted to protect her. Take care of her. I felt like I had let her down over that army cover-up. All she wanted was the truth. An apology from Washington. All she got were evasive answers."

"Dad, sympathy and love are two different things."

Robinson chortled. "Now the son lectures the father."

"Just when you need it."

"When I drove off from Meagan's, I went straight up the mountain and spent a couple of days at Sun Mountain Lodge—arguing with myself about going back and talking with her."

"Did you?" Robbie asked.

"Would it matter?" Robinson tousled his son's hair as he had often done when Robbie was a boy. "Let me know if you find her, Robbie. I'd like to see her again. If what you say is true, then this whole miserable life has come full circle for Meagan." He stared down into the pool at their faces reflected there, but the face he kept seeing in his mind was Meagan Juddman's. "I'm not certain she could take it—having some army officer or chaplain knocking on her door again and opening an old wound. I guess I'd like to be there for her."

"I intend to be, Dad."

"I need to warn you. That article I did on Juddman—I didn't print the whole thing. There was the possibility that he was linked to an intelligence fiasco. Rumor said he volunteered for a special mission—one he couldn't possibly survive. But I couldn't print rumors. I needed facts."

"He'd be daring enough to volunteer for a risky mission."

"Juddman was mechanized infantry. He wasn't up to being a hero. He was just doing his job. Duty. Honor. Country."

"And what thanks did he get, Dad?"

Robinson fixed his gaze on the pool. He had to trust Robbie to follow his own instincts. No blocking him. "Do you remember when I taught you to swim?"

"Yeah. As I recall, you tossed me in the Delaware River."

"I guess I did." Robinson moved his broad hand to Robbie's back and shoved.

Robbie came up sputtering, angry, sopping wet. "What was that all about?"

"It was time for your Saturday bath."

"That bad, eh?" Robbie splashed water in his father's face. "Well, come on in, the water's fine."

Robinson glanced at his watch. He stood and slipped back into his shoes. "Gotta fly. I have a live report to make. Call me at the hotel before you leave town."

"Sure, Dad. Tomorrow maybe."

In spite of his heavy Kevlar vest, Robbie dove beneath the water and swam across the pool. Robinson whirled around before Robbie could swim the length of the pool again and see tears in his eyes. He loved his son, was proud of him. He was grateful to Robbie's God for bringing his son safely to Baghdad. But he didn't envy his son locating Meagan Juddman and finding that an army chaplain had been there before him.

Every time the death of another soldier hit the airwaves, Meagan Juddman dreaded that awful memory of staring down at the spit-shined boots of the Fort Riley chaplain.

These days she poured a cup of coffee at work and forgot to drink it, made appointments with prospective buyers and forgot to keep them, listened to the office phone ring and fought down the fear that welled within her. This morning she stole glances at the television on her boss's desk, dreading the news it would bring.

She felt her boss's presence before she saw him stroll across the room. He spoke into his phone before she realized it had rung.

"Cragg's Real Estate. Bob speaking." A slight pause. His voice tensed, his words emphatic. "Yes, she's one of my agents. No, not here—"

His words were muffled now, as though he had cupped the mouthpiece. The call ended. His chair creaked as he stood. He came toward her and rounded her desk to face her.

"Was the call for me, Bob?"

His eyes turned wary. "Did I say that it was?"

Bob was forty-five. Thick-shouldered. As always he was in casual dress, with his shirt collar open and his beard trimmed. He leaned into her desk, his broad hands flat on the desktop. "Meagan, you forgot to meet with the Branson family." His tone was firm but not unkind. "It's not like you."

She reached for her phone. "I'll call them at once."

"Don't bother. I handled the deal for you. You ought to take a few days off. Go on home. Get hold of yourself."

"I'm fine. Really, Bob."

"I'd be hard put to know it."

"The phone call was about me, wasn't it? It wasn't the Bransons— or any other of my clients?"

"Meagan, go home. You need strength for tomorrow."

You're keeping something from me. That phone call.

She was afraid to ask; he was unwilling to tell her.

"Meg, you need to hit the sack and take a long nap. Take time for a full meal."

"I can't. I have to keep busy."

"We have to keep selling. That's your job here. If you can't keep up with it—"

"Bob, I'm your best salesperson. You know that."

"You *were* my best salesperson. But these last three weeks you're gloom and doom itself."

"I'm sorry."

He reached across her desk and brushed a strand of hair from her forehead. "Look at you. Half-moons under your eyes."

She'd already seen them. Even the Lancôme concealment cream couldn't hide them. She'd rolled out of bed this morning after another sleepless night and stared in the bathroom mirror. Each morning the circles beneath her eyes were larger, darker.

The morning shower and shampoo had long been her eye opener before facing the day. Standing under a stream of hot water, almost blinded by the steam, was the luxury she permitted herself each morning. The answering machine picked up her messages. The bed remained unmade until after breakfast. There was nothing more refreshing than lathering down in the shower. Massaging her scalp with the tips of her fingers and letting the most expensive shampoo in town wash over her shoulders, down her back, over her toes.

Sometimes she'd sing or hum. More often she practiced her first liners to new clients. But never, never did she have trouble expounding the virtues of the Valley. Nor did she stumble over finding words to describe it. God, she had to admit, had painted a magnificent valley with mountains rising above it, layered with a forest of conifer trees and all of nature to delight her. This was Owen Wiser's smiling country, but it was hers as well. She knew its history, knew where the rivers merged, was on a first-name basis with the townsfolk. It even felt safe to wave at strangers.

She'd step from the shower ready for anything. But not these last few weeks. Not since the threat of war in Iraq had tangled her thoughts. Terrified her. Bob was right. She was out of it.

She glanced up at the man who had taken her under his wings a dozen years ago when she first came back to the Valley as a single parent. "I need a job, Bob," she had told him.

"You've got it." Just like that . . .

Now she choked out the words, "I can't lose this job."

"You won't. I told you we'll cover for you for a few days."

"I haven't slacked off. You know I've listed several new properties along the Twisp River and the Methow Valley in less than three weeks."

"Have you made any sales?"

"I've shown perspective buyers the glory of the Valley."

She saw concern on his brow.

"Have you looked at yourself in the mirror lately? Have you been sleeping at all?"

"A little," she admitted.

"No news?"

"Only what I see on television."

"Our troops have been on the move, Meagan. I doubt there are any public phones en route to Baghdad."

"But they've crossed into Baghdad, and I still haven't heard."

"I know." Bob turned and flipped the television channels until

43

he saw Robinson Gilbert reporting live from Baghdad. Again he reached out and patted Meagan's shoulder. "Time is in your favor, Meagan. They reached Baghdad in twenty-one days."

But what about the men in her life? Where were they?

"Please. Go home, Meg. We'll cover for you today."

S ince the day Ryan had left for the Middle East, she had dreaded going home. She'd stayed away until late at night, like an ostrich with its head buried in the sand. If the house was dark, empty, how could a chaplain knock on her door?

Robinson Gilbert's voice again. "The coalition forces took another casualty today . . ."

"No!" she blurted out. "It could be—"

Bob snapped the television off.

"Don't, Bob. Leave it on. I know that reporter. He reports the truth. He said there's another casualty—"

"You're letting your imagination get away from you. Whatever happens, that soldier was doing what he wanted to do. What he believed in."

Bob was practical, straightforward. A man who could hardly think beyond *sell, sell, sell,* yet somehow he understood.

"That phone call a moment ago—you know something."

"Go home, Meg. Take a few days."

He knows. She grabbed her purse and keys. She couldn't remember getting into the car or turning on the engine, but her tires squealed as she roared across the road and drove parallel to the river.

Years ago, somewhere along this stretch of Highway 20, she and Cameron had found their way to the river at dusk. She pulled off the highway now and walked the last few yards to the river. By the time she got there, her legs were scratched by the twigs and vines. Gray clouds hung low overhead. The distant mountains were in shadows. The wind whistled through the towering trees.

Yet a comforting stillness hovered over her. She braced herself on a slippery rock. The Valley was in spring meltdown the way it had been when Cameron was here—the river rushing pell-mell toward the Columbia, wrapping itself around the trunks of the towering trees, its deep ripples backslapping against themselves. The river made its own sounds: Bubbling. Gurgling. Slurping. Slapping. Rippling. Lapping the shoreline. Racing through shrubs embedded in the river, over the rocks. She sat there for most of the afternoon, her only companions the bubbling water and the crickets crying out the same refrain: *Go home. Go home.*

Bob was right: no matter what happened, life went on.

Meagan's boss had never met Cameron. She'd only been eighteen—and Bob Cragg a family friend whom she knew by name—when Cameron made his one visit to the Valley. Cameron, twenty-one and handsome in his uniform, had come to propose to her. He'd come to the Valley as a stranger to everyone else, and he'd left without any of the townsfolk getting to know him.

She'd brought Cameron to this very spot, perhaps this very boulder. She had looked away, unable to bear the thought of never seeing him again. "I don't want you to go away, Cam."

"Then go with me."

"I can't leave Twisp. I'm happy here."

"Without me?"

She watched the river race around the distant bend. Cameron was like the river. Always in motion. Eager to go with the flow. Meagan loved the river, too, and never wanted to leave it. But she wanted to stay close to shore, to never leave her comfort zone.

Before darkness set in, Cam's nose had crinkled; the merriment had reached his eyes. "Go away with me. I promise you, I'll make you happy. And when I leave the army—"

"Twenty years from now?"

"Seventeen," he corrected. "Maybe we could come here for our *family* vacations."

"Family vacations?"

"We do plan on a family, don't we?"

"You're crazy."

"About you."

She had looked up into those gorgeous gray-green eyes. Cam was promising her the world, the moon, and the stars, but she feared in her heart that they would never come back to Twisp together.

He had brushed the grass and twigs from his hands and stood, a tower of strength, as he grabbed her hand and swung her to her feet. Caressed her. "Look, there's a falling star. Aren't we supposed to make a wish?"

"I think so."

"I already made mine, Meg. I want you to marry me and join me in Germany as soon as I can find a place for us to stay."

"Germany." A gasp stuck in her throat.

"I have new orders. Germany this time. I didn't want to say anything—I didn't want to spoil this time together."

"When?"

"Soon. In less than a month. I'll find you the nicest love nest in Heidelberg. You'll be happy there, Meg."

"I don't speak German."

He put his arm around her waist and drew her closer. She came shoulder height, little more. Her cheek had rested against the coarse threads of his worn jersey. She slipped her arm around him, her hand against the middle of his back. She felt his strength, his uncertain breathing. He wanted her to be a soldier's wife and follow him to an overseas posting.

As they stumbled over the twigs back to the car in the dark, he promised her the moon, the world. Even an overseas posting. And now all she had left was a fallen star.

CHAPTER 4

The sun was setting when Meagan slipped off the boulder and made her way back to the car alone. Thinking about that long-ago time with Cameron strengthened her. Now she allowed herself to think of Cameron's grandfather, the feisty old man who had always sided with her.

She and Conaniah were two of a kind. Independent. Blunt. Headstrong. Indifferent to the Juddmans' God. But inside both were sensitive, vulnerable. The two of them had been at constant odds with Cameron's parents. His parents were good people, hard workers, determined to keep the family farm manageable. Fran was plain, country-style, little makeup; Aaron was rugged and frugal. But they were well liked in the community, pillars at the little church, God-fearing. And fearful of any outsider who wanted to marry their son. Meagan had not been their choice for Cameron. The elopement had poured salt in the wound.

Conaniah's record was not much better—even worse in a way. He had married three times—an embarrassment to Aaron. Conaniah didn't even darken the church door for a funeral but buried his first two wives at the grave site. The third, a likeable, good-looking woman, tried to take him to the cleaners, but in the end the marriage ended on amicable terms. Conaniah was left with a mansion twenty miles from the farm, where free from marital commitment, he went on accumulating his historical record of World War II paraphernalia.

Meagan and Conaniah had shared a fierce loyalty to Cameron

and a deep love for Ryan. Would the old man still be alive? If so, he didn't know that another Juddman was crossing the desert of Iraq. Would it even be fair to tell him, to worry him?

When she reached her house, she parked in the driveway and ran up to the side porch where the winter fireplace logs were stacked. She grabbed the spare key from the top ledge, not bothering to search for the key ring at the bottom of her purse. Running her free hand flat along the inside wall, she flooded the interior with light at the flick of the switch. Her gaze fled past the wood-burning stove and the open living room drapes to the photograph on her desk by the windows.

She kicked the louvered door shut, tossed her purse on the table, and crossed the room to stare down at Cameron's handsome face. He looked somber in his uniform, but the photographer had caught the twinkle in his eyes as he gazed at the infant in his arms. Forcing herself to look away, she rummaged through her desktop for the old address book with his grandfather's Kansas number still in it. Before she changed her mind, she dropped onto the cushioned sofa and dialed Conaniah.

The phone rang several times before a singsong greeting came through. *"Buon giorno."*

Her courage slipped. *"Buon giorno.* I—who are you?"

"Roberto."

Italian. That familiar lighthearted greeting with laughter in the voice. She could picture this stranger guiding a gondola through the waterways in Venice. Young, barefoot and singing, a red neck scarf around his throat. Not a care in the world in his smile.

But who are you?

"Per favore, who are you, *signora?"*

"Meagan Juddman . . . Roberto, *non parlo bene l'italiano."*

"Then we will speak English. How can I help you?"

"I'm trying to reach—" She hesitated. *Perhaps he's died. He'd be in his eighties, or ninety by now. Maybe an Italian family has taken up residence in Conaniah's old mansion.* "Is Conaniah Juddman there?"

THE TRUMPET AT TWISP

The musical voice half-sang again. "You have come to the right place. To Conaniah Xavier Juddman's residence. Who shall I say is calling?"

She cleared her throat. "His—his . . ." For want of a better word, she explained, "His granddaughter."

"But he just speaks of a grandson. A great-grandson."

"I was married to his grandson."

"Meagan?" A gravelly voice had joined them. "Where the dickens are you?"

"I'm calling from Twisp."

"Is that young man with you?"

"No, Conaniah . . . He's in Iraq."

"That old already?"

"The army thought so."

"Is he safe?"

"I don't know—that's why I'm calling. I'm worried."

"Roberto, you can hang up now."

"But, Signor, it is time for a snack and then a walk in the garden so you will sleep well."

"So I will freeze in the evening air. And I can't be bothered with sleeping. It is time for me to talk with Meagan."

She protested. "I don't want to interfere, Conaniah."

"The walk can wait. All I have left is time. Plenty of that. It's been a long time, child."

"Four or five years, I think. My fault. I should have invited you back for Christmas."

"Don't like flying—not since 9/11."

Meagan smiled. "You didn't like flying before that."

She pictured him in that vast study of his, relaxed in his leather chair, content to be on terra firma. A proud man—straight-backed and tall when she met him. His skin as olive as the familiar tweed jacket that barely covered his thick chest. His pursed lips were always sucking on an unlit pipe.

The last time he came for a visit, his skin was cratered with age.

Deep wrinkles had set in, his chin doing double time. Now, though she could not see him over the wires, she knew he'd grown old by the tremor in his voice.

Yes, she should have invited him back for Christmas. Each year. Every year. *But I was exhausted trying to sell real estate and struggling to get Ry through his teens at the same time.*

She stretched out on the sofa. "You're still living in the same place, Conaniah?"

"They can't throw me out, and I won't move."

"Are you well?"

"I'm old."

"And Cameron's parents?"

"Aaron still works the farm. It comforts him. And Fran—you wouldn't recognize her. She's never been the same since—"

"Neither have I."

"Fran's gone gray, but she's sweeter somehow. I'm still her prized project. If she nabs this old agnostic—this old *reprobate*, as she calls me—she's bound to get the crown she's looking for."

"That's cruel. And you're not an agnostic, Conaniah. You're just stubborn."

"And lost, according to Fran."

"So they're staying on at the old homestead."

"I'm the rightful owner, but I want no part of it. I would have given Aaron anything—he was my only son. He had only to ask. I had plenty to give."

Conaniah's voice warbled. "I offered him university training—anywhere he wanted to go. Or financial backing for a business venture. But all Aaron wanted was the farm."

"Give him credit, Conaniah. He made a success of taking that turn-of-the-century place and making it thrive."

"Yes, been in the family for generations. I should tell Aaron how proud I am of him—before I forget it."

Her tone became wistful. "Conaniah, when you see Fran, will you tell her that I understand about the Ivory Palaces now? About what she and Cameron always wanted for me?"

50

The old man cleared his throat, but the gravelly tone lingered. "So you're not on my side any longer?"

"We'll talk about it when I see you again."

"I'd like that, child."

"But who is Roberto?"

"My timekeeper. He times everything I do. Naptime. The walk in the garden. Fifteen-minute showers sitting in the nude on an old wire bench. We keep quite a routine. He's a good boy—came from south of Rome."

"Anzio?" she guessed.

"Yes, close to there."

"Do you still have your display tables in your study?"

"I'm sitting here right now looking at them. At least trying to— my glasses must be dirty."

Or your eyes failing. To her he had been handsome, his strong bone structure and deep rich voice passed on to Cameron. But Conaniah's eyes were unsmiling. Pensive. A clear but frosty blue. And now with poor eyesight had they faded?

"Nothing has changed, Meagan, except me. I'm just plain growing old, and I can't stop it. They call these *the golden years;* I find them tarnished. But at least I have Roberto reading my history references when he isn't arguing with the cook or painting. We talk long hours about what he reads. Smart lad."

"He paints?"

"He uses the room next to mine as his studio. He's quite accomplished. Probably never sell a thing, but he's happy."

"Are you?" she asked.

"I am now that we got rid of those white-starched nurses who tried to run the place three months ago. Aaron and Fran's idea. I fired them and hired Roberto the day he delivered my groceries . . . Now tell me about yourself. You're well?"

"I . . ." Her tears fell. "I'm worried. I'm sick of this war."

"I don't watch the news much. I'm weary with war. But I saw that journalist friend of yours—whatever his name was."

"Robinson Gilbert. I've seen him reporting live from Baghdad

too. At first I couldn't turn the television off. Now I'm too frightened to even hear the news. Every time they report another soldier killed—oh, Conaniah, I'm glad when it's someone else's
loved one."

"And then you feel guilty?"

She hung her head. "Yes."

His body might be deteriorating, but not his mind. In some
things he sounded sharp as ever. "Natural reaction, Meagan."

"But I'm still ashamed."

"My dear child, you've suffered enough already . . . After my last
visit to Twisp, Fran asked me what you did with Cameron's trumpet. Whether you put it out in the Goodwill bin."

"No, I stored it when Cameron went away to the Middle East.
I'd never give his trumpet away—but I won't look at it either.
Haven't ever since—"

"It was an expensive instrument, Meagan."

"Is that what Fran told you?"

"No, my dear. I bought it for Cameron in Germany. It's a Wurl-
itzer. Perhaps it's time to take it from its hiding place. To let it
make music again."

Her voice was flat. "There's no one here to play it."

"Cameron wanted his son to play it. Promise me it won't stay
locked away."

She heard exhaustion in the old man's voice. A slight slur to his
wording. "I'll think about it, Conaniah. I must go. We've talked
long enough—you're growing tired."

"Not long enough. My dear, you won't forget me this time?"

"No, I'll let you know as soon as—"

"Will you come see me?"

Her fist knuckled. "When this is all over."

"You could come for my birthday. I'll be ninety-two next time
around."

"I'll be there."

"Will you bring Ry?" he asked.

"I pray so . . . Or better yet, come see me."

"I'd never make it up to that loft of yours."

"I still have a guest room. We could wait this war out together. I'd like that, Conaniah."

He chortled. "My dear girl, I'd need a truck to get me there. Wheelchair. Walker. Urinal. Half a medicine cabinet. And Roberto to take care of me."

"No problem. Just come."

Long after the call ended, Conaniah remained ensnared in his brown leather chair, too weak to push himself to his feet without Roberto's help. For months now he had been pleading with his daughter-in-law's Maker to free him from the entrapment of this worn-out body. But he had lived one day too long. One war too long. War was a curse on the Juddman family, and it was happening all over again. Poor Meagan. Would wars never stop destroying young men? Cutting them down in the prime of their lives? Leaving their families with nothing but memories? Hadn't the Juddmans given enough without Operation Iraqi Freedom?

He shivered. In spite of the warm evenings Roberto had set a fire in the fireplace. The logs crackled and burned. Popped and snapped. In Conaniah's ears it sounded like bombs exploding. The sounds of war. Was he never to be free of that nightmare? Or had the noise of memory grown louder as he grew older?

God, where are you? Are you listening to me? Or are old men's voices too powerless to reach your ear? Oh, God, I should have died in that Bloody River—in the defeat at the Rapido. Then there would have been no Cameron. No Ry. No terrible pain for Meagan. No shattering of the Juddman lives.

Back in the forties Conaniah had almost lost his life in the Bloody River in Italy. Half the men in his platoon died, his friends included—all of them expendable to those in command determined to get the Fifth Army to Anzio and on to Rome. But at what a price! The road to Rome was a deterrent for the Germans. The real focus was the second front in Normandy. But men like Eisen-hower and the brash, outspoken Clark, a mercurial general, planned the battles from a safe distance. They weren't sloshing through the mud in Italy or clawing up the cliffs in the dead of win-ter under enemy fire.

Before he'd ever reached the battle in Anzio, Conaniah had led his platoon of forty men into a deathtrap. Sixty years later, the Rapido crossing still haunted him. It was his nightmare, a shock-ing defeat. Conaniah tried to rub warmth back into his thighs, his gnarled hands numb with cold. The river had been at flood stage, a torrent of rushing water; the operation ill-fated from the start. Casualties were heavy. Many dead. Hundreds wounded. Too many missing and never accounted for.

They advanced in heavy rains, freezing in the melting January snows. In pitch darkness they slid down the steep embankments, the fog so thick they couldn't see the soldier in front of them. Some waded into the waters. Others climbed onto rubber rafts and ply-wood boats. The second they broke shore they were at the mercy of the river and the German machine guns and mortar. The remains of a footbridge crashed into Conaniah's raft, tossing them into the raging, bloodstained river.

Those who crossed the river never came back.

Roberto bounced into the room, whistling, an evening snack bal-anced in one hand. Conaniah's red-rimmed, rheumy eyes struggled to focus. "Jack? Carl? Swim, boys, swim."

"Conaniah, it's Roberto. You're safe. You're here in your own study."

Not in Italy. Conaniah forced himself to look beyond Roberto. The room was the same as it had always been—his shrine to Anzio, to the Rapido crossing. His touch with memories. He was no longer in command of a platoon of soldiers. He was an old man with nothing but possessions and family and friends waiting for him to die so they could claim them. Yet he wouldn't be able to leave anything to Cameron, anything to Lieutenant Rebecca Armenson, the combat nurse who took care of him on the beachhead at Anzio.

He turned toward the sepia photo on his massive desk as Roberto placed the tray on the end table. Roberto's presence was vibrant like a field of poppies, his actions quick and alive, but his gaze had followed Conaniah's. "She's beautiful."

The old man smiled. "Becky had beautiful eyes, but she was never glamorous in her uniform . . . Her parents gave me that picture of her after the war. It's all I have left of her."

"You have your memories."

"Not enough, Roberto."

In the middle of the room lay a glassed-in display table with its relief map of the Italian Campaign. Behind him lay his vast library on World War II. The shiny mahogany bookshelves recorded the Italian Campaign within its pages.

"Roberto, have you read Blumenson's *Anzio: The Gamble that Failed*? It's on the second shelf, midcenter, west wall."

"I'm reading the one on that Bloody River of yours."

"The Rapido? So I've already told you about that?"

A slight smile touched Roberto's lips. "Once or twice."

As Roberto added a packet of sugar to Conaniah's coffee, the old man rasped, "Two packets, boy. Maybe it will help jar my recall. It's difficult to remember these days what I've told you, and what has been left in the crevices of my memory."

"What shall it be this evening, Conaniah? The Budapest Philharmonic Orchestra? Vivaldi? Verdi? Ponchielli?"

"You choose."

"Ah! I know your favorite. Rossini's *The Soldier's Dance*."

Roberto leaned over and flipped on the CD player. As the classical music of Italy filled the room, Conaniah touched his lips to his cupped hands and listened.

A few minutes later, Roberto whipped a linen napkin from his hip pocket and tucked it around Conaniah's neck. Lifting the spoon toward Conaniah's mouth, he pointed to the phone. "This Meagan Juddman . . . you never told me about her."

"I thought she had forgotten me." Conaniah shoved the spoon away. "But I was wrong."

"Then she must call again. Or you must call her. I'll dial for you whenever you say."

"You're a good man, Roberto."

"But a lousy cook. I heated up a little ravioli and snagged a fresh pot of coffee before the cook complained."

"My doctor will have a fit."

"Sì. Let him have his fit."

"My son won't like it either."

"Then we won't tell him," Roberto promised. "I brought some hot mush to keep them both happy . . . Conaniah, why do you think so much about that war so long ago? There is more to Italy than that."

The bite of mush slid down his throat reluctantly. "Yes, I know. I'd like to go back."

"To my country? Then I will take you."

"I'd be a burden."

"You pay me well. You would love my village. My mama would cook for you. No mush. You'd have all the pasta you want. And the sun and the sea." There was a dreamy look in Roberto's eyes.

"With my eyes I'd barely see them."

"You will feel it with the sea breeze on your face. You will see it with your heart—with the music. You would not be an old man there. You would be the grandfather of Roberto. You would celebrate the festivals with my family."

"A trip like that would kill me."

"Then we will bury you there with a big celebration. We would celebrate your years and what you did for our country. Come, Conaniah. Let me take you back to Italy. Then you would have something to live for."

"I think I have found something to live for. My grandson's wife needs me. I call her my granddaughter. I think of her as my granddaughter."

Roberto spooned some more mush into Conaniah's mouth. "Then we will take your granddaughter with us."

"It's a long journey."

"Worth every mile," Roberto claimed.

"You said your village is made up of dirt roads and cobbled streets. I'd have difficulty walking."

"*Sì!*" Roberto shrugged. "No problem. We'll take your wheelchair, and if the wheels give out, I will borrow my brother-in-law's goat and wagon. We will go everywhere." He grinned, shy for the first time since Conaniah had met him. "You will meet my girl. I must marry her before someone else does. She is lovely like the sunflowers. Like your Lieutenant Armenson."

"Yes, I would like to meet her. If we go to your country, can we go to Nettuno—to the American cemetery?"

Roberto shot a glance to Conaniah's desk and the sepia photo. "Is she buried there?"

"Yes. Becky is there, along with several of my friends."

"I will take you there. And then we will go back to my village. Mama will take care of you while I court my beloved Teresa."

"What will you want in exchange for all of that? My property? My house? My money?"

Roberto waved the spoon, splattering some of the cold mush on the floor. "I want none of this. You have given me so much already. My studio. A chance to follow my dream."

"You would leave your painting for an old man?"

"For you, yes. You are my American *padre*, my *famiglia* in this country."

Conaniah sputtered, unwilling to accept another spoonful of mush. He pushed the spoon away. "Let's try some of that ravioli instead."

"Then we shall go into the garden and walk and talk about our trip. Should I call your granddaughter?"

"Not yet. And after we walk, I'd like to sit in your studio and watch you paint."

"Wait until morning when the curtains are wide open. The sun pours in. You are tired now. The studio is not a place to doze."

As Roberto helped him stand, Conaniah felt alive again. Hopeful. Yes, Italy sounded beautiful. He would go there once more. He felt Roberto's strength steadying him. The boy was like Cameron. Like Ry. Like part of his very being.

Meagan's hand slid from the phone. Conaniah, of all people, understood her, but did he understand why she could never touch Cameron's trumpet again?

She argued with herself for an hour. For two hours. For three. Just before midnight she rummaged through the storage closet in the guest room. Boxes tumbled from their hiding places until she came to Cameron's trumpet in its faded blue case. For a second she recoiled, not wanting to fill the house with memories.

At last she picked it up. Taking it back to the sofa, she dusted the cover with her hand and with trembling fingers flung back the lid. The trumpet looked as shiny as she remembered. Time and the weather had left their imprint but had not destroyed it. Cam had been born with music in his fingertips. From jazz to hymns, he played them all.

His medals were there, too, crammed into the case. She unraveled them from the soft cloth where they lay and spread them out on the end table beside her. Cameron's Purple Heart. His Army Service Ribbon. The Good Conduct Medal with two knots—yes, Cameron of all people would have earned a Good Conduct Medal. And the Bronze Star that she would have given back to the government if Conaniah had not intervened.

Straining against the lump in her throat, Meagan picked up the trumpet and attached the mouthpiece as she had seen Cameron do so many times. She rested her thumb on the hook and fingered the three buttons one by one. They resisted. She tried again. Her mouth felt dry as she pressed the trumpet to her lips. She blew. Nothing. She blew again and managed a squeaky, muted note.

Surely it could make more music than that. She laughed and then cried over the trumpet as she turned it in her hands. She polished the bell with her sleeve and turned the instrument upside down to peer inside. A folded letter had been taped there—a letter in Cameron's familiar scrawl.

> My darling Meagan,
>
> I leave for Saudi Arabia in just a few hours. I love you and Ryan more than anything in this world. I had to tell you that once again—but tonight was not the right time. I sit in this old farmhouse—the place where I grew up as a boy. It has always been a happy place for me, but I realize now that you long to be elsewhere.

She paused, as he must have done before writing.

> Dear, dear Meagan, you have always been the joy of my life. Someday you may find this letter. If you do, you will know what it means . . .
>
> But if anything happens to me . . . if I fall on the field of battle . . . know that I was doing what I loved doing. I never wanted to be anything but a soldier. To serve my country.
>
> But being a soldier blinded me to your needs. Right now, with all the memories rushing at me, I think the last time we were ecstatically happy was that week we spent on the Italian Riviera. If I survive, will you go back there with me after this bloody war?

CHAPTER 5

Outside an evening breeze stirred. A tree branch scraped against the open living room window. Inside the only sounds were Meagan's thudding heart. Her sobs. And Cameron's letter shouting his love across twelve silent years.

He loved her. She never doubted it. Somewhere in that last night together he had found time to steal away and write his love letter to her.

After all she had done to him.

She tried to remember the good times—meeting him at the high school prom in Kansas, loving him, marrying him. Both of them had been too young for marriage. A couple of ecstatic kids. Cloud-flying like a couple of turtledoves. Rhapsodic in their love. Her grandmother would have called them an impulsive pair with barely two farthings to rub together.

They drove in a friend's borrowed old rattle trap to Coeur d'Alene. Cameron had sped along the highway southeast of Spokane into Idaho's panhandle with one hand on the steering wheel, the other holding hers. They were oblivious to the August heat blowing in through the open windows. They had each other. The army couldn't take that from them.

As they rode past the lake and into a city framed with steep mountains and clear rivers, Meagan exclaimed, "Oh, Cameron, what a beautiful little town!"

In the early days it had been a logging town with rich silver mines up in the mountains. They asked for directions to the court-

house and the nearest walk-in clinic and then, with marriage
license in hand, they rode past the wedding chapels, searching for
a church. She wanted to marry in a church.

Cameron chose a little church with a brick facade and a sign
that boasted Sunday and Wednesday services, a Baptist affilia-
tion, and the pastor's name: Owen Marshall. Cameron parked out
front and they ran hand in hand up the steps into the empty
sanctuary.

Cameron broke the silence with a shout. "Anybody home?"

Meagan giggled and sobered when a short, stocky man appeared
from a side door, mopping his brow. "May I help you?"

"Will you marry us?"

The reverend's eyes twinkled behind horn-rimmed glasses. He
wiped his brow again. "I'm already married."

"Sir, we're in kind of a hurry."

This time Reverend Marshall peered over the top of his glasses.
"No need to hurry. I've been married forty years. It's a long haul,
son. Not to say they haven't been good years." He dabbed at his
perspiration and scrutinized Meagan. "You're not . . ."

Her cheeks flushed. "No, Reverend Marshall."

"It's all up and up," Cameron assured him.

"Good, but you'll need a license and a blood test."

Cameron waved the license. "All taken care of, sir."

"Then guess your mind's made up. You'll need witnesses . . . oh,
never mind. I can supply those too. And I'll give you my summer
rates."

Cameron looked crestfallen. "How much, Reverend?"

Beads of perspiration had wedged into the fat creases in his face.
"Oh, thirty dollars. We can set up a payment plan if you need to."

As he turned, Meagan noticed the bedroom slippers and the
limp. "Oh, sir. You're hurt."

"Just a bunion. My wife stepped on my foot too many times in
the last forty years. It won't interfere with the ceremony."

"Maybe you didn't move fast enough, sir."

He chuckled, belly deep. "Think you might be right, son. Come along. Bring that bride of yours with you."

A plain, ordinary man with a big heart, he had led them into his study, called in his secretary and wife as witnesses, and performed the ceremony without fanfare. There were no flowers except the lone pink rose the secretary plucked from the pastor's desk and put in Meagan's hand. Meagan had no clear recollection of what she had promised, but Cameron had towered above her, his hands sweaty as he held hers, his eyes never leaving her face. When they left, Owen Marshall made them promise to stay in touch.

"But we're going overseas, sir," Cameron had explained.

The pastor rubbed his jaw. "Then—say in ten years you get back to me. Let me know how you're doing."

So many good memories flooded back. She must call Reverend Marshall someday and tell him . . . tell him what? That Cameron was gone?

No, she would tell the reverend about the excitement in those early days of packing up and moving to Europe to be with Cam. That crazy little apartment in Heidelberg. The unforgettable trip to the Italian Riviera. The brilliance of Cameron's eyes when he held Ryan for the first time . . .

Her old bitterness pushed the good memories away. She stared out the window. The blackness of the sky left her weak with fatigue. Cameron always said it was the darkest just before the dawn.

Right now she remembered the darkness, not the dawns. She had spent almost eight years as an army wife, and much of that time she resented being a *dependent wife*. She disliked being dominated by the military. Sometimes they lived within the walled city of an army base, moving into Cameron's world with the sound of marching troops and the sight of those gun-toting guards at the checkpoints just to go to the commissary. She'd brought Ryan up with an ammunition dump a block away or a military jet flying so low that it rattled the windows when he was napping.

All that time she had longed for a home of their own with lace curtains in the living room window and a big backyard where Ryan could run free and have a swing set and a puppy to romp with. She'd wanted an all-boys room for him where he could keep his books and trucks and have a desk when he went off to school. And she had longed for a pretty pink nursery for the baby girl that she and Cameron had both wanted.

At midnight she lowered Cameron's trumpet case to the floor beside her and placed the shiny trumpet in the folds of its velvety liner. As she read and reread Cameron's letter, the clock chimed the hours.

Midnight.

One o'clock.

Two.

Before the chime could strike three, she stretched out on the sofa and pulled her grandmother's quilt over her legs. She pillowed her head with one hand, clutched Cameron's letter with the other.

For the next three hours she slept. Drifted and dreamed. Awakened and cried. And dozed again. A persistent knocking awakened her in the early morning. She frowned, perplexed by the letter clasped in her hand.

Cameron. Cameron.

The rapping came again. Was it the pounding in her head—the pain like a migraine thundering between her temples? No, something outside the house.

Had the young deer wandered into her yard again? Or boldly stepped up onto the porch? Two days ago she'd leaned out the window to study him. Proud and stately, he'd stared back and then turned and fled back into the woods, his antlers pointed skyward.

The knocking persisted.

She blinked as the morning sun streamed through the open windows, its beam of light forming a brilliant path across the rug.

The trumpet lay in its path. The glare of the sun against its golden rim blinded her.

The banging grew louder. The front door this time. If a salesman had come to sell her something at this hour, she'd send him packing. She thrust her grandmother's quilt from her legs and pushed herself to a sitting position. She stood, wobbling, as she tucked Cameron's letter beneath a sofa pillow.

"I'm coming."

She had mumbled the words through a dry mouth and considered stopping off at the bathroom to splash her face and run a toothbrush over her teeth. But the violent knocking forbid it. She stared down the hall, but the closed louvers made it impossible to see who was there.

She padded to the door in stocking feet. Stood tiptoe. Peered through a crack in one of the louvers.

Spit-shiny black boots!

No. No, Lord. Not again. You can't do that to me again.

The toe of one shiny boot stirred, revealing a uniform trouser leg. The man's fist banged on the door again.

A chaplain? An army officer? Go away. Go away.

Meagan collapsed against the doorjamb, her tears brimming.

Once when she was eight, she had almost drowned. She was drowning again . . .

As a child, she had kicked off her shoes and waded barefoot to the edge of the water where the Twisp and Methow Rivers merged. Giggling. Ignoring her father's warning as he stood at the top of the bank. With a defiant shake of her curls, she had stepped deep into the water. But the racing current caught her off balance. She stumbled against a large boulder. Caught in the swift-flowing current, she was swept away.

She screamed for her father.

Her father's desperate voice echoed behind her.

No one else seemed to see her.

She was part of the river now, too far in its path to reach either shoreline. She was swept over twigs and rocks.

Swallowing water.

Gasping for air.

Her face and hands scraped on the rocks.

The water was deeper now.

Her footing gone.

Her thoughts spinning.

Every time she came up for air, more of her childhood flashed before her. A party. A spanking. Quilting with her grandmother. Her bed unmade. Her mother scolding. The church bells. The death of a friend.

She was drowning . . .

And now she was drowning again. Gasping for air. Being sucked under by her fears. Caught in a whirlpool unable to break the surface. Her prayer for peace and strength swirled in the maelstrom.

As a child a firm hand had grasped her shoulder, yanked her from the river, and protected her from being swallowed by the current and swept along to the Colombia River.

Cameron had marveled at her when she'd told him about her father rescuing her. "He was saving you for me, Megan."

Right now she wanted to block out the pounding on her door. To shut out the worried voice on the other side, saying, "I know you're there. I must talk to you."

All she saw was the spit-shiny black shoes.

All she could think of was Cameron. She would never have met him if she had not moved to Kansas for her senior year of high school.

Meagan had only to open the door. To put her hand to the knob and turn it. She could not move. Could not dog paddle. As she floundered, wave after wave of dread swept over her. Panic caught her in its undercurrent. Engulfed her in its riptide.

She was drowning in her memories, remembering all too clearly what had brought them together. What had separated them forever.

PART 2

The Muted Trumpet

The Lord is my shepherd, I shall not be in want.
He makes me lie down in green pastures,
he leads me beside quiet waters,
he restores my soul.

—Psalm 23:1–3

CHAPTER 6

DECEMBER 1982

Most of the year the Methow Valley stretched out in seasonal colors of mossy jade and Kendal greens, with a bluish-purple on the lower slopes. But that morning, as seventeen-year-old Meagan Norris stared out her bedroom window, the Valley was layered in snow mounds, the craggy Cascade peaks covered with winter's glow. Sunlight streamed through the Valley, reflecting on the icy river as it meandered over the rocks and past a forest of conifer trees. The top branches of the forest bent, heavy with snow; the lower boughs remained an emerald green.

A thousand feet higher the mountains were thickly powdered with a fresh snowfall. To her delight more snow was predicted, a blizzard that would blanket the whole countryside. A good day for cross-country skiing. But last night Meagan's secure world had crumbled. How could she face her high school friends on the slopes today and tell them the devastating news—that she wouldn't be here in June to graduate with the rest of them?

She practiced the words. "Oh, didn't I tell you? My family is moving to Kansas. Dad has this marvelous job offer. Once we get there, he promises to find us the prettiest house in town."

The words stuck in her throat. She didn't want a fancy home on the best street in Junction City. They had a Twisp address in the Methow Valley, a ramshackle two-story with narrow windows that her mother had turned into a home.

Meagan pressed her forehead against the windowpane. Some way, somehow, the day she turned eighteen she would find her way back to this Valley, nestled staunchly against the jagged North Cascades. She belonged here; her life meshed into the very fiber of the land. She felt a part of the hills and knew every twist and bend in the river, every slope and mountain peak. Meagan and the school valedictorian at Liberty Bell had plans of their own, their future already mapped out. What right did her parents have to tear her away, to kidnap her from everything she held dear?

As she tugged on her boots, she heard her parents talking downstairs. No, they were arguing again, shouting at each other, their heated words shaking the rafters. Her meek mother's voice rose. "You can't be serious about leaving the Valley? It won't be the same, John. Meagan has spent the last five years with her classmates. She's set on graduating with them."

"It can't be, Em. I have a job offer near Junction City."

"Junction City? Where in the world is that?"

"Kansas."

A zillion miles away. Meagan snatched up her backpack and ran down the steps in her ski wear. At the foot of the stairs she grabbed the rail to catch her balance and heard her mother say, "Please, wait until summer, John. Think of Meagan."

"They have schools in Kansas. She'll fit in. I can't keep going from job to job, struggling to put food on the table."

"We've managed."

"No, we've existed. They'll hold the job until Tuesday. Meagan and I can go on Saturday. I'll get her enrolled in school. You can pack up and follow us."

"But, John, she has plans for the fall—for her future."

"I want to enroll Meagan in Kansas State University next year. I want her to have a good education."

The farthest Meagan wanted to go was Spokane or Lake Chelan. She didn't want any degree from Kansas State. Storming into the kitchen, she announced, "I won't move with you, Dad. I'd feel like a fish out of water in a big university."

He turned, his eyes soulful. "You have to go, sweetheart. We can't leave you behind."

"I'll be eighteen in July. July twentieth. By then they may be ready to expand Sun Mountain Lodge. They'll need good carpenters like you. Please stay."

"Are you blind, girl? They'll be talking about renovating the lodge for the next twenty years. We're living in an economic depression here. I haven't had real work for weeks."

"Someday they will enlarge the resort. You can help build it, Dad."

"Someday is not soon enough. I promised you last night that I'd buy you and your mother the prettiest house in Junction City on the best street in town. Sit down and we'll talk about it, sweetheart."

"Let her go, John. She plans to spend the day cross-country skiing with her friends. At least give her that much."

He caught Meagan's hand as she passed him and put his truck keys in her palm. "Drive with care. And try to understand, Meagan. We have nothing here in the Valley."

You're wrong. She ran down the squeaking front steps to his truck. *Everything I've ever wanted is here.*

What more could she want than skiing all day, or soaking in a hot tub with school friends, or going to the rhythm and blues festival in July or the Apple Pie Jamboree up in Pateros? What would Kansas have to offer? She knew the Methow Valley from a hundred mountain trails in the back country. She'd soared over the dry powdered snow on her Nordic skis with the crisp air brushing her cheeks and felt the exhilaration of downhill skiing at Loup Loup Bowl. In Kansas she would not be able to hike Mount Gardner with her friends or sleep under the stars in the Okanogan foothills or go cross-country skiing among conifer forests or discover the tracks of a cougar in a bushy canyon. She knew nothing about Kansas and wanted nothing to do with strangers who would treat her as an outsider.

This was what was familiar. The ponderosa pines on the lower hills. Fir trees covering the granite slopes. Hawks or bald eagles soaring overhead. The golden hues of the aspens in bloom along the river. Exploring the crumbling Marsh cabin up the mountain. Hiking through miles of forest and along the rivers. Where else

71

could she watch deer nibbling in her backyard? Meagan liked being part of the legend of the Valley. She didn't want to be torn from her roots, didn't want to go away.

She pulled the truck off the road, bumped over the slippery gravel, and parked by a small bridge that led down to the Twisp River. Her grandmother Norris had brought her here when she was seven—to holiday for the first time in the Methow Valley. Her grandmother had crunched along beside her in wide white boots, leaning on her cane with one hand and wrapping her free arm around Meagan's shoulders. Now Meagan crunched over the same snowy trail and found the large boulder with her grandmother's initials carved on it. She sat on the rock and clasped her hands much as she had done as a child. As she rested there, the long golden hair beneath her snowcap fell softly around her shoulders.

The trees by the water lay barren, the shore on both sides of the river strewn with rocks and pebbles of every size. In either direction the Methow River surged, flowed, and rippled, twisting and turning with each bend. Sitting here in her grandmother's favorite spot was like stepping back to the simpler times of a century ago, when small towns sprung up as trading posts and travel was done by foot, in a carriage, and on horseback or muleback. Back to the time when drinking water for the family had been hauled from the well and served, as her grandmother had told her, from the finest china in town.

From this vantage point, the Valley stretched wild and free; it beat with Meagan's heartbeat. She knew everyone; liked almost everyone except the teacher who had forced her to memorize Poe's "The Raven." She didn't care what the raven did.

But like her grandmother, Meagan felt a kinship to the land and the people—to the first white trappers who had moved in on the Indians. To pioneers in calico dresses, to miners bewitched at the prospect of growing rich, to homesteaders staking their claims. She imagined the lure of gold that brought more men to the fork where the rivers merged. Whatever brought them, they stayed on to fight the elements and the inconvenience, considering it a small price to pay in exchange for the beauty that this land offered.

Her father had moved back to the Valley with reluctance, the dutiful son who came home to wait out his mother's old age with her. Until three months ago Meagan had sat at her grandmother's knee and watched her quilt, hand-sewing each patch with her crooked arthritic fingers. Now that she was dead, they were running out on her. Putting the house up for sale. Acting as though she had never existed.

As the temperature dropped, Meagan's tears felt like tiny ice chips on her cheeks. In the distance she heard friends calling, shouting her name as though she were lost. She pushed herself to her feet so she could see them coming down the trail toward her. Just before they reached her, Meagan took in the Valley once more, scanning the mountain ridges, naming them. The December wind snapped at her ski pants and brushed her face with snowflakes, leaving her cheeks flushed and chapped. How could she face the exuberant chatter of her friends? She wanted to listen to the wind whistling past her, to etch in her memory the calls that echoed across the Valley.

Her friends saw her now. The high school valedictorian trudged through the snow and put his arm around Meagan's shoulder. Wanda, her best friend, put her hands on her hips. "Meagan Norris, we've searched everywhere for you. You were supposed to meet us at the lodge."

The lodge. Sun Mountain Lodge. One of their favorite places to gather. A tourist's paradise. A diner's delight. Banana bread that melted in your mouth. Inside the lodge the beams were of Douglas fir, the stone floor of Idaho quartz. Outside, mountains and valleys and wilderness stretched as far as the eye could see. Jack Barron's and the Haub brothers of Germany's mountaintop dream.

Usually the mention of Sun Mountain Lodge excited Meagan. But all she could do was manage a warm smile. "Wanda, I'm sorry. I must have lost track of time. I just stopped off here for a few minutes."

"You've been thinking about your grandmother again?"

"I feel close to her here. She loved this river."

"I know, but come on. It's a great day for skiing. The others are waiting for us up at Sun Mountain."

Meagan stuffed her hands into her pockets and bent toward the chill. Hours later, after a day on the slopes, she left the others by the fireside in the lodge and stepped outside alone. The beauty of the Valley and the utter vastness wrapped around her.

She was numb with cold, her fingers stiff even in the mittens. But she did not seek the warmth of the lodge. She listened instead to the wind as it howled across the Methow. Looked instead to the patches of blue in the sky and the North Cascade Mountains shouldered with snow, with majestic Mount Robinson to her left. This was where she belonged. Her father had other plans. She could stand her ground against the elements but could not stand against the inevitable.

Inside the building Wanda screeched with laughter. Outside Meagan fought back tears. It was still too soon to tell her friends that she was leaving on Saturday. Instead, she made a promise to herself. Someday, maybe when her world was falling apart even more than it was at this moment, she would come back to the Methow Valley and the mountains—back to utter freedom—and find herself again.

CHAPTER 7

JANUARY 1983

Meagan sat on the passenger side of her father's truck and glared at the dreary desolate land. In the field, a barbed-wire fence with stone posts cut through the prairie grass, and bands of limestone and flint rock covered the gentle rolling hills that stretched out in front of her. But they were not her beloved Cascade Mountains with their forests covered with snow. Here red cedar evergreens were still full of growth, but the cottonwoods and elms had lost their leaves. Some wispy tufts of cottony seeds lay on the hard ground and the vaulting branches of the elms drooped lifeless in the January morning. Why had her father brought her here to the brown and tarnished gold of a Kansas winter?

Her father chatted as he drove past a farmstead nestled in a sheltered valley. To their right barren trees leaned into rock walls. A stone church sat empty, its steeple bell silent. Everywhere they drove rocky outcroppings dotted the rolling Flint Hills.

"We're going to be happy here, Meagan."

"I'd rather be skiing with my friends back home."

"Try to be happy for your mother's sake. She'll be so pleased that it isn't all flat prairie. She will love these rolling hills. And the majestic sky—oh, Meagan, so much sky."

Yes, Mother will put on a happy face to please you, Dad. "It's just not home. It's not where I want to be." She hunched down farther into her seat, determined not to be content.

"But I have a good civil service job over at Fort Riley. I'll be able to provide things for you and your mother."

"We were happy in Grandma's old house in Twisp."

"I couldn't find steady work back home."

Meagan averted her eyes and stared straight ahead. She loved her father yet felt ashamed that he worked so hard and failed so often. But had he failed? Five years ago he'd sacrificed gainful employment at the post office in Portland, uprooted his family, and moved back to Twisp to take care of his aging mother. He had held things together with temporary jobs—mucking out barns near the Chewuch River, driving snowplows in winter, and scooping ice cream for Gene Walker in the summer or clerking at the Trading Post in Winthrop. Her dad, sweet as he was, remained cash-poor. Yet he had spent a lot of time with Meagan, showing her the mysteries of the river, pointing out the beauty of the trails, teaching her how to cross-country ski, how to swim. All that time in Twisp he had cared for his mother. In those last few weeks of her life, he had lifted her from the bed to the commode, spoon-fed her, read to her, and sang to her in his rich tenor voice. Meagan treasured these memories.

As they drove farther and evening fell, shadows formed on the tall prairie grass. The shadows in her own heart deepened as well. Tears welled in her eyes. With her resentment over the move to Kansas, she had wounded this kind man once more.

He reached over and patted her hand. "I love you, Meagan."

She nodded and whispered, "I love you doubly."

Not far from the city of Manhattan, the "little apple" of the West, he turned into the Porters' cattle ranch, where they were staying. The ranch, nestled in an orchard grove, had its seasonal apples and cherries, an abundance of wildlife and nature, and a pond where they'd fish for bass in the spring.

"Dad, I don't want to live in Junction City."

"Then we're in agreement about something. I don't want you near the fort, dating soldiers or marrying one."

"Oh, Dad!"

"I'm serious, honey. You've got a good mind. I want you to go to the university to prepare yourself for a steady income. When Mother gets here, we'll let her decide where we buy a house. But it'll be spring before I can afford a place of our own."

Meagan guessed it would be even longer than that. Reaching the porch of the limestone bunkhouse—the place they were to call "home" for a while—Meagan glanced back. Giant oaks and sycamores formed a backdrop for the ranch. Once Meagan's mother arrived, she'd turn the cramped quarters into a cozy setting. The living room and bedrooms were crowded, the kitchen congested, the refrigerator moaning, but her mother would make the place homey in a day.

"It's okay, Dad. Mother will make do at the ranch. But she won't like it here in the winter."

His chin quivered. "Spring's coming, sweetheart."

It was not until spring that Meagan began to settle down. As the seasons changed, she borrowed her father's four-wheel pickup and took to roaming the woods, where she spotted her first whitetail deer. Inching closer, an opossum scampered across the trail, stopping long enough for Meagan to see its white snout and beady eyes. On the third Saturday in March, she encountered her first rattlesnake sunning itself on a pile of rocks.

After that she donned her father's high-top socks and long-legged pants and allowed the bespectacled ranch owner's son to accompany her on her outings. Tad Porter had a lopsided grin and an Indian mother. He knew the wooded trails behind the ranch, could identify the footprints of a coyote, and showed her the Collard lizards beneath the rocks. When the wildflowers poked their faces above ground, he knew each one by name.

Tad eased his own workload by teaching Meagan how to mend the fence with a bullsnake slithering by, and how to make friends with a horse by feeding him apples over the barbed wire. He taught her to fish at the deep end of the creek and to fry the white filets on an open fire. Most important, he took her under his wing at the school some ten miles east of Fort Riley.

April awakened the hillsides, turning the barren fields into enormous, lush-green lawns. Herds of cattle grazed the hills; others lazed around the ponds. At school they talked of graduation and the prom in mid-May. As late spring broke with its balmy weather, the golden strands of wheat decorated the countryside and Tad invited her to the high school prom.

As they danced, he pressed his cheek close to hers. "Now that we're graduating, what are your plans, Meagan?"

"My folks want me to go to Kansas State."

He caught his breath. "That's where I'm going."

"Not me. I have plans of my own."

His arm tightened around her. "I hope you change your mind."

"We'll see."

But no matter what Tad wanted or her father said, she was not staying in Kansas. She was going home again . . . home to Twisp.

As Tad swept her past the bandstand, a handsome young man lifted his trumpet and filled the room with the sweet tones of "Mood Indigo." Moments later he changed tempo and played "Tuxedo Junction."

"Tad, who's that? I never saw him at school."

"Cameron Juddman." Tad's eyes darkened as he led her to the sidelines. "Thirsty?"

"Later. Tell me more about the trumpeter."

"He likes the music of the forties and fifties and religious stuff. He graduated two or three years ago. Kids liked him, but I kept my distance. He was always carrying his Bible—or blowing that horn of his up on the hills."

"He plays well. Does he live nearby?"

"Interested?" Tad teased.

"I'm just curious."

"Yeah. But I'm not worried. He won't be much competition. He's in the army. Came home to see a sick grandfather."

"Then he's not stationed at Fort Riley?"

Tad's tone sharpened. "Don't sound so disappointed. It's fortunate for me he's stationed somewhere in Georgia. Oh no. Trouble on the way . . . Excuse me, Meg, I'm going to the refreshment table."

Meagan glanced over her shoulder and saw Cameron Juddman approaching with an amused twinkle in his eyes and two cups of punch in his hands.

The day after the prom Cameron appeared at the Porters' ranch with a rose in his hand. Meagan felt certain he had broken it off from the bush out front, but she smiled.

He grinned, his merriment reaching his slumberous gray-green eyes. His skin was a bronzed tan, a direct contrast to her creamy complexion.

"Hi, Meagan. Remember me? I played the trumpet at the dance last night."

"Yes, you brought me a glass of punch."

"And I tried to get you to ditch Tad Porter, and you wouldn't do it." Cameron Juddman was long-limbed and muscular, his voice rich and lyrical. "I spotted Tad out in the fields tending the horses, so I thought you and I could spend the day together."

"How did you find me?"

"I asked around. Even my mother knew who you were."

"But I don't know you, Mr. Juddman."

"If we spend time together you'll know me."

As she took the rose, he touched the back of her hand. "Do you believe in destiny? You see, I believe we were meant to meet. Why else would my grandfather be ill and the army compassionate enough to send me home to his bedside?"

"Then why aren't you with him?"

"He's much better. He told me to spend the day with you. Gave me the keys to his car. Will you come? I'll even introduce you to him just to prove to you that I have a grandfather."

She twirled the rose and smiled. In July she'd be eighteen and looking for an excuse to leave Kansas. A day's outing meant fun. Less boredom. It was just a date. He'd be gone soon, back to his army post, and she was leaving Kansas, wasn't she?

Except for his close-cropped hair, no one would know he was a soldier. His powder-blue sport shirt and pressed slacks were casual. He appeared honest, trustworthy. His lips were thick—maybe from blowing his trumpet—but sensuous, kissable. Overall he was charming, good-looking. There was no need to explain him to her parents. They were gone for the day.

Forty minutes later, as they drove through the visitor's gate at Fort Riley, Cameron talked of the frontier days and the Civil War. Of Indians and bison roaming the prairie. Of settlers coming and going. Of the importance of the mounted cavalry when soldiers rode horses into battle.

"Kansas has a long history, Meg." Cameron parked the car and offered her his hand as she stepped from the passenger side. When he didn't let go, she was pleased. "We can claim some biggies. Buffalo Bill Cody. Wild Bill Hickok. George Armstrong Custer. George Patton. Dwight Eisenhower."

He took her by the chapel and the Irwin Army Hospital. They browsed through the museums and looked down on the hump-shouldered bison from the observation point. Cameron knew every inch of the fort. At the Custer House he squeezed her hand. "Custer and his wife, Libby, lived in a limestone house much like this one."

Cameron's eyes were brilliant. "Custer was second-in-command at one time. He took his stand against Sitting Bull and Crazy Horse and Black Kettle—and his last stand at Little Big Horn in 1876 . . . Meg, at the end of that battle a horse named Comanche was the sole survivor. They never rode Comanche again. Like an old soldier, he hung on for a long time. He was buried here at the fort with full military honors."

"You're getting excited about a four-legged horse? What about Custer's wife? She must have been lonely in this isolated fort."

"She was a soldier's wife, Meg."

"And forced to move into his world? Away from her own family? With the wind howling over the prairie? Her husband riding off to battle? What did she give up, Cameron? The comforts of a home in the East? The living standards of a socialite family? Must the army always come first?"

"Yes, when you're a soldier."

"So you marry the army?" She felt flattered by his attention—after all, Cameron Juddman was a handsome twenty-one-year-old—but his career angered her. "I don't think I'd like being a soldier's wife."

He laughed. "Then I better not ask you to marry me."

Calming down, she bantered back, "Wait a month or two."

"Too long. I fly back to Georgia in the morning."

She tried not to think about it.

His tone took a more somber note as they walked through the Fort Riley cemetery, where rows of graves were marked with rounded white headstones standing in formation. "Some of the markers date back to the 1800s. Victims of the cholera epidemic. Soldiers from the Civil War. POWs from World War II."

"Prisoners of war?"

"They were soldiers, too, Meg. When the time comes, I'd like to be buried here at Fort Riley with full military honors. Close to where I was born. I don't dare mention being buried here to the folks. They never wanted me to be a soldier."

"What then? A soda jerk?"

"Mother wanted me to be a doctor. Dad wanted me to take over the farm. But I always wanted to be a soldier."

She liked the pride in his voice. The casual way he laughed. The quizzical way one brow arched higher than the other. The way he looked at her. The way he gripped her hand.

"I don't expect you to understand, but even as a boy I loved hearing the bugle call at sunrise and the measured cadence of troops marching. Mother hated those sounds. In the summer, after my chores, I'd ride my bike over to the fort or go out in the fields and practice marching."

"All that way?"

"I enjoyed it. My grandfather served in the army. Maybe he's the reason I wanted to be a soldier."

"And if another war comes along?"

"I'll be the first one to volunteer."

"You'll be the first one to get yourself killed."

"I'll be careful now that I've met you, but I love this country and would not be ashamed to die to keep her free."

Later she'd remember these moments and regret not listening to that first inner warning: *I always wanted to be a soldier.* Cameron loved the army. The fiber of his being was military. Committed. She didn't want to be a soldier's wife.

Leaving the fort, Cameron drove into the country. Scattered farms dotted the land. The sun turned the wheat fields to gold. Horses and cattle munched the clover.

"See that big silo? My folks own that land. The farm's been in my family for generations. We date back to the pioneer days. One of my distant relatives rode cavalry here in the Civil War. Another helped lay the Santa Fe rails. We still have a picture of Wild Bill Hickock with one of the first Juddmans in the territory. We go back a long ways, Meg."

She sucked in her breath and exhaled when he drove past his parents' farm. "I was at your place once."

"You know my parents?"

"My mother and I joined the Quilting Bee when we first moved here. They hold a luncheon every month at your mother's."

"How did that go?"

"Not very well, Cameron. She asked me about going to church, and I told her that God wasn't in my plans."

"I've gone to church all my life."

"My grandmother was like that, but not the rest of us. I guess we've been too busy."

"Too busy for God? I'm sorry. You were saying . . ."

"One of the ladies at the luncheon told your mom that the next time you came home on leave she'd introduce us."

"Not good."

"No, your mother informed her that when her son married it would be to a nice little girl from the church—and she was bound to be born and bred in Kansas."

His jaw clamped with a irritation that surprised her. "When I marry, I will make my own choice. Mother knows that." His hands tightened on the wheel. "My parents are pillars of the church. God-fearing people. That's how they brought me up. But Mother is blunt. If she offended you, I'm sorry."

She laughed. "She meant well. Your dad came in for the luncheon and brought a basket of fresh apples. He didn't say much, but he had a splendid smile." She risked the truth. "Cameron, I'm glad you didn't drop by your parents' place just now. I bet it would make your mother nervous seeing us together."

"I'm afraid you might see her at my grandfather's place. That's where we're heading."

"We are?"

"Yes, I promised him we'd swing by. She planned to take lunch to him. Be forewarned—she and my grandfather are two sparks. But since he's been sick she says she can't let the old reprobate die without Jesus."

"Will he?"

"He's more apt to die from Mother overfeeding him. But I pray he'll live for a long time. Right now he's gaining weight on her home-made soups. She may be spooning some lentils into him right now."

"He can't feed himself?"

"He likes steak. There. There's my grandfather's place."

She shielded her eyes and looked for another old farmhouse with Black Angus cattle grazing by the fence. But Cameron pointed toward a magnificent gated property, shrouded with trees: a three-story mansion with an entry of limestone rock.

Cameron turned in. "Here it is."

A brass plaque bore the owner's name: Conaniah Xavier Juddman. Above the iron gate, in the shape of a bridge, loomed the words The Rapido Crossing.

"Cameron, is that the name of a river around here?"

"No. The battle for the Rapido River turned into one of the greatest defeats in World War II. They suffered massive casualties when they tried to cross the river."

"Was your grandfather there?"

"Yes. And at Anzio. When he first built this mansion, Gramps planned to call his property Hell's Half Acre, after the beachhead at Anzio. But my folks threw ten cat fits."

With a click of the remote, the massive gates swung open. Cameron drove through and up the winding road.

"It's so big for one person. Were there no children other than your dad?"

"Just Dad. But Gramps had three wives. The first one was buried down at the fort. Another buried in her home state. Wife number three left him."

"She didn't take the mansion with her?"

"There was a good settlement, but she considered this property too eccentric."

"But you like it?"

"Of course. I've spent much of my life here with my grandfather. I have a host of friends, but Gramps is my best friend."

"An old reprobate?"

"Judge for yourself when you meet him."

Cameron parked the car by a row of sycamore trees and dashed around to open the door for her. "Let me warn you. Gramps can be quite crotchety. But he'll just be testing you." He reached out and broke off a piece of bark from the tree. "This reminds me of my BDUs."

"Your what?"

"My battle dress uniform. Just look at the green and yellow blotches against the brown."

Meagan looked at Cameron instead, and when their eyes met, she blushed. *I don't want you to fly back to Georgia in the morning. No one ever made me feel this way before.*

He drew her back, saying, "Whatever you do, Meg, don't mention the name Mark Clark to my grandfather."

"Mark Clark? I don't even know him."

"You're such an innocent." His merciless teasing was back. "Clark was an army general in World War II. As far as Gramps is concerned, General Clark designed the Rapido crossing."

"But he didn't plan on the losses."

"He insists Clark knew there would be heavy casualties. Guess that's the prerogative of the men who design battles."

He ran up the steps to the house and walked in, without knocking. She followed and heard his voice echo in the vaulted entryway: "Gramps, it's Cameron."

"In here." The voice was low and gravelly.

They traced the sound into the elegant study. Conaniah sat in his leather chair by the window with a thick history book balanced on his lap. He whipped off his reading glasses and studied his guests. "I was afraid your mother was back."

"Did you have a row?"

"I wanted steak and she gave me that!" He pointed to the unfinished bowl of broccoli soup that lay on the table beside him. "I told her to get out and go cook for the homeless. A man grows weak on soup and crackers."

"Gramps, Mom means well. So what's wrong with you?"

He scowled. "You want a diagnosis, or what I think about doctors—or your mother?"

"The latest medical report."

"The doctors voted on double pneumonia and a weak lung."

"What did they say about your old war injury?"

"I have to explain *everything* to those young doctors. The medical schools turn out men in white coats who aren't even dry behind the ears. I have to diagnose my own condition for them."

Cameron chuckled. "They're probably relieved. But you know what I mean. Your doctors ordered bed rest if you came home."

"And what do they know? I'd die in that miserable hospital room. I'm content here."

"You do look a shade better."

"Have you forgotten your manners, Cameron? Who's the young woman cowering behind you?"

Cameron grabbed Megan's hand and pulled her forward. "Gramps, this is the girl I told you about."

Bushy brows knit together. "You were right. She's pretty." He seemed to study her now. "But you're not too smart spending the day with this scoundrel."

"Cameron says you're stubborn and rich. And buddies."

Conaniah chuckled, the harsh lines on his face softening. "That about covers it. The old reprobate and the trumpeter. I thought he was going to show you the sights around Kansas."

"We compromised. A trip to Fort Riley, then here. He wanted to prove to me you were a grumpy old man—who didn't like soup." Meagan was surprised at her own brashness.

Conaniah chuckled again. "Cameron, I like this girl of yours. She'll have to come visit me when you leave."

"I'd like that, sir. Maybe I could cook a steak for you."

He winked. "With baked potatoes and mounds of sour cream."

"What else is on your *don't eat* list? I'll make that too."

"Strawberry shortcake."

"With whipped cream."

"Meagan, my girl, I'm glad you came, but Cameron should have taken you to Milford Lake. We've been fishing there ever since he was a boy. And hunting together. Pheasant. Quail. Deer. I taught the kid everything he knows."

Everything that would make him want to be a soldier. Meagan frowned. "I don't think animals should be killed." She didn't add, *Nor soldiers.*

"Then how do you propose to make me that steak? I have a cook, but she leaves off the salt. Won't put butter on my plate. And refuses to bake pastries."

"I still don't like killing animals." She glanced at Cameron for support.

He shrugged. "Okay, Meg, we won't go out for hamburgers at Grizzly's or have steaks at Clyde's this evening. We'll have soup with Grandpa."

"No fighting, you two." Conaniah pointed to the center of the room with his bookmark. "Show her my war, Cameron. The Bloody River of Rapido and Anzio are there."

Cameron held Meagan's hand as they stared down at the glassed-in display tables with relief maps of the Italian Campaign. "Gramps planned this whole thing."

"Not that bloody war, Cameron, just the display tables. Don't ever line me up with the generals, boy. They're the ones who sent my men to their death." He pointed back to the display tables. "But the record's all there. It took me years to complete the project . . . It'll please some museum someday."

She glanced at Conaniah. "Won't your family want it?"

"We'll see."

"Gramps handcrafted everything—from the camouflaged landing craft that unloaded them at Anzio to the soldiers."

"That's right. I hired an artist to craft the soldiers: the Americans and Brits, the fighting Polish, the French, and those shrewd warriors from India. Good fighters, all of them."

Pointing to one relief map, Cameron explained, "This is the muddy road to Rome with its rugged terrain and steep cliffs where the Germans hid. And that's the ancient stone Benedictine monastery—that building with its narrow cell windows."

It was all a work of art. The battle aid station staffed by the Army Medical Corps lay on the beachhead. The medical tent city cared for the wounded on portable operating tables while the enemy, in German pillboxes, fired down on the tents with their bright Red Cross markings on them.

"That's where Gramps met his friend Becky—there on the beachhead. The nurses called it Hell's Half Acre."

Cameron kicked a hassock to his grandfather's chair and sat down. He beckoned for Meagan to leave the display tables and join them.

For the next few hours she watched them reminisce. Conaniah boasted about making his money on the oil wells of western Kansas. He talked about the train sets he'd made for Cameron, about parades and war heroes and the history books that lined his shelves. He spoke of the Rapido crossing and the bloody Anzio beachhead. Of friends lost in battle and the nurse who saved his life, and with great bitterness of Eisenhower and Clark, the men who designed the war plans.

At the mention of the nurse again, his lip trembled. Cameron reached out and squeezed his grandfather's hand. "Meagan, Lieutenant Armenson was Granddad's first love."

Conaniah recovered. "Go on with you, boy . . . but he's right. I would have married Becky there on the Anzio beachhead if only . . ."

Meagan pitied him. *If Lieutenant Armenson had lived, you never would have married the others.* "I'm sorry, Conaniah."

"Don't be. That brief time of knowing her was worth it."

Cameron talked of boyhood memories at his grandfather's side. Of their trip to Italy when Conaniah at last made peace with himself. Of his grandfather crafting the display tables here in the study with their historical references to World War II. Of skiing with his grandfather in Colorado.

Later Meagan would remember the affection that passed between the two men—of the close-knit bond between the old reprobate and the trumpeter. She found herself liking them both— the one who described himself as hellbent, the other whose commitment to God and army had merged.

When they stood to leave, she smiled. "I'm glad we came to visit you, Conaniah."

The old man gripped her hand. "You will come back, Meagan?"
"I promise."

I t was past midnight when they reached the Porters' ranch again.
She had missed her father's curfew.

"Will you write, Meagan?" Cameron asked.

"I don't think we should."

"I don't want it to end here. I want to keep in touch."

"Libby Custer made the mistake of keeping in touch."

"It's because I'm a soldier, right? How is it you can accept the soldiers of the west or an old soldier like my grandfather, but not me?"

"They seem less threatening."

He stepped up on the porch with her. "That may be your father
peeking out the window. No—no. Don't look."

"Does he have a shotgun?"

"If so, I hope *he* doesn't believe in hunting down animals."

She giggled. "You'd better go. I loved spending the day with
you. And meeting the old reprobate . . . Well, soldier, be good to
yourself—don't volunteer for any special missions."

Cam leaned down and sang in that lyrical voice of his, "I'll be
seeing you in old familiar places."

He brushed her tears away, stole a kiss, and ran down the steps.
Halfway down the path, he turned and waved. Then he was gone,
a silhouette swallowed up in the darkness.

Behind her the door opened. "Good evening, Meagan. Mother
and I think you need a new battery in your watch."

"Time just got away from me, Dad."

"Tad tells me that young man is a soldier."

"Yes." She walked through the door ahead of him. "He's been
home on leave to see his grandfather."

"You've been gone all day. No note. No phone call."

"I'm sorry, Dad. I've been to Hell's Half Acre and back."

"You've what?"

"I'll explain in the morning."

Inside the house, he took a ticket from his pocket. "We planned to give you your graduation present this evening, but Mother couldn't wait up any longer. It's a round-trip airfare to Washington. Mother and I thought—*I* thought—you would like to spend the summer in Twisp."

"To keep me from dating a soldier?" She thrust a strand of hair from her cheek. "There's no need to worry, Dad. Cameron goes back to Georgia in the morning."

"You know I only want the best for you."

"I know." Relenting, she gave him a quick embrace. "Good night, Dad."

"Good night, Meagan."

In her tiny bedroom with the moon shining through the window, she pictured Cameron's face. She never expected to see him again, but she could still hear him singing, *"I'll be seeing you . . ."*

Would he? Would they be looking at the same moon and seeing each other?

CHAPTER 8

SUMMER 1983

Twisp, Washington—back where people still waved at strangers. Meagan was once again in Owen Wister's smiling country. The top branches of the conifer trees caught the sunlight. Craggy peaks begged her to climb them. The meandering rivers gurgled and bubbled as they always did. Aspens lined the riverbed. Wildflowers dotted the hillsides. Mount Gardner still wore its snowcap. The ice-cream store was doing a booming business and buzzing with wasps. The pioneer days of calico and denim, and mining for gold, were gone. Now tourists in shorts and sleeveless blouses strolled through the town.

Other things had changed too. Some of her old friends had moved on, and now Wanda wore the high school valedictorian's engagement ring.

New owners had painted her grandmother's old house with a fresh coat of paint, but her grandmother's best friend, Mrs. Bishop, had rented her a room for the summer in a yellow country house with a couple of cows, an old workhorse, and a dachshund. From day one, the dachshund slept at the foot of Meagan's bed and huddled in her arms when she stood at the window looking at the stars and thinking about the soldier down at Fort Benning, Georgia.

Here, in the Valley that she loved, she spent her eighteenth birthday quilting on the sofa beside Mrs. Bishop. They had cake and ice cream to celebrate, just the two of them.

Two weeks later Mrs. Bishop called from the foot of the stairs. "Meagan, you have company, my dear."

She stirred in her bed. "Who is it?"

"He didn't give a name. Said it was important."

"Tell him to go away."

Mrs. Bishop's shrill voice rippled with laughter. "Said he won't budge until you get dressed and get down here. He's good-looking . . . if that helps."

Meagan rolled out of bed and tugged on a pair of old jeans and an ice-blue blouse. Running a comb through her tangled hair, she grabbed her shoes and socks and left the room. As she ran down the steps, her heart skipped a beat. Cameron, so handsome in his uniform, was kneeling on her doorstep. He looked up and grinned. "I've come to marry you, Meagan."

"Did you go AWOL?" she teased.

"No, I inveigled a three-day pass. So there's no time to waste. Put on your shoes and come away with me. Marry me."

"You're kidding. Your parents won't like that. Nor mine."

"I'm not marrying them."

He didn't propose again until that afternoon. He had pulled on his grubbies and they had gone down to the river.

"I'm too young to get married, Cameron. I just turned eighteen."

"I know. I brought you a diamond for a birthday present. Just a wee solitaire, but it's all I could afford. We can drive to Coeur d'Alene and be married by the justice of peace."

"My grandmother would want me to be married in a church. I'm sorry, Cameron. I'm just not ready to settle down."

"I'll be gone for two years, maybe three. I want you to be with me."

"Gone? You're leaving Fort Benning?"

"Yeah. My first overseas posting."

"You know I just came back to Twisp. I plan to stay here."

"We'll visit when we get back from Europe." He was promising her the sun, moon, and the stars . . . and his spur-of-the-moment, unquenchable love. She thought him crazy, and yet she'd thought of no one except Cameron since the day she left Kansas.

They sat together on a huge boulder on the river's edge talking, laughing.

An hour later he took her hand. "Meagan, I'll give you one more chance. Will you marry me?"

"I don't think it would work. Your mother doesn't approve of me. I . . . I don't believe the way your family does."

His eyes clouded. "I know. But you've told me your grandmother was a God-fearing woman."

"She was. Granny Norris was always singing hymns. Going to church. Reading her Bible. She loved God, and He snatched her away from us. She suffered so much those last few days."

"Things like that happen, Meg. Normally, I'd agree with my mother. But I'm going away for a long time. I don't want you falling in love with someone else. I want you to be with me." He paused, his eyes intent on the river. "My folks can't stand in our way now."

She turned his face back to her. "I'm still not good enough for them."

"You're not religious enough for them. That's all. Once we get to Germany, we'll go to chapel on the army post. I'll ask the chaplain to talk to you—you'll come around."

No, she would not come around, but she could pretend. But would that be fair to Cameron? "Come back when you're a civilian, and we'll talk about marriage then."

"I'm a soldier, Meagan. Long-term."

Meagan watched him slip into a moody silence. He seemed both sensitive and caring, flirtatious and daring. And yet there was a part of him that was aloof, distant, caught in some tangled commitment in his military life that he could not share with her. She looked out, over the land she loved. Dipped her hand in the river. "I don't want to leave here."

Meagan ached as she watched him try to find the words to tell her that Twisp was not the place for him. Not even when he left the army. It was clear he was lured by the prospect of an overseas duty. The Valley that she loved was too constricting for him. He loved being a soldier. But she knew that the army, being a soldier's wife, would smother her.

"It won't work, Cameron. My folks want me to go to the university."

"I want you to go to Heidelberg with me."

Europe. Heidelberg. It sounded like a dream come true. She'd be crawling out from parental control. Let Wanda have the valedictorian.

And then with that impulsive, coquettish nature that ruled her, she agreed. "Why not?"

There was a tender gleam in his eye. "You won't be sorry. I love you."

She wasn't certain what the words meant. She just knew she was ready to spend her life with Cameron Juddman. "I . . . I love you too."

He slipped the sparkling diamond on her finger. It was small, yes, but it was more than her mother ever had.

And with that swinging-on-the-stars elation of the young, they borrowed Mrs. Bishop's old rattletrap of a car and drove to Coeur d'Alene, Idaho.

Three weeks later, with both sets of parents infuriated with them, but Conaniah amused and delighted, Cameron left for Europe. "Write, Meg."

"I will."

"As soon as I can arrange for housing, I'll send for you."

"I won't have the money to come."

"Sell my car. That should do it."

In October both sets of parents and Conaniah were at the Kansas City Airport to see her off on her first lap of the journey to Cameron. Even Tad Porter showed up to wish her well. She pressed her face to the window and waved long after the jet was airborne.

As the plane neared Heidelberg, Germany, the captain lowered the jet beneath the high billowy clouds. In the distance a forest fire raged. Flames leaped from the burning hillsides. Plumes of smoke darkened the sky. A fire whirl rose like a tornado, its exploding force scorching more trees. Outside the plane window a ring of fire encircled the sun.

The nerve endings in Meagan's stomach did a twittering jig-jag dance. What if the distant fires had closed the airport? What if they were not cleared for landing in Frankfurt? How would Cameron find her?

Two weeks earlier she'd told him, "Cameron, you must meet me."

"Sweetheart, I can't. I'll be off for ten days on a special training mission."

"Where? What have you volunteered for this time?"

"An air base in Italy. But I'll be back the night you arrive—and we'll be together. Just follow the instructions I sent you. You'll have no trouble finding our place."

But she was having trouble finding the paper with the address on it. The jigs in her stomach multiplied. *Turn around. Fly home again. How dare Cameron expect me to find my own way to the apartment!*

When she heard the captain's voice, she fastened her seat belt. Her fingers locked as the Lufthansa airliner tilted to the left and circled above the airfield. She saw little more than a haze until the plane braked and came in for a landing. The sign Rhein-Main Frankfurt Airport reassured her. This was not an emergency landing.

Heidelberg was eighty kilometers south of Frankfurt.

Until that moment the thrill of flying to Europe on her own had kept the adrenaline pumping. But stepping from the Lufthansa jet, her stomach churned. She rushed along with the throng to passport control. Her lips went dry. What had the customs officer asked her? What had she answered?

"Traveling alone?"

She nodded. *Why not? I'm eighteen.* It sounded wretchedly young to her. Five months ago she had nothing to concern her but finishing high school and mending the fence with Tad Porter.

"Tourist?"

"No, I—Yes, I guess I am. I'm joining my husband."

"A German national?"

"An American soldier. We'll be in Heidelberg two years."

"Dependents?"

Dependent wife. Already she disliked the army jargon. The label. The restrictions. "No children." She blushed. "We've only been married two months."

Why hadn't Cameron arranged to meet her? Why didn't he ask his commanding officer for time to meet his wife? She stared down at the solitary diamond—the thin gold wedding band—and remembered his words: *"It's all I can afford."*

The rings calmed her. She was married now. An American abroad, but married. The minute she saw Cameron everything would be all right. She just had to collect her luggage at the baggage claim and locate a taxi.

She waited her turn in the queue before a young taxi driver helped her into the backseat. With his foot heavy on the gas pedal, he jerked the car forward for the drive to Heidelberg. As fast as they rode on the autobahn, Mercedes sped past them.

Thirty minutes later she stepped back in time to a quaint city made up of clustered buildings with multicolored facades and magnificent baroque cathedrals. The ruins of a medieval castle dominated the skyline. It stood high above cobblestone streets and old stone bridges. Beneath the bridge flowed the swift River Neckar, with wooded hillsides rising from the shoreline.

The driver maneuvered around the narrow streets and squealed to a stop in front of a drab cement building. "This is it, *Fräulein*."

She looked down the street at the charming homes with colorful facades, then back at the three-story dwelling. "You must have the wrong address."

"This is the address you gave me."

"It just can't be—I was expecting—"

"Ah! You are an American? A soldier's wife?"

"Yes."

His gaze turned sympathetic. He gave a wave at the cement building. "This is the housing that the soldier can afford."

At least the drabness of her new home was broken by window boxes of geraniums. He swung her luggage from the trunk and waited, hand extended. She paid him in Deutsche marks and picked up her bags and negotiated the five cement steps up to the door.

"Güten Tag. Frau Juddman?"

She glanced back to the sidewalk where a broad-shouldered boy of twelve or thirteen stood. He was Nordic in appearance with his mop of thick blond hair and intense blue eyes. "I'll help you."

He came up the steps, grinning. She had no railing to lean against as she relinquished her luggage. As he swung her suitcase up into his hands, what had seemed iron-laden to her appeared featherlight to him. "I'm Karl. My mother is your landlady. My father works at the army post with your husband. Your husband will be home in thirty minutes."

That would be Anna and Wolfgang VonHoekle. In thirty minutes? She must change into something special just for Cam.

Karl bounded up to the third floor. She dragged herself behind him, stopping to catch her breath with each landing. Once inside the flat he pointed out the small kitchen, the living room, two bedrooms, and a bathroom at the end of the hall. He deposited her luggage in the smaller bedroom. It was all right. They could rearrange things when Cam came home.

She tried to tip him.

"No, *Frau Juddman*."

"Then that will be all. Thank you for helping me."

"*Dänke*. You tell me *dänke*. I tell you *bitte*."

She expected him to leave. Instead, he dropped down in a chair in the living room and picked up the copy of the *Rhein-Neckar Zeitung*.

So Cam is already learning German . . .

"Where do you live, Karl?"

Karl glanced over the top of the newspaper. "Here."

"Here? On this floor?"

"*Ja*."

She was waiting at the bottom step, outside, when Cameron, as tall and handsome as she remembered, came home. She ran to meet him. He embraced her and kissed her right there on the curbside.

When they reached the house, he stopped. "Wait."

"Is someone coming?"

"No, I'm catching my breath. You are so beautiful—I've missed you, Meg. I felt awful asking you to travel so far alone."

"I managed."

"No one bothered you?"

"Of course not. But I had lots of attention and several offers to help with my luggage."

"Didn't you tell them you were married?"

She gave him a coy smile. "When someone wants to lift my luggage from the overhead bin, it's not the appropriate time to show him my wedding band."

He swept her up in his arms.

She kicked at the air. "Put me down. What will the VonHoekles think?"

"Don't know. But this is our first real home. Those few days with my parents don't count. That means I carry you over the threshold."

"You carried me over the threshold in Idaho."

"On our wedding night? That doesn't count either." He started up the first flight of steps.

"Cameron, we live on the third floor."

He groaned under her weight. "In my dreams you were light as a feather."

She giggled. "I tip the scale a bit more than that."

They'd reached the first landing.

"Cam, your back—"

"Just two more flights."

Meagan was worried. As physically fit as he was, he struggled to catch his breath. "Let me walk the rest of the way, Cam."

"Can't break tradition." He leaned against the banister. "I should have rented a room on the first floor."

"Why didn't you?"

"Wasn't available."

She wiggled free and faced him, her arms around his neck. "I lost a shoe on the way up."

"I'll get it later."

He was about to sweep her in his arms again. She protested. "Wouldn't a piggyback ride be easier?"

He roared with laughter. "Now, why didn't I think of that?"

They paused every few steps, laughing.

"What did you tell your landlady about your wife?"

"That you were fat and sassy—no, I told her you are young and beautiful—and crazy."

He boosted her bottom higher and went the last flight of stairs. "Do you have your key, Meagan? Mine is in my pocket."

She slid off his back. "I left the door unlocked."

"Anna VonHoekle won't like that."

"Why should she care? It's not her place."

His smile faded. He led her into the sitting room. "There's something I need to tell you, Meg. I was afraid your parents wouldn't let you come."

"We can't afford the rent?"

"I've got that one worked out. It's—well, we're sharing this flat with the landlady."

"With the landlady?"

"And her husband and twelve-year-old son Karl."

"We're sharing the bathroom with all three of them? Sharing that old tub with the claw feet?"

"I'm afraid so."

"I didn't see a lock on the bedroom door."

"Wolfgang promised to fix that this weekend."

"Then fix it yourself," she insisted.

"I won't rattle his cage. Anna says *he's* the handyman."

"And that funny little white bowl in the bathroom?"

"It's called a bidet."

"A who?"

He grinned. "Don't ask. But it's sort of like a sitz bath. We won't bother using it."

"There's only two bedrooms. I went on an inspection tour."

"They have one. We have the other."

"And they're sharing their room with their son?"

He ran his fingers over his buzz cut. "I didn't stop to think about that. Just about us."

"Cam, the one spot that's really ours is the bedroom?"

He looked away and nodded.

"We have to find another place."

"We can't—it's *imperative* that we stay here." There was a strange firmness to his tone that Meagan hadn't heard before.

"But the whole top floor belongs to the VonHoekles."

"I know, Meagan. I work with Wolfgang at the army base. When I told him you couldn't join me until I had a place off base and a refrigerator—"

"But just one bedroom."

"I searched all over Heidelberg, Meg. And then Wolfgang offered to make room for us here. The VonHoekles always seem strapped for cash, just like soldiers."

To stave off her argument, he swept her back into his arms and carried her across the threshold into their bedroom. When he set her down, she stood by his side, surveying their quarters.

"You're disappointed, Meg."

"What did you expect?"

"I wanted you to be happy."

In a cubbyhole smaller than their bedroom in Kansas.

"Cameron, isn't there any housing on the base?"

His mouth twitched. "For sergeants and above. I thought you understood. We had to be *command sponsored* to have housing on the post. With my rank I don't qualify."

"That's what you meant by unaccompanied—unsponsored."

He nodded.

"I thought you meant I was flying over here alone."

"You've got to listen to me." His tone sharpened. "You've got to understand. I'm on a short tour—two years. I was responsible for bringing you over. That means we live *on economy*—in civilian quarters. I guess I wasn't totally honest with you. But I wanted my wife here in Germany with me, not halfway across the world."

They were having their first big quarrel.

"Oh, Cam, let's not fight." She giggled through her tears. "It's just that we don't have any place to cook. Your mother insisted that I bring a cookbook. What will we tell her?"

"As little as possible. Maybe I could talk Wolfgang and Anna into a couple of hours in the kitchen. But they've given up so much already just to help us out."

"Cameron, I put my suitcases in the hall closet. I guess I'd better bring them in here."

"There's space under the bed. We can put them there."

She fought her tears. "Along with the cookbook."

"I did order a two-burner hot plate at the commissary. It hasn't come yet. But we have to keep it in our room."

"No roasts. No big meals."

He shook his head. "Do you think you can make it on cans of spaghetti and meatballs? Maybe when they think we're starving, the VonHoekles will give us kitchen time."

Seeing his distress, she reached up and cupped his cheek. "We'll work it out, Cam. I'll get a job."

"It's not likely here in Heidelberg. Once they find you're a soldier's wife . . ."

"Well, it's just for a year or two."

A massive bed filled most of the space. A soft easy chair and floor lamp occupied one corner. A five-drawer dresser edged the wall by the door. Someone had nailed a full-length mirror to the back of the door.

Cam gave a sweeping bow. "Just for you, my lady."

"Nice."

She eyed the bed that dwarfed the room. "Where did you get that?"

"Before one of my officers rotated back home, he gave me a good buy on the bed and the chair." He grinned. "He threw in the lamp and the mirror at the last minute."

"And this?" She fingered the chipped corner of the dresser.

"A bargain on one of the back streets. Wolfgang helped me haul it upstairs."

"Mother sent a dresser scarf, and I can line the drawers if we can find some shelf paper."

"The commissary has everything. You'll be okay. Right? I got you one of those Heidelberg cards. You can travel all over. You can do a lot of walking in this town too."

"Really, Cam, I'd like to get a job. So I can help out."

"The officers' wives have a better shot at that." He reached out and took her hand. They walked to the window that overlooked an empty cement square.

"Why don't they put a garden down there, Cam?"

"It gets noisy sometimes. That's where they held the Oktoberfest before you came. But you're here in time for the *Karneval*. That starts the first day of Lent, with everybody wearing crazy costumes and throwing confetti. They'll parade down there in the square wearing wooden masks and necklaces with clanging bells. There's lots of music and merrymaking until early morning."

She groaned. "A nice quiet neighborhood, right?"

THE TRUMPET AT TWISP

"At least the festive Christmas Market is held in other squares. Honest, Meg, I wanted to do more for you."

"It's okay, Cam. We'll make the best of it."

"Will you be happy?"

She leaned against him. "You're here, aren't you?"

Early that evening Meg glanced at the bed again. "I'd better make that up."

"I already did. I bought sheets at the commissary."

She pulled down a corner of the bedding and blinked at the striped beige and brown sheets. They reminded her of a zebra. "A little bit wild. Do you have another set?"

"No, there's nowhere to put them."

"Dad gave me some money when we said good-bye at the airport. I'll use some of that for a bright set." In her mind's eye she pictured a floral print with a lacy or ruffled edge that could fold back over the eiderdown.

"Anna loaned me some towels. You may not like them—they're pretty coarse."

"Don't worry, Cam. Mom sent some pretty sets with me."

That night she discovered the color of dark striped sheets didn't matter. She fell asleep in the crook of Cameron's arm, secure and loved. Puffs of frothy clouds, looking like frilly, lacy linens, filled her dreams. Deep in her subconscious she determined to make this little corner in Germany—small as it was—a happy place for Cameron.

CHAPTER 9

Meagan vaguely remembered Cameron whispering in her ear the next morning, telling her he was leaving. She just wanted to sleep. But the faint sound of church bells awakened her at eleven. She sat up and stared at herself in the mirror—a ghastly sight of droopy eyelids, tangled hair, and no makeup. Far below her open window the symphony of bells turned to a grating clanging.

She gave up—got up. As she pattered barefoot over the hardwood floors in the hallway, she met her landlady at the bathroom door. Meagan had expected a matron with harsh features and a freckled face, but Anna was tall and well-figured, her eyes a pensive, curious blue.

"*Güten Morgen.* I'm Anna. And you must be the bride."

"*Güten Morgen, Frau VonHoekle.*" Meagan brushed her sleep-tangled hair from her face. "I just woke up."

"Your young husband left hours ago."

Singed by the reprimand, Meagan wrapped her negligee snug about her. She considered escaping by going back to bed, but decided she had made a bad enough impression on Anna. "I won't let it happen again. I mean, I won't oversleep. I guess I was bogged down with jetlag."

Anna surveyed her with a scowl. "Now it will be another thirty minutes before there's enough hot water for a shower. But once you're dressed, I'll show you Heidelberg."

"I'd like that . . . but Cameron won't know where I've gone."

"If he's anything like Wolfgang, he won't care. Besides, they won't be back until this evening. So we'll have a late breakfast in town. I'll call the *Zum schwarzen Walfisch* for a reservation."

A reservation for breakfast? Meagan let that one fly by her sleep-deprived mind. She had expected to spend the day alone. But, except for the candy bar melting in her purse, there was nothing in the room to eat. "I'll just take a cold shower."

"That will wake you up." An amused twinkle lit Anna's tired eyes. "And if you're looking for your shoe, I found one on the landing last night. I started to knock on your door, but the light was out."

Meagan turned scarlet. "I dropped the shoe on the way up. And then we got so busy—we ate some crackers for supper . . . and . . ."

"I know. And turned in early. Jetlag can be so exhausting." The teasing smile softened the sternness of Anna's face. "When you're ready, I'll be on the balcony."

Later, as they settled across from each other at the *Zum schwarzen Walfisch*, Anna pushed the menu aside. "This is the best place in all Heidelberg for breakfast. My son and I come here often."

But not Wolfgang? Meagan wondered.

Savoring the "Sugar & Spice" breakfast, Anna talked with pride of her city. She spoke of walking the lush wooded hillsides with her son, of her dreams for him to go to Germany's oldest university here in Heidelberg. "I don't want him to study in Argentina."

"Argentina?"

"That's where his father studied engineering."

As Meagan noted the streaks of silver that crowned Anna's blonde head, she modified her first impressions. Anna was graceful, her face square, her mouth wide, her expression sometimes harsh, yet none of these features hid the fact that Anna had once been attractive. Now the facial lines were more pronounced—the effect of being forty. Or were they the worry lines of a troubled woman?

As she finished her second *der Kaffee*, Anna propped her wrists on the table, folded her smooth hands, locked her slender fingers. She wore a thin wedding band on her right hand, a plain watch with a black strap on her wrist. "If you'd like, we'll walk through the old town and go to the castle before we go home."

"Oh, I'd love to. The castle was the first thing I saw when we drove into Heidelberg."

"I'm afraid our town is famous for those old ruins."

"Was it bombed in the war?"

Anna's crystal blue eyes frosted. They were judgmental as she met Meagan's gaze. Meagan froze. Had Cameron persuaded Anna to spend the day with his wife? Or had Anna come with deeper motives?

"We were spared the Allied bombings, Meagan. We weren't destroyed like other cities."

"I'm sorry."

Why was she apologizing? She hadn't been alive back then, and Anna would have been too young to remember the war and destruction.

But she sensed in Anna's tone a controlled resentment. "Keep in mind that good people like Beethoven and Wagner and their magnificent music came out of my country."

"And Johannes Brahms. He's a favorite of mine."

"And the Gutenberg Press—we wouldn't have books if it hadn't been for him. And the Gutenberg Bible, as your husband likes to remind me." Anna's locked fingers tightened. "I'm sorry. I just don't like such a strong American presence in my town. But Wolfgang says that Heidelberg has always been a high-level headquarters for your military. Tell me, Meagan, does your husband work for American intelligence?"

"No, he expected to be a squad leader when he moved here."

"Then why is your husband chauffeuring for a senior intelligence officer these last few weeks?"

Meagan cocked her head, surprised. "I'm certain you're wrong . . . Anna, if you dislike Americans so, why is Wolfgang working for the U.S. Army?"

106

"I tried to persuade him not to go there. It's no secret that I'm not crazy about Americans, and neither was Wolfgang's family. They fled Germany just before World War II ended. Wolfgang was eight then—six years older than I am. It was a good thing for his family to move to South America—to get away from the Allied occupation and the terrible destruction of our country. Many of my people went to Argentina and Bolivia and Brazil."

Meagan tried to sort it out. *The ordinary German didn't flee at the close of the war. But some of the German leadership did.* She jerked her attention back. "So your husband speaks both German and Spanish."

"And English and French. That's why the Americans hired him. They didn't want his engineering background, but he is of untold value to them as an interpreter."

"And you, Anna?"

Her voice was curt, defensive. "I was born in 1943—just two years before the war ended." Her tone sharpened. "I assume your good husband has already told you. Today's society considers me illegitimate. Back in the forties I was one of Heinrich Himmler's perfect Aryan children." She shoved back her chair and stood. "Come, Meagan. It's a strenuous walk uphill to the castle, but you're young."

As they left the restaurant, the castle loomed down on them.

Meagan shaded her eyes. "We're going to walk up there?"

"Why not? Wolfgang and I get around by walking. Of course, if you don't like the exercise, we could catch a tram or bus."

You're testing my endurance. "We'll walk, Anna."

Once inside the courtyard, Meagan realized that the castle had been built in different styles. Its gardens, with their waterfalls and beautiful flowers, resembled an English park.

"Meagan, come back with Cameron some evening when the castle is lit up. It's romantic. Wolfgang brought me up here when we were first married. The best views are at the top. We'll save that for a clear day when we can see all the way to Mannheim."

"I think Americans are stationed there too."

"No doubt. They seem to be all over my country." She glanced at Meagan's shoes. "You'll want to wear trainers that day because we'll walk back down through the woods—but the only danger will be the mountain bikers who don't like pedestrians."

Meagan grimaced inside. *Any better than you like Americans.*

Once they'd hiked back down from the castle into the old town, Meagan stopped to browse in a window. When she looked up, Anna was gone. Twenty minutes later she found her landlady sitting on a bench in the Bismarckplatz.

"I thought you had gone on home without me."

"I intended to. But you're a guest in my country."

Meagan touched Anna's wrist. "Anna, I want to be your friend. Mother is sending me some of my quilting squares so I can make a quilt of my time in Germany. I want you to help me."

The blue eyes brimmed with tears. "I need to be honest with you. It was Wolfgang's idea to make room for you in our flat. I fought it all the way. American soldiers aren't always popular here in the neighborhood. But once Wolfgang makes up his mind, there's no changing him."

"I'm sorry that we took your son's room."

"That makes no difference. Wolfgang is busy these days—very involved in his job. The evening meal is of little importance to him. He drops off for drinks with his friends. That young man of yours won't even taste a glass of beer at the festivals down in the square." Her words wavered. "On Sundays Corporal Juddman goes off early in the morning to play his trumpet at the base chapel. He's invited us to go with him—but Wolfgang said I would have to go alone. He isn't in to things like that, but Karl went once."

"Anna, perhaps we could go together sometime?"

"I'd like that."

Meagan wanted to tell Anna about Cameron and his grandfather. She wanted to make Anna laugh by calling them *the old reprobate and the trumpeter*. But before she could do so, Anna stood and linked arms with her.

"Yes, you're right. We're both lonely. And I think we can—should—be friends."

"Oh, Anna, I think I'm going to love Heidelberg."

"Your Mark Twain did."

That evening, as Meagan lay in Cameron's arms, she spoke in hushed tones. "Anna doesn't trust us—at least she doesn't trust you."

"Doesn't trust me? She hardly knows me."

"She says you're chauffeuring an intelligence officer around Heidelberg and between army bases."

He sucked in his breath. "I am, but how did she know that?"

"Wolfgang, I suppose."

He lay back on his pillow and stared at the darkened ceiling as he tried to block out the music and dancing down in the square. Six weeks before Meagan had arrived, his commanding officer had called him in and asked how well he knew Wolfgang VonHoekle . . .

Well enough to drink with him, sir," he had replied. "But I don't drink."

"The two of you are quite friendly?"

"Here at the base. And he has shown me around Heidelberg."

"Do you know anything about his background?"

Cameron knew little about Wolfgang's past. Even less about his wife. "No, sir."

"Does he discuss military matters outside of the post?"

"I don't know, sir—at least not with me."

"We want you to get better acquainted. He works in a sensitive area where someone is leaking intelligence data."

Cameron had filled in the rest. "And because he's German—"

"We want to make certain he can be trusted . . . We need you to do two things, Corporal." And then his commanding officer had spelled them out, promising that the duty would be temporary . . .

Now Cameron told Meagan, "My chauffeuring is just temporary."

"What happened to being a squad leader?"

"I guess you could say I volunteered for this job."

"Are you—are you with intelligence?"

His ribs quaked with laughter. "I'm infantry. You know the only thing I want to drive is a Bradley fighting vehicle."

"Then why the limousine service?"

"They asked me to help out. It's all I can tell you."

"Is Wolfgang VonHoekle trustworthy?"

"I thought so. That's how I got into this mess."

"Cam, did you know Wolfgang's family fled from Germany before the end of World War II? That's what Anna told me today. Wasn't it only the Nazis who fled the country back then?"

He laughed. "Meagan, do *you* work for intelligence?"

"I don't understand everything she told me. Anna said she was one of Heinrich Himmler's perfect Aryan children. She sounded so bitter when she said it. What did she mean?"

He blinked in the darkness. He wanted to be as honest as he could. "Himmler wanted babies with perfect Nordic traits to build up the German race, so he promoted illegitimacy between the *Schutzstaffel* and selected young women. His state-registered program was known as Lebensborn."

"But why is she so troubled by it forty years later?"

"Wouldn't you be, Meg? I suppose it would have been swept from the records except that the children of that program grew up to be outcasts, misfits. When Wolfgang married Anna, he didn't know she had been conceived in this manner."

"And now he rejects her. Poor Anna."

"She's a good mother. A good wife. And she needs a good friend."

"That won't be difficult. I like Anna."

"Good, because we have to stay here at least a little longer. And now, my lovely, can we forget Anna and Wolfgang and talk about us?"

In March Cameron was gone for three weeks on maneuvers in Italy. When he came home, he swept her into his arms and waved a travel brochure. "It's official."

"Oh, Cam, did you get a promotion?"

His smile cascaded. "I hope that comes later." He put the brochure in Meagan's hand. "I put in for a three-day pass and added some leave time. If my commanding officer approves, we're going to spend seven whole days on the Italian Riviera."

Morning sickness swept over her again. "Not today?"

"No, early in June. I'll take you on a honeymoon."

"It's a little late, Cameron. I'm . . . I'm pregnant."

His mouth gaped. "Pregnant! We're going to have a *baby*?"

She was close to tears. "Yes, and it wasn't in my plans. I wanted to go to college first. And see as much of Europe as we could."

"Why didn't you tell me about the baby?"

"I thought I had the flu . . . hoped I had the flu. Then you were going to be away on maneuvers, and I didn't want to worry you."

"Worry me? I could have boasted to my buddies while I was gone."

"Oh, Cam, how can we raise a baby in just one room?"

His hands dropped to his side. "Then you haven't been happy here? We'd find another place—except I'm still committed to staying here. Until . . ."

Meagan didn't want explanations. She knew that his army

commitments came first. Perhaps his commanding officer had asked Cameron to remain at the VonHoekles. Was Anna right? Did the military have a particular interest in Wolfgang Von-Hoekle?

As Anna trudged down the hall toward them, Meagan whispered to Cameron, "Is there any chance of finding another place to live?"

"We'll work it out. But the baby . . . I'm glad. I always wanted a son."

"I don't want to be pregnant."

Anna reached their side and shook her head. "Child, child. I keep telling you—the first little kick you feel, you'll want him."

"It might not be a him." Meagan knew her voice sounded defiant, but she didn't care. "I—" She flew down the hall, her hand to her mouth.

Cameron started after her. Anna stopped him. "Let her go. By the time you go to the Riviera, this morning sickness may ease off."

"Are you sure?"

"Karl wasn't my only pregnancy. There were four others. Sick each time just like Meagan. Miscarried every time."

He gripped her arm. "That won't happen to Meg?"

"She's young. Frightened. Away from home. But she's strong." Anna glared at him. "You're busy, but *I'll* be here for her."

"I'm grateful. But we won't always be in Heidelberg. We may have to move."

"My place isn't good enough for you? So why have you insisted on remaining in these cramped quarters, Corporal? Your wife will always be welcome, but you? I'm not sure of you. I don't know what my husband has done, but I think you are watching him."

"Anna, we started out as friends."

"He doesn't sleep well since you moved in."

"I'm worried about him too. He has to be more careful on the job. If he doesn't measure up—"

"I told him never to work for the Americans. If he didn't work for your people, he'd be free to travel. He likes to travel, you know." Her voice filled with longing. "Once a year Wolfgang flies back to Argentina, but he never takes Karl and me with him."

"Wolfgang sometimes talks about the Italian Riviera," Cameron prodded.

"He does?" She hesitated. "I've told him we could move there with him. He goes two or three times a year to check on those olive groves of his."

Cameron scowled. *Wolfgang? Wolfgang is always strapped for money, or so he says.* "He owns olive groves, Anna?"

"Not really. But a friend of his from Argentina owns a big olive grove. Wolfgang worked the olive fields for him long before we met. He could work there again."

"That's what he told me." Cameron glanced toward the bathroom door. "Are you certain my wife is all right?"

"Of course. And we were talking about my husband. He's good at languages. He insists the Americans need him. But he's trained as an engineer."

I know. Trained in Argentina and flies back there once a year too. Never takes you or Karl with him. Two or three times a year he flies to the Italian Riviera, claiming he's checking on some olive groves. Wolfgang is a worried man, and I cannot tell Anna. Cannot warn her. I'd be breaking my own cover—endangering the job I was sent to do.

"Is that why you chose the Riviera for a vacation?"

She was close, but wrong. He wanted Meagan to see the land that Conaniah loved.

Again he could hear Meagan retching behind the closed bathroom door. "She'll never forgive me."

"Would you blame her? When I got pregnant with Karl, I didn't speak to Wolfgang for weeks—until I felt the baby kicking inside of me. You go on with those plans for the Riviera. Spend some time together."

"Anna, there's another problem."

She scowled. "You don't want the baby?"

"I'm thrilled about that. But my commanding officer offered to put in for a transfer for me. Maybe to Vilseck or Baumholder."

"But Meagan loves Heidelberg."

"We both do. But I don't think there's a hospital in Vilseck, and now with Meg pregnant—"

"We have excellent medical care in our country."

"Anna, I didn't mean to offend. You see, in the beginning I was never slated for here. I'm mechanized infantry. I want to do what I was trained for."

"But you've been driving a senior officer around."

"I drove him around a few times back at Fort Benning, in Georgia—as a favor. When he heard I was coming to Europe, he requested my services. It was supposed to be temporary. Never this long. And now he's being rotated back to the States."

"Is that what you want?"

"Not exactly. I'd be sent on as soon as a transfer came through."

Anna stiffened. "And Meagan? She'd go with you?"

"That's the problem."

The toilet flushed and then sounds of Meagan's retching came again.

"If we couldn't find housing—"

"She could stay here with me," Anna offered.

"We couldn't afford housing in two places. There's no base housing for my rating. That means Meagan couldn't go with me. We'd be separated . . . She'd likely be sent home."

Anna glared at him. "Your wife is pregnant, and you'd send her home? Then turn the transfer down."

"I can't. In the case of a promotion or a transfer, the army has a fast rule about things like that. Up or out. I take this transfer or I could be out of the army."

114

"Meagan would like that. But whatever happens, you should not leave her, now that she's pregnant."

The bathroom door opened. They both turned, waiting. Meagan's face was ashen. She pushed her damp hair back from her face and leaned against the doorjamb. "I don't want to be pregnant—not if it's like this."

Cameron smiled in sympathy as he went down the hall to her. "Anna tells me that you should feel better by the time we go to the Riviera."

But he was worried, worried about the transfer. What if they couldn't be together at a special time like this? And then he was there, holding her against him, and she was crying.

CHAPTER 10

Two days before the Juddmans left for the Riviera, Wolfgang Von-Hoekle disappeared without a word to his wife.

"Where is he, Anna?"

Anna cast a brief glance at Meagan. "Wherever he is, I don't think he's coming back this time."

"Why do you say that? Something must have happened to him!"

"I think he's deciding where his loyalties lie."

A chill ricocheted off Anna's icy words and crept along Meagan's spine. "His loyalties should be here with you and Karl," she argued.

"He may not be strong enough."

Not strong? Strong was the first word Meagan would use to describe Wolfgang. A brawny type, tough and hard-nosed. Unyielding in his political views. In all the months she'd been in Heidelberg, Meagan still knew little about her landlady's husband outside the home. She could describe his physical appearance if someone asked. A guarded smile. A black mustache. Thinning hair at the temples. Forty-six years old. She knew because they had celebrated his birthday a month ago. A crooked front tooth, and yet pleasant looking . . . except for his eyes.

His eyes were calculating, dark, his manner crusty. For all her months in Heidelberg, she had known when Wolfgang was coming up the steps. Like an old soldier, his booted feet made a resounding *thud* on the uncarpeted stairs. He came in with a copy of the

Buenos Aires Herald under his arm, and his clothes and breath smelling of beer. Anna was always there with a weary smile and his supper plate on the table as he walked through the door.

He joked with Anna and his son through dinner—and with Cameron and Meagan when they were invited to join them. Then, in the middle of a sentence he'd stand, carry his dirty dishes to the sink, and disappear into the sitting room to collapse in his easy chair and devour the international news.

On the weekends he seemed quite different. Companionable to his son. Ready for a game of tennis with Cameron. Willing to sit in the living room with his wife and watch television or to take his family to the festivals in the square, where his uproarious singing could be heard above the crowd.

A complex man. Cameron liked him. With Meagan, Wolfgang's conversation was provocative but moved to defensive whenever she mentioned Argentina or the old Germany. Three nights ago, when Meagan was talking about their upcoming holiday in the Italian Riviera, Wolfgang had tossed the paper on the floor and stomped from the room.

Now Meagan looked at Anna and asked, "Do you think I offended him in some way the other night?"

"You? No, Meagan. He's been afraid that his job at the post was at risk. Once or twice he suggested that Cameron was here to spy on him. When he gets like that—unsure of himself—he always goes away. He took the suitcase he always takes when he flies to Argentina. He packed lightly, but he took his best clothes."

"Why would he go there without telling you?"

Anna twisted the black band on her watch. "His father, Erich, is alive and living there. Erich is not at all well, but still dreaming of the Third Reich rising again."

Rising again? Forty years later? That had to be pure rumor. The Allies had won. Meagan was ashamed at her own lack of knowledge. It had been part of the history books, but she'd memorized just enough to come out with flying colors in high school. Now she wished she'd remembered more so she could comfort Anna. If only Conaniah were here. With his vast historical library, he would understand this troubled woman. He might not like her, based on his personal loss on the Anzio beachhead—after all, she was a German and the product of a Nazi—but he still would offer wise counsel.

Meagan's youth stood against her. She had known no pain as deep and cutting as the pain Anna knew. Her deepest grief had been the death of her grandmother and her resentment against the family's move to Kansas. So all Meagan could offer was a listening ear. She sat down on the sofa beside Anna. "Maybe Wolfgang has just gone on a family visit."

"I wouldn't know. I forbade him to mention his father's name in this house. I know it's been forty years since the war, but I don't want Karl to ever know the despicable things his grandfather did when he worked with Heinrich Himmler."

"The man who organized the mass murder of the Jewish people?"

"Yes, the man who wanted the perfect Aryan race. The group I was born into. I've borne that shame."

"Anna, that was a long time ago. You're a good person. A dear friend."

"With a pathetic background. Ever since Wolfgang discovered I was born into the Lebensborn program, he has become more distant. We both know his father would have been involved in that program—he was one of those proud *Schutzstaffel* officers."

"The SS?"

"Yes." Anna struggled to her feet and paced the pint-sized sitting room. "I think Wolfgang made a choice over these last few months. It has always been his father or me."

"But you've been together so long."

"With his father always between us. Himmler died at the close of the war. If only Wolfgang's father had been kind enough to do the same." She sighed. "You think me cruel, Meagan? Selfish? But

Wolfgang's father and Himmler were the cruel ones. And to think they both started out as sons of Catholic schoolmasters. Good beginnings. Little more."

"What happened?"

"With Wolfgang's father I don't know. Himmler joined a paramilitary organization, and that started it for him."

"You and Wolfgang were happy before we came, Anna. That's what your son told us. It's all our fault—overcrowding you like this. It's upset your family."

Anna stared out the open window where her flower box was blooming with brilliant red geraniums. "Will the American military look for my husband?"

"Even if they did, I would never know."

"Cameron wouldn't tell you?"

"Not something like that. Last night he said it would be up to your local police to find him. The crime rate here in Heidelberg is low, and there's no evidence of foul play. That makes it more hopeful."

"If your military asks, it's Wolfgang's father and friends who are high-risk. A threat to us. Not Wolfgang. The organization is not dying out. Not fast enough. By now they're men in their sixties and seventies, but no less dangerous. The Third Reich will never rise again—but they are still clinging to world domination."

"Anna, you're frightening me."

"When the time comes, it is not Wolfgang who will be important to you, but his father. The last time I knew, Erich was using the name Franz Mueller. Once before he was called Jens Nehmer. Franz Mueller and his friends were never tried for their war crimes. Now they never will be. Argentina wouldn't allow them to be extradited. There's something else your American military might want to know—Wolfgang's father has new interests. Reinstating the Third Reich has failed. But their goals of superiority are just as strong. They're investing their wealth in other projects."

"Other projects?"

"Perhaps in funding training camps for terrorists, for one."

"Anna, I'm going to talk to Cameron. I think we should cancel our trip and be with you."

She whirled around. "No. Karl and I will be all right."

"For your sake, we must know the truth. Wolfgang worked for the American military, and if what you say is true . . ."

"When you come back, perhaps Cameron could go through Wolfgang's papers. Perhaps he would find something."

"Will you still be here, Anna?"

"I won't run. My son is too important to me."

That evening, as Meagan and Cameron sat on the edge of the bed in their tiny bedroom, she urged him to cancel their trip.

He gave her a reassuring hug. "We're going. Just the two of us."

"After all I've told you?"

"Wolfgang's going away has nothing to do with us."

"Cameron, did the army order you to go to the Riviera?"

He laughed. "The villa where we're going was my idea."

"And if all the things that Anna said are true—"

He kissed her into silence. "All I can tell you is it's best if we're gone. Anna will be all right—I have my . . ."

"You have what?"

". . . my commanding officer's word on that."

"Anna is my friend."

"Wolfgang was my friend. I still want to believe in him."

"After all I've told you, Cam?"

"I knew those things already, Meg. But it's just a gut feeling— I think when the truth is known, he will be all right . . . Sweetheart, it's going to be all right. Whatever happens, we've never betrayed the VonHoekles. Now promise me—when we reach the Riviera, we'll put Heidelberg behind us. Our time there is going to

120

be a memory of a lifetime." His arm tightened around her shoulder. "I love you, Meagan. Whatever happens, remember that."

That same week, back in the States, a Washington reporter packed for his latest assignment abroad. He glanced at his son—a weed of a kid. "About packed, Robbie?"

"Yeah. I squeezed everything in."

"You going to call your friends again and say good-bye?"

"Already did. Just didn't tell them I'd be in Paris for three years or more."

"You'll make new friends."

"Yeah. That's what I did in London and Tokyo."

Robinson winced at Robbie's casual shrug. "The American Academy in Paris is a good school, Son."

"Hope they don't expect me to speak French right off."

"They won't. And you won't have any trouble learning the language . . . Son, am I making it hard for you by taking this assignment?"

Robbie shrugged. "You always tell me travel broadens me."

And it isolates you. It's turning you into a loner. You're more at ease talking to my friends, one on one, than kids your own age. You're a kid, but not a kid.

Robbie was in constant motion like prairie grass caught in the wind with its glint of gold swaying back and forth. Young as he was, he was already shooting up like a beanpole. Given enough time, the boy would match his own six-four. Already Robbie's gangly legs kept pace with his. The boyish, froglike voice cracked at times as it began to show signs of deepening. Robinson wondered what the outcome would be. Rich? Resonant?

Robbie was so much like his mother. Catherine's voice had been sultry, one of those things that had attracted him to her. The worse thing about their wretched divorce had been losing Catherine, as strange as that sounded. Yet reflecting on it, as he often did, she had never been completely his. He'd caught her on a rebound, at the tail end of the Vietnam War when her fiancé was killed days before the Americans pulled out.

He'd been there as a war correspondent. An arrogant twenty-three-year-old thinking himself invincible. Cocksure of his journalism skills. Confident that he could handle the war zone.

On that first helicopter flight over the jungle, the copter in front of them went down in a smoldering wreckage. The copter he rode in took flak and wobbled; in outright fear Robinson lost control of his bladder. After that, the survival instinct took over. He was there to do a job whatever the cost. But friendships were temporary. One day he was in a foxhole with Dwight Evans, talking about Dwight's fiancée, Catherine. The next he was penning a note of sympathy to her. He'd called her when he got home . . .

Robbie caught his eye.

He shook himself free of the jungle. "I have one more surprise for you, Son."

"Yeah?"

"We're going to the Italian Riviera."

"Not Paris?"

"This is an extra. We'll fly into Paris, get our things settled at our flat, and then take a car rental and do a bit of Europe. You'll like the Riviera."

"What's there?"

Robinson considered spouting the intricacies of life. A sun-scorched beach with bathing beauties. Sipping Italian wines. Instead, he explained, "I'm tracking a story."

The boy's brows arched. "What kind of a story?"

"Would you believe it? I'm looking for a Nazi."

"In Italy?"

"Years ago Bernhard Grokov served in Germany's *Waffen SS* in World War II. He was on the Allies' wanted list, but they never found him. It seems he disappeared. Surfaced years later in Brazil . . . then Argentina. Am I going too fast?"

"No, but you're not making sense." The boy flopped on the bed and stared at his father. "Are we looking for an old man, Dad? Why don't we just leave him alone?"

"Robbie, he's wanted for war crimes. A long time ago, I grant you. But we can't let a man like that hide behind his age. I do know that he spends several months a year on the Riviera. Owns an olive grove there."

"Maybe he likes olives. You do."

"Maybe our mutual interest in olives will give me a chance to talk with him. But Grokov wasn't the kind of man who would turn to farming. I want to know what he does with his time when he's not in Italy."

"Got any proof he's a war criminal?" Robbie asked.

"He's like the man in that novel I read—about a spy coming in from the cold. I got interested in Grokov when I started reading reports about him popping up in Brazil and Argentina. And now the Riviera. I've tracked him down. That means Germany knows where he is too. That means they know he has become financially independent with his olive groves. But it doesn't account for why they don't go after him." He chanced explaining further. "Don't know why I'm surprised. A number of those suspected of war crimes went free."

"What we gonna do when we find him? Shoot him?"

"No, interview him. Only I plan to interview him on my own."

"What about me?"

"You'll make new friends there."

"Yeah, with goats? I bet there aren't any kids my age."

Robinson shoved his hands in his pockets. "I could make arrangements for you to stay in Paris. But I thought we could have some downtime together."

The boy braced against the pillows. "A minute ago you told me I was on my own. That I'd have to find some friends. Dad, know what I'm gonna do when I finish school?"

"I haven't a clue."

"Gonna study journalism. Then maybe you'll let me help you interview a man like Bernhard Grokov."

"Hit the sack, Son. We have to be on the way to the airport by three."

His son had crashed in Robinson's bed. Those piercing eyes of his boy's had shut in sleep. Someday a young woman would come along and be taken by Robbie's good looks. And once she got past those eyes, she'd realize what a treasure she'd found. Robinson was sure of it.

CHAPTER 11

As they sped through the isolated villages on the Italian Riviera, Cameron took the hairpin turns on the two-lane highway with reckless abandon. A dizzying drop-off lay to their right. Jagged alpine peaks rose to their left. The convertible responded to Cam's command as he downshifted on the serpentine curves and challenged the oncoming traffic.

From around the next bend came the blaring horn of an approaching bus. Cameron paled. Meagan screamed. She gripped the handle and placed her other hand over their unborn child. If they collided, it would plunge them over the rocky precipice and straight down into the azure Mediterranean, where fishing boats lazed in the harbor.

Neither vehicle slowed. The crowded yellow bus appeared—its headlights like monstrous eyes. The driver shook his fist. Cameron swerved onto a limestone outcropping. The bus raced by. As Cameron accelerated, he laughed. "That was close."

"Our vacation could have ended right there. Slow down!"

"Sweetheart, this is Italy. We drive like the Italians."

This was a new side of Cameron, and Meagan wasn't sure she liked it. His disciplined life had dissipated into a wild invincibility. In the sweltering Italian sun, he looked swarthy like a native, a direct contrast to her creamy complexion that was fast becoming sunburned. But when he stole a glance her way, those gray green eyes danced with delight. When he was gentle she forgot how strong he was. How stubborn.

She calmed herself by admiring the landscape. Honey-colored farmhouses. Romanesque churches. Colorful homes cleaving to the cliffs. Towns carved from the rock. Tiny shrines along the road. At last she loosened her grip on the door handle. "You're going to get us killed if you keep driving so fast."

"No, my love. I intend to enjoy these seven days. This is the first time since Coeur d'Alene that we've been alone. Just the two of us." He reached over and patted her tummy, barely a pooch to it. "Although it's obvious we spent *some* time alone."

She flushed even in the sunshine and placed her hand over his for just a second. "The baby's kicking."

"I know. Cameron Ryan junior."

"He may be a girl."

"Not a chance. We'll have a girl next."

"Watch out, Cameron. You can't sightsee on this road."

"And I can't stop looking at you. This will be our first real honeymoon."

"But I'm pregnant."

"I know. And you're glowing."

"You don't mind?"

"I've never been happier. I've always wanted to be a dad . . . and I'm in love with his mother."

As the utter freedom changed Cameron, so the senses came alive for Meagan. The smell of the sea as they drove along. Basil-scented gardens along the roadside. The sea breeze brushing her cheeks. Hillsides resplendent with flowers. People along the road in peasant attire—laughing, chatting, waving.

She couldn't distinguish the intoxicating scents. Perhaps a mixture of orange lilies and lavender. The linden trees or the tangled bushes of roses. The village was secluded by a forest of trees rising on the hills behind it. A jasmine hedge hugged the stone wall on the winding driveway up to the house.

As they neared the top of the hill, the villa came into view in an apricot-orange with bright green shutters and a tile roof catching the glint of the sun. A young boy with unruly hair looked out from the iron balcony on the second floor.

Robbie Gilbert leaned against the railing and watched the shiny convertible roar up the sledge of a road. As the woman passenger looked up and waved, Robbie, even young as he was, was beguiled by her smile. When she stepped from the car, it was into the waiting arms of the dark-haired driver.

"Anything interesting?" his father called.

"Yeah, a bright red convertible. It's gotta be a Rolls-Royce or a Mercedes."

"There's a difference, Son."

"Power. That car has power. Classy rims. Leather seats."

"I suppose that's what you plan to drive when you grow up."

Robbie faced his father, who had stripped to his undershorts and stretched out on one of the beds with his head crammed against the Ligurian bed board and his toes an inch beyond the mattress.

"Is the Rolls-Royce your car choice of the week?"

"Yeah."

His father chuckled. "Then you'd better start working now."

"But you promised me a car when I get my driver's license."

"A secondhand car, Son. And I have several years before I have to face that headache . . . Any human attached to that dream car of yours?"

"See for yourself, Dad."

"I'll pass. I'm just about to have my siesta."

"She's pretty. Pretty like Rosalie at the reception desk."

His father swung his legs over the side of the bed.

"Don't bother. She's already taken, Dad." Robbie walked over and sat on the edge of his father's bed. "Do you have plans for dinner, Dad?"

"You mean Rosalie? No. I'm having dinner with you."

"Can I ask Arturo to put them at our table? You talk to the pretty lady, and I'll ask the man to give me a ride in that car."

His dad tousled his hair. "You don't go riding off with any stranger."

"But, Dad, the way we country-hop for your jobs, everybody we know starts out as a stranger."

"Off with you." He rolled over and made himself comfortable. "You check with Daniela while I get some sleep."

Daniela fluttered into the room and, with a wave of her hand, pushed her daughter, Rosalie, aside. "The Juddmans, is it? Now let me show you where you will be staying. The Riviera is everything Italian. You need go no farther than our villa."

Cameron and Meagan exchanged amused glances and followed. It was a typical Ligurian country house with tiled floors and frescoed ceilings, whitewashed walls, and simple yet elegant handcrafted furnishings. Everything had Daniela's fingerprint—most of all, her kitchen. She led them through it to reach the staircase.

Meagan was drawn to Daniela. Plump and loving, she spoke in rapid Italian. Her energy was boundless. In the first fifteen minutes, she'd spoken with her hands and cried at the slightest provocation when she wasn't stirred to laughing and singing. A large white apron covered her simple peasant dress. Two braids of shiny black hair—as black as her eyes—were tied in the back with an orange ribbon. She was quick to inform them that she was cook and hostess, troubleshooter and tour guide.

"I do my own cooking and serve my own guests. My husband, Arturo, and Rosalie, my daughter, help me."

She studied Meagan and patted her tummy. There was a quick embrace against her ample bosom. "Bambino!"

"You told her, Cam. But I didn't think I showed that much."

"Only to the practiced eye," he teased. "And no, I didn't tell her."

Daniela showed them to their bedroom on the second floor. "So you can have the best view of the sea."

The double bed was smaller than the one back in Heidelberg, but it made the room look larger and quaint with its wrought-iron canopy. A bamboccio chest of drawers took up most of one wall. Carved figurines of the nativity sat on top.

"The chest is seventeenth century," she announced with pride.

There was a decorative macramé fringe on the bedspread and towels and a lace scarf on the top of the chest of drawers.

"You will have to sit on the bed," Daniela told them.

"No problem," Cameron assured her with a glint in his eye.

Daniela left.

Within minutes her daughter appeared with fresh flowers and a dish of pine nuts. "Mother insisted I remove the chairs from your room. She does that for young couples." Rosalie lingered for a second. "Mother said to come down to the meal anytime. We have two other Americans with us. The Gilberts." She blushed as she mentioned their name. "They come down early—the boy is always hungry. His father is writing a story about olives and the man up the hill, I think." She pointed to their open back bedroom window.

From outside came the sweet scent of wisteria. Clumps of wild-flowers and blue cornflowers could be seen beyond the fence. From there the hill climbed upward, past a terraced rose garden to the shimmering silver-green trees high on the mountain.

"Our neighbor owns that olive grove up there. Robbie tells me that Mr. Grokov is a Nazi. But who's to believe a young boy? Madre says it's better to be a Nazi than a Fascist, but she despises them both."

Cameron frowned. "I've heard about the man—and men like him. It angered my grandfather that they could be shipped out of Germany at the end of World War II to save their hides. They're called neo-Nazis now. A lot of them helped shape the politics in South America—in countries like Argentina."

"They're allowed to do that, Cam?"

"Powerful enough, honey."

"You'd think they'd be dead and gone by now."

"Some of them are, Meg. But if the man up there is one of them,

I'll let my commanding officer know." Cameron looked out the window again, up at the innocent-appearing fields. "I'd like to visit that olive grove."

"Then go with Mr. Gilbert," Rosalie told him. "He's going up one day this week."

When Rosalie left and shut the door, they were alone at last.

"Cam, how can we afford this vacation?"

"You'll be angry."

"Not if you didn't steal the money. It's embarrassing enough that you borrowed the convertible. Everyone will think we're rich."

"We are. We have each other. But the truth is, Gramps sent the money. Told me to take my bride to Italy."

"Dear Conaniah." She rested her hands on her tummy. "I hardly feel like a bride."

At the crack of dawn Meagan awakened to find Cameron standing at the window looking out. "What's wrong, Cameron? What are you doing?"

"Nothing's wrong. I'm watching Daniela go off in her black shawl, carrying her prayer book."

She yawned. "What time is it?" He turned, and she saw his smile in the early light.

"I don't know what time it is."

"Look at your watch, silly."

"Can't. I had Daniela lock our watches away in the safe downstairs. All we have, Meg, is time." There was a sadness in his voice that went beyond this room. "We have one week here. One week and a day if we count yesterday. Daniela told me we can eat when we want. She won't mind. No one knows where we are. No one can find us. Just us."

"What about Daniela and Arturo, with his lemon-scented cologne? And Rosalie and the Gilberts?"

"They don't count." He strolled across the room in his bare

feet and took her in his arms. "Time is all we have, Meg. And it's all ours."

Each morning the sound of the sea awakened them, and they'd stand at their bedroom window looking down on the narrow inlets as the mist rose above the pristine sea. With barely a ripple the tiny fishing vessels pulled to shore with their morning catch. In either direction painted houses clung to the sheer cliffs. Their days were sleepy and peaceful. Unhurried. They ate when they pleased. Napped in the heat of the day. Hiked. The sea lulled them to sleep each night.

Midweek, as Daniela and Rosalie left the dining area, Cameron pushed aside his breakfast plate and turned to Robinson. "You've been too outspoken these last few days. Talking about an ex-Nazi living here in the village."

Robinson slammed his cup down. "Not down here." He nodded through the open window and pointed. "Bernhard Grokov lives up there in the olive grove . . ." His words turned caustic. "He's a war criminal. One of Goebbels's boys."

"So you're after a story?" Cameron lowered his voice. "I'm looking for a man who may be working for him."

For several minutes Cameron fixed his gaze on a hillside overrun with bougainvillea blossoms. High above that was the shimmering glow of Grokov's olive trees. Cam turned back to face Robinson. "I still have to warn you. He offers the villagers gainful employment. A few months back he replaced a water system down here in the village."

"Hush money?"

"Not according to Arturo. He tells me they respect Grokov's right to privacy, and he provides funds during their festivals."

"You sound well informed."

"Arturo can be quite informative," Cameron explained. "The people consider Grokov a loyal friend."

"Then they have no idea what he once was."

"Some of them do—Arturo for one. They just go on living in peaceful coexistence. So they won't thank you for ruining Grokov's reputation with a story. Not if it sends the villagers into economic disaster."

"Cameron, you have no idea how many lives were lost while Grokov was a *Waffen* SS officer."

"That's forty years ago. It's not important to these people now. Let me report it to the military when we get back."

"If he suspects anything, he'd be gone by then."

Cameron stood. "My wife decided to sleep in this morning, so if you don't mind the risk we're taking, it looks like a good day for a hike."

"Shall we go gather some olives for Daniela's kitchen?"

"That's as good an excuse as any." Cameron looked at the clock on the wall. "I'll be ready in ten minutes."

For forty-five minutes, the men climbed the abrupt cliffs, up past the shepherds' huts, and on through blackberry brambles. Weeds ran rampant along the way, but at the end of the steep path, they found the stone steps they were looking for. As they mounted them, they sniffed the intoxicating scent of freshly crushed olives. Just ahead lay the fenced-in olive grove.

After flicking off a scorpion with a stick, Cameron shoved open the rusted iron gate. "What do you plan to do if it is Grokov?"

"Get an interview maybe. I'm a World War II buff. I'll play that angle, but I still recoil at what Nazism did for so long, to so many people."

"If this village is a refuge for neo-Nazis, we're walking on dangerous ground." Cameron shaded his eyes and took in the beauty of the land. "Strange to think that such evil exists here."

Robinson nodded. "You don't have to go all the way, Cameron."

"Too late. That may be the owner coming our way now."

"You're right. That's Grokov." Robinson patted his shirt pocket. "He looks like the news clippings I brought with me."

The man approached, his features menacing. He was a powerful-looking man, though short and stocky of stature. His eyes were like steel, his tone just as rigid. "This is private property."

"My name's Cameron Juddman, and this is a friend of mine, Robinson Gilbert. We're vacationing in the villa at the foot of the hill. You must be Mr. Bernhard Grokov."

Grokov's gaze slid to Robinson, then back to Cameron. "We make it our business to know who's staying at the villa. But we don't want uninvited guests up here. We've an olive business to run." When he closed his mouth, his upper lip twisted, as though years of snarling had left an indelible imprint. "So what do you want?"

Cameron decided to be honest. "The truth is, my friend wants an interview. And not about the olive grove industry."

The man glared at Robinson. "You're a reporter?"

"An American journalist." Robinson extended the yellowed news clipping. "I'm interested in your business ventures in South America. I'm told you make your home in Argentina most of the year—have done so ever since you left Germany after the war forty years ago."

Grokov's jaw clamped. "You have the wrong man."

Robinson squinted at the article. "Don't think so. This is a picture of you in your SS uniform. See—that's Goebbels and Hitler on either side of you."

Grokov snatched the article from Robinson's hand, but Robinson pressed on. "I'm sure the name Goebbels must mean something to you. Or Adolf."

"Should they? I think not. I export olives. Now leave."

Cameron pictured him back in the war—an arrogant *Waffen* SS officer in the distinctive black shirt and boots, wielding a heavy stick in his hand. Grokov was still arrogant. He was still waving a verbal stick.

Grokov shredded the news clipping and toed the scraps into the ground. "How dare you associate me with such savagery. Leave. Both of you," Grokov ordered.

Robinson snarled, "Sorry, Grokov, I keep copies of that article on file."

Cameron tried to warn Robinson, but the journalist pressed on. "Have I stirred up a dark past, Mr. Grokov? I've done my research."

"And made a terrible mistake coming up here. But for your record, Mr. Gilbert, Nazi Germany made a great contribution to Argentina and other South American countries."

"Yes—Bolivia, Chile, Paraguay, I believe."

"We had the right to start over," Grokov fired back. "To contribute our training and experience as industrialists, scientists, and military advisors."

"I'm just wondering what your future holds?"

Grokov's voice rose. "We have a future, gentlemen. National reorganization. Whatever false accusations were made against us in the past are lies. All lies."

Cameron saw nothing but rage on the man's face now. His denials and lies were a mockery. *What about recruiting former Third Reich operatives and their heirs?* he wondered. *Innocent? Upright?* He would like to unleash his grandfather, Conaniah, on this man.

But Robinson was holding his own. "Have you no remorse, Mr. Grokov, for the long years of intolerance? For the death of—"

"None . . . Get out. Leave my property at once."

Cameron was enjoying himself. "What do you think, Robinson? Should we leave? I came up looking for someone myself. He used to work the olive fields in this area. Perhaps you know him, Mr. Grokov?"

A voice came from the shadows. "I believe these gentlemen are looking for me, Bernhard." Wolfgang VonHoekle stepped out and faced Cameron. "You don't seem surprised, Corporal?"

"Not surprised. Just disappointed."

Grokov's fury exploded. "You fool, VonHoekle. Now I'll leave it up to you to get rid of them. One way or the other I want them gone. And don't return." Then he disappeared into the olive grove.

When he was out of earshot, Cameron asked, "Why, Wolfgang? You had good employment with the Americans."

"I know." Wolfgang almost seemed apologetic. But it was clear he was worried. "What will happen to my wife and son now?"

"I don't know. You could go back and turn yourself in . . ." Cameron's voice grew stern. "Wolfgang, you know as soon as I get down to the villa, I will notify the American and German authorities."

Wolfgang's reply was swift. "It will do no good. I have no choice. I'll be flown out of here in a private jet, perhaps even before you gentlemen can reach the villa again. Now go, and take this American journalist with you. Both of you are in danger . . . And you have put my life at risk as well."

On the day that Cameron hiked up the mountain with Robinson Gilbert, Meagan wandered into Daniela's kitchen. Daniela looked up. Smiled. Without a word she put a dish of homemade noodles in front of Meagan. Meagan took a spoonful of the pesto sauce and nodded her approval. With a satisfied smile Daniela went back to stretching a sheet of dough with her long rolling pin.

Her kitchen was stocked with pickled zucchini and herbs. With tomatoes and eggplants. Her shelves were filled with sea biscuits and garlic, beans and marjoram, thyme, and rosemary. Her pans and kitchen tools hung on brass racks on the wall. But it was easy to identify Daniela's favorite spot—the wooden table where she crafted her noodles. Her antique mortar and olive-wood pestle were as old as the Ligurian hills.

Meagan savored the vegetables stuffed with basil leaves, but Cameron tried everything—as long as Daniela cooked it. Ravioli was the mainstay, but Cameron allowed Daniela to introduce him to stuffed veal or goat or wild boar saturated with olive oil and lemon dressing, and flavored even more with walnuts and herbs. But while he nibbled fava beans, he turned up his nose at the dried codfish smelling of white wine and parsley and only tolerated the tender young artichokes simmered with garlic. At breakfast Cameron always opted for coffeecake with candied fruit. But his all-time favorite was the veal chops and pepper cooked in a plain tomato sauce.

At the end of the day Daniela wiped her brow. "In late fall the heat will be gone. So will the crowds. But I won't want to see you and Cameron go. I think you have been happy here with us."

"Never happier."

Robinson and Robbie stood by the Juddmans' convertible, saying their good-byes. Meagan reached out her hand and tousled Robbie's hair. "I hope my son will be as bright and sweet as you have been to me."

Robbie exchanged a glance with his father. "That's not how Dad describes me."

"No, more like rambunctious. But he's a great companion," Robinson put in. "Well, you two, drive safely."

She grinned. "Oh, we will. If you're ever in Heidelberg . . ."

"And if you visit Paris," Robinson announced, "remember, we'll be there three to six years."

Cameron donned his dark glasses. Twirled the car keys in his fingers. "We'd best be going."

"The army awaits us."

"Yes, so it's back to being a soldier's wife for you, sweetheart."

"Hold it." Robinson rummaged in the pocket of his khaki shorts, then extended a card to Meagan. "Here's my business card—the Paris address as well as my home office in Washington DC—in case you ever need me."

She lifted an eyebrow. "We are not newsworthy."

Robinson stood back. "You never know."

She laughed and leaned over to kiss her husband on the cheek. "Cameron will never be a general."

"But he might be a hero."

She shrugged and tucked Robinson's business card in her purse. "Until then, Mr. Gilbert."

As their convertible roared down the narrow roadway and turned right, Cameron glanced back for a last look at their villa, lost now behind the sage and lavender hedges. Then they were once again riding the serpentine curves.

"Meagan, I love you. I've never been happier than this time together. I want to grow old with you. And when we're old, I'm going to bring you back here."

"And we'll walk the roads and pick the flowers."

"That too." He grinned. "Meagan, I'm going to love you forever."

Yes, that time in the Riviera had been so happy. It seemed like they would go on loving each other forever. But forever only lasted seven-and-a-half years. Years that took them from army post to army post. From Heidelberg to Fort Stewart. From there, two years later, to Fort Irwin. From California to Fort Hood in Texas, where Meagan miscarried their second child. And then, to Cameron's delight, back to Fort Riley in the fall of 1990, where they were just a stone's throw from his boyhood home.

CHAPTER 12

WINTER 1990

The early December dawn lay silent.

Soundless.

Ominous.

Then a shattering burst of light filled the stormy sky. Against the backdrop of the fading Evening Star, the Kansas sky was awash with brilliant swirling lights, sketching cloudlike faces in the heavens. A gauzy haze of blue and orange-red vapors spewed from its center, fanning out in a zigzag pattern.

Coiling.

Winding.

Looping into diaphanous circles and overlapping trails.

Meagan watched the mystical glow as unburned fuel and water droplets played havoc in the atmosphere. Slowly the dazzling vapors receded, then vanished into the snow clouds.

Unlike the silent households around her, Meagan viewed the phantom apparition with the practiced eye of an army wife. She knew that a rocket missile had left the launch pad at a nearby military installation, destined for a coral island in the Pacific Ocean. Yet she sensed intuitively, felt with a certainty, that this one had misfired.

Shattered like her marriage.

The missile carved its mistakes in the sky. But Meagan wanted to erase her own blunders and write her dreams across the heavens.

138

She ached to carve a place for herself, to control her own life, to distance herself from the confines of the military. She longed to break free from Cameron's commitment that true and honest valor could only be found as a soldier.

Her young son and husband waited for her on the farm just outside of Junction City. But all she wanted to do was go back in time to the remembered happiness of her childhood. Her years of marriage had all but squeezed the memory of the Methow Valley from Meagan's mind. Seven-and-a-half long years and the mossy jade of the Valley, with its pristine lakes and rising mountain slopes, had faded. The way home had always ended in detours. She no longer kept touch with the friends of her youth. Could no longer trace her godly grandmother's features or remember the sound of her voice.

She was Meagan Juddman now. Wife. Mother. A twenty-five-year-old still living on the wintry plains of Kansas, her dreams as numbing as the bitter cold weather.

Meagan gripped the wheel of the Ford pickup. A sudden braking on the sleet-crusted road would send her skidding into the snow-drifts. The plows had been out all morning, but a rare blinding storm had blown in while she shopped at the all-night market. Nature's fury left the Flint Hills covered in a billowy whiteout and Fort Riley barely visible in the distance.

She hunched forward, her anger lashing out like the weather. The army belonged to Cameron's world, not hers. Yet she lived in the shadow of the military. As she crept along the unguarded bend of the country road, her windshield wipers squealed back and forth, pushing away the snow flurries. Jamming. Starting again. Squeaking again. She squinted into the grayness, trying to pick out the cutoff that led to the farm. She knew she was close. Five minutes or less, just beyond that dangerous twist up ahead.

Suicide curve, Cameron called it.

Meagan shivered at the thought of the truck plummeting over

the edge. She played out the scenario in her mind. The truck landing upside down. The roof caving in. Snowdrifts engulfing her, trapping her in the cab. Unchained tires still spinning. The engine sputtering. Her scream stolen by the winds.

She imagined Cameron's voice accusing her of wrecking his fathers pickup, his face a mixture of rebuke and concern. The seconds ticked away. The truck inched along. She spotted the silo at last, then the chimney poking up from a foot of snow on the sloping rooftop. The tire treads crunched over the snowy fields as she pulled into the driveway.

The knobby porch railings of the Juddman farmhouse were encased in mounds of snow. Icicles clung to the cottonwoods, the barren branches scratching against the frosty windowpanes. The snow-laden thorn hedge blocked out Fort Riley. Last year's Christmas wreath hung on the door, and the snowman that Cameron had built with their son stood by the side of the house, its twiggy arms outstretched, its button eyes and mouth borrowed from Mother Juddman's sewing tin. Then she spotted one of Cameron's army hats cocked on the snowman's head.

The army—the bane of her existence. Was there no part of their lives free from the military? Cameron and his unit were stationed at Fort Riley. That made their fifth—or sixth move from army post to army post. She was beginning to lose track. They had come back to Cameron's boyhood roots and the farm outside of Junction City where he had grown up.

The day after they moved in with his folks, Cam put in for permanent housing at the base. In another month they would be forced to move again into the dismal cramped housing reserved for enlisted personnel. But Meagan would not go with him, not this time. No, she was leaving Cameron. She was taking their son, Ryan, and fleeing as far away from the bitter bleakness of a Kansas winter as they could go.

Meagan turned up her collar as she stepped from the car. Everything looked familiar. Poignant. Painful. She felt cold inside, her spine numb, the beat of her heart sluggish as she plodded toward the porch. She loved this old place, loved the young man who had grown up in this house. But she was walking out on him, going her separate way and taking their son with her. She'd turn in her ID card that labeled her a *dependent wife.* No more of the army's rigid caste system. Many wives loved it. She hated it.

No matter how much she tried over the years to enjoy the company towns and cities where they lived, nothing compared to the beauty of the Valley she had left behind. She found pristine lakes and historic trails everywhere, and for this she was grateful, but as her marriage to Cameron grew shakier with each new assignment, she became consumed with the longing to return to the Methow Valley.

As she reached for the doorknob, she heard the clear sweet notes of a trumpet playing "Out of the Ivory Palaces." She glanced up toward the corner bedroom that she shared with Cameron. He was home early. With each note the crack in her heart widened. Her first picture of Cameron was of a handsome young man stand-ing taller than his peers, his vivid gray-green eyes seeking hers as he lifted a trumpet to his lips and filled the room with music. Was it to be her last memory as well?

She waited for her heart to quicken. Waited for the lump in her throat to go down. In the days ahead she knew she would remem-ber that song and weep, but now the thought of Cameron and his trumpet angered her.

Once inside the entryway, she slung her coat and scarf on a peg and stared at the snow flurries that formed a puddle on the floor. Conscience suggested mopping it up before her mother-in-law came home. But this time Meagan shrugged and glanced at her wind-chafed cheeks in the oval mirror. With a toss of her head she tried to throw off the snowflakes that had turned her tawny hair a silvery white.

Peeling off her gloves, her gaze dropped to yesterday's mail stacked on the hall table. She spread the letters. It was still there—the attorney's letter with its announcement for Cameron that she was filing for a divorce. It was over. Almost eight years slipping through the drainpipe. Gone. Down the tubes.

Meagan's throat tightened again. The envelope had been opened; contents stuffed back inside. Had Cameron tossed it there for his mother to read? Snowdrops and tears balanced on her lashes. *He knows. He knows.*

She twisted the solitaire diamond on her finger. When they married, she thought the ring was beautiful because Cameron had given it to her. It was all that any twenty-one-year-old could afford on army pay. He had stood there in his uniform, his eyes sparkling. His words still rang in her heart: *"This is forever, Meg."*

And now she would give the diamond back.

Meagan mounted the steps, one at a time, and understood how her mother-in-law must feel climbing the stairs on her thin, arthritic legs. She stopped at the entrance to their room. Cameron sat on the foot of their bed polishing his trumpet, his strong, handsome face turned away from her. His army duffel and neatly folded government-issued underwear and uniforms lay on the bedspread behind him. Not the sharp-looking uniform he wore to the base chapel on Sunday mornings, but camouflage pants and shirts the color of the desert sands.

"You're going away."

"You are, too," he mocked, without looking up. "The letter stated irreconcilable differences."

"The attorney's choice of words, Cam. Not mine."

"Did you have to choose a family friend, Mother's friend?"

"He was the only lawyer I knew. Would it help to know he suggested a trial separation?"

"But the paper said divorce."

"I told him it was the only way to get your attention. We talked about it before, Cam. I don't make a good army wife."

He worked that firm, steady jaw. "I wouldn't make a good civilian. Being a soldier is all I ever wanted to do. You knew that when I married you."

"I didn't know I would feel so isolated. So constantly uprooted." Her bitterness tasted like grapes plucked too soon. "I don't want the army to dominate my life another minute. Never a home of my own. Just army-issued. A drab, colorless existence. Raising Ryan next to an ammunition dump. That's not what I want for him." Her words shot out like the *rat-a-tat-tat* of a machine gun, and she could tell by the pain in Cameron's eyes that they hit their mark dead center. "All Ryan knows is the bugle blowing. Troops marching. Daddy not coming home because he's off on maneuvers. Off playing his war game."

"Have you really been that unhappy, Meg?"

Flashes of yesterday caught her unawares. Running off to Coeur d'Alene without a care in the world. Their first Christmas together in Heidelberg and him carrying her up to their cramped one-bedroom housing on the third floor. Holding hands and dreaming of growing old together on their trip to the Riviera. The utter joy on Cameron's face when he first held Ryan. The comfort of her son when Cameron was off on maneuvers. She bit her lip, looked away.

"I love you, Meg. I know we've had our ups and downs. I know you had bad experiences living on the base at Fort Stewart— especially your confrontation with the officer's wife at the commissary. My interfering—your snatching Ryan up in your arms and walking out without the groceries."

"That's water under the bridge."

"It may be in my record somewhere. You didn't have to choose the commanding officer's wife."

"I didn't choose her," Meagan snapped back. "She marched right up to me—all perfume and dangling earrings—and insisted on being at the head of the line. They had their lines for the officers' wives. Why come to mine?"

"I have no idea, but once you walked out, she demanded my name and rank and reminded me that rank had its privileges. That my wife needed to learn that."

"She didn't."

"She did. After that, whenever we drove into the base, you called it 'a border crossing into an alien land.' Meg, I've been so blind to how much you hated this life. I've been sitting here for the last two hours, thinking of all the things that might have brought us to this moment."

"It wasn't just one thing, Cam."

"I know. A whole duffel bag full. I used to tease you when you buried your head under the pillow at Fort Hood—or was it Fort Irwin—so you wouldn't have to hear the cadence of marching men. Or the times you flew to Ryan's room at Fort Hood when the planes swooped overhead and rattled the toy shelf in his room."

"I still do that—even here in the safety of your parents' farm." She walked across the room and glanced out the window, her back to him. The wintry haze veiled Fort Riley, but it was still there, standing between them.

"Meg, look at me. Please."

She turned, her eyes meeting his.

"Have you ever forgiven me for that time at Fort Irwin when I couldn't take you and Ryan to Disneyland?"

"You never asked for forgiveness."

He seemed immobile sitting there except for his hands—strong hands gently buffing a trumpet. Except for his voice resonating across the room. "I was too proud. I expected you to understand that I was on lockdown—on special duty. There'd been terrorist threats to the safety of the base."

She lashed out at a strand of hair that had fallen across her cheek. "Why didn't you tell me?"

"You know I couldn't tell you. You stood there flicking a strand of hair behind your ear—just like you're doing now."

It all came back . . .

H er screaming, "Then you won't go?"

Cameron calm, saying, "I can't. The army—"

She had grabbed Ryan's hand, piled him into the car, and driven off. When she saw Cameron again forty-eight hours later, he was sitting at the kitchen table blowing his trumpet, practicing a hymn for the chapel service. He had lowered the trumpet, wiped his mouth, and asked, "Did you have a good time . . . ?"

H er temper flared. "Life in the army will never be normal for me. You may think the uniform makes the man, Cameron, but it destroys the wife."

He stared behind her. "I haven't made it easy for you, have I? Coming home to Fort Riley and living with my folks and waiting for base housing hasn't been easy either. But, Meagan, I love you."

If he didn't stop repeating it, she would scream. She loved him too. That's what made it so pathetic. She waved her hand at the stacked items on their bed. "Is that what this is all about? Base housing has opened up? I won't go there with you. It's over, Cameron. You're a good man. A wonderful father. You've never looked at another woman."

He offered her a sheepish grin. "I've looked. But that's all. Maybe even flirted once or twice. But you're the only woman for me. I loved you from the day I met you."

That word again. "I know. The high school prom. You playing in the band because your folks wouldn't let you dance."

"You know that isn't true. I was on leave from Fort Benning— filling in the evening with what I did best. From the moment I spotted you, I connived ways to keep you from dancing with anyone else."

"The glass of punch did it."

"It chased Tad Porter away. But I almost lost it when I spilled some on your dress."

"It didn't matter. I never wore that dress again."

He gave the horn another buff. "That night I practiced every speech in the books so I could propose to you before I returned to Fort Benning."

"You knew that soon?"

"I knew the instant I saw you. There's never been anyone else."

"I'm so sorry." That lump in her throat rose again as she glanced at the army shirts stacked on the coverlet. "You don't have to leave tonight just because of that letter."

"It wasn't the letter. The army sent me home to pack."

Light dawned. She saw his shiny, dark boots. The bulletproof vest. A gas mask. His helmet and Boonie desert hat hung from the bedpost.

Across the room he met her gaze, his sensitive eyes unblinking. "My unit's been called up."

"To the Gulf?" she whispered. "Before Christmas?"

"Saddam Hussein doesn't celebrate Christmas." His wisp of a smile faded. "I'll be in Saudi Arabia for Christmas—unless the war starts sooner."

"But Ryan—wants you here for Christmas."

"We could let him open his presents tonight. I don't have to report in until three in the morning. It means I would have to stay over this evening. I could sleep on the couch."

"No, this is your room—our room . . . I didn't think your unit would have to go."

"They're still building up our troops in Saudi Arabia. They need more engineers and tanks and Bradley fighting vehicles. I tried to tell you."

"I know you did."

"I just didn't know we'd go before Christmas."

For days Meagan had avoided the daily headlines and the evening news on television. She'd switched off the channel whenever the commentator mentioned the military buildup in Saudi. As though stopping her ears would stop the war. Now all that she had ignored flashed before her: guns and cannons, rocket-launchers and Tomahawk Cruise Missiles, land mines and the walls of sand that hid them. High-tech payoff with F-117 Stealth fighters, digital mapping, and Bradley tanks.

And gas suits and gas masks. All of those things that Cameron had tried to talk about. And the things he had never mentioned:

the growing stockpile of body bags at the Dover Air Force Base and the gunmetal gray caskets that would bear the heroes home.

She felt the color drain from her cheeks. "I don't even know where Saudi Arabia is."

"I'll let you know as soon as I get there. But I hear it's nestled between some sand dunes."

"Why is the president sending you over there?"

"I'll have company. My own unit and the thousands of other men and women already there."

"Don't tease, Cameron. This isn't some training mission."

"I know. It wasn't my idea for the Iraqis to invade Kuwait."

"That happened last summer."

"August second, to be exact. We're just going to take back their land for them."

And die in the process. "It's more than that, Cameron. The president wants to protect our oil supply. He wants to keep the black gold flowing between those sand dunes."

Meagan saw agreement in Cam's eyes, but he looked down and went on polishing the wide rim of his golden trumpet.

She folded her arms. "Are you taking that with you?"

His shoulders and the trumpet shrugged together. "This? I'm packing it away so you can give it to Ryan someday. I don't want any of the sand or black gold to damage it."

"You can give it to him yourself."

"I'll be away. Remember?"

"You'll be back."

His unsmiling face betrayed him. "And you'll be gone."

"I'm sorry. Like always, my timing is off."

A nervous tick ran along his jaw. "Better to get your lawyer's letter now, right? Better than getting it in the desert?"

Her words were barely a whisper. "I wouldn't do that to you."

"Then I'm sorry they didn't send me sooner." He went back to polishing his trumpet. "I thought we had worked things out."

"It's over, Cam. I just can't go on being a soldier's wife. I hate it.

I hate always packing up and moving to a new base. I didn't mean for it to happen this way. I intended to be gone before you got home this evening."

"Forever?"

"No, just for a three-day weekend. Your mother offered to take care of Ryan while I'm gone."

"She knows?"

"I'm certain she's guessed. Your mother is a wise woman. She's picked up on the strain between us . . . and given a mother's loyalty, she will side with you. You're her son."

He looked up. His eyes held hers. "Where will you go, Meg?"

"Back to Twisp and Winthrop. Back to the Methow Valley. I want Ryan to know something about my childhood roots too."

"Eastern Washington? Don't leave me, Meagan. I love you. Wait until I come home, and we'll go together."

"You've said that before. And we've never gone."

"I mean it this time, Meg. I'll only be gone six months, max."

"You expect to free the oil fields that quickly?"

"I expect to free the Kuwaitis," he corrected. "You and Ryan could stay here with my folks while I'm gone."

She stared out at the snow-covered woods and the backyard, where the clover and daisies and Sweet William would bloom in the springtime. But winter stared back at her. "I hate Kansas."

"I thought you liked it here on the farm."

"It's peaceful—like my home in Twisp. But your mother would expect to take Ryan off to Sunday school and expect me to go as well."

"Would that be so bad?"

How could she tell him that God seemed farther away than the desert? His faith had never been enough for her. She still couldn't believe in the Juddmans' God. "Kansas and church are your memories, Cam. I always feel like a stranger here. I hate the winters. Hate it when the sunflowers are buried beneath the hard-packed ground."

"The flowers will bloom again. They always do."

"You used to tell me it was always spring and summer here."

"That's the way it seemed when I came home."

"I want a home of my own, Cameron, not endless military housing, not borrowed furniture."

"We'll have all of that when I retire from the army."

"Nine or ten years from now? You're a twenty-year man. I want a sprawling backyard with enough room to grow vegetables and plant flowers. A house bought and paid for, with frilly curtains in the windows and back trails where Ryan can ride the horse he wants."

"He'll have those things. I promise. For now he has my parents' old plow horse, and they promised to get him a new saddle."

"Don't you understand? It's not the same. I want him to have one whole year without moving and a music teacher who can teach him to play the trumpet the way you play it at Sunday morning chapel."

"You'd let him play hymns?"

"If he learned to play the trumpet the way you do."

She wanted these things for her son. Or did she want them for herself? Dear Cameron. He meant well, but he was army. Eleven years. Sergeant First Class. E-7, enlisted rank. Would they ever build the kind of home she wanted on that kind of salary? She slammed him with what bothered her most. "You must bypass opportunities to advance, Cam. Some of your friends have gone on for officers' training."

"Maybe they know their congressmen better than I do. This war in the desert may please you. Maybe I'll get a battlefield promotion," he threw in. "What do you want, Meg? Master Sergeant? Sergeant Major?"

"Stop it, Cameron."

"I *like* working with my men. And the truth is, I don't see myself as officer quality. Lieutenant. Captain. That wouldn't be me."

"You sell yourself short. You could blow your trumpet. They'd follow you."

His pained, transparent gaze drifted, then came back brighter, more alert. "A trumpet to me is music. I played it up in the hills as a boy. Up there with just God and me. I see my trumpet as an instrument of peace, not a battle cry."

"They roll you out of the sack every morning with a bugle."

"Yes. As a boy I used to poke my head out my bedroom window just to hear that bugle call in the morning."

"And the trumpet is the last thing you'll hear—someone blowing 'Taps' over your grave?"

A veil swept over his eyes, a sadness that she had never seen before. "'Taps' is played for the living, Meg."

She had pushed him too far. Belittled him. Humiliated him. Now he was frightening her.

"I considered putting in for specialty school twice. The first time Ryan had pneumonia. And recently—"

"You didn't tell me."

"I kept it for a surprise."

"What happened?"

"The Kuwaiti Invasion happened. Some transfers were denied. Mine included. Like it or not, my unit is needed . . . Forget the divorce, Meg. As soon as this deployment is over, I'll apply for specialty school again. I promise."

Another promise. "But you'll still be army."

He nodded. "For me it's honor and valor all the way. For you the army is misery and moving." He flexed his muscles. "Somebody had to hold up the bottom ranks. Somebody had to be at the bottom of the high school class."

"You were nowhere near it."

It was the same old argument. They'd been kids when they married, Cameron twenty-one and already committed to the army the minute "Pomp and Circumstance" stopped playing. Meg had stargazed every time she saw him. Back then she'd seen the military as travel and adventure. As standing by her man.

College had never been in the books for Cameron. It stabilized him to know what he would wear the next day, to bargain shop at the post exchange, to pull up roots and travel on Uncle Sam's say-so. Cameron—her rock-steady, broad-shouldered, six-foot trumpeter—the army's twenty-year man. If he made it to the Gulf and back, what did Cameron want besides nine more years in the army—years she didn't want to share with him? She knew his heartbeat for their son. Cameron wanted to live long enough to see his son grow up. And another child . . . yes, they had both wanted that. But she knew that something else was the root of their troubles. It was what angered Meagan most: Cam wanted her to believe, as he did, in a creative God and his Son on the cross.

"Cam, let's call it quits while we still care about each other. While we can still be friends."

"Not now. Wait until the Gulf business is over. We'll talk about it then. I love you, Meagan. I love Ryan."

"We've been holding this marriage together too long now."

"Just a little longer for Ryan's sake."

"He won't thank us for pretending."

"I'm not pretending, Meagan. I'm still in love with you. I always will be. It's just—"

"Don't say it. Don't tell me that if we believed the same way, it would work out."

He fingered the keys, then lifted his trumpet, and the sweet clear notes of "Out of the Ivory Palaces" rang out in the room again. His favorite hymn. Meagan understood the music, but not the words. Cam had built his faith on them, content in his Savior's "great eternal love" for him.

Cameron placed the trumpet in its case and strolled across the room to Meagan. He took her hand in his. "Someday, Meagan love, you will hear the clarion call. And like a burst of sunshine, you will understand. You'll believe in the Man on the cross as I do."

She put her fingers to his lips, gently, because she did care for him. "I need more time."

"I may not have any time left to give you . . . Maybe I'll do you a favor this time and I won't come back."

She turned away from him. Outside the frosted windows the snow flurries whipped in the howling wind. Through the haze she saw her father-in-law's workhorse plodding toward the barn, pulling an eight-foot sleigh over the ice behind it. Hours ago, before the weather turned sour, she had bundled Ryan into a parka and boots and sent him off with his grandparents. Mittens had covered his stubby fingers, and his face had almost been hidden by a wool cap and ear muffs.

His dark mahogany eyes—her coloring, Cam's intensity—had shone as she stooped to kiss him. "Have fun, sweetheart. Do what Grandma Fran tells you."

Now Ryan looked like nothing but a bundle of blankets huddled against his grandmother. Meagan glanced over her shoulder. "They're back, Cameron. What will we tell Ryan? He'll cry when he hears you're going away."

Cam slid his hand over his buzz cut. "Let me tell him."

"He's too young to know that you're going off to war."

"Then I'll tell him about the oil and the sand dunes."

CHAPTER 13

That night Cameron tucked their son in bed. Whatever promises he needed to make to Ryan, Meagan didn't want to intrude. She was still cleaning up the festive wrappings and clutter when Cameron came back into the living room and stood by the crackling fire.

"I couldn't pry the army truck loose, Meg."

She met his watery gaze. "He's not sleeping with that?"

"Afraid so. I did turn off the siren." He sounded pleased.

"I'm glad, Cam. He managed to get his old teddy bear drenched in the snow today."

"He's not still carrying that around? Meg, he's six years old."

"I know. Six years, three months. But who's counting? Besides, Fran tells me you had an old stuffed bear for years, so he's following in your footsteps. You wouldn't give it up. You even hid it in your closet when your little friends came over."

"I'd forgotten about that. My grandfather gave it to me."

"That makes sense. Half the toys under the tree were from Conaniah. So don't worry, Cameron. Ry is all boy. He hasn't cuddled that old bear for a long time . . . But Fran said he took it out the last time we were quarreling."

"He heard us?"

"Little big ears. He doesn't miss much." She sighed. "And this morning he insisted on taking it on the sleigh ride with him. It's a sopping mess, but trust your mother. Fran hung Old Sarge up to dry above the wood stove." She put her fingers to her lips and swallowed the emotions rising there.

"Ry said he wanted a two-wheeler from Santa Claus. I can't believe he didn't pay attention to the bike the folks gave him." Cameron shook his head. "Dad stayed up all last night putting that together for me."

"You can't take a bicycle to bed with you—nor ride it in the snow . . . The truck will always be you to him, Cam."

"Thank you for telling him it was from me and not from Santa Claus. I just didn't have time to go shopping this year."

"You never go shopping." She scooped up another torn sheet of wrapping paper and crinkled ribbons.

He held out his hand. "Forget the cleanup. Can you? In the morning all of that wrapping and tinsel on the floor will still remind me of Christmas." He waited for her to take his hand.

She lowered her head so he wouldn't see her suck in her lower lip. But she snatched up her Christmas present from him and followed him up the stairs to the bedroom. She tried to ignore the signs of his leaving. His uniform hung in the closet. His locked duffel stood in the corner of the room. His polished boots sat by the bedside.

"It was a nice Christmas, Meg."

"But no turkey and dressing." She laid his Christmas present down on the bed.

"No problem. Ryan likes hot dogs better anyway. And the army will come up with some freeze-dried substitute for our holiday . . . It was just being with you and Ryan that mattered. I wanted to watch him open his presents one more time." His words were muffled as he pulled his wool sweater over his head. "Thanks for letting me stay tonight."

"It's your house, remember?"

"My folks', actually."

"Did you tell them good-bye?"

"Yeah. It was tough this time. So we agreed to just give each other a big hug and let it go."

"Is that what you want from Ryan and me in the morning?"

"I think so."

She stood there looking at him, feeling flushed and uncertain, the way she had in the Coeur d'Alene hotel room on their wedding night.

From across the room he leaned against the dresser and smiled. "Will you wear my Christmas present tonight?"

"Do you want me to?" She looked down at the sheer black negligee lying on the corner of the bed. "I might be cold with winter's frost on the windows."

"I'll be here."

She felt the burning flush hit her cheeks again. She grabbed up her Christmas present. "I think I'll shower first. There won't be time in the morning."

He nodded. "And I'll run downstairs and check the fire."

"You just did."

"I want to make certain. And I have a couple of business items to tend to."

It was past midnight when they crawled into bed. She turned her back to Cameron, but she could not sleep. As Cameron's cheek pressed against her bare shoulder, she felt his tears on her skin. In all their struggles, she had never known Cam to cry. She ached for him and longed to tell him that she still loved him, but the words would not come. She did love him. But she did not want to live with a soldier. Not now, not any longer.

"You can't say it, can you, Meg?" His voice was husky, strained. "Is it so hard to tell me you still love me?"

In the dark she turned and went willingly into his arms, her face buried in the curve of his neck.

Meagan stirred as the alarm rang. Silencing it at once, she turned on the bedside light and glanced over at Cam. He went on sleeping, his muscular arms stretched above his head, his bare chest rising and falling rhythmically, his expression relaxed and peaceful. She watched him in silence for a moment, wondering whether she would ever see him this way again—that familiar face with those dark lashes and full lips and tiny mole to the side of his mouth. She leaned down and brushed a kiss across his bristled cheek. "It's time to get up."

A groggy voice snarled back, "We just went to bed."

"It's 2:15. You have to report to the base in forty-five minutes. You know, holiday time in the sand dunes."

"Oh, that. Call the airline and cancel my reservation."

She thumped him with her pillow. "Get up."

"Watch out, woman. I'm not the enemy." He pulled her down.

She pulled away. "The army has its own time clock, remember? I'll put the coffee on."

"There won't be time." He flipped the covers back and sat up. "*Brrr*. Right now the desert sounds good."

"It won't when you get there . . . You're sure you won't take coffee?"

"I'll pass. Let Ryan sleep. I'll just shower and leave."

"No. Ryan and I are going with you."

Meagan fought tears as he strode off to the bathroom, straight and unflinching. She wanted to remember the set of those broad, muscular shoulders. Those narrow hips. That quick, easy stride. The way he had of never looking back. It took the sound of water running before she went to awaken Ryan.

He was curled in his bed, clutching his new truck, his features so much like his father's, his face angelic. The angel part of him snapped as he opened his eyes. "Go away."

"No. You have to get up. We're going to see Daddy off."

She pulled his snowsuit over his pajamas. He fought her, hating the morning as much as she did. He yanked the woolen cap off, doubled his fists against the mittens.

"Ryan, your daddy—"

"My daddy is going away."

She wouldn't be able to threaten Ryan with Cam's discipline, not for six months or more. She tackled the mittens and skullcap again. Cameron returned in time for the boots.

"I guess this is it. How do I look?"

Like the army, she thought. "Good looking."

She hated the camouflaged uniform. Hated what it implied.

He dumped the duffel bag by the door and grinned at his son. "Soldiers wear boots, so let's get yours on."

Meagan pressed her cheek against Ryan's as Cam parked the pickup by the fence near the olive drab buses.

"Are they school buses, Daddy?"

"No, soldier buses. They will carry the men out to the airstrip. See that gigantic old airplane out there?"

Ryan's nose already looked like Rudolf's. It was running, as if a cold were on its way. "I don't want you to go, Daddy."

"I know." He handed Meagan the car keys and wrapped her fingers around them. Then they piled out of the car into the wintry morning, closing ranks with hundreds of other soldiers in dark parkas and helmets, their families shivering beside them.

"Write. Write every day, Cam. Let us know how you are."

"Don't forget to pay the car insurance. I left a list of things to do. Dad can help you."

Nearby a distraught soldier stared down at his family of three. "I'll be okay," he promised, "but just in case, the army had me up my life insurance—and sign my will."

Cameron gripped Meagan's arm and steered her to a less congested spot. "We should have said good-bye at the house." He stomped his boots against the snow-crested ground, his canteen and gas mask swaying at his hip. "You and Ryan will catch pneumonia out in this weather."

"Your folks will have a fire going by the time we get home." Meagan looked up into Cam's face—into those long-lashed eyes. "Come back," she whispered.

He nodded. "Six months isn't long."

"Make it less."

"I will if I can." He crushed Ryan, that replica of himself, to his side, but his eyes were on her. "Honey, I thought you wanted me to go away permanently."

"That was last week, when you didn't come home for pot roast and gravy—and three months ago when you missed Ryan's birthday cake."

"We were on tactical alert."

"I know. I know that now."

His voice lowered. "What about yesterday's letter from the lawyer?"

She fibbed. "I tore it up this morning."

"You're willing to try again?"

"I promised until death do us part." Meagan bit her tongue at the choice of words. It was their old joke, their famous makeup line when the quarrels were put behind them.

"I plan to be around for another fifty years," he vowed. "Can you make it? Are you willing to wait for me?"

"Do you have to have a reason for coming back?"

"You and Ryan have always been my reason. Will you wait?"

Here in armyville? She wouldn't, but she didn't want to send him away to war that way. Her timing was off. It always was. The army and Cameron always won out. Had he forgotten that she wanted wide open country to settle down in? A quiet town somewhere in the middle of nowhere, as far away from military bases as she could get? Fort Riley might be the Home of America's Army, but it wasn't her home. Never would be. She belonged in the Methow Valley and longed to go back.

The officers began to bark their orders—to line the men up for that ride to the plane where they would climb on board and head for the desert sands a world away. She had to convince Cam that she would wait. He had to have a reason to come back again. Yes, until now, Ryan and Meagan had always been his reason.

"Don't be gone long, you big ox. I can't stand a long Kansas winter without you."

"You'll stay with the folks?"

She nodded. "They'll insist on it."

"You're sure?" Boyish eagerness lit his face. He searched her eyes. "We can work it out, hon."

The same sincere words. The same unspoken prayer.

His fingers touched her cheek. "We can work it out." He'd said it a hundred times before.

She nodded assent as he scooped Ryan into his arms.

"Meg, we're a good threesome."

"Come back, Cam," she repeated, her voice urgent. This time she was afraid for him. Not for herself. "Just tell them Ryan has a birthday coming up."

"They'd check the records and find out he had one in September."

"Then tell them you're allergic to sand."

"The generals won't care." He slipped his arm around her and kissed her, his lips hard on hers. "Take care of yourself." He gave Ryan a bear hug. "If anything goes wrong, Son, be a good boy for Mommy. A brave boy for me."

"Fall in," a sergeant yelled.

Meagan reached up and kissed Cam again, dropping some genuine tears on his broad shoulder.

He cupped her chin and looked straight into her eyes. "Honey, it's always the darkest before dawn."

"Go, Cam. Or they'll demote you."

"Just a stripe or two."

Ryan's voice piped up. "Daddy, will you come back tomorrow?"

Cam's eyes brimmed with tears as he let go of his son. "Soon. I promise, Son. As soon as I can."

He saluted and, without turning back again, set his face like a flint and marched to the bus. They waited in silence—Meagan biting her lower lip, Ryan clutching his brand-new truck.

She stared at the bleak, gray sky and tried to dwell on those good times—meeting Cameron, loving him, marrying him. The excitement in those early days of packing up and moving to a new base. And Cam's indescribable joy when he first saw his son.

A little voice piped up. "The bus is yucky, Mommy."

The fumes from the bus died away as it moved toward the wide-body airplane that would carry Cam above the icy fields of Kansas on a ten-thousand-mile journey to the desert.

"Why isn't Daddy waving at me?"

Because he's crying, Meagan thought. "He saluted as he left. Wasn't that enough?"

One by one the other soldiers climbed the steel staircase and, with one final wave, disappeared inside the gaping door. Cameron was swallowed up too. The plane groaned under the weight of its cargo as it lumbered down the Tarmac. Its wings wobbled, barely clearing the telephone poles. Then it lifted skyward, carrying Cam with it.

CHAPTER 14

Far from the plains of Kansas, the plane rumbled and roared as it flew above the ocean. Cameron's neck felt stiff. He'd tried to sleep in the miserable jump seat, with his stomach taut from the seat belt and his long legs cramped from lack of space. Tanks and trucks were secured down the middle of the plane.

War. He was heading to war.

He took a plastic folder from his parka and stared down at the faces of his wife and son.

"Missing them already, Juddman?"

Sergeant Max Cranston's voice sounded gruff, but when Cam turned, he saw the man's rugged grin. The ridges around the sergeant's mouth were cut deep, a result of sunbaked skin and long tours of duty abroad.

"I keep wondering when I'll see my family again."

The sergeant nodded. "I've been wondering the same thing for twenty years. But the wife and young'uns—grown now—have always been there when I got back."

"That's the point. Getting back."

"Oh, you'll get back, all right, Juddman, with plenty of Saudi sand in your boots and nostrils. But you'll get back. We've got the president's guarantee. We'll have Saddam Hussein in the palm of our hand, quick as a flash."

"It won't make much difference. Meagan and my son won't be there."

As they flew through a darkened sky, the chaplain made his way down the wide aisle, swaying in an unsteady gait, catching his balance from tank to truck. Sergeant Cranston reached out to stop him. "Here, padre. Take my jump seat. Juddman here could do with a chaplain right now."

Meagan stood in the freezing cold until Cameron's plane was less than a speck in the sky. Ryan crushed against her, not saying a word, waiting. She took his mitten hand in hers and smiled down at him.

"Can we go home now, Mommy?"

He meant the farm, his daddy's birthplace, the place his daddy always came back to. She thought instead of the Valley and the sloping hills that rose into the Cascade Mountain Range, thought of the rushing flow where the Twisp and Methow Rivers merged.

"We'll be going home soon. But first, let's go see Grandpa Conaniah."

"Why, Mommy?"

"So we can tell him Daddy went away."

"Didn't Daddy tell him?"

"I don't think so."

Conaniah came to the door with a pipe in his mouth, dressed in his familiar tweed jacket and green vest. He'd knotted his frayed university tie tightly at his neck and wore cuff links on the sleeves of his white starched shirt. He looked such a formidable giant standing there that Ryan shrank against Meagan.

"Morning, young man." His raspy voice was even more frightening. "Well, you'll freeze like a snowman if you don't come in."

As he stepped back, Meg urged Ryan inside.

In the alcove Conaniah scowled at them. "Good thing I'm an

162

early riser. But what's that child doing still clad in his pajamas in this kind of weather?"

"We left the house in a hurry."

"Did Fran throw you out?"

"No, Conaniah."

"Did she feed you this morning?"

"No. We came to tell you that Cameron left for Saudi Arabia two hours ago."

Ryan lifted his gloved hands and slapped them together. "Daddy went in a big plane that swallowed him."

"A C-140 or C-17, I think, Conaniah."

"He left without saying good-bye to me?"

"There wasn't time."

High bushy brows tented his pensive eyes. "I'm the one who should be going away to war, not my grandson."

"He loves you, Conaniah."

"I know. And the truth is we never say good-bye. We always expect to see each other again. Take your boots off, young man," Conaniah ordered, "and you can warm your feet by the fire."

"I can't get them off."

"Then it's high time you learned."

Ryan plopped down on the floor and tugged. At last Conaniah leaned down and helped him. "First thing we're going to do in your daddy's absence is get you a new pair of boots. Boots that fit. He's growing like a weed, Meg."

A short weed, she thought. *But given time he'll take on Cameron and Conaniah's stature.*

Conaniah led them into the library—his war memorial, as he called it—and sank into his plush leather chair. "Sit down any-where. And, young man, the soldiers are over there on that table." He pointed with the stem of his pipe to the display he had created in memory of Becky Armenson.

"It's all right, son. Grandpa Conaniah said so."

Ryan tore off his snow jacket and flew to the middle of the room. "Can I move the soldiers?"

"Can you put them back where they belong?"

Ryan's face clouded. "I don't know. I don't know which ones are the good soldiers."

Conaniah's brusqueness melted. "Never mind. I know where they go. Just slide back the glass top—gently now."

"Why is this soldier lying down, Grandpa?"

"The soldier is dead."

"My daddy is a soldier."

"I know . . . But I'll help you later. Let me talk to your mommy first. And, Ryan, are you hungry?"

Ryan's eyes went wide. "Can we have flapjacks?"

"I'll have my lady get your breakfast right away." He rang and his housekeeper appeared. "Sophia, can you make some famous flapjacks for my great-grandson and his mother?"

"Shall I set a table by the French windows?"

"It might be warmer by the fireplace."

He sighed as she left. "She's a good woman. I don't know why she stays on when I'm such a grumble."

"Because she likes you and wants to please you."

He met Meagan's gaze. "I hoped Cameron wouldn't have to go. That boy has been my whole life."

"He adores you too." She pulled a chair over beside him. "What's it like, Conaniah—going to war?"

"Dear child, you don't want to know that."

"I want to know what Cameron faces if we go to war."

"The battlefield is a man's world."

"Not this time. Women will be on the front lines too."

"At the Rapido and Anzio it was cold. Bitterly cold. For Cameron it won't be the snow and ice, but the heat of the desert and a foe greater than the ones we faced." He sucked at his pipe and sent a smoke curl into the air. "We had nurses in our war—but they listed them as noncombatants."

"That's unfair. They were there in the thick of it too, weren't they?"

"Very much so."

She glanced at the sepia photo that always sat on his massive desk. "What was she like, Conaniah?"

"Becky?" He sucked his pipe with pursed lips. "I wish I could tell you she was youthful and beautiful like you. But I never saw Becky in a dress. Never got to pin a flower in her hair and take her to a dance. We never went out to dinner together. Yet as long as I live, I'll remember her."

"Tell me about her, Conaniah. Right now I can't bear going back to the farmhouse. Do you mind if we stay?"

"You have to ask?"

"I don't want to face the empty bedroom. I don't want to talk to Fran and Aaron."

"They can be a bore sometimes, can't they?"

Glancing at Ryan, she lowered her voice. "Conaniah, I'm afraid something awful will happen to Cam this time."

He tapped the bowl of his pipe and put it in the ashtray. When he took her hand in his, his skin felt rough against her own. "You must not think that way. You must be brave for Cameron's sake. And for the boy. You'll have to be strong for both of them. And for me."

As she put her head down on his arm, her cheek brushed the coarse tweed of his jacket. "Oh, Conaniah, I told Cameron I was going to divorce him."

Conaniah chuckled. She looked up at him, startled. "This is a small town, my dear. The lawyer is a personal friend. I go to him every time I want to rewrite my will. He handled probate for me for my first two wives, and when I divorced my third wife, he handled that as well. He kept her from lynching me."

"When did he tell you? I just told Cameron yesterday."

"He called me when you left his office. Asked me if there was anything I could do to change your mind."

"He's overstepping client privilege," she snapped.

"My dear girl, he meant well. He knows how much Cameron means to me—how much you mean to me. It's a common thing for couples to threaten divorce. What's important is that Cameron thinks you're waiting for him to come home."

"Why are you so good to me?"

"I like you, Meagan, almost as much as my grandson does."

"Will you tell me about Becky?"

He opened his tobacco pouch, packed his pipe, and lit it again. As he puffed, he stared across the room, far beyond where his great-grandson played. "In January 1944, Ernie Pyle reported in the *Stars and Stripes* that thousands of American and British forces had gone ashore into a tiny fishing village called Anzio. I followed them a few days later . . . I've told you before about the disaster at the Rapido River crossing."

"Where so many men in your platoon lost their lives?"

"That happened about the same time our men went ashore in Anzio—putting them smack behind the enemy lines. A handful of us asked if we could be transferred to the Anzio beachhead. They needed men. We had battle experience. So they sent us."

His pipe seemed to comfort him as he glanced at the photo of Becky Armenson. "What was glossed over in many papers and barely touched upon in the *Stars and Stripes* was the story of more than two hundred nurses who went ashore five days behind the invasion."

Again he stared in the distance, but this time he was smiling. "I was there when they came ashore. I hadn't seen a woman for months, and here they were coming ashore with steel helmets shoved on their heads and fatigues and boots that hid their shapes. And we thought they were beautiful."

That January in 1944 Becky Armenson lay on the deck of the landing craft and prayed to go ashore. She preferred the deck to the crowded quarters below where other nurses were seasick and using their helmets for an emesis. They had joined the convoy in Naples eight hours ago, but it seemed like an eternity. Now, along with destroyers and battleships and cargo vessels carrying dynamite, they bobbed in the harbor in total blackout. In total fear.

What had once been an Italian seaside resort for the wealthy had become a battlefield, a narrow strip of land that would cost the Allies and the enemy great casualties. Warning sirens screamed in the night. German shells exploded all around them, causing whirlpools of water to lash at their landing craft.

Five days after the soldiers landed, Becky and the first of the medical team went ashore with German artillery shells falling all around them.

Soldiers, shocked at the sight of them, begged them to go back. "This is a death trap."

One lieutenant stopped in his tracks. "This is no place for a woman. Get back on that ship and get out of here."

"And face being seasick again?" She shouldered her duffel. "Show me the hospital."

He shrugged. "Touché. They've put up a makeshift tent east of Nettuno. We didn't have time to build a modern medical center. But I'm telling you, lady—"

"Lieutenant Armenson to you, Soldier."

"Lieutenant to you too, Nurse."

Armenson and the other nurses were trucked to the medical tents with the Germans firing down on them. The same soldier was at the wheel. "I don't have the hang of driving this thing. The driver was killed on the last run in. I warned you to get back on that landing craft, Armenson."

"And I told you, Soldier, I hate being seasick."

"Well, if you ever have any free time, let's watch the German fireworks down by the shore. It goes on twenty-four hours a day."

"I won't have time. I'll be busy, Lieutenant."

There wasn't even time to unpack or comb her hair. They went right on duty, tending the wounded as troops in battle dress unloaded the supplies. The hospital clamored for space amid armored tanks and trucks, with the fear that the ammunition dumps beside them would blow under enemy fire. It was hours before they had time to set up sleeping tents for the nurses. Two to a tent, their palace away from home. It was much longer before the nurses were able to stretch out on their cots for the first time and sleep through an air raid.

The lieutenant made several more runs with the wounded before he was moved on to the front lines. Each time he reached the evac station, he saw her. Each time he asked, "How about a date, Lieutenant Armenson?"

"I'm busy tonight. Sometime when you can stay longer, we'll talk about it."

The lieutenant smiled and drove away, leaving her to face the boiling cauldron on the beaches of Anzio. Night after night the blasts shook the ground. Wobbled the tents where they had set up their hospital. Parachute flares zeroed in on them. Still the ambulances bounced over the bomb craters to take the casualties to the aid station. Litter after litter arrived of the mud-caked wounded, their bodies bloody, mangled. The stench of blood and death hung in the air. The used urinals and bedpans added to the stench.

On the front line that same lieutenant pitched forward, rolled over. The pain in his chest was unbearable. When he put his hand inside his jacket, it came out bloody. He tore at his clothes to retrieve a packet of sulfa.

"Here, sir. Let me help you." The soldier's voice was young. He poured the sulfa into the lieutenant's wound as he called, "Medic! Over here." Then he nudged the wounded man's shoulder. "Excuse me, sir. I have to go fight a war. The medics are here now. I'm leaving you in good hands."

The medic jabbed the lieutenant with morphine.

The lieutenant could no longer talk. He could only hear the sucking sound of his chest wound and the muffled words of the medic. "That will help the pain, sir. Hopefully you won't feel the quagmires on the way back to the hospital. What these Italians call roads, we call Pockmark Highway."

The lieutenant drifted off . . .

He awakened as they carried him into the surgical ward on the beachhead. "Hi, Lieutenant."

He heard her sultry voice and tried to focus on her face. "Becky?"

"Yes. I didn't think we'd meet again this way."

"I'm—"

"You're going to be all right."

"I'm not dying, Armenson?"

"Not on my shift."

"What are you doing?"

"Cutting off your blood-soaked uniform. You're a mess," she teased. "You have an inch of mud on your boots and clothes. When did you shave last, Lieutenant?"

He tried reaching for his jaw, but his hand fell limp to his side.

"Trust me—you have a week's growth. I'll tell them to shave it off in surgery."

He would have fought back with words, except he saw tears in her eyes.

"Breathe, darn you, Lieutenant. I told you you're not going to die on my shift."

When she wiped his brow her hand was gentle, cool. And then she was whispering in his ear, "The surgeons are ready for you now. I'll see you after surgery—don't forget we have a date afterward."

He saw her every day for the next ten days, sometimes from a distance as she leaned over another wounded soldier. But she always came back to him. When he got the word that he was shipping out to a medical station in Naples in the morning, he crept over the soft, wet sand to Becky's tent. It was off-limits, but he went anyway.

He slipped through the tent flap, hoping she'd be presentable, and almost hoping she wasn't. She was sitting on one of those deplorable cotton-filled mattresses in the middle of her cot with her mosquito net folded back and two army blankets serving as her writing table. Her roommate's cot sat against the tent wall. Fuel was scarce, but the tent had a potbellied stove in place of a furnace. A forty-watt bulb swung from a wire above her; the tent smelled like mildew and unwashed clothes.

She huddled in an olive-drab woolen shirt, her long legs covered by baggy pants. But this was the first time he'd seen her without her helmet on, and he thought her even more beautiful. Her hair was short and curly, her face scrubbed clean.

Unlaced combat boots lay on the foot of her bed, leaving her red, swollen feet exposed. Her feet looked like the soldiers who had come back from the foxholes. It was at that moment he realized how much suffering these nurses faced so the wounded could go on living.

He sat on the empty cot and faced her. "Hi, Becky. Where's your roommate?"

"On duty." Her dark eyes flashed. "And you shouldn't be here, Lieutenant."

"I had to see you. They're evacuating me to the military hospital in Naples in the morning."

She averted her gaze. "I delayed your transfer as long as I could. But we need more space for the wounded coming in."

"Becky, you won't be in Naples."

"And you can't stay here, Soldier. The nurses' quarters are off-limits."

"I had to know you were all right. Two of the nurses—"

"I know. They're dead. That's why I'm writing to their families to tell them what happened."

"They'll censor your letters."

"Let them. I have to tell the truth. Go back, Soldier. I'll see you in the ward in the morning—before you leave."

"With the shells falling like they are, you might not live to get there. I had to tell you—I love you."

She shook her head. "You don't even know me. Love? Look at me. I'm a mess."

"You're beautiful."

Suddenly she was crying. "I'm scared, soldier. My ears ache from the sound of antiaircraft guns exploding around our hospital. I want to go home. I want to leave all of this behind me." He moved to her cot as swiftly as his bandaged chest permitted. "I'm sick of blood and mangled bodies. Sick of cold water and sponge bathing in my helmet. Sick of eating C-rations and taking care of the dying. I'm sick of being so lonely . . ."

His arms went around her . . .

The next morning, before he was evacuated to Naples, they went to the chapel, hand in hand. They sat on a flat board bench as the chaplain eulogized the dead nurses. A medic played "Taps" off-key. They sang "Amazing Grace" while the bombs exploded all around them.

One of the shells landed on the chapel.

And when he wiped the dust from his eyes, Becky Armenson was dying.

I'm so sorry, Conaniah."

He didn't seem to hear her but went on recounting his nightmare and the pitiful loss of the young woman he loved. "I was that soldier, Meagan."

"I guessed." She tried not to cry. "Oh, Conaniah, I can only hope that if something happens to Cameron, there will be a medical team like that to care for him."

"The best. Trained and qualified. Sophisticated equipment. There will be field stations and hospital ships like the *Comfort*. But we won't let our thoughts go that way—drumming up the worse. Our boy will come back to us."

Will he? she wondered.

As she faced him, Conaniah's shrewd eyes looked wary. He patted her hand.

He knew. She knew.

A place had been set by the fireside for breakfast. She stood and held out her hand to Conaniah. "You really loved Lieutenant Armenson, didn't you?"

His stance was proud, defiant. "I stayed with her that night. Does that shock you?"

"No."

"I left her tent before her roommate came home from the operating room. I didn't care whether they caught me and court-martialed me or not. I wanted to be with Becky. I wanted to hold her in my arms."

CHAPTER 15

JANUARY 16, 1991

Captain Tharon Marsh—twenty-seven, handsome, tall, and confident—glanced around the War Room, studying the faces of the other officers. As he waited for the conference to get under way, his thoughts veered back to his wife, Kips. The beautiful girl with a weak heart. Once a successful model, still good-looking, his mainstay. She had handled his tour to the DMZ in Korea like a trooper. Kips still kept pictures of him standing in that demilitarized zone in no man's land. It was one of the most fortified borders of the world—with land mines on either side of the road where he stood.

But Kips had wept when he left for the Gulf. Always before she'd been his shining star, proud of him. Sending him off with words of encouragement. This time she had clung to him, not wanting him to leave.

The colonel beside him leaned forward, his hawklike eyes on the general standing in front of them. Within seconds blood surged through Tharon's body as General Schwarzkopf's fist doubled around the latest memo from Washington.

Without a word from the general, Marsh knew. This was it. The zero hour. The war was on. He felt ready for it. He shoved his concern for his wife to the back burner.

He'd itched for real action since the day he had graduated from West Point as a fifth-generation soldier. The third generation to commit to a military career. He expected to succeed, to lead. The army suited his tastes. Built his ego. Schwarzkopf was the kind of

173

man Tharon admired, respected. He'd follow the general into hell itself. This was what they were here for, wasn't it? To do battle with the Iraqis. To nail Saddam Hussein. To liberate Kuwait.

And after that, he could think about his wife. Go home to her. By then those miserable headaches and fainting spells that Kips was having would be gone. Surely medication would help. Perhaps the threat of an open-heart surgery would not be necessary. He'd forgotten in the rush of packing to ask her what the doctor had said. But if it had been important, important enough to keep him home, she would have said something. They were always up-front with each other.

He patted his inside pocket where he kept Kips's picture. *Okay, baby, I'm about to make you proud. Your hero is going to war. No doubt about it.*

The Army Special Forces had already made their stealthy entry over the border.

Before dawn of the seventeenth, the Screaming Eagles, known for their cavalier bravado, climbed aboard their Apache attack helicopters. Engines revved up. Aircraft from seven nations took to the airways simultaneously from ships and military bases. The first shots were about to be fired. Those white tents in Saudi Arabia were about to come down, the men and camouflaged vehicles ready to move out. In those minutes before the hell of war broke loose, the chaplain prayed, and the strains of "God Bless the U.S.A." echoed in the War Room. The coalition forces would keep their promises to Saddam as they followed Stormin' Norman into the frenzy of war.

Cameron remained upbeat in his letters and e-mails to Meagan. Humorous in his descriptions of life in Saudi Arabia. Hungry for news of home. Overflowing with plans for the three of them. Yet between the lines Meagan read something different. His apprehension, his loneliness reached her.

Time crept in slow motion as the troop buildup fueled the rumors. Meagan kept busy, trying not to panic as the country drifted toward war.

But on January 17 Desert Shield erupted into Desert Storm on a moonless night. Bombs fell over Iraq. Tomahawk Cruise Missiles launched from warships. F-117 Stealth fighters took to the air. It was no longer training in Saudi Arabia. It was war. Her fears were real now. It was inevitable that Cameron would be caught up in the storm.

His last letter reached her on February 24, the day the ground war began. He sent his love and added, "Never let Ryan forget me."

On February 27 the armored Infantry advanced in the Euphrates Valley. Cameron walked across the small berm, using the moon as his light. He felt comforted that the same moon shone down on Meagan and Ryan, the two he loved more than anyone else in this war-torn world. Several officers with flashlights huddled at the front of a Humvee, poring over the map spread out in front of them.

Colonel Corbin waved him over. "Sergeant, we need a volunteer for a reconnaissance mission."

The colonel spelled it out. Detailed enough for Cameron to wish he had not been out on a pit stop when they were looking for a hero. Colonel Corbin had a thousand armored tanks and vehicles in his command, stretched out on the desert sands for miles. Once Cameron had questioned Corbin's leadership. His judgment. He questioned it again. "You want us out there maintaining radio silence? My men would be sitting ducks."

"The rest of the tanks will be three or four miles behind you. Once you lure the Iraqis into sight, we'll be there," Corbin told him.

"We haven't broken any speed limits on the desert, sir. The

Iraqis have Russian-made equipment. They'd spot us in a minute."

"That's the idea, Juddman. It's the high price of honor. So far intelligence can't tell us their exact location or their numbers . . . Some of our equipment is faulty in these sandstorms. We don't know what lies over the next hill. With our computerized navigation system down, we have to put a Bradley crew up front—"

"You're asking me to put my men at risk?" Cameron frowned.

"I'm *ordering* you to do so. There's a war going on."

"Sir, you're asking us to maintain radio silence. How are we going to send a message back to you when we sight the enemy?"

"What do you want, Juddman?" Colonel Corbin barked. "To announce to an Iraqi tank that you are just north of them?"

Cameron felt belligerent. Defiant. Not at all like himself. But he didn't trust the colonel's plan. Rank had its privileges. But there was a madness in Corbin, a self-motivated man who wanted promotion and glory. Cameron wanted to live long enough to go home again, but he had soldiered long enough to know he had to obey.

Weary, he finally agreed. "I wish we had an electronic identification system, Colonel. A laptop computer screen that plots our own units. Maybe I'll invent something like that when I get home."

At the front lines, Captain Tharon Marsh—the young career officer, a soldier respected by General Norman Schwarzkopf and a personal friend of Colin Powell—received a message from home that his wife was going in for emergency open-heart surgery. A fifty-fifty chance for survival. *Kips. Kips.* The news distracted him, blocking his awareness of the green glow of the high-tech machines in front of him. A moment in time that he would regret forever.

Under cover of darkness Tharon used his night-vision goggles. A lone vehicle was beached on a dirt berm. He radioed in the coordinates. He didn't like Colonel Corbin. Didn't like depending on his judgment.

Corbin snapped, "If they don't have a fluorescent orange marking on the roof to identify them as friendly, take them out."

A second of silence, then Tharon asked, "Are there any friendly tanks in the area, Colonel? Our radio frequency codes aren't always the same."

"Marsh, we have your coordinates. I've called for air power. None is available. You have your orders, Captain. Obey them."

"But, sir . . ."

A string of expletives pierced Tharon's ear. "Repel that attack. It has to be an Iraqi tank. Take it out."

And so Tharon gave the order. "Fire."

Two Bradley fighting vehicles responded. Mortars shells blasted into the night. His own gunner was jubilant. "We got him, sir."

"Fire again," Tharon ordered.

In the dust of the desert, the cry for help erupted. An American voice desperate, pleading. "We're a friendly. We're a friendly. You're firing on us. Listen this is R-2-1—"

A *Bradley.* Tharon stared through his night goggles. "He must have drifted off course. He's alone. The fool is breaking the rules giving out his location, pleading for survival."

"Captain Marsh," the gunner warned, "there are other tanks approaching from the south. Enemy tanks. I'm sure of it. They look like the Russian model."

"Cease firing," Tharon roared. "Cease firing."

Fire exploded around Cameron's Bradley. The sky lit in fiery balls of orange and red. Inside the Bradley Cameron took courage. He had been trained for this. To meet the enemy. To take them on. These men riding with him were his responsibility. So were those tanks and vehicles stretched across the desert three miles behind them.

"It's not the Iraqis firing at us, sir. We're being attacked by another Bradley."

Tony was right. Cameron knew enough that their own men were firing at them. They were doomed. In the isolated sand dune their Bradley was expendable. The crew expendable. He was expendable.

In a desperate attempt to save his men, he attempted a coded radio contact. Static. The wires connected. "This is R-2-1—"

The deafening roar of another shell took their communication out. In the open hatch above them, his gunner lay limp across his weapon. They had been ordered to maintain radio silence. They had no choice now. Cameron knew Colonel Corbin had sent them out to die by their own people.

He took a deep breath. "Men, the gunner is dead. Our orders are to stay here, to hold our position. To wait for the enemy. I may not be able to get us safely back to base. But I can get us safely HOME." He felt like something had lodged in his throat. "For God so loved the world that He gave His one and only Son—"

"Have you gone mad?" an angry voice shouted. "Get on the horn. Call for air cover. Don't you understand?"

Cameron understood. Radio communication was dead, silenced by a stray bullet.

"Come on, man. Let me try to wire it," one of his men insisted. "They're trying to blast us to kingdom come, and you're pulling a prayer?"

"That's what I'm talking about. Kingdom come. 'For God so loved the world that He gave His one and only Son that whoever— Jim, Tony, Melvin—believes in Him—'"

The tank rumbled and shook as another shell whizzed across the tank top. Another voice was heard above the blast, frightened and desperate. Tony praying. "Hail Mary. Full of grace . . . Blessed art thou . . ."

Tears coursed down Cameron's cheeks. Ahead of them. Behind them. Nothing but sand dunes. Dead ahead, Iraqis. To their right their own men firing on them.

Ryan, my son. I will never see my son again.

"What's the rest of it, padre?" Jim cried.

The cry shocked Cameron. *He means me.* "For God so loved—that whoever believes in Him shall . . . have eternal life."

Melvin, the declared atheist among them, mumbled, "'Our Father, which art in heaven'—oh, God, do you exist here in these sand dunes?"

Cameron ducked instinctively as another blast exploded inches from them. Gunfire raked across the Bradley, penetrated their armor. In the distance he saw a tank blown off course. A Russian tank manned by Iraqis. It erupted in flames. He knew that everyone on board was dead.

Oh, God, where are you? I will never see Meagan again. I love her. "*That whoever believes in you shall not perish but have—*"

The blast hit full force. Cameron's words were left unfinished. Metal and limbs exploded into the Iraqi sky. Fell in tiny fragments to the ground. Flames danced against the sand dunes. Lapped against the fragments.

Cameron opened his eyes to a brilliant light. To total peace. He was alone. The other men gone. A trumpet played. Music from the Ivory Palaces. A voice—majestic, awesome—saying, "Well done, my good and faithful servant."

Cameron examined his body. His tattered uniform was gone. His body weightless. Changed. He was peaceful. Cameron was Home.

Captain Marsh had called for the guns to stop. The firing to cease. Now he could see the lone tank in infrared lights. The armor of the Bradley lay partly demolished, an upside down V on the front panel. A *friendly.* Bodies were strewn around. American bodies. There was no movement. Only death.

"Come in, R-2-1," Tharon pleaded.

There was no answer. Only stillness.

The gunner could barely form his words. "They're dead, sir. They were caught in the crossfire. They didn't have a chance. Sir, I mistook him for an Iraqi."

"You were following orders."

So was he, but Tharon was not certain where the blame lay. Kips had been on his mind. Visibility poor. Tensions at a peak. They had known of no friendly tanks in the area. Colonel Corbin had told them to take the tank out. But in his mind, Tharon had failed *to confirm the target before firing.* Had fired before correctly identifying the target on Colonel Corbin's order.

The blame was his own. The chain of command would cover for the colonel, the son of a hero. Tharon too came from a military family. He'd been trained to obey. Had prided himself in obedience. And *he* had made the decision. Given the order to fire.

His gunner was ashen, already bearing his share of the guilt. "Captain Marsh, we've got to go out there and get them. You know we try not to leave anyone behind."

Tharon looked at the distraught expression on the young man's face. He nodded. But they could not rescue anyone—even dead warriors—not in the heat of battle. More Bradley fighting vehicles were moving in, putting the Iraqis to flight. Colonel Corbin hollered over the radio, "Did you take them out, Marsh?"

"Yes, but, sir, they were *friendlies.*"

In the War Room in Riyadh, they reviewed the fierceness of the battle, the casualty list. The tally of Iraqi losses. The cessation of war. Tharon Marsh was a time bomb waiting to go off. Part of the high command was missing. General Schwarzkopf away on a special session with the Saudi Arabians, the British commander in the Gulf, and Secretary of State Dick Cheney en route home.

Taking advantage of his commanding officer's absence, Colonel Corbin reported that the Bradley tank had been destroyed by enemy fire. Marsh tried to shout down the lie, but the beginning of a political cover-up had begun even before the plane bearing Cameron Juddman's remains began its flight home.

CHAPTER 16

In Kansas, when a vehicle—the color of a staff car from Fort Riley—turned in at the farm, Meagan knew with terrible certainty. She felt icy inside. Her legs were immovable. Just this morning the media had talked about an immediate cessation of hostilities. About the ground war ending.

"Ryan, I want you to go inside and tell Grandma we have company."

"I don't want to. She's got her ladies in there."

Meagan's throat tightened like a stretched rubber band. "Her quilting bee, sweetheart, but the ladies like you."

He sensed her fears. His eyes had turned dark and frightened, the smile of five minutes ago gone. The ball they'd been tossing dropped from his arms and rolled down toward the car. He gave her that tragic look that said, *Mommy, what did I do wrong?*

"Ryan, now. Please."

His jaw jutted forward, a smaller version of Cameron when he wasn't going to budge on an argument. The army vehicle moved up the winding drive like a funeral dirge. Like Cameron's funeral dirge.

Chaplain Whitford stepped from the vehicle first, then another officer—someone she did not know. That was good. She didn't want bad news from someone she knew.

She waited. It seemed important for Chaplain Whitford to adjust his cap. Then he came briskly toward them.

"Go, Ryan. Mommy said go."

"That's Chaplain Whitford. He's Daddy's friend."

"I know. But not Mommy's friend." She leaned down and hugged him. Kissed the top of his head. Wet his thick dark hair with her tears.

"You're squishing me, Mommy."

"Because I love you. Now go."

He ran, a hurt expression on his face. He glanced back and gave an uncertain wave to the chaplain. Whitford nodded.

She focused on the officer's spit-polished black boots as he stepped closer. They were inches apart now.

When she looked up, the chaplain's kind eyes were somber. "I asked to be the one to come, Mrs. Juddman."

"Yes, that's good that you did . . ." The voice was not her own. "When?"

"We just received word this morning."

"How bad?"

He glanced around. The laurel hedge seemed to catch his attention. "We should sit down, Mrs. Juddman. On the steps perhaps."

"No, I would never be able to get up again. Tell me," she insisted.

"He's gone, Meagan."

The chaplain's use of her first name surprised her. In a strange way it comforted her. This was Cameron's friend.

"How did he die?" Her voice sounded hollow even to herself, as though it came from the far end of a tunnel. Her words were too rational, too calm, as though she were inquiring about a stranger. But no, this was Cameron. Her husband. "How, Chaplain?"

Chaplain Whitford hesitated. "Hostile fire. His entire crew."

On the sand dunes. "Was it a scorching hot day?"

"I don't know. I can find out."

"No, don't. It won't matter. He died at the hands of the Iraqi. Did you know that he wished them no ill?"

"We talked about it more than once," the chaplain admitted. "Cameron cared about people."

The stranger—the other officer—gummed his lip. "Iraqi mortar shells hit the Bradley, Mrs. Juddman. Destroyed it. Enemy fire pre-cluded an immediate search. But there were no survivors . . . Sergeant Juddman was killed instantly."

For a moment she feared he would be more detailed. Describe the fragmented Bradley. The mangled bodies. She rubbed her palms together and didn't know how to stop. The other officer kept looking at her. She held him at bay. She wanted him to leave. To not speak her husband's name again. She wanted to go on pre-tending that Cameron was alive.

"Chaplain Whitford, I never said good-bye properly."

"You saw him off."

"Yes, and I wanted to see him come home again."

"You will," the chaplain explained gently. "I don't know when. There's some delay. But as soon as we hear—"

"Delay? Why?"

"I don't know. But, Mrs. Juddman, your husband used to tell me that one day he would hear heaven's reveille. That's the first thing I thought when I heard."

"And that's supposed to comfort me?" Her voice shook.

He took her hands in his. To steady her. To let some of his strength flow back to her. "He said to me—if anything happened, he wanted me to conduct the service."

Service? He was talking about a funeral. And Cameron was still in the desert. Or where did they go when they died? They had never discussed that. Now the tears came. A salty taste. Inside she was angry. Scared. And here on this bright, clear day in Kansas she could see Fort Riley in the distance. She hated the army. Hated them for making her a widow.

"Cameron"—she said his name. Forced it between dry lips— "Cameron's parents will want to have a private burial."

"Of course."

"No. That's not what I want. On our first date he told me that he wanted to be buried with full military honors. He wanted to be a hero."

"From all accounts he was."

"I do have the right to make the decisions, don't I?"

"Yes, you're his widow."

She swayed at the word. *I'm his wife*, she wanted to scream.

His grip tightened. "Your mother-in-law is on the porch right now."

"I can't tell her. Cameron was her only son. Her only child."

"She already knows. I see it in the way she's standing there. Is there someone else I should notify?" Chaplain Whitford asked, his tone compassionate.

"Cameron's grandfather."

"Conaniah Juddman, the elderly gentleman. You're asking me to tell him? I usually don't—"

"Yes. But would you?" she pleaded.

Chaplain Whitford watched her, his growing concern evident in his gentle manner.

She tried to assure him. "I'm all right, Chaplain."

The women from the quilting bee came down the steps. In twos and threes. One or two hugged Fran. Meagan drew back, not wanting them to touch her. Not wanting to feel or see their sympathy. "Chaplain, would you take Ryan to the neighbor's for me? It's the nearest farm—his best friend lives there."

"Shall I tell the child's mother?"

"Yes, that would be good. Then I won't have to phone anyone. She's like that you know. Spreads any news quickly. But she makes Ryan's favorite cookie. Did you know that, Chaplain?"

A faint smile touched his lip. "That same woman brings me cookies on Sunday now and then."

"Thank you for coming, Chaplain. Cameron would be grateful that you're the one who told me."

She saw tears in Whitford's eyes. And felt pity for him. "I'm going out to the barn and tell Cameron's father."

"You're all right?" he asked.

It was an odd question. *My husband is dead and you ask me if I'm all right?* Yet that would be a chaplain's job. She did not answer but turned and walked away. At the porch she stopped and met Fran's gaze. "Mother Juddman, it's bad news."

"He's gone? My son . . . is gone?"

"Yes, killed in combat . . . by hostile fire."

Fran had her arm around Ryan as though without each other they would not stand. Fran's soft, straight hair touched her shoulders. Color had drained from her cheeks. Long lashes blinked back the tears. "When will my son come home?"

"Chaplain Whitford doesn't know."

She called over Meagan's head. "When, Chaplain?"

"As soon as more word comes through, I'll call. And, Ryan, I'm to drive you over to your neighbor's. Would you like that?"

"Mom, I don't—"

"It's okay, Ryan. You can go. You can play with Jackie. I'll come for you in a few hours."

Whitford held out his hand. "Come along, young man."

Quietly he left, taking Cameron's son with him. As they drove away Meg looked at Fran. "I'm going out to tell Aaron."

"He's been afraid this would happen."

"We all have."

Cam's mother leaned against the porch rail, stoic in her grief. But there was a strange peace on her face.

Meagan screamed inside, *Your son is dead and you're calm? What's wrong with you?*

But for the first time she realized that Fran was plain, yet pretty. Wounded deeply, yet strong. Weeping, yet confident in her son's destiny.

Meagan shaded her eyes and saw Aaron coming to them. They went to meet him. Tomorrow the pain would begin. Today she felt dead inside. And more angry at the army than she had ever been.

Days later Meagan stepped from the front porch into a brisk, cold day with rain clouds hovering in the distance. In spite of the chilly weather she had worn her white summer hat with the wide brim and navy blue ribbon. She hoped it would hide her swollen eyes and the deep dark circles that blotched her skin.

Cameron had teased her mercilessly about her hat. "You mean Mother talked you into a hat for her Quilting Bee Tea?" And when she seemed hurt, he added, "Thank you for pleasing her—and me. You look so lovely. Wear it someday just for me, Meg. Maybe when I go away—or when I come home. And I'll stoop down and kiss you under the brim of your hat and tell you how beautiful you are."

I'm wearing it, Cameron. Just for you. For your homecoming. Do you see me—do you see me from where you are?

Aaron waited with the car engine running, but at the end of the path she saw a yellow flower blooming in Fran's yard. She leaned down and touched its soft petal. She must tell Cam about the first bud of spring in her next letter. Cam loved springtime in Kansas . . . But no, there would be no more letters. No more e-mailing. No more phone calls. Yes, Cameron Juddman was coming home early, as he had promised.

Ryan grinned at her as she slipped into his grandfather's car. "You look pretty, Mommy."

"And you are handsome, like your daddy."

Spring in Kansas was coming, but it was winter in Meagan's heart and winter all around her. They drove to the airport in silence. Conaniah rode in the backseat with Meagan, Ryan between them, and Cam's parents riding silently in front. Conaniah sat unbending. Straight as an arrow for his grandson's sake. Yet he looked ashen, like death itself, as though he were once again crossing the Rapido River.

She reached over and patted his knee. "My parents aren't coming today, Conaniah," she whispered. "They sent their love—but Mother has been down with the flu, and my father is staying with her."

"It's best," Conaniah replied.

They rode on in silence and arrived early—they always did with Aaron in the driver's seat. Even so the school band and the honor guard arrived ahead of them.

She stiffened when they saw the plane coming in for a landing. Ryan looked up into her face. "Is Daddy coming home, Mommy?"

"Yes, today. Just like I told you."

"Will he remember me, Mommy?"

"He will always remember you."

She crushed Ryan against her. She did not tell him that Cameron was coming home in a flag-draped box. Meagan's eyes remained glued on the belly of the plane, staring at the rigid stance of the men as they lifted the flag-draped coffin. A box. A gunmetal gray box. Cameron hated boxes, hated confinement, had hated even the sand that had clogged his nostrils and ears.

His mother sobbed beside Meagan and collapsed against Aaron. A hand reached out to touch them both, but not Meagan's hand. A broad, strong hand. A gentle hand. The hands of Cameron's boyhood pastor. The preacher was a family friend. But not Meagan's friend.

He tried to take her hand. "Mrs. Juddman, if there's anything I can—"

"Leave me alone," she threw back at him. "Save your platitudes for the memorial."

He had asked her for some thoughts on her last days with Cameron. "Just some words of hope for the congregation, Mrs. Juddman—for the people who knew your beloved husband when he was a boy."

"Make them up" had been her only reply.

Words of faith? Is that what he wanted? They hadn't talked about Cameron's beliefs those last few hours. They had talked about divorce, words that left her wreathed in guilt.

The high school band formed a grim, crooked line by the fence. Cameron's old band. The shiny blue-and-gold uniforms, like the one Cameron wore. Their somber music permeated the air. One boy blew his horn. Another his nose. A tall boy beat solemnly on the drum. A neighbor boy dug at his tears.

On command six young soldiers from Fort Riley steadied Cameron's casket. Six unknowns to Meagan, perhaps unknown to Cameron as well. As the soldiers balanced the box that held Cameron, the Stars and Stripes were no longer askew. They were straight, even. A cloak of honor for Cameron. A symbol. A symbol of a hero's homecoming.

The soldiers marched in step. One sandy-haired young man stumbled and regained his footing, bracing his white-gloved hand against Cameron's box as they carried it to the hearse..

Ryan's lower lip trembled, his saucer brown eyes glistened with tears. "Is Daddy in there?"

"That's how he came home."

"But I can't see him, Mommy."

She bent down, cupped his trembling chin in her gloved hand and, whispering in his ear, tried to make a six-year-old understand the casualties of war. The brim of her wide hat shaded them both. "Daddy talked about what might happen. Remember? He wanted you to be brave."

A lone trumpeter began to play as the hearse moved slowly down the Tarmac.

"What is that man doing with Daddy's trumpet?"

"It's not Daddy's. Daddy's trumpet is in the closet—where he put it before he left."

As she drew Ryan to her, Meagan focused on the hearse again. She knew Cameron was not in that box. His body, yes, but not his spirit. Not the Cameron she knew. Not the Cameron she remembered.

Ryan cried out as the long white van drove away. "Where are they taking my daddy?"

"To a big house." She hated the thought of the mortuary. Her arm encircled her son. "And then on Saturday he's going to lie beside his great-grandpa at Fort Riley."

"Won't he come home again, Mommy?"

"No, Ryan. He went to God's house."

Yes, that was what Cameron would want her to tell their son. Cameron Juddman was in God's house.

Afterward, Fran and Aaron drove away with their pastor, and Conaniah left with his old lawyer friend. Gripping Aaron's car keys, Meg and her son made their way back to her father-in-law's car. A young man in uniform limped toward them. "Mrs. Juddman."

He was clean-cut, fresh-faced, and had a terrible pain in his eyes. "I accompanied your husband's body home."

"Thank you. I didn't realize . . ."

"He was my friend. I brought some of his personal effects with me. There were only a few things. Cameron's ring, pictures . . ."

To hide her tears she opened the door and settled Ryan in the youth seat, then turned back. "You were there with him?"

"Yes, ma'am."

"When he—"

"Yes, ma'am. I was assigned to his Bradley."

"I don't understand. They said all of you died in combat that day."

"No, ma'am. When that last shell hit, I was wounded, but I was blown free. The others died."

The young man had to be wrong. He was grieving for a fellow soldier. Confusing the facts.

"I didn't even ask your name."

"I'm Jim. I wanted to be here for the funeral."

Ryan had fallen asleep. "Where are you staying, Jim?"

He scratched his temple. "Haven't even thought of that."

"I don't want my son to catch cold, so come back and stay at the farm with us. You'll have a warm bed, food. My in-laws—Cameron's parents—would want you to be there."

"I'd be grateful."

They rode back in silence. Once there Jim lifted Ryan into his arms.

"It's the room on your left," she whispered.

Jim carried the boy upstairs and came back smiling. "He woke up just for a second, then went back to sleep. I took his shoes off and put some blankets on him. He looks like his father—even has that mischievous glint in his eye."

"Yes, that's what people say."

"Except for those dark eyes—they're like yours, ma'am."

"That's what people say. Jim, why don't you call me Meagan?"

"Yes, ma'am."

They were talking. Speaking of the one Meagan loved, the one this young man respected. Yet they weren't really talking. Or crying. Or laughing. Instead, they tiptoed around the house, skirting their thoughts, because someone had died.

Don't you understand, Jim? That someone was my husband.

Everything had slipped into past tense. Meagan had worn her summer hat for Cameron. She had touched the first spring flower. But inside she was dead, lifeless, because Cameron had died.

She took her hat off and shook her hair free. "The sandwich and milk are for you. We'll have more later. Everyone has been bringing food. I guess they don't know what else to do."

"Your husband was a good soldier, ma'am."

"He always wanted to be a hero."

"He was a hero in my eyes. He'd be glad to know I made it."

"They told me Cameron was killed confronting the enemy— that there were no survivors. That all of you were killed by hostile fire."

"Who told you that, Mrs. Juddman?"

"The chaplain—no, it wasn't the chaplain. It was the officer who came with him."

"You're certain?"

"Yes, he described it in full. He said there was an engagement with Iraqis. You were outnumbered."

"No, ma'am, they lied to you. We were out there all alone. Sitting ducks. The Iraqis were approaching, but our own men took us down."

"Our own men?" In utter shock Meagan furniture-walked the living room and collapsed in a chair. "Our own people?"

"Yes. He was killed by friendly fire, ma'am. Killed before the Iraqi tanks moved in."

"Please. Please don't make up stories," she begged.

"I'm not, ma'am. I was in the Bradley with your husband."

In her confusion she reiterated, "But they told me all of the men with Cameron died."

"Like I said, ma'am, I'm the only one who made it out alive. We were sitting out there in the middle of the desert, trying to lure the Iraqis out of hiding. When it happened, Sergeant Juddman knew it was our own men firing on us. He tried to radio. Tried to tell them to stop. But the radio went dead."

The truth, the bitter truth, even before she could bury Cameron.

Someone turned the latchkey. Fran and Aaron were home. When she could keep her voice from trembling, she leaned toward Jim. "You must not tell Cameron's parents what you've just told me. Not until I can talk to someone at Fort Riley. But they will want to know you accompanied his body home."

He looked uncomfortable. "Ma'am, that isn't how it happened. I knew which flight he was coming on from Dover. So I booked the same flight. It was like being with him."

"Cameron would have been grateful. I know I am—for your honesty. Your loyalty to my husband. Someday I will want to tell his son the truth."

The front door slammed shut. Footsteps approached.

"I wasn't supposed to tell you what happened to Sergeant Juddman," Jim whispered. "The military warned me to keep everything under wraps."

"You'd be in trouble for telling me the truth?"

"There'll be an investigation. There always is on things like this. I think it's already under way. But they'll consider their report classified."

"Then I'll get in touch with an old acquaintance—a journalist friend back in Washington."

"Ma'am, I won't talk to a reporter."

"I won't quote you."

She glanced up. "Oh, Mother Juddman. Dad. You're home. I want you to meet someone—this is Jim, a friend of Cameron's."

Fran's arms went around the young man. Her cheek to his. Her tears dropping on his uniform. "Thank you for coming, Jim."

Aaron studied his son's friend through wide-rimmed glasses that were far too large for his tired, grief-stricken face. He wore the faint smell of the barn on his skin no matter how often he tried to scrub it away. This morning the faint scent comforted Meagan. It took her back to the familiar—to Aaron and Cameron milking cows together. Laughing.

Meagan stood. "Perhaps you two could visit with Jim for a while. I need to check on Ryan and make a phone call."

I n Washington DC Robinson Gilbert sat at his desk, buried in paperwork, his mind racing with the late-breaking news when the phone rang.

Why that particular ring set itself apart—lingering long after the call ended—he would never know. But in the clatter and clutter and the vocal shouts and phones ringing off the hook, that particular ring caught him off guard.

He adjusted his hearing aid. "Gilbert here," he shouted.

"You won't remember me—"

Here we go. "Then enlighten me."

"We met in the Italian Riviera."

His mind did a double take. A soothing voice. A young voice. There had been brief encounters on some of his foreign assignments. But not in the Italian Riviera. His son had accompanied

10

him there. The one thing he had promised himself was to live honorably in front of his son.

"Mr. Gilbert."

He rocked forward in his chair. Feet spread. A lock of silver hair sprawled over his wide forehead. "Go on."

"You and your son were staying in the room next to ours."

"Yes. Yes, of course." He scratched his head, trying to retrieve the name without begging her for it.

"My husband and I were on holiday there. You were tracking down an old enemy of the Allies."

Bernhard Grokov, the German who had disappeared at the end of World War II. "He got away."

Now he heard the tightness in her voice. The confusion. The panic. "Mr. Gilbert, when we left the Riviera, you gave me your business card."

"Juddman. Meagan Juddman." He was glad the name came back.

"You said if I ever needed you—"

His brawny hand curled around the phone. "How's that young soldier-boy husband of yours?"

"He's dead . . . He's dead, Mr. Gilbert."

He whacked his forehead. Felt her dismay. "Not in the Gulf War?"

"Yes."

"I just got back from there myself. Was he killed in action?"

"Mr. Gilbert, he was killed by friendly fire—by his own compatriots. I want the truth exposed. Will you come?"

For a story, he thought. *I've gone around the world for a good news story, but for one dead soldier?*

"Please come to the funeral. I need your help. The government lied to me."

CHAPTER 17

Meagan insisted on going to the mortuary alone. Cameron's body had been accompanied from Dover by another sergeant—a man she did not know or trust from the moment she met him. He was, in her eyes, part of the lie, part of the cover-up.

"I want to see my husband. I want to say good-bye."

The sergeant stepped forward. "That's not possible, ma'am. His casket is sealed."

"Then break the seal."

"Ma'am, the army—"

"My husband no longer belongs to the army. He gave you his life. The army sent me back his remains."

The sergeant cast a worried glance at Seymour Mackey, the mortician who had known the Juddman family all his life. Seymour nodded. "Give her a second or two, Sergeant."

She stared the sergeant down. "Ten minutes. I want ten minutes alone with my husband."

"Ma'am, I have orders to remain—"

"Alone. And don't worry. No one will ever know what passed in this room. My friend Seymour here and I made the decision. You will not be disciplined for disobeying."

"But I'm in charge."

"No, right now I am." She stared into space as the lid to the gunmetal casket was propped open. She did not move until the others left the room.

The smell of the floral wreaths sickened her. It would have

sickened Cameron too. She stepped forward and looked down at Cameron's lifeless, chalky-gray face. He lay wrapped in a green army blanket, his dress uniform draped over his body. She was enraged. He had not even been given the dignity of wearing his uniform for the last time.

Had he been so badly wounded? So mutilated?

Meagan focused on his face again. She ran her fingers over the closed eyes and long lashes, down along the waxen skin to the tiny brown mole. Had the army used that to identify him?

She whispered in the empty room, "I'm so sorry. We would have worked it out, Cam. I know we could have worked it out." And then she leaned down and kissed his cheek and those full pale lips, the lips that would never again play a trumpet and send its clear, sweet notes across the room. "Good night, sweet prince. You kept your promise. You came home again."

She heard the door opening behind her, the quick sharp steps of the sergeant approaching. His voice was terse. "It's been fifteen minutes, ma'am."

She met his gaze, her eyes as hard as his. "How thoughtless of me."

He stopped on a dime, unsure of himself now.

"Sergeant, I want my husband buried in his uniform."

"But, ma'am."

"He died in his uniform, didn't he?"

"Yes." The word dragged out.

"Then that's how I want him buried."

The sergeant knew trouble when he saw it, and this widow spelled the word in bold capital letters. He was on orders to get Sergeant Juddman under the ground as fast as possible, to sweep away all evidence of death by friendly fire.

But across the coffin he met that angry gaze. *Humor her. Do as she asks, and get it over with.*

He considered diverting her by telling her about Juddman's

heroic death by hostile fire—about his Bradley tank being out-numbered by the Iraqi Guardsmen. But he had no idea whether Juddman was in or near his tank. He had not a clue as to whether he was in or near Kuwait. Whatever he told this widow would only be lies and added fuel to the fire in her eyes.

He stole a glance at the local mortician. Mr. Mackey looked miserable.

The sergeant squared his shoulders. "Do as she asks." Then he turned back to Meagan. "If you would step outside for a few moments, ma'am."

"No, I'll wait here. And, Sergeant, I want to put his wedding band back on," she insisted. "The young man who served with Cameron in Iraq returned it to me with his personal effects."

The sergeant winced. The harshness in his voice softened. "Mrs. Juddman, your husband's left hand was blown away."

He caught her as she swayed. Now his concern was more than military courtesy. More than pity or his own need to finish the task at hand and get out of town. He broke into a sweat. *Does this widow know something is askew?*

"We could put the wedding band in his pocket, close to his heart."

She gripped the open coffin with both hands. "That would be good of you, Sergeant. Thank you—I . . . I gave the ring to Cameron the day we married."

When else would you have given it to him? he wondered. But he restrained himself from further comment. "Yes, ma'am. It's good that Sergeant Juddman kept it with him always."

Meagan went mechanically through the next few days. She rallied long enough to welcome Robinson Gilbert and his son and to thank them for coming. Once there, Robinson became the main-stay for all of them. Taking care of food deliveries. Phone calls. Riding out to Fort Riley to make certain everything was arranged as Meagan wanted it. Robbie, now a teenager and handsome like his father, became a tower of strength too. He took Ryan under his wing and together they played catch. Or Robbie would piggyback Ryan out to the barn to help Aaron milk the cows.

The night before the funeral Robinson, Robbie, and Meagan reminisced about the Riviera.

"I can't believe how grown up you are, Robbie," she murmured. "You were so rambunctious in the Riviera."

"I'm seventeen now."

Robinson nodded. "Robbie likes to remind me he's almost eighteen."

"I'm starting university in the fall to study journalism."

"My son plans to take the media world by storm," Robinson added, the pride evident in his voice. "Do you have plans, Meg—after this is over?"

"Over? It will never be over. But I'm leaving Kansas soon—I know that for certain. I told you on the phone that I'm riddled with guilt. I planned to divorce Cam when he came home. I'm angry at him for dying so young. But it's the government's deception that's tearing me apart. If he died by friendly fire, why not tell me? Why lie to me? All Cam ever wanted was to serve his country and to honor his God. And they dishonor his memory."

She rocked in her hardback chair. "Whenever Cam was away on maneuvers or on duty at the post, Ryan would bring his teddy or toy and sneak into our big bed. Until Cam found out. He put his foot down. Since . . . since we got word on Cam's death, he sneaks into bed with me every night. Somehow I think it comforts him to be with me. Maybe it makes him feel closer to his daddy."

"I used to do the same thing with this young rascal. When my wife and I first separated, Robbie had trouble sleeping. Bad nightmares. I'd pick him up and take him to bed with me. It's not a bad thing when you're both hurting."

"Fran doesn't agree." She looked up, her gaze steady. "Robinson, I need your help. I've been given bits and pieces of the truth. I know the Bradley is equipped with weaponry. Antitank missiles.

Coaxial machine gun. Why didn't they fight back?"

"They were taken by surprise," Robinson theorized.

"At first the army told me they were up against Soviet-made vehicles. That the crew died at the hand of the Iraqis. Jim said they were hit with mortar shells and armor-penetrating bullets from the American side."

"What is it you want me to do, Meagan?"

"Find out the truth and publish it. I want to know who gave the command to fire on Cameron and his men. What kind of miscommunication went on. I've been to Fort Riley. They're stonewalling me. They're full of excuses. Paperwork lost? What paperwork? Documents missing when Cam's body came home? I don't know anything about the morgue in Saudi Arabia—I don't even know whether it exists, so why would they start a chain of errors? The military has given me excuses. Nothing but excuses. Will you find out what really happened?"

Robinson took a breath. "It won't bring your husband back, Meagan. I can't take on the bureaucrats in Washington. Honestly, there's nothing I can do."

Her eyes narrowed in defiance. "Then why did you tell me to contact you if I ever needed your help?"

"Mrs. Juddman is right, Dad," Robbie announced. "I've never seen you back away from a good story. She needs your help. That's reason enough to take on Washington."

Ironically, the day of the funeral proved a day of celebration. In this both Meagan and Fran agreed, for they were celebrating Cam, celebrating his life, celebrating a man whose life, though cut short, still exuded patriotism even in death. It was a simple ceremony—sad yes, but the exact kind that Cam with his dancing gray-green eyes would smile upon. He wore his dress uniform with a new stripe sewn on. He was going out with a shout, according to Fran. With full military honors, according to Conaniah. Going army all the way.

Everyone seemed pleased. Even Meagan was calm, for she imagined Cam saying, "Oh, Meg, this is Kansas at its best. Spring coming in. Rain clouds running away. Flowers beginning to deck the Flint Hills. And that boy of mine tugging at the bugler's coattail, asking after me."

Chaplain Whitford had kept his word, planning down to the last detail all that would have pleased Cam. For the hometown boy the horse-drawn caisson carried his remains from the chapel to the grave. Two horses: one mounted; one symbolically empty with Cameron's shiny boots over the empty saddle. An honor guard with their own spit-shined boots.

The men's chorus from the chapel sang "O God Our Help in Ages Past." Fran's choice. Past ages—not this moment in time for Meagan. She had chosen "Proud to Be an American," for that was so typically Cameron. No matter how much she felt betrayed by the country he served, it could not diminish Cam's love of America.

The honor guard removed the flag from Cameron's casket and with meticulous care folded it thirteen times. The first fold as a symbol of life. The eighth fold for Cameron—the tribute to the one who had passed through the shadow of death. The thirteenth fold that left the stars on top. The lieutenant pressed the folded flag into her hands. She accepted the flag as she sat in the folding chair and, upon seeing Fran's deep distress, leaned over and placed it in her gloved hands. In the end seven men fired their twenty-one gun salute. The shots cracked out, leaving the smell of cordite in the air. The cocking of rifles made ready. A second volley. A third. And then the mournful blare of "Taps" echoed among the crosses.

At the sound of the haunting melody, she whispered, "All is well. Safely rest . . . Good night, my darling. Rest well."

Ryan, bored with the long procedure, wiggled. Squirmed. Scooted from the folding chair. And stood by the bugler. "What are they doing with my daddy? Why did they put him in that box?"

The bugler continued to play, eyes straight ahead, his other arm embracing Ryan.

A thorn pricked Meagan's finger as she tossed the crushed white rose into the hollow ground. She heard it thud against Cameron's casket. And then a trumpeter from Fran's church played "Ivory Palaces"—for no celebration would be complete without the song that Cameron loved. As the trumpeter played, the crowd moved over the lush green grass and past the rows of crosses.

Meagan turned abruptly as Cam's friends came toward her. She waved them off—in the same way that she had waved her husband off two months ago—and hurried away. Not speaking. Not wanting any of them to know the secret she carried in her heart. They had come as Cameron's friends, reaching out to her in love and sympathy. But none of them knew she had planned to leave her husband, not welcome him back as a dead hero.

The shame overwhelmed her. The beat of her heart thundered against her ribcage. What if Cameron had been unguarded, careless even for a second? What if her threat of a divorce had sent him to an early grave? She stumbled blindly over the uneven ground of the cemetery, Ryan's small hand clasped in her own.

"Meagan, wait. Don't run away." It was her mother-in-law.

Meagan turned back and saw that Fran Juddman's usual strong features were crumbling.

"Don't go away, Meagan. Not now."

"We're not leaving for a few days."

"If you would stay, we could get through this together. Dad and I need you. You need us. Stay a few weeks at least. For our sake . . . We lost our son. Don't take our grandson away so soon."

Meagan looked at the ashen face. "Oh, Mother Juddman, how could you think of having me stay? Don't you realize I was planning to leave your son when he came home?"

She nodded. "It doesn't matter now. He loved you, Meagan." Her voice caught. "You loved him once."

"I still do. But . . ." Meagan spread her hand at nothing in particular as Cam's mother reached out and put her thin arm around Ryan's shoulders.

"He's all we have now. Don't take him from us."

"We'll be back for visits." Meagan squeezed her mother-in-law's hand. "And you can come and see us once we're settled."

But even as she extended the invitation, Meagan doubted that Fran would ever cross the Kansas borders. She had never flown—never strayed far from the farm or her small circle of friends. Meagan glanced back at the crosses and knew that Fran would never go far away from her son.

"Then you're never coming back here to live, Meagan?"

To what? The bleakness of Kansas? "Fran, Cameron is dead. I have to leave. Please understand. I have to go back to where I was once happy." *To the place where I trust and pray I will be happy again.*

"But not tomorrow. Please, Meagan."

"Not tomorrow, Mother Juddman."

She saw a fresh bout of pain each time Fran looked at Ryan. He was so much like his father. But in the end Meagan would have to do the only thing that could possibly set her world right.

When Robinson called Meagan three weeks later, she asked, "Do you know his name yet? The monster who killed my husband."

"I know that he's a career officer. A fifth-generation soldier. The nephew of a retired general."

"And we would not want to ruin his career?"

"More likely they will want to protect it."

"Then no one in a command position has been affected. No ribbons torn away. No career tarnished. Just several innocent men dead."

"They'll call it a covert mission or a betrayal of trust for them to release sensitive material to you."

"I can't get past the gate at Fort Riley anymore. All they throw at me is military parlance. 'We're still looking into it, Mrs. Juddman.' If only the man had come and said he was sorry."

"We have one shot in the dark, Meagan. One chance to go public. A House Subcommittee is willing to meet with you. I convinced them you have a right to decry the military's lack of accountability in the death of your husband."

"So they hear me out to silence me?"

He bypassed that one. He'd already delved in enough to know that Juddman and his Bradley had not driven off course. He was precisely where his commanders had sent him. Robinson was willing to gamble that they knew he wouldn't survive the mission. Make that into a headliner and it could explode into a full-blown war between the government and the families who had lost loved ones in less than a week in the ground war. Meagan blamed one man. Robinson was convinced that the incident went beyond that. Higher in the ranks. Not one mishap, but two.

"Meagan, I have a copy of the report on the army's investigation regarding the notification process. In your case, they admit no error. They blame paperwork for your conflicting reports regarding Cameron's death. You have to understand they're not going to make it easy for you."

"I'm a fighter. I've been a soldier's wife for years."

"Good."

By stealthy contacts, Robinson had uncovered the detailed account of the wreckage and the recovery of the bodies. He'd been privy to copies of the photos taken at the scene and later recorded in the Identification Laboratory in Hawaii. It would not be a pleasant picture for Meagan if the House Subcommittee showed them: A boot sole. A ring? Cameron's ring perhaps? No. She had told him that Cameron's ring went to the grave with him.

There'd been pictures of the fragmented remains of charred bodies. Personal effects from the crew. Dog tags. And Cameron's mangled body—but his handsome face intact, as though God had preserved him for the journey home.

Robinson knew his way around Washington. He had reviewed documents obtained through the Freedom of Information Act— and traced the path that Juddman's Bradley had taken. It was out there in the middle of the desert with no other vehicles around it. He'd kicked that one around for a good while, pounding himself with questions. Didn't they usually spread out? Move into battle together? There was no indication that Sergeant Juddman had strayed—been lost. He was beached on that berm with the full knowledge of those in command. The poor devil and his crew were fighting to claim a piece of the desert.

"What do you think, Mrs. Juddman? My paper is interested in the story. They'll stake you to a hotel suite. A freebie all the way. Or Robbie and I would be glad to have a houseguest. If you could tolerate a couple of bachelors."

"For Fran and Aaron's sake I'd better stay at the hotel."

Robinson met Meagan Juddman when her flight arrived at National. "Are you okay, Meg?"

She looked dreadful. "Like I told Conaniah, if my tears were diamonds, I'd be rich. The family opposed my coming, Robinson. Fran and Aaron want no publicity. They want me to put it to rest. How can I? It's as though Cameron is calling from the grave for justice. Fran sees it as Cam shouting with joy in heaven. And I asked her if he was rejoicing that he's no longer with us."

"I'm sorry."

"You're my sole ally. His family insists that nothing will bring Cam back. As though I don't know that. As though I don't cry myself to sleep every night. But I want accountability. The government has no right to withhold the truth from me."

The hearings lasted for hours. The committee blamed the losses in the war on poor visibility, with both sides wearing the same camouflage uniforms. The chairman acknowledged that in an effort to bring the ground war to a quick end, there had been friendly fire casualties.

"In a war against terrorism, we can't defeat terrorists without major loss of life, Mrs. Juddman. Friendly fire happens."

"Then it's up to you to halt these casualties, sir," she insisted.

She had been so brave when Robinson phoned to tell her that she would have the opportunity to meet with the committee investigating the incident. But neither of them had envisioned that with the elected leaders in Washington, the review process would be one-sided. It was Meagan and Robinson who became the enemy, not friendly fire.

Robinson worried about her. Meagan had lost weight in just three weeks. She sat beside him stony-faced, her eyes sunken, hollow. Her hair had lost its sheen. Her attention drifted when he spoke to her. She'd start to answer the chairmen and then leave the sentence unfinished.

He put his hand on her shoulder. "It was too soon to put you through this. You look like you've gone through a wringer."

"The old-fashioned hand washer?" She smiled, the lines on her face repositioning themselves. "Robinson, I miscarried at Fort Hood a few years ago. I miscarried again ten days ago. No one knows. But what if it was the baby girl that Cameron wanted—we both wanted? She would have been my last link with Cameron."

The House Subcommittee had reconvened. "Mrs. Juddman, we are doing our best. In the future Allied tanks will be outfitted with special identification thermal panels. Pilots will look through infrared devices and identify them as American. Studies are under way for vehicle-to-vehicle communication, where answers will come back in less than a second."

"I'm grateful, Congressman, but not soon enough to save my husband or the men who rode with him."

The congressman's power seemed to lie in his frown. "No, for that we regret your deep pain."

A second congressman spoke up. "We have a computer system in the planning stage that will give every armored vehicle the same picture of the battlefield. Blue for the friendly tanks. Red for the enemy. Spot an enemy tank. Plot it on a computer screen. Our gunners will tell at a glance whether it's safe to open fire . . . We'll have it all for the next war."

"I thought we just had the war to end all wars. I'm glad for tomorrow's soldiers, but I'm concerned about the war just ending. The losses we suffered without these computers."

"Are you aware, Mrs. Juddman, that Stonewall Jackson died as a result of friendly fire?" There was a Southern twang to the congressman's voice. "He was a much-loved, brilliant Confederate wounded by his own men. That incident may have changed the course of the whole war."

Robinson slammed his pen on the table. "Is Sergeant Juddman of any less value, Congressman? I think the army wants to silence this widow. To sweep everything about her husband's death under the table. You demand silence regarding the incident that took her husband's life. For security reasons? How can her silence protect her husband? He's dead."

The chairman ignored Robinson's outburst. He kept his attention on the widow. "I see your husband was promoted to Master Sergeant."

"Posthumously, sir. Four days after he died. And they gave him a Purple Heart and a Bronze Star for Valor—valor for being killed by his own people?"

Outside the windows, mockingbirds twittered. Inside, government officials lied. People, Robinson decided, grieved in different ways. And this beautiful widow was falling apart. He leaned closer. "Meagan, you won't get anywhere badgering the committee. Remember your son."

Her response was stoic. "That's why I'm here. So I can face him in years to come."

The chairman took a swallow of water, but it didn't eliminate the gruffness in his voice. "Sergeant Juddman had an exemplary career."

"Our whole family has been ripped apart by this war, Mr. Chairman. I have a six-and-a-half-year-old who doesn't understand why his daddy isn't coming home to tuck him in bed or to build a snowman with him. Your ground war, sir, lasted less than a week, and yet it took everything from us. Just a handful of days. Cam had to lose his life while you sit here in Washington trying to pacify widows. My husband always wanted to be a soldier. But families are casualties of war too. And we deserve accountability."

The chairman was blunt. "Why are you doing this, Mrs. Juddman? You're torturing yourself. Putting yourself through needless pain. Robbing your husband of rest. The government needs closure."

"Sir, I need closure."

"I would think that the press attention you're receiving would appease you. You've been quite vocal. Outspoken. The beautiful grieving widow from the plains of Kansas. So what is it you want from us, Mrs. Juddman?"

"An apology for lying to me. Or better yet, give me back five weeks ago when my husband was still alive."

As they waited for her plane back to Kansas, Robinson knew that the widow was choosing to step away. But he still smelled a story of deception. Of governmental cover-up. Tragic incidents had been labeled classified. "Meg, I told you when you flew to Washington that the review might not go in our favor."

"But I hoped there would be some disciplinary action taken. I thought such action would block any future promotion for the officer involved or even force him to early retirement." She shrugged. "They call this a military investigation when no one is held responsible or charged with negligence?"

"I can resubmit an application to the Army Board for Correction of Military Records on your behalf."

"What good would it do?" Meagan's voice was resigned.

"It might get you the government's apology in writing."

"I'd go on with the search, but Cam's parents are bitterly

opposed. If you learn the truth, you can have your story. And maybe I'll have closure."

He switched the subject. "What are your plans?"

"I'm going home to Twisp."

"Your in-laws won't like that."

"I know, but it will be best for all of us."

"And if I find anything in this fight for justice?"

"Let Conaniah know. He's stronger right now than I am."

"I'm sorry I couldn't do more."

"You tried—that counts with me."

Meagan sat by her husband's grave and watched the dusk over Fort Riley turn to darkness. She was cruelly aware of time in a place where time did not exist. There were no tears left, only sadness for her beloved soldier who had loved life. The miserable loneliness of widowhood taunted her. But she did weep for their son.

"What have you done to us, Cam, dying like that? I hated the army, but I don't know how to make it on my own."

"What are you doing here, Meagan?"

She jumped up from the white cross and stumbled into Conaniah's arms. "I've been scolding Cameron for dying so young."

He seemed to have aged since the funeral. "You're leaving, aren't you, Meagan?"

She nodded. "Soon. There's nothing left here for us."

"I'm here."

"But you won't be long, will you?"

He thumped his chest. "The old ticker is playing out."

"And I won't stay and watch you die."

"Will you stay in touch with us, Meagan?"

"I'm not good with letters. Cameron hated that about me."

He lifted her hand, his grip like rough sandpaper as he touched her fingers one at a time. "You can still use the phone."

"As soon as I get a phone . . . Perhaps you would come and see us in Twisp. I don't want Ryan to forget you."

"I'd like to come."

"I'll take you to Winthrop—that's another quaint town. They don't have cattle drives anymore, but they have ice cream and fishing and steak houses and . . ."

He held her hands in his. "You loved him, didn't you?"

"But I was going to leave him."

"Is that important now?"

"Fran knows . . . How can she ever forgive me?"

"Have you asked her? She has a big capacity for forgiveness."

"That sounds strange, coming from you."

"My daughter-in-law proves her mettle when the chips are down."

"But Mother Juddman and I don't have much to say to each other," Meagan insisted.

"Surely you know Cameron was her whole life—until Ryan was born. Then she divided her affection between the two. If you take him away, Fran will have nothing left."

"If I stay, it would destroy me."

"You will let Ryan visit them?"

"Yes, of course. I told Fran that we'd come back for visits. And they can come to the Methow Valley to visit us. Oh, Conaniah, I don't want to say good-bye."

"Of course not, child. We Juddmans never say good-bye."

Part 3

Going Home Again

Why should we be in such desperate haste to succeed,
And in such desperate enterprises?
If a man [or woman] does not keep pace with his companions,
Perhaps it is because
He hears a different drummer:
Let him step to the music which he hears,
However measured or far away.

—Henry David Thoreau, conclusion of *Walden*

CHAPTER 18

Two weeks later Meagan and Ryan crunched over the snowy trail to the Methow River and stood just beyond where the rivers merged—gurgling and flowing with seasonal intensity. Spring was late in coming to the Valley this year, but Meagan didn't care. Coming back to the place of her youth was the memory of yesterday, a return to the rolling lavender hills of eastern Washington that her grandmother had loved.

She pointed to a large rock in the river. "Ryan, my grandmother carved her initials on that boulder a long time ago. We call it the Norris Rock."

Ryan's brows puckered. She was confusing him with foreign words. Boulders and initials. And her maiden name, Norris.

"Grandma Fran?"

"No, Granny Norris. My grandmother. When the weather turns warmer, we'll wade out to the rock and sit on it. I used to do that when I was young." Her throat constricted. "She was such a special lady, Ryan."

Her grandmother had never shed her British accent or lost her love of living and singing. Meagan never tired of Granny Norris talking about finding her American businessman on a foggy day in London. Falling in love with him. Marrying him. Moving to Seattle, Washington, and spending her summers and holidays in the Valley. She had come back here as a widow to live out her years in the little house in Twisp. Meagan remembered that she kept her curtains open because her living room windows faced the mountains, her kitchen looked down on the river. Even when Granny Norris was dying, she was still witty and vibrant. Her eyes sparkled whenever Meagan walked into the room.

She'd lift her head from the pillow. "Oh, child, come here. Let me tell you about my Jesus again—before I go away."

The night she died, Meagan had run outside and waved her fist in the darkened sky. "Why, God? She loved You. She never hurt anyone. We need her. Why did you take her from us?"

Now it struck Meagan like the snap of a twig. *This time I am the widow coming home to the Valley.*

Right now, her grandmother's face seemed as real and lifelike as though she had stepped down from heaven to sit with Meagan— to counsel her, to love her. Perhaps here as the seasons came and went—the seasons that Granny Norris had called God's painting on the landscape—Meagan would find peace, for the Valley and her grandmother were one.

The icy river rushed over the rocks and wound its way through the Methow Valley. All around them, the sloping hills rose to snow capped peaks. On the other side of the river—high in the mountains—a gushing waterfall formed a trail of its own as it cascaded over the snowbound cliffs.

"Like living water," her grandmother would say.

Meagan caught her son in her arms and whirled him around. Clumps of snow fell from his mittens and rubber boots. As he patted her face, the snowdrops chafed her skin. But it didn't matter. She was back where she belonged.

"We've come home, Ryan. We've come home."

Ryan's eyes widened as the winding river roared. He clapped his hands as the bubbling waters rushed past them and crisscrossed the rocks.

"They go so fast, Mommy."

"Rivers do that. It will slow its pace when spring comes. Right now the river is caught between two seasons." She kept babbling. "You will love it here, darling. The mountains were meant to climb, the trails to explore, the rivers and streams to follow. And the budding leaves to pluck. We'll do all those things together."

"I'm just a little boy, Mommy."

"I know. And very dear to me."

As she looked at Ryan, she saw Cameron, and the pain came roaring back. They had come to make a new life for themselves, to shut away the stench of war. In time she would take Ryan to the small cemetery where her grandmother was buried. And she'd take him to the smokejumper base and teach him appreciation for the forested mountains and about the danger of forests burning.

I want the Valley to come alive for you, little darling, in the same marvelous way that my father made it live for me.

They'd ride Highway 20 so Ryan could learn about the towns that made up the Valley. Twisp merging into Winthrop. Winthrop into Mazama. He'd love the main street in Winthrop with its Old West frontage and the ice cream store on the corner. She remembered those many times of walking into the Forest Rangers' office beside her dad to learn about the Cascades and Sawtooth Mountain, about Goat Wall Overlook and Buttermilk Butte, about the hiking trails and how the three rivers merged.

Oh, little darling, like my daddy did for me, I will teach you to ski at Sun Mountain and swim in Patterson Lake.

There was so much she wanted to show Ryan so he would love the Valley, but his nose had turned red. His lips trembled with cold. "Can we go home to Grandma Fran now, Mommy?"

His request startled her. "Someday. Not right now."

"Is Daddy coming to see us?"

"No, he's in heaven. Remember?"

She'd come back to the Valley to place a stake in the land and erase the memories of Cameron's death and sacrifice. But for Ryan, Cameron was still very much alive.

The war made her a widow. She wanted only to survive—something that had eluded her young husband. She wanted financial success—something her young husband had failed to achieve in his short life. She wanted acceptance in the Valley, to be recognized and remembered for her contribution—something that her soldier husband received posthumously.

Ryan's squeal of laughter pierced her ears. Meagan ran to pull him back from the edge of the surging river. She crushed him against her. "Ryan, that's a no-no. You never go near the water's edge without Mommy there."

"I told you I was going."

Had she been listening? No. Her sudden grief over Cameron had wrapped its miserable tentacles around her. Her fears, her pain brought back her deceased husband's words: *"I don't know what it's going to take, but someday, Meagan love, you will hear the clarion call. And like a burst of sunshine, you will understand. You'll believe in the Man on the Cross as I do."*

He was wrong. She felt nothing but fresh anger at Cameron's God.

"Mommy, who made the river?"

She answered grudgingly. "God did."

"And that big mountain?"

"God."

She shivered. Had Cameron's God followed her to the Valley? No. Her grandmother had found God in the Methow. Perhaps, as she understood it herself, she should teach Ryan about her grandmother's God. Yes, Cameron would be pleased if she did.

As they followed their footprints back to the car, she felt part and parcel of this land. She determined to place a stake in the Methow, and do everything she could to erase the memories of Cameron's sacrifice and her bitterness against the government's cover-up. But how could she block out the guilt that she had planned to divorce Cameron when he came home from Desert Storm?

Impulsive by nature like her dad, Meagan had given little thought to making a living. She had Cam's insurance, but what with the move and settling in, that wouldn't last forever. It might not last until the next winter.

She had to work.

But how to get a job with no training and no experience here in the Valley where people were often cash-deprived? Jobs—any job—were at a premium. Selling ice cream in Winthrop wouldn't put nourishing meals on the table for Ryan. So she drove to the realty office to ask a favor from an old family friend.

When she walked in, Bob didn't even get up from his desk, but his grin was welcome enough. "Well, Sunshine, you've come back to God's country."

"I thought it was Owen Wiser's old smiling country."

"True enough." Bob pointed to a chair across the desk from him. "Have a seat, Meagan. Rest those hundred twenty pounds of yours . . ." His tone changed, his words less cheery. "Look, Meg, I'm sorry about your loss."

She nodded, not wanting to begin life in the Methow with grief as her entry.

"The paper ran a piece on him. Picture and all. I'm sorry I never met him."

"I am too. You would have liked him."

"What mattered was you did." He went on leaning back in his leather chair, his arms stretched back, his head supported by locked fingers. He'd propped his feet on the desk, a size thirteen boot at least. He looked like a man too comfortable to stand.

"I need a job, Bob."

"You've got it." Just like that.

"I want to sell real estate."

Bob was barely into his thirties. With his wife at his side, he had built the business from scratch. He was practical and hard-working, too heavy and too busy to climb the mountains at his back door. And obviously too busy to shave. He sported a thick black beard that would look better trimmed. A toothpick switched from one side of his mouth to the other, its tip swishing across his whiskers like wind across the prairie grass.

"What's your work experience, Norris?"

"It's not Norris these days, Bob. The name's Juddman. Cam's

death didn't change that. And I can only boast high school honors. Travel experience to Germany and Italy. For the last seven and a half years I've battled the army, and since Cam died, I've fought the government."

"So you're feisty and two-fisted. And pretty, I might add. All three qualities work for me. But selling homes and property is hard work, Meagan. I have one motto in this office. *Sell, sell, sell.* Seal that in your mind. We joke at the water cooler and that's it. Otherwise this is a hard-working outfit."

"I know I can do it."

"The apprenticeship is costly."

And her bank account dwindling.

"There will be a tough study program ahead, Meagan. An intense course at Rockwell. Then a state licensing to hurdle before we could hang your license on this wall." He pointed to the space above the water cooler. "Once you get that, we'll frame it over there. Your picture beside it will look good. Clients like a pretty young face."

"How much commission, Bob?"

"Usually nothing for the first year. But out here where the houses and Valley sell themselves, maybe six months max."

"There will be a salary to tide me over? Right?"

"Zilch. Those are the terms. A tough first year, maybe more, with all the preparation for the job and the clock hours for continuing education and license renewals."

She felt defeated before she started. "How many hours? I have a son to think about."

"I thought you were going to ask me when you earned your first vacation. We work around individual schedules here." He chewed on his toothpick as he considered her dilemma. "If you want to succeed in this field, you won't be sitting on your bottom. You'll put in time—every day. It's your call. You can't play games—can't fly in and out of the office and expect to make it." His eyes were piercing, challenging. "How old is that boy of yours?"

"Ryan is still six. He'd be in school during the school year."

"And during the summertime and school vacations and between school and when you'd get home from work each night?"

"I guess I haven't thought about those things."

He called over his shoulder to his wife. "Honey, can you bring Meg Norris and me a couple of Cokes?"

"Meagan Juddman," she corrected. "And I prefer root beer, if you have it."

"Make one a root beer, honey." He hadn't budged his position. "Meagan, let's work it out. You'll need a place where the boy is safe. Loved. Cared for. This isn't a nine-to-five job. It's a twenty-four, seven."

She swallowed her dream. "I could do housework."

He brushed the idea off with a wave of his hand. "And you'd still be scrubbing toilets twenty years from now. No, you can build a livelihood in real estate. You just have to have guts and determination."

Bob's wife appeared from the back room with two cans of pop in her hand and a smile on her pleasant face. Her eyes were sympathetic as she swept around the desk and hugged Meagan. "We're glad you're back . . . we're sorry—"

"Sweetheart . . ."

"Okay, Bob. I'm going. See you later, Meg, but what about dinner on Sunday? Our place. Bob can cook the steaks on an outdoor grill—I'll toss the salad. Bring that boy of yours. We can give him his first riding lesson."

Meg fought back the tears burning behind her eyelids. "Yes, thank you." She turned back to Bob.

He popped the can open for her and shoved it across the desk. "Where are you staying, Meg?"

"At a motel in Winthrop."

"That's no place for the boy."

"I didn't have anyplace else to go. We have no furniture. I just brought our clothes and Ryan's toys and a few linens."

"You're well equipped. Sounds like when they muster you out of the army, you go barehanded."

"I was just an army wife. Just a widow now. There was nothing left for my husband to give. He was dead."

"You need to board in one of the country homes so Ryan can have space and playmates and someone to oversee his care when you're not home."

"But I plan to be there for him."

"Wrong, Meagan. This is a sixty-hour work week until you're really into the business. After that, you'll set your own pace. If you can scrape two farthings together, you should consider a place of your own. You'll need to place a stake in this land, and down the way we'll be able to help you do that." He turned back to his wife. "Honey, I know you've been listening to everything we said, so what do you think? Anyplace where Meg and her boy can board?"

His wife called back, "I'm already on it. I left word for my sister to call me. She's bound to come up with some suggestions. Right now I'm thinking about old Mrs. Bowers. She could do with the company and the money. She'd be a good one to watch over Ryan."

And so it was settled and so it began.

Ryan was eight when he took his first flight back to Kansas. The thought of sending him alone proved unbearable, so Meagan took vacation time to go with him.

Both sets of grandparents met them at the airport, but the biggest surprise was Tad Porter there to welcome her. Meagan flew into her mother's arms, both of them laughing and crying at the same time.

Beside them, her father knuckled Ryan's chin. Tilted it up. Winked down at his grandson. "We've waited a long time to see you again, boy."

Off to the side, Meagan caught a glimpse of Fran and Aaron standing stoically, waiting their turn. She reached out and squeezed their hands, but she was not ready to go out to the farm where Cameron was born.

Oh, Lord, I'm just not ready for that.

Conaniah was right. They'd grown older, grayer. Fran's face seemed softer, Aaron's ridged with a lingering sadness—their lives forever imprinted with the loss of Cameron, their only child.

In the crowded airport terminal, Tad's eyes sought hers. "I can't go with them," she mouthed.

"You won't have to. I've arranged everything." He nodded toward the Juddmans. "They'll drive Ryan out to the farm themselves. And I, pretty lady," he announced, grinning, "have the privilege of taking you and your parents back to the Porter Cattle Ranch. So say your good-byes and let's go."

Leave my son? We haven't been separated since—

She knelt down and hugged Ryan. "Now, you be good for Grandma Fran and Grandpa Aaron."

A crazy warning, little man. You're impish and into everything. Curious and delightful . . . stubborn and reckless . . . and if you break any of your grandmother's china . . .

She hugged Ryan again as Fran Juddman edged toward them.

"We really must go, Meagan. Ryan will be fine. Don't fret over him. We're losing precious time with our grandson."

Fran tried to take Ryan's hand.

"He's outgrown that, Mother Juddman."

She stiffened slightly. "I see." To Ryan she said, "You're going to be staying at the farm where your daddy grew up."

Ryan turned back to Meagan. "Mom, I think I remember the farm. Daddy and I built a great big snowman."

Just before your daddy went away, Meagan thought. She leaned down and kissed him again.

"Ah, Mom." He wiped her kiss away.

He was Cameron all over again—she could see it in Fran's and Aaron's eyes. They looked at their grandson, but they were seeing Cameron, and indeed she saw it herself. The brilliant eyes—her coloring—but Cameron's sensitivity, daring, his excitement at life.

As Ryan went out the terminal exit between them, Meg saw a little Cameron walking off, never looking back.

Tad picked up her luggage. "He'll be all right, Meagan. They just want a little time with him."

Meagan spent her mornings sitting on the porch enjoying the view. She found herself excited about the familiar—looking at the countryside that Cameron had loved. The golden wheat fields. The Flint Hills. The cottonwoods. The clover and daisies and Sweet William still in bloom.

Tad showed up every morning for breakfast at her parents', which pleased her mother, and came by every spare hour he had, begging Meagan to go fishing with him or horseback riding.

"I can't, Tad. I need to stay close in case Ryan calls."

Ryan's calls grew shorter. His voice radiated happiness. "Grandpa and Grandma took me to Fort Riley today to see Daddy's grave . . . We saw the old reprobate today. He's got a big collection of soldiers in the middle of his library. I think I remember the soldiers. He calls it the Anzio landing or something like that. I don't think Daddy fought there. It was Grandpa Conaniah's war . . . Conaniah's coming to see us at Christmas . . . Boy, that means more presents for me. Maybe he'll make a snowman with me . . . Sorry, Mommy. Got to go. Grandma is taking me to her quilting club. They're making a quilt for me with photos of Daddy. She says it will make me feel close to him."

Another time: "Gramps and I are spending the day fishing . . . Tomorrow we're going back to Fort Riley to see the chapel where Daddy played his trumpet."

Ryan was rapidly outgrowing her, not needing her. She resented Fran for this, and yet understood why. The little man in the house was becoming independent. Cameron all over again.

On Thursday's phone call, an overcast morning, he grumbled, "Grandpa says I can't get the hang of milking a cow. Grandma says I'm just like my daddy . . . Am I all right? Yeah, but Grandma says

I'm coming down with a cold because I got my feet wet fishing yesterday . . . We just had a farmer's breakfast, and Grandma promised chicken and dumplings for dinner."

Between calls from Ryan, Tad appeared. His eyes said everything. Aloud he said, "There was never anyone but you, Meg."

She put her finger to his lips. "Please, Tad. We're just friends. That's all it can ever be."

"I'm willing to wait."

"Please don't, Tad. I care about you but—"

His eyes shadowed with disappointment. "Friends then . . . And if you want Ryan to stay another two weeks with your folks at the ranch, I'll accompany him on the jet ride home—as your friend. As Ryan's friend."

Two weeks later Tad arrived on her doorstep in Twisp with a wild, happy child on his hands—a boy looking the spitting image of Cameron. Ryan did not remember his father except for little snippets of memory, but after that visit to Kansas he charged into the house, dropped the suitcase on the floor, and ran to the guest room.

"Ryan, I didn't even get a hug."

A muffled voice called back. "I'm looking for my daddy's trumpet. Grandma Fran told me to play it."

"You don't know how to play it," she argued.

"I'll learn. Honest I will, Mommy."

She stood in the bedroom doorway, Tad just behind her. "Come out of that closet right now, Ryan Juddman."

He came out with a frown on his forehead and dust on his face. "I can't find it."

"It isn't there."

"But Grandma Fran wants me to play Daddy's favorite song about ivory palaces. I think I remember Daddy playing that. Where is it? Grandma Fran wants me to have that trumpet, Mommy."

"It isn't your grandmother's to give away. Now come over here and give me a hug. I've missed you."

She dreaded the thought of Ryan learning to play his father's trumpet and hearing the sweet clear notes of his favorite hymn: "Out of the Ivory Palaces." That song would remind her of God, and she still wanted nothing to do with Cameron's God, even though the picturesque valley spoke clearly of His creativity.

CHAPTER 19

SPRING 1999

Ryan came sleepily to the breakfast table, a gangly teenager now, his dark brown hair tousled, his mahogany eyes bright and shiny—almond-shaped like Cameron's. He slid into his chair, scarfed down a glass of orange juice, and reached for a refill.

She smiled at him. "You're the handsome one this morning."

He hand-brushed his hair back from his forehead. "I'll run a comb through it before I leave for school."

"I wasn't thinking about your hair. You're looking more and more like your daddy."

"Should. I'm a man now." He gulped down another glass of juice and nagged her again. "I'm fourteen. I think I'm old enough to have my father's trumpet now."

"Please. Let's not talk about that again."

"Why?"

She twirled her coffee cup. "I couldn't bear looking at it, Ryan."

"It's been eight years, Mom. When are you gonna grow up?"

"That's my line."

"And that's my trumpet."

But even now she could not tolerate the thought of the sweet sounds of a trumpet playing.

"It's mine. Grandma Fran told me that," he insisted.

"Your grandmother talks too much. You have the wide open spaces and a horse of your own to ride. Thanks to Mrs. Bowers. That should be enough."

"That's Mrs. Bowers's aging nag, not mine." He mashed his

scrambled eggs and popped a forkful into his mouth. "They're cold."

"You should have come down when I called you." Meagan stared at the frilly curtains hanging in the windows of their rented house. "I have my eyes on a place for us to buy. I'm negotiating the down payment."

"You've said that before." But he eyed her curiously and took another bite of breakfast. "Will I have a room of my own?"

"You have your own room now. But yes. The owner calls it a cabin, but there's a loft."

"And I'm supposed to use a ladder to get there?"

"No, there's a narrow staircase and an old wood stove and a fair-size yard."

"For me to mow."

"I'd be grateful if you did."

"What happened to that mansion you promised?"

"That's still down the road. But owning a piece of land will be a step in the right direction."

"I'd think Bob—"

"Uncle Bob to you. And he has helped us. It's his idea for me to start with a smaller place. It's a good investment."

Should she tell him? Lately she'd made some good real-estate sales, but she had her eyes on the property on the mountaintop above Winthrop. Sell that one and she might have a down payment for her dream house and enough left over for Ryan to really own his own horse . . .

"Do you remember me mentioning the old Marsh property?"

"You talk about property all the time. Uncle Bob said you ought to date someone and get a little variety in your life."

She shook her head. "Ryan, we've been over that too. There's no one around that I'm interested in. No one who would even begin to measure up to your father."

"You liked him like that, eh?"

She flicked a row of crumbs on the oilcloth. The remembrance of filing for a divorce—even thinking about it—burned in her chest. Ryan must never know the truth. "He was a wonderful person, Ryan. But we were talking about Rodman Marsh's property up on Buck Mountain."

He wiped his milk mustache with the back of his hand. "You gonna buy that?"

"No, I'm going to sell it."

"There's an old trapper's cabin up there."

"How would you know that, Ryan?"

He avoided her eyes and lunged for the milk carton.

"Ryan, don't put your milk in your juice glass."

"You only gave me one glass."

"You have two feet. But the Marsh property—you were up there?"

"Once or twice."

"Not with those kids—"

"Yeah. The truant bunch. The ones who do drugs, as you call it."

She touched his hand. He pulled back. "You're not—"

"No, I just went up to look around. They had a car. I went with them."

"Ryan, you're only fourteen. I don't want you riding with underage drivers and especially not on that uphill road. It's not safe . . . And you can't skip school."

"We were bored."

"I'm sorry. I've been late coming home at nights."

"No problem. I'm getting good at opening cans."

"I told you, I'll always cook dinner for you, no matter what time I get home."

"I'm hungry when I get home. If you've got a growling stomach, you feed it." He looked at his watch. "Got to run. The bus will be here any minute."

"Mrs. Bowers said you promised to chop some wood for her."

"I just didn't tell her when."

"Ryan, she's getting old. She's been good to us. She took such good care of you when you were a little boy. Made a home for us. Baked you cookies. Called you her little man."

"Yeah, I know. She's okay. She still bakes cookies. When she runs out of steam for that, I don't know what we'll do for munchies. But what about that old Marsh property?"

"There's some legal obstacles. I'm working on them."

"Somebody must own the land."

"Somebody did. The original owner was one of the pioneers. His heir hasn't been heard of for seven or eight years. When the old man was alive, the heir used to visit."

"Why visit? There's no place to sleep up there. But the old cabin still takes the winter winds." His gaze shifted from his watch back to her face.

"Ryan, it's been rumored that the heir died back in the Gulf War. Time's in my favor. The city planners would benefit too. If the rightful heir never comes back, then the land reverts to the city."

"Lucky you. What are you going to do with the wad?"

"It's called a commission, Ryan, and I'm going to spend it on improving our lives."

He shoved back his chair and stood.

"I'll be home on time this evening, Ryan," she promised. "I really will. I think I'll pick up a couple of steaks for us."

"Mrs. Bowers won't be able to chew them."

"I'll buy chicken for her and drop it off on my way home."

"She doesn't see too good, Mom. We should have her over here to eat. She just lives down the street. I wave to her every morning, but she still gets lonely."

Do you get lonely, Son? I thought life would be so perfect when we moved to our own place. The rent is higher, but we were getting to be too much for Mrs. Bowers. She was getting too old.

"I promise I'll cook you a fancy meal this evening."

"I promise to wolf it right down. And I promise I won't skip school today."

Long after he left, Meagan sat at the table thumbing through the photo albums that she had made since coming back to Twisp. What had happened to her sweet little boy? Why the streaks of defiance? The evidence of rebellion? Her fault, she knew. But she had no choice. The job took long hours. It put food on the table and a roof over their heads, but it had wedged a distance between them.

Meagan had filled the albums as Ryan's birthdays flew by. Hundreds of snapshots of him growing up. Ryan at five. Ryan at seven. Ryan at eleven. A small boy bundled up for Christmas. A child boarding a yellow school bus and never looking back. A grinning, growing boy tearing the Christmas wrappings off of another weapons carrier, another armored truck from Conaniah. Ryan sitting on Granny Norris's boulder and carving his initials beside hers. Pics of hiking in the woods together with her son. Meagan on the sidelines as he played Little League. Ryan throwing a fishing line. Ryan holding up a dead rattler. Ryan riding a horse. Ryan making the basketball team.

Ryan with his grandparents and great-grandfather.

And there were the pictures that Fran and Aaron had sent—snapshots of Ryan's second summer in Kansas when he turned eleven and flew alone. The Christmas album had several photos of Conaniah—when the old reprobate came to Twisp for Christmas, five holidays in a row. She laughed at the memory of him huddled in front of the old wood stove. She turned to the pages of Cameron's parents—they came twice between harvest seasons, and she had been glad to see them go. Aaron disliked her cooking, and Fran constantly ran her finger over the furniture, checking for dust. Her mom and dad had only come once. It was all they could afford.

She closed the last of the albums. Meagan's greatest joy was her son. But she had spoiled him rotten since his father's death and given him everything he wanted except his father's trumpet. She associated the sound of a trumpet with her broken dreams. But it was Ryan, *his daddy's boy*, who had held her together since her world fell apart.

Meagan knew the mountain. She'd surveyed the land more than once. Now, for Ryan's sake, it was time to ride up the rutted dirt road and put the FOR SALE sign up on the mountaintop.

She studied her surroundings before stepping from the car. People didn't worry her, but cougars and coyotes did. Over there, to her left, stood the crumbling Marsh cabin, a ramshackle building where the old town crier had lived for decades. It was backed up against a scattering of pine trees and balsam root. The property was a choice parcel of land, but it remained unclaimed since Marsh's descendants could not be located.

What she really wanted was a single buyer. But if necessary she would divide up the acreage and sell it to the top bidders. If a man wanted solitude and beauty it was all here. He could build his own place, heat the home with solar energy, and dig a well for water. There were no power lines up here, but kerosene lanterns were available down in the towns. She wouldn't mention those drawbacks to a potential buyer. She'd keep the focus on the magnificent scenery.

Meagan could not afford the land herself. Would not want it. She'd seen a black bear—in the distance—on her first trip up here, and she wasn't into arguing with bears. The rangers had warned her that bears didn't like surprises. She didn't either. Nor did she like coyotes. She'd heard them the last time she was up here just at dusk. Whitetail deer were more to her liking. But she didn't want the land to lie there under a tangle of sagebrush, untended, where only the wild animals found shelter and refuge.

She dragged the FOR SALE sign from the back of her truck, took a heavy rock, and hammered it in.

In Heidelberg, Germany, an older Anna VonHoekle stood on the top step and watched her son carry his luggage down the long flight of stairs. Her shoulders drooped. She owned this cement complex with its three floors, but ownership brought her little joy. At least it had a new facade like the houses down the street and rails on the front steps. Karl had insisted on these.

She only saw the frescoed paintings on her own house when she went shopping. Other than that she stayed in her flat, waiting for the renters to pay her each month. On those days when her mood was lighter, she quilted. Meagan Juddman had taught her how to quilt. It was the only pleasure she had except her pleasurable indulgence in her son. But Karl had grown into a shrewd, selfish, and secretive man—like his father had been. He was a brilliant student, but why this move to America?

He was back a few minutes later, running effortlessly up the steps to her.

"Must you go, Karl?"

"I'll write, Mutter."

"It won't be the same. No one will cook your kraut and bratwurst for you the way I do. Or make your favorite strudel."

"I know."

"And no one will make *Flammkuchen* for you."

"*Ja.* It won't be a square pizza, but they do have pizza in America with tomato. I'll miss your cooking," he admitted. He brushed her hair back from her face. "You'll have time now to have your hair done and to buy some new clothes. Promise me you will do that?"

"What for?"

"So you will be the beautiful woman you once were."

"One of Himmler's beauties?"

His eyes narrowed. "I do not blame you for your beginnings. Why blame yourself?"

"I thought—I thought perhaps—"

"You thought Father left you because of that."

He guided her back into the living room for their good-byes. Long ago she had rid herself of Wolfgang's easy chair, but the room was still comfortable, well dusted.

"I want you to stay in here." He turned on the television. "I don't want you to watch me leave."

She clung to him and asked again, as she had many times, "Why must you go to America, Karl?"

"I want to finish my university studies."

"You have your degree from Heidelberg. There are other schools here in Europe if you want to study more. But it would be better for you to get a job."

"Or better for you, Mother? You don't want me to go away."

"You're all I have. Karl, have you ever seen your father since he left us?"

"Why would I look up a man like that?"

"Because you loved him. When I dusted your room and picked up your clothes, I found airline stubs. One when you went to Argentina and—"

"And no doubt the one when I flew to the Italian Riviera the last time. You know that's my favorite vacation spot."

"Your father's as well. But there's one big difference—you never liked olives, Karl. Go get your luggage. I'll unpack for you. Please, Karl, take a job in one of the architectural firms here in Europe."

"I told you. I have the promise of a job in America with a German firm once I finish my studies."

"What could you design there that you couldn't right here at home?"

"The Schmidt and Ludwig Architect Firm serves my purposes." His cold glance caused her to shiver. "You see, Mutter, I plan to design a war memorial for Cameron Juddman."

"Sergeant Juddman—Meagan's husband? He's dead?"

"*Ja*. Didn't I tell you, Mutter? I've done some research on that Gulf conflict. Cameron Juddman lost his life in that war."

"You seem pleased."

"Wasn't it Sergeant Juddman who drove my father away?"

"It wasn't the Juddmans who shaped your father's politics."

"But they ruined his reputation."

"Your father made his own choices. The Americans gave him a decent living."

"That sounds strange coming from you, Mutter. You've despised the Americans from the day my father disappeared." He pressed some euro currency into her hands. "I won't need this. I kept enough for the tips at the airport. My friend will bring the car back to you. You'll be all right."

No, she would not. She dreaded eating alone. Then her resolve strengthened, for she could see the lush, wooded hills and the swift-flowing Neckar River from her living room window and the Heidelberg Castle from her desk in the bedroom. And Karl would write. He would call. He would never disappear from her life as his father did.

CHAPTER 20

In the spring of 1999, when the cherry blossoms were in full bloom in the District of Columbia, Major Tharon Marsh resigned his army commission. He'd tendered a resignation two months before, requesting separation from active duty and a transfer into the Individual Ready Reserve. Quitting was not his nature, but he had a plausible excuse for moving on. It was time to claim his inheritance on Buck Mountain.

As he explained to his commanding officer, time was running out on the Marsh property left him by his great-grandfather. "It's claim it or lose it to the city fathers, sir. I'm not throwing my career away, I'm salvaging my future."

"You're not still running from the loss of your wife?"

He had not answered. With all of the time that had passed since her death, he still couldn't bring himself to talk about it. Kips and the army had been his life, his reason for living.

But claiming his great-grandfather's land would give him the peace and solitude he craved after fourteen years in the military. The army had been good to him, but he was leaving at a time when he was eligible for another promotion. Moving up in the ranks had been his career goal from the time he graduated from West Point as a generational West Pointer. On his first overseas posting, he'd been promoted to first lieutenant while on duty on the DMZ zone in Korea. Had advanced to captain—a company commander—during Desert Shield and Desert Storm. He'd served in an advisory capacity in Kosovo while NATO considered sending in ground troops and been promoted to major during the ongoing Balkan tinderbox just before being assigned to the Pentagon. Sometimes it seemed as if he had spent the whole fourteen years sitting near the flames of war, like a career officer serving in some outpost forever under siege.

Along the way he'd collected the medals and ribbons that recorded his service time. He wore them proudly . . . except for the Bronze Star for valor in Desert Storm. This he kept in a castaway box. Because of one split-second decision in the Gulf War, he was not proud of his service time there.

He chose not to leave Washington in the snarled morning traffic but to wait until the city was silhouetted in the night sky. That sight had pleased him from the day he accepted duty in Washington three years ago. Tonight he was subdued, somber like the granite walls of the Vietnam Veterans Memorial. Nearby, at the Korean War Veterans Memorial, statues of soldiers marched in full battle gear. Memorials abounded in this city, but none honored the Gulf War or the Balkan Conflict in the same way. Nor had a monument ever been erected to the families grieved by friendly fire.

Or to the men who gave the order to fire.

His condo lay in darkness as he strolled from room to room, gazing out the windows at the lights flickering from the dome of the Capitol and at the white marble shaft of the Lincoln Monument that housed a majestic, unsmiling Lincoln. The troubled face cast in marble seemed to reflect the entire weight of a country.

Moments later he tossed the last suitcase into the Range Rover, along with his best tools, personal papers, his favorite pictures of Kips, golf clubs, and his rifles. He covered these with his sleeping bag and blankets. It was seven when he eased his lanky body into his vehicle and drove through town. Light streamed from the south portico of the White House and beamed across the lawn and flower beds. He'd been inside once, enjoying the simple elegance of the president's home. In the distance lights from the John F. Kennedy Center cast their golden streamers on the banks of the Potomac.

Funny that the lights were so important to him when he was

Doris Elaine Fell

destined for a mountaintop cabin with no electricity, no running water. He remained resolute that he had made the right decision as he sealed the sights of the city in his memory.

Everything about the city stood for honor, duty, country—cruel reminders that he had resigned a post at the Pentagon, hung up his uniform, closed out his condo, and left no forwarding address for anyone. He kept two bank accounts open—one for direct deposits and the other with funds to cover the association fee at the condo and the end-of-the-year taxes. Rumor had it that the White House was unhappy about his departure. The committees on which he had worked to lessen the risk of death by friendly fire felt threatened that he was slipping away with intelligence secrets tucked away in the back of his mind. The rumors were unfounded. He was leaving because the cover-up on friendly fire still rankled him.

Because life never felt the same without Kips.

He sped across the bridge with its well-lit lampposts and headed for the outskirts of town. As he reached the expressway, he glanced once more in the rearview mirror, accelerated, and nosed his Range Rover northwest for the three-day journey to the mountaintop.

Tharon timed his drive to reach the Methow Valley in the early morning. He picked up some food supplies at the country market in Twisp and found himself whistling as he sped along the highway. He'd forgotten the beauty of the Valley with mountains hemming him in. No wonder his great-grandfather stayed so long.

He almost missed the turnoff. The marker with the words Rodman Marsh imprinted on them was missing. Putting the Range Rover in park, he stopped long enough to undo the chain lock and open the small privacy gate at the bottom of the road. Safe on the other side, he secured the gate and looked around. Bushes. Wildflowers. A noisy black-and-white magpie scolded his intrusion, and hawks dropped low in search of food.

236

Branches of the trees that had not weathered the last winter storm lay crisscrossed on the road. Recent tire marks had gone around them. He could ride around them in the same way, but why not clear the drive now? He rolled them toward a compost pile to his right and booted it, not wanting to be surprised by marmots or rattlers, not wanting to surprise them. He found the old marker facedown. The sign and a rotted mailbox had stagnated together. He'd come back later and take the sign into town. He'd have a new one made: Rodman Marsh & Great-grandson.

He got back into his Ranger and drove up the narrow rutted road to Rodman Marsh's land, high in the Methow Valley. His land now. What Tharon found was a ramshackle trapper's cabin, smack in the middle of long-neglected land. But the view of the Valley and the mountains was without equal. And there, just off the road, was a FOR SALE sign. He stepped from the car and strolled over. Yanking it from its place with his bare hands, he leaned it against an aspen tree.

Standing there, looking down at the picturesque valley, Tharon's thoughts vacillated between his great-grandfather and Cameron Juddman's widow. He had known for more than a year that she made her home in this valley. He wondered now how much her presence had influenced his decision to claim his great-grandfather's property. He hoped the years had treated her kindly. He would not look her up, but perhaps with a community geared toward friendliness, their paths would one day cross. Perhaps then he could tell her he was sorry.

Tharon tapped the weeds and grass with a stick as he made his way to the cabin through a trail overrun with sagebrush, bitter-brush, and wild grasses. He was glad he had worn his high boots and made a mental note to purchase a machete to help clear the land around the house.

The roof had caved in. Two crumbling walls made a gallant effort to remain upright. Yet his great-grandfather had loved this old place. When had he seen the old man last? It had to be that summer he came back from Korea. How much time had he given his great-grandfather? Two or three days. Four at most. A recluse living in a cabin. His clothes threadbare, unkempt. But he was content; that's what Tharon remembered. Rodman Marsh looked as aged as some of the fir trees, but he was a happy man.

Tharon still could recall their hike out to Buck Lake, a quarter of a mile away . . .

The old man set the pace. He pointed out the prints of a cougar and smiled when they discovered a whitetail deer in the bushes. He named the songbirds as he shuffled along and paused once to let a magnificent butterfly rest on the back of his hand. They'd stayed by the lake for an hour, sitting on a log. Rodman Marsh talked about bears and their habits, about the moose he had seen at the lake on his last time here. About the round, plump grouse with the mottled feathers. And the snowshoe hare that came in the winter. He spoke of them as old friends.

Tharon made the mistake of asking, "Grandfather, do you do much hunting up here?"

Horrified, the old man shook his head. "These animals are my friends. I would never kill them."

When they reached the cabin again at twilight, they dined on canned goods because Rodman Marsh didn't get down to town much anymore.

Tharon shook his head to clear the images. In the end it had been one of Rodman Marsh's loved creatures—a bear—that had mauled him to death.

Amidst the ruins, Tharon found the remains of what had once been a trapdoor—the place that Rodman Marsh had long used as a bank. Over the years he had sold plots of land to others and on those rare trips down the mountain had allowed his lawyer to invest the money for him.

Other than those few boyhood visits, Tharon had spent little time with his great-grandfather, so why had the old man left his entire estate to Tharon? Enough money to buy a condo in Washington. Enough money to order a foreign model car. And this glorious piece of property.

Yes, Tharon would take refuge here, start construction on a house of his own, and stay forever. He'd nestle his home against the scattered pines and fir trees and let them absorb the winter winds. From the looks of it he'd have a woodpecker for an alarm clock and the possibility of enough animals to keep him company.

He'd have to build the house with a long, sloping roof to take the snows, and solar panels to provide the luxury of heat and energy that Rodman Marsh had never known. If the winter snows grew too deep, Tharon would drive down to the Valley and wait out the weather.

He went back to his vehicle and took the blueprints from his glove compartment. Turning them this way and that, he decided to have the front of his three-room cabin facing south.

It was well past noon when he drove back to town to find a motel for the night. Tomorrow he'd look into obtaining a permit for his guns and purchase lumber and sacks of cement and aluminum roofing. He'd need some estimates for drilling for water, and then he'd find a construction crew brave enough to take the hill to build him a house.

The land had been cleared and the foundation marked off when Tharon faced his first uninvited guest. The sturdy teenager leaned forward in his saddle and eyed Tharon curiously. "You'd better put that FOR SALE sign back up," he warned.

"The place isn't for sale."

"Says who?"

"Me." Tharon dug his shovel into the hard ground. "I've staked my claim. Nobody's selling this place."

"My mom is."

"Your mom?" The kid had appeared from out of nowhere, coming up the steep mountainside on a horse. Disgruntled at having his privacy invaded, Tharon asked, "What would your mom want with a place like this?"

"It's worth a pretty penny."

Tharon scrutinized the boy. "Doubt there are many takers."

"She just needs one. If you're interested in buying the property, I'll tell her. She might even give me a commission."

The horse and its rider grew restless. Tharon wiped his sunglasses, weighing the boy's suggestion, smothering his own amusement. "No need to buy something if you already own it."

"You must not know anything, mister. The land up here belongs to the Marsh family."

"I know. Belonged to them for generations. Ever since the first homesteaders came."

"Buy a piece of land and you get a bit of history. That's what my mom tells me."

"She talks a lot, doesn't she?"

"Has to—she's in real estate." He brushed a lock of dark hair from his forehead. "Do you have any kids my age, mister?"

Tharon considered for a moment. "None that I know about."

"You one of those dads who ran away?"

"Would it matter?"

"My mom might want to know." He pointed toward the house under construction. "I know she'll want to know why you're building a house up here."

Tharon's gaze swept the high mountains, the Valley far below. "Because I want a place with a view."

"But there's no electricity up here. And no water."

"I like it that way. And if it's so inconvenient, why is your mom trying to sell the place?"

"She'll tell them to put in solar panels and dig a well. You want to be up here all alone? Don't you have a wife, mister?"

"Just a few coyotes and rattlers." Immediately Tharon's con-

240

science stabbed him. It was a flippant answer that sent Kips's memory even further into oblivion. "Look, son, I had a wife once. Now get out of here."

The horse dug his hoof in the ground. "What'd ya do with her?"

Tharon nearly choked on his answer. "I buried her."

"What for?"

Irritation ripped at his gut. "She died."

"I know that, mister. I ain't stupid. I just wondered why?"

"Are you the kid with a thousand questions?"

"Mom tells me that's how I find my answers. Besides, I ain't no kid. I got another birthday coming up in September. And I was just being polite about your wife."

His answer proved as grudging as his mood. "My wife had heart trouble."

"That's a tough one. I'm sorry I nosed in."

"Don't be. It was fast. Zip. Gone." *And my whole life with it,* Tharon thought.

For now, total isolation comforted him. He was accountable to no one. It had been eight years since his wife's death, but he still missed her.

The lad adjusted his weight in the saddle. "Do you have a bum heart too? Is that why you're holed up here all alone?"

Heart trouble? Only if you count the crack that developed when Kips died. The one that seldom goes away. On his last army physical, Tharon had passed with flying colors. Not even an ingrown toenail. "Not that I know of. I just like to be alone."

The kid shrugged. As he scanned the horizon, he pointed in the distance. "Twisp and Winthrop are down there."

"Yes, I shop at the open market once a week."

The dark eyes narrowed. "I never saw you there. And I know everybody in town—except the tourists."

"Even tourists get hungry."

The kid was good-looking. Dark hair. Dark eyes. An easy way. He seemed like a nice kid. Intelligent. He guessed that the boy only used *ain't* for the fun of it.

"Do you buy the farmer's cinnamon buns when you go to market?"

"Matter of fact, I do. Have one of those going stale right now." Tharon thumbed toward the old run-down cabin. "Want to come inside for a bun and some tea?"

"Nope. My mom tells me not to talk with strangers or go anywhere with them."

Tharon gave an uproarious snort. Was this kid for real? He looked tall for his age, his patched jeans a size too small, his lettered T-shirt dragging over his buttocks, his boots well-polished. "Don't talk to strangers? What do you call what you've been doing for the last fifteen minutes? Killing time?"

"Nope. Being neighborly. Besides, I'm just checking up on my mom's business. She's selling this property, you know."

No, he didn't know. And how could she? The place belonged to Tharon. He had the papers to prove it. "Are you supposed to be up here, kid?"

"Nope. It's one of those forbidden privileges. I ditched school today. Had to do something to kill time, so I borrowed one of Mrs. Bowers's horses."

"Borrowed?"

"Well, she lets me ride sometimes," he explained.

"Look, I'm busy."

The kid pulled in the reins and nudged the horse's flank, turning him toward the narrow rubble of a road. "Okay, I can take a hint. But you'd better put your best shirt on. My mom's bound to come up here and check you out. See ya, mister."

"Look, do me a favor."

"Depends."

"Depends on whether it's worth it?" Tharon reached into his jeans' pocket.

"Nope. On whether it's something I can do." An impish grin spread across his face as he nodded at the money in Tharon's fist. "Can't take money from strangers either."

Tharon reached up and slapped the five-dollar bill in the boy's palm. "Look, just don't mention seeing me up here. Your mother wouldn't have to know right away, would she?"

"Why? You hiding from the law?"

"Actually I'm hiding from myself. I just retired from the army."

"My dad was army."

Was? The kid talked about his mother but not his father.

"He retired?"

"Nope. Died. And, mister, you shouldn't be on this property. It isn't honest."

Tharon nodded at the shack behind the unfinished house. "My great-grandfather lived there."

"You mean old man Marsh?"

"You sound like you knew him."

The boy grinned. "He died long before I knew he lived up here. But my mom met him. Dear old Rodman Marsh, she called him. Used to think her grandmother was sweet on him."

"Did you know he was one of the first pioneers up in these hills? I inherited this place from him."

"Then how come my mom's been trying to sell it?"

Now the worry was on Tharon's face. "She can't do that. I have the papers to prove my ownership."

"Mom says it's up for grabs. She says the guy who owns this place died back in the Gulf War."

"I'll work that out with your mother. Okay?"

The boy shrugged. "That won't be easy. She has her heart set on selling this place."

Tharon heard the wistful catch in the boy's voice.

"If she can sell this one, maybe we can buy a house of our own. Better than what you're building up here. I'm telling you, once she gets wind that the FOR SALE sign is down, she'll fly up this mountain."

"By horse?"

"No, she's got an old Dodge truck."

"But I just bought your silence."

"Want it back?" the boy offered.

Tharon glanced at the boy's ragtag jeans. "No, keep it."

"See ya, mister." The boy and the horse began to amble off, down the mountain.

"Wait." Tharon sounded gruff even to himself. "What's your name, son?"

"It ain't 'son.' It's Cameron Ryan Juddman."

At the name Juddman, Tharon sucked in his breath.

"But everybody calls me Ryan. Except those times when Mom's really mad I get the whole shootin' caboodle."

Tharon wiped his sweaty palms on his jeans. "This riding up the mountain on a borrowed horse, won't that be one of them?"

"Could be."

Tharon knew the truth now, but he had to ask. "And your mother's name? In case I come down the mountain to meet her—"

"Meagan Juddman. And she's not interested in dating."

Ryan put his boot to the flank of the horse and rode off, fast-paced, leaving the dust and rubble blowing in Tharon's face.

"Cameron Juddman. Meagan Juddman."

The names stuck in his gut, almost doubling him. "Dear God, I asked you to help me find them, but not this way."

Tharon had been caught defenseless. With his guard down. He had known there was a child, but he had pushed that knowledge to the back of his mind. Left it there, nameless, without personality or human form. But this kid was personable. A handsome face. A bit on the skinny side. A kid with a name now.

And the young man had a mother—the widow of Cameron Juddman.

Halfway down the mountain the boy turned and waved once more. Tharon could not respond. His peaceful solitude above the Methow Valley had just been shattered.

CHAPTER 21

Meagan was furious.

Enraged.

Out of control.

How dare this stranger take over the property on Buck Mountain? She checked her appointment book and found a free slot. She refused to enlist Bob's help. She'd solve this one herself. When the hour arrived she called into the office and left a phone message: "Checking out one of my properties."

As she rode over the rutted road to the mountaintop, her back wheel spun. She panicked, but with her foot heavy on the gas pedal she lunged forward. If she could only close her eyes and shut out the downward plunge to her right. Straight down. A guaranteed death warrant. She gripped the wheel tighter and finally made it to the top.

A Range Rover Defender was parked in the wild grasses, its sides covered with dust and mud, its wheels high off the ground. She knew enough about cars to know this wasn't an economy model. European. British, she believed. So the mountain intruder had exclusive tastes. She pulled in beside the Rover and glanced around. The old trapper's cabin had been torn down and a cement foundation laid. Bags of cement and lumber were piled near it.

He had obviously cleared a large portion of land. The grass and shrubbery had been cut back. Rocks rimmed an outdoor fire pit. The fool had to be risking the whole mountainside cooking his meals up here.

Still she saw no one. But the FOR SALE sign lay propped against an aspen tree.

She slid from her car and peered in the Rover window. Blankets and a sleeping bag. Pillows and a pile of folded clothes. Groceries. The fool. Didn't he realize this was grizzly country? Bears were lured by the smell of food. Or maybe he was smart enough to assume a cannonball position and play dead.

Meagan paused again, listening. Wondering where the person was. She stole over to the FOR SALE sign and dragged it back through the wild grasses to the hole in the ground where it had stood. She struggled to upright it. Picking up the nearest heavy rock, she began to hammer it down, inch by inch.

"What are you doing?" The metallic voice boomed through the stillness.

Meagan started. She hadn't noticed the man even being there, but he tossed an axe on the ground and charged like a bull, covering the distance between them in seconds. He glared at her with steely clay-cold eyes. "What are you doing here?"

"I came here to ask you the same."

He jammed his thumbs in the pockets of his drab, washed-out jeans. His bleached work shirt lay open at the neck, the sleeves rolled almost to his armpits. Curly auburn hair and perspiration covered his bare chest. "Ma'am, get off my property."

"Yours? I'm Meagan Juddman. I'm the real-estate agent selling this place. If you want to discuss the price—"

He looked lean and mean, yet his shoulders were broad, muscular. He worked his jaw, his thin nostrils flaring. "I'm serious. Get off my property."

"I have the approval of the city council to sell this property. The owner is dead."

"The heir is alive."

"He can't be. We were told he died in the Gulf War."

His expression turned grim, his smile spare. "You've been misinformed, Mrs. Juddman."

She tossed a five-dollar bill at his feet. "I believe this is yours."

"I believe I gave it to your son."

A breeze thrust it into a tangled bush. He made no attempt to retrieve it, but his right foot did a devil's tattoo, a steady thumping on the hard ground. "I thought your son would tell you I was living up here before this. It's been two weeks."

"He only admitted the truth yesterday—after the principal called to tell me he'd been expelled for truancy again. He wasn't supposed to be up here that day."

"Skipping school is not a wise move, but I believe he's a good lad."

"I don't think the two go together."

He tilted his head at a rakish angle. "I had a bit of experience with skipping school myself. But I started my truancy much younger. Once I was twelve and set my eyes on West Point, I didn't do that again."

Her stomach soured. Yes, he did have a military bearing. "West Point? You were in the service?"

"Yes. Fourteen years."

She didn't dare ask. He could have served in the Gulf War, and it only made her despise him more. She nodded to the fire pit. "You shouldn't be cooking up here. You'd need a permit."

"And what makes you think I don't have a permit?" His smug gaze sized her up. "Actually the nights turn cool. It's a good way to keep warm and to keep wild animals at a distance. Once I wear myself down, I crawl into the Rover and sleep."

"It's not safe up here at night."

"Is that concern in your voice?" he mocked. "Don't worry about me. I have to be on hand when the workmen arrive. I pay them double to come at the crack of dawn."

"There's no electricity or water."

"But have you noticed the view?"

"Of course. It's the best selling point."

"That and solitude. I like being alone. That's why I'm building up here."

"Then stop building until you can prove who you are and whether you own the land or not," she insisted.

"Oh, I own the land all right. I'm Tharon Marsh, Rodman Marsh's great-grandson. His only living relative. I'll be down in a few days to settle this problem of ownership with the city fathers. Perhaps we can work out our differences then as well." He took her elbow and turned her toward her car.

She pulled free. "I can navigate on my own, Mr. Marsh."

"Then leave now, Mrs. Juddman. But if I can ever help you with your son—"

"Help me? You're not the kind I want around my son."

"I'm not a bad sort. I might even be able to come up with some references. In the past I knew some of the town fathers. And I am good in history and math."

"Are you equally gifted in legal matters?" she countered.

"I believe I will be able to hold my own, Mrs. Juddman."

Hi, Mom. We've got company for dinner," Ryan called out in a happy voice.

"I brought Chinese vegetarian soup," she announced, kicking the door closed behind her.

"Oh, Mom," Ryan complained. "My stomach growls all night from that stuff."

"I prefer steak and potatoes," the man said as he turned to face her. "If I'm going to help your son on his schoolwork, I'm going to want a good square meal. And on time."

"Mr. Marsh!"

"Yes, it's been a month since we met. I keep missing you when you ride up to put the FOR SALE sign back up."

"Then why don't you stop taking it down?"

He was blunt. "It confuses my workmen. I tell them I own the property. Your sign contradicts that. But now that the paperwork has been filed with the city fathers, it's not likely you'll be up Buck Mountain again."

She glared at him. "Why don't you leave, Mr. Marsh? We really have nothing more to say to each other."

His smile was fractional. "But we're going to see a lot of each other, so call me Tharon."

Her thoughts raced in surprise. *What? What does he mean "a lot of each other"?*

While she recovered from her shock, he made a point of looking at his watch. "The two of us will want our meals on time." He included Ryan with a quick gesture. "And, Meagan, I'm not a free-loader. I'll pay for half the groceries. But no leftover casseroles or canned dinners. Meat and potatoes."

If Meagan had despised Tharon Marsh on the mountaintop, she could not begin to describe her emotions at his audacity. At his intrusion into her home. Into their privacy.

"I think you'd better leave," she warned.

"That was my line up on Buck Mountain."

"He can't leave, Mom. I invited him in. He made an agreement with the principal," Ryan explained. "I get back into school, and Tharon here oversees my studies."

Absolute fury rose in her. "*You* talked to the principal about my son without my permission? How dare you!"

Mr. Marsh was calm, maddeningly calm. "He was a very nice man. We hit it right off. Once I explained to him that I owed the boy one."

Her eyes narrowed. "You owe us nothing."

"But you're wrong. I've had a commitment to the boy's father for a long time, and I intend to fulfill it."

Her fury abated. "You knew Cameron?"

"In a way, yes. We served in the same war."

"You drove a Bradley?"

"No."

But I was there, Tharon remembered, *when the medics wrapped his remains in a body bag and carried him away. Yes, I owe this boy something for robbing him of a father when he needs him most.*

He had given an order, and a boy had lost his father.

Tharon had to look away, pretend to be absorbed in Ryan's text-book. "I don't think any kid should be expelled."

"The school thinks differently. You don't go behind the school and smoke pot or drink beer—"

"Were you there, Meagan?" Her name wrapped around his tongue.

Meagan Juddman was beautiful. Fiery. And in her fury, still graceful like a deer. Her hair was between gold and tawny. What-ever color, it was a soft, silk halo. He imagined her body, slim and attractive, behind those sacks of groceries.

"Help your mother, young man. She doesn't seem to know her way to the kitchen. From now on, you help her carry in the groceries—and it wouldn't hurt you to put them away."

She winced. "He'd leave a disaster zone like he does in his bedroom."

"Guidance," Tharon admonished. "Just a little guidance."

She sighed. "You don't have teenagers, do you?"

"No children. But I did have a couple of dogs, and they learned to 'Sit up' and 'Stay' on command."

"I'm not under army jurisdiction any longer. I'm just a mother struggling to make a go of it."

"I'm here to help you. It's my way of saying I'm sorry for your sake that the property on Buck Mountain isn't for sale."

"I'd rather not discuss it. I had such plans . . ."

He nodded. "So Ryan tells me. But on Saturday this young man and I plan to mow the yard."

"We dooo?" Ryan sounded like something had lodged in his voicebox.

"Oh, I didn't mention that?" Tharon grinned at Ryan.

Ryan hedged. "I plan to play baseball with the boys."

"Then we'll have to do the yard at the crack of dawn. We'll be cleaning out the flower bed too."

"Why bother? Mom never has time to plant flowers."

"Then this is her golden opportunity. Impatiens and petunias grow quickly. We can ask the gardener what else."

Meagan frowned as she shifted the grocery sacks. "Are you trying to take over our lives?"

He considered her question. For the first time since Kips's death, he found himself interested in someone else. He wouldn't want to take over their lives, but he'd like to be part of them.

Then that awful day in the Gulf seared back. He was looking at the beautiful widow of Cameron Juddman. Looking at Juddman's son, who had gone without a father because he had ordered his men to fire at the wrong time. No matter that Colonel Corbin had outranked him. That he had sent Juddman and his men on a fatal mission. Tharon was all army; he knew he had to follow orders. But he had wondered all these years . . . if he hadn't been thinking about Kips, would Cameron Juddman still be alive? Would he have doublechecked the identity of the Bradley before firing?

Ryan sauntered over to take the groceries from his mother and disappeared into the compact kitchen.

Tharon stood still, as if frozen. He still hadn't answered his own questions—never would.

He noticed she was looking at him with concern. "Are you all right, Mr. Marsh?"

"Fine. I think I'll clear the table for you."

"You can't. It's loaded with real-estate business."

"So where do you eat?"

"There." She pointed to the cozy living room with the black wood-burning stove adding to the quaintness.

"Meagan, would you mind if we sat around the table this evening? My wife and I always did. And for some reason I'm missing her more lately. She was a professional model when I married her. After her heart started to give out, I insisted that she not work. Perhaps physically she couldn't. So keeping house and making it special for me was Kips's main concern."

"Ryan told me she's dead."

"Yes. Her heart finally gave out. And when it did, it broke mine."

He was grateful she didn't respond. It gave him a minute to control the crack in his voice. "Believe me, Meagan, I don't want to pry. I don't want to take over. That's not my purpose here. But I think you and your son were victims of the Gulf War too. And like I told you, I owe your husband one. I hope you will let me keep my promises to the principal."

Mealtime proved awkward, but Tharon kept the conversation going. When it was time to leave, he smiled down at her. "I'll be here Sunday morning, bright and early, dressed in my suit and tie. Could you have Ryan in his best bib and tucker?"

"And where are you going?"

"To church. And we expect you to go with us."

She answered quickly. "I have an appointment that morning."

"Change it until midafternoon. That will give us time to have dinner at the Freestone Inn. It's out on the highway."

"I know where it is, Mr. Marsh." Meagan frowned.

When she kept frowning, he added, "It has a grand view of the Cascades. They've got a good food selection. Rib eye. Pan-roasted pork. Rainbow trout. There will surely be something you like."

"Do they have soup and salad?" Ryan piped up. "That's Mom's standby."

"Mr. Marsh, you can't afford that place."

"Do you have any money, Ryan? We could go Dutch treat."

The kid's eyes were downcast. "Nope."

"Then you'll go as my guests—right after church. That'll put you back in the sales business by midafternoon, Meagan."

Her answer was curt. "I don't go to church."

"I've been missing myself. Ever since Kips's death, I've kept myself busy. Sundays included."

"Which means you stopped going to church."

"I stopped trusting God for a while, but now I have a new responsibility." He nodded toward Ryan. "That was part of the agreement with the school. Ryan gets a five-day tour of duty without skipping. And we put in an hour. An hour and a half at most at church . . . My wife and I always went to church when I was home. I got out of the habit when she died."

"I never made it a habit."

"For your son, I think we will."

She raised an eyebrow. "Do you have a particular service in mind?"

"Yes, I've spotted a rural church. It sits up against some evergreens. On a clear day it's a perfect view. The sign had Bible Camp and Christian in it. That sounded stable enough for me."

"You're crazy."

"No, quite serious. You do have a pretty dress to wear?"

"Several."

"Ryan here will help you pick out a pretty one. He may even guess which colors I like best."

Tharon Marsh stood in the doorway watching Meagan as she poured the cartons of vegetarian soup and noodles into her best china bowls. She opened the refrigerator and peered in. "Mr. Tharon, I can make you a hamburger."

His spare smile widened. "This time I'll settle for soup."

Ryan wiggled his nose. "You'll regret it, Tharon."

She had not seen her son so happy in a long time. Tharon was an amazing man, but even in his kind moments still crusty, authoritative.

But I don't know squat about this guy. How on earth can I trust him with my son?

Ryan was beaming, laughing, soaking up everything Tharon said. She didn't like the way he had swept in and taken over. But inside she knew that Ryan needed a male role model before he got into serious trouble. Part of her was willing to try anything, even if she wasn't crazy about Tharon Marsh. The irony was he was a soldier, but she desperately needed his help. So why not give it a try? After all there was something both trustworthy . . . and unnerving . . . about Tharon Marsh. In what was once the safety of a small town, Meagan had not been prepared to encounter a man as competent and rugged.

She kept stealing glances his way, trying to see the value that Ryan had already placed in him. Tharon's skin looked a permanent sunburn, with a smattering of ginger freckles across his cheeks and on the tips of his ears. His eyes were hazel, the color of autumn in the Valley. She fussed over the place setting on the table—not wanting her own creamy complexion to take on the flush of a sunburn.

This evening his speech had been crisp and unbending. A month ago on the mountaintop he had been bullish, imperious, and threatening. But tonight his evident caring about Ryan had snuffed out his anger at her for trying to sell his property.

It was strange—even now, as she placed the takeout dinner on the table, she was thinking about tomorrow's steak and potatoes.

Months later, when summer had settled on the Valley, Tharon sat at the table with Meagan, dutifully drinking one of her Suisse Mocha sugar-free, fat-free instant coffees, and wishing it were a percolated black. She was not Kips. Didn't look like her. Didn't cook like her. Still he found himself longing to be more than a mentor to Ryan. But memories of the Gulf War had drifted like windblown sand dunes between them.

"Tharon, whenever I ask you about your career in the army, you're vague. We don't really know anything about you."

"You know I was married. That I lost Kips."

"Is that all that happened between West Point and Buck Mountain?"

He stared out into space. "Wasn't that enough?" He pushed himself up from the table, looking much older than a man in his thirties. "I graduated with honors from West Point. Did you know that?"

"Ryan told me."

"I was career military."

"So was Cameron."

"Like I told you, I had fourteen years in when I resigned. I qualified for another promotion, but I gave up my career. End of story."

"I thought you loved the army. Cameron did. He gave them eleven years of his life. Actually he gave them his life. He didn't quit. He died. A week later they promoted him to E-8."

Tharon feared she would crumble at the table. Tears balanced on her eyelids. He wanted to wipe them away.

"We sent my husband to war as a sergeant first class, Tharon. He was a good soldier—always ahead of the pack. A man so committed to the army that he willingly died for them." Her voice wavered. "We buried a master sergeant. His mother sewed on that stripe for his funeral. I couldn't see to thread the needle."

Tharon winced. How long had this been building inside her? Or had his presence dredged up the pain?

"The truth is, Meagan, I tired of the politics in Washington. That's why I handed in my resignation."

"Cameron never got a chance to resign."

"I'm sorry. Meg, it wasn't easy for you to start over again. But you're well-suited for your job. I was trained for mine. Planned on staying until I was too old to march. It didn't work out that way . . . But you're a natural for your job. You have a winsome smile, a gift of gab, a mental calculator that runs on fast speed. You love the land. It's easy for you to persuade others to move to the Valley."

She sipped her coffee and absently mentioned, "The mocha is cold. No matter. I came back here to get away from everything military. I dreamed of bringing up my son in peace and solitude."

He took a gamble in defense of her son. "Ryan has a dream of his own. If he follows it, he risks defying your wishes."

"I don't want another loved one in the military."

That eliminates me too. "What about retired soldiers? Never mind. Just tell me why you dislike the military so much."

She threw up her hands. "You're a fine one to talk. You resigned. You disliked their politics. I hated their lies."

He had stirred up an old bitterness. He wanted to lean over and take her in his arms. Hold her. Comfort her. When Kips was hurt or wounded, he simply held her. When she was dying, he had held her. When she was dead, he had held her and wept.

But Meagan pushed him away with her words. "The army lied to me. At first they told me Cam died by hostile fire. I fought them for months, begging them for the truth, when one of Cameron's friends told me he died by friendly fire. And the army had the nerve to give me Cameron's Bronze Star for his heroism under fire."

"He still died in combat, Meg."

"I've never been able to tell my son that his father died by friendly fire—that some American monster killed his father. Some monster who has gone free all these years."

"Awful things happen in war. Accidents. Mishaps. I don't defend them. I can't explain it."

"I'd like to know the officer who took my husband's life."

"And if you did, Meg, would you forgive him?"

There was a long pause. "I don't know. My son would. Cameron would. But I don't know that I could."

"I've known of families who thought their loved one died under enemy fire. Then when the government found the truth—maybe within twenty-four hours—they immediately informed the family."

"That's not how it happened for me, Tharon. They stonewalled me the whole time. Different excuses. Different stories. They had a mock investigation. What good did it do? When they covered up the truth, they grieved me all over again."

"I think there should be a memorial wall for wives and children," Tharon commented. "You're as much victims of the battle as the soldiers. I see that now. I ache for you, Meagan. I only wish that the sand of the desert would blow away for you—one particle at a time. We're both smothered by the ashes of the war. I'm like you, Meg. I have never come to terms with friendly fire."

"So you quit. It doesn't sound like you, Tharon. Inside you're still committed to the army."

He smiled. "My commanding officer convinced me to go out with an unqualified resignation—an IRR status. That means Individual Ready Reserve. I'm subject to a presidential recall in the event of another war."

"You'd go back in as a major?"

"Yes."

"I don't know whether you're helping or harming Ryan. All he talks about now is going to West Point. His grades won't warrant that." Her next words sounded almost pleading. "Why are you giving him impossible dreams?"

"Without impossible dreams we drop by the wayside. His grades are better. He just wants you to be proud of him, Meg, and yet he's convinced he has failed at every turn."

"I didn't know—"

"Ryan wants to blow his father's trumpet. Wear his father's medals. Walk in his father's shoes—just to please you, Meg. Don't take those dreams from him. If it comforts him to dream, what does it matter? Right now he's on the edge. He's staying in school because I've told him that if he doesn't, I'll drop out of his life and head back up to the mountaintop. He can't risk that just for a bottle of beer behind the school."

"He's still getting in with the wrong kids," she worried.

"They say men work with half a brain—left side genius. It's likely that teenagers get only a fraction of that. His thinking is warped, yet he's on target. He has an artistic flair. When he visits me up on the mountain, he whittles animals out of the chunks of wood I give him. I'm going to check it out at Liberty Bell and see if they offer wood shop. If not, we'll line him up with one of the craftsmen in town."

She stared him down. "Oh, Tharon, sometimes I think you're so arrogant, so certain the world revolves around you. *The major*

257

speaks. Everyone stops and listens."

"Rank has its privileges, Meg."

She rolled her eyes. "You should have had a son of your own."

"Ryan is as close as I will ever get. Kips was not well enough to bear a child. She was willing. But after two miscarriages the doctor warned us that her heart couldn't take a full-term pregnancy."

"I'm sorry."

"Ryan reasons that going military will draw him closer to the father he never knew. Meagan, he wants to have his father's medals."

"He can't wear them."

"But he could hang them up in his room. If you won't give him Cameron's medals, I will give him my own Bronze Star."

"So you were a hero too."

Anything but, he thought.

"And please give him his father's trumpet. It's the only memory he has of his father."

He saw her lips tighten. "Ryan was too young to remember Cameron."

"What he describes is vivid. His father in the chapel—probably Fort Riley—playing hymns."

"His grandmother must have put those thoughts in his mind."

"No, that memory belongs to Ryan. Don't you think it's time for the trumpet of Twisp to make music again?" He slid his hand across the sofa cushion and gently touched her fingers. "His up-and-coming birthday would be a good time to trust him with his father's instrument. Let him follow his dreams, Meg."

Her next words were cold, distant. "I think you'd better go, Tharon."

"You're afraid, aren't you?"

Tharon was right, and Meagan despised him for it. As the door slammed behind him, she pounded her fists on the sofa pillow. She couldn't reward Ryan's behavior with a gift. No matter what Tharon said, it was up to her to protect Ryan from his ill-chosen friends—and from following his father's career, playing his father's trumpet, believing in his father's God. Tharon was a newcomer in their lives. What right did he have to draw the battle lines? This was between her and her son.

So why did she long so much for Tharon's approval?

CHAPTER 22

SEPTEMBER 1, 2001

An hour after arriving in the Methow, Robinson Gilbert left a message on Tharon Marsh's cell phone. While he waited at an ice-cream parlor for the major to return his call, he pictured Marsh from their first visit: an army major in uniform, ginlet-eyed and guarded. He was tall, impressive, his smile and attitude somber. When Robinson later learned that Marsh had recently been widowed, he regretted their blunt confrontation.

An hour ticked away before Tharon Marsh called back.

Robinson plunged in. "I'm Robinson Gilbert, Major. We met in Washington."

"Yes, several years ago. You're a journalist." The voice was as steely as the man Robinson remembered.

"I want to interview you again, sir."

"The answer is the same. No interview."

"I'm still researching battlefield errors. Fracticide. Amicicide. Friendly fire. Whatever term you prefer, Major. I have enough information to make you glad you moved away from Washington."

"Sorry. No interview."

"Wait, Marsh. This is about Cameron Juddman's widow and families like her, victims of friendly fire. Mrs. Juddman makes her home here in this area. Go back to Washington with me, and let's see what can be done to help these families. I'd like to interview you and Mrs. Juddman together."

Marsh groaned on the other end of the wire. "Impossible. I gave the order to fire upon her husband's Bradley."

"Then we need to talk, Marsh, for Meagan's sake . . ."

They made strange bedfellows, meeting over dinner in a crowded restaurant.

Marsh prodded his steak. "You know the statistics. A number of the Gulf War casualties were likely hit by friendly fire. It happens in every war." He bathed the meat in steak sauce and popped a piece in his mouth. "In the fog of war, soldiers are tense and fearful. There's miscommunication and defective equipment. There's confusion from smoke and noise and dust. They mask the visual field. But no family is prepared to hear these excuses. So don't open old wounds for Meagan Juddman and her son."

"That isn't my plan. She's a friend of mine too. But recently other families filed lawsuits. They want to know what happened. And they want to know what's been done to prevent similar accidents in the future."

"Suits against the government? Good luck. It never works. And yes, there have been advances made on equipment and uniforms in an effort to deter friendly fire incidents. But we both know it's never enough. Never enough. For families it's small comfort knowing that friendly fire deaths exist in every war."

As they finished their dessert, Robinson studied the man across from him. The major was different out of uniform, casually dressed now like the locals. But he seemed even more guarded and somber than on their first meeting.

Robinson gambled that Marsh was directly involved with Meagan Juddman. Somehow. He nailed that possibility. "The government's damage control left families like Meagan Juddman's in limbo. There was an investigation into Juddman's death and then what Meagan called 'the government's cover-up.'"

Marsh quirked an eyebrow. "How so?"

"The usual—everything was declared classified."

"What good would it do for her to know the truth? The vehicle Juddman was riding in was out there in the desert like a sitting duck. No backup. No air cover. I know about damage control, Mr. Gilbert. The families never seem to recover. Juddman's young son has spent a lifetime missing the father he barely had a chance to know. His mother works sixty-hour weeks to support them."

Robinson signaled for coffee, bringing the waitress back on the double. She filled their water goblets and left again. "Didn't the government kick in, Major?"

"The insurance doesn't last a lifetime. I was in the army for the long haul. A lifer. During one of those Washington heat waves, I decided to build a new life for myself on the mountain property my great-grandfather left me. Money runs out quickly."

"So you threw in the towel before admitting to burnout?"

The major's smile lit his rugged countenance. "Burnout is not in our vocabulary."

"At least not something an army officer admits to. As a rule, you're Type A personalities. There's nothing you can't handle. Exposure risks the reputations of other career officers who served in the Gulf—whose battlefield errors have been swept from the public's view and locked away in secret files."

"Along with mine. I don't want Meagan to know the truth. When we first met, we did battle over the land, over politics and the military, and the rearing of children. I won't add to her pain now."

"There's another problem, Major. I traveled from Washington with three other men. They're not the usual tourists looking for the scenic route. I should warn you: one is a career officer involved in friendly fire deaths himself."

"Not Colonel Corbin?"

"His father actually. He's a retired general. Has no intention of his son being wiped out of the service or denied promotions."

"Let him earn them."

"The problem is that both Corbin and his father fear your coming back to Washington and working on any committees that

might expose his tarnished career. I'm afraid the younger Corbin—
well, a man in his forties—wants your disappearance to be permanent. The second gentleman is actually a congressman from your
district. He didn't identify himself in that capacity, but I know he
wants to send you back into battle again."

"I don't know of any congressman with a grudge against me."

"He maintains that wars are inevitable. He wants someone on
the front line who's acquainted personally with friendly fire incidents."

Marsh put his elbow on the table, his fist to his lips.

For a few seconds Robinson matched his silence. "Since the
Gulf War, there's been research. New ways of marking men and
equipment to keep them safe—to distinguish them from the
enemy."

"Soldiers will always die by friendly fire." Marsh's penetrating
gaze held Robinson's. "And the third stranger?" he queried.

"A German, a young architect from New York who wants your
support to get a Gulf War memorial off the ground. He considers
Mrs. Juddman's presence in Twisp a bonus to his project. Frankly, I
think his business is in Washington—not here in Twisp."

Robinson laid out his credit card to cover both meals. "Don't
blame yourself for Juddman's death, Major. Perhaps the generals'
war room in Riyadh left you in the dark. One brief message from
them and you would have held your fire. It's obvious you were not
informed about the Bradley sitting in the middle of the desert."

"It sounds like we both know the truth about his death. So how
can my relationship with his widow end in anything but pain?"

"Consider her pain, Major. Her husband was sent on a special
mission."

"A mission that killed him."

Meagan stared wide-eyed as four men from Washington con-
verged on the realty office, crowding into Bob's work space.

Looking surprised at the professional entourage, Bob swung his legs off the desk. "May I help you, gentlemen?"

One of them flashed a government badge. Meagan questioned its legality. Bob seemed to accept the strangers, but he scowled at the tall silver-haired man nosing around the office.

Robinson Gilbert winked at Meagan, gave a quick shake of his head. So she was not to recognize him. What had happened to an old friendship? She kept an eye on Robinson, her ear tuned to the conversation going on at Bob's desk.

The spokesman of the group handed Bob a photo. "We're looking for this man."

The toothpick in Bob's mouth stopped swishing as he studied the photo, then handed it back. "An official visit?"

"You'll understand when I say something like that is classified."

"I have places like that for sale. Perhaps I can interest you in one. Meagan, you're free, aren't you? You can show them a cabin set against the woods. Or a two-story family home. Or if these gentlemen are looking to just buy land we can show them a place east of Winthrop or in Beaver Creek. Rolling hills. Pines. Aspens. You might even take them up to Buck Mountain."

So they were looking for Tharon. Good of Bob to warn her in this way.

"Excuse me, Bob. Could I talk to you in private?"

"Mrs. Juddman, you see I have guests."

"But I need to go over several morning appointments with you," she argued. "I don't have time to go up to Buck Mountain this morning or escort these gentlemen around the Valley."

The government man's aggravation mounted. "We're not looking to buy."

Bob bought more time for her with his sales pitch. "We have charming places in the country. Or riverfront homes overlooking the Methow. Log cabins. Stucco homes. Sweeping views. Your pleasure." As he gave them a spitfire rundown of the Valley market, they grew more aggravated. "If you want solitude, we have an outstanding piece of property among the aspens."

"Sir, we're *not* looking to buy property. We are looking for this man." The lead man from Washington slapped the photo on the desk.

Meagan stretched her neck and saw Tharon's rugged face.

Bob rose to his feet in his casual unhurried way. "Excuse me, gentlemen. I have to get my colleague squared away on today's listings." He escorted Meagan back to the water cooler. "What's up with the man living in the shadow of the mountains?"

"Don't tell them that Tharon is in town," she whispered.

"They seem to know that already."

"I have to warn him."

Bob cocked his head. "He's that important to you?"

"He's important to my son."

"I know." Bob tugged at his whiskers. "Classified."

As she rushed from the realty office, Robinson Gilbert followed her. Out of earshot of the other men he said, "Thanks for not giving our friendship away."

"I thought for a moment you were denying it. Are you here as my friend, Robinson, or not?"

"I want to be more than that." His tone was wistful.

Meagan shielded her eyes as she sat on top of Buck Mountain, waiting for Tharon to show up. As far as she could see, the Methow spread out before her—a beguiling valley nestled against the jagged peaks. Today the mountains seemed like steep rolling hills loping down lazily toward the sun-scorched bales of hay.

She picked out Twisp and Winthrop and the Methow River wending its path through the Valley. To her south the Sawtooth Range looked razor sharp in the blinding sunlight. Pioneers and homesteaders had looked down on this same valley. Back then men with mule packs forged the trails in their lure for gold. Now SUVs broke the speed limits on Highway 20.

Up here everything was majestic. Breathtaking.

A God thing.

Something more majestic than the landscape. More breathtaking than the tree-lined mountains. The time had finally come to make her peace with Cameron's God. She just had to do it. As much as she'd tried to ignore Cameron's God, He'd been sneaking up on her, making His presence known through the beauty of the Methow Valley.

No wonder Tharon loved his mountaintop. Up here the birds sang. The wind whistled. The eagles and hawks took flight, their wings spread. Earth sang all around her, the woodpecker off-key. But she felt like they were playing "Taps" and putting finality to her past, burying it, and allowing God to change her completely. Her heart thumped as though she had run up the hill. She could hear her grandmother humming over a sink full of dirty dishes . . . and remembered snatches of phrases from those songs.

Was this thumping of her heart a clarion call?

She broke off a twig and scratched at the hard soil, her heart longing for peace. Cameron and her grandmother had found the way. Even her mother-in-law, as troublesome as she had made life for Meagan, was soundly on God's side.

What had Cameron said on that last night together? *"'Taps' is played for the living, Meg."* And when he packed his trumpet away, *"Someday, Meagan love, you will hear the clarion call. And, like a burst of sunshine, you will understand. You'll believe in the Man on the Cross as I do."*

"Oh, Cameron. You were right. I do believe as you did."

In the far distance a cross poked its message into the sky. It had to be that old abandoned church, discarded and crumbling like some of the old barns off the highway. Months ago Bob had listed that parcel of land for sale, but the environmentalists were at war about any commercial project replacing it. The old-timers wanted it kept as a historical landmark. She'd buy the property herself, but her funds didn't amount to much.

Not knowing how to pray, Meagan took a real-estate brochure from her briefcase and scribbled her thoughts on paper.

Lord, I sit here in awe and with all of my heart
Cleanse me and free me in my innermost part.
Set my soul free to worship, my heart free to sing
To You who created everything.
I've fought You forever, but deep in my soul
Please, please make me whole.

Meagan flinched. This would be a laugh a minute for her colleagues hanging around the water cooler. As the water jug gurgled, they often discussed clients or boasted a choice sale. Or told the inevitable jokes. Out of that maze of memories, she remembered one that wasn't a joke. It was the story of a little boy who was lost until he saw the church steeple. Then he told the police officer, "Take me to the cross." And from there he knew his way home!

Her colleagues had laughed over that story. But suddenly, to Meagan, God and the cross were no longer a laughing matter. She never could have explained to anyone just how God had grown in her heart, in her life, over the past months. But now she found that it was impossible to ignore Him any longer. It was time. Time to make her peace. Time to stop blaming Him for what the army had done to Cameron.

She gripped her pen and wrote,

The cross. Your cross.
Not three crosses on the hill, Lord.
Not the one in the valley, but Your rugged cross.

She was hearing His invitation. Hearing heaven's reveille, Cameron's clarion call. "Lord, Cameron told me about lost sheep. I am one of them, a wandering prodigal who wants to come home . . ."

Tharon slipped up soundlessly behind Meagan and dropped down on the wild grass beside her. He stretched out his long legs. The knees of his worn jeans were in dire need of a good woman with a needle and thread.

"I thought you were alone, Mrs. Juddman."

"I am. Except for the songbirds and butterflies."

"But I heard you talking out loud."

She flushed, her face heated more from her embarrassment than from the sun. "I was sort of . . ."

"Crying out from your heart? Praying, maybe?" He was silent for a minute. When he spoke next, his voice was gentle. "I've done some of that myself lately . . . It is magnificent up here, isn't it? My great-grandfather and I both came here to escape the world down below. Now I know why he stayed. No electricity. No heat. Just the mountain with a view like this."

Tharon turned. Their eyes met. "What made you think about God?"

"A little lost boy."

"Your boy?"

"No, a story they talked about around the water cooler at Cragg's Realty. It's the story of a police officer and a child who didn't know his way home."

When she told him the story, he nodded. "Sounds like me, Meg."

When he rested his hand on hers, she didn't pull free. The warm pressure of his hand on hers increased.

"The story came from the Internet," she continued. "But I'd like to know if it really happened. It makes me think of my own prodigal; I pray that Ry will see the Cross and find his way home. But I was judging my son's destiny when I hadn't settled my own." She found the courage to glance his way. "My grandmother was like the child. She liked the book of Daniel, especially where he said, 'Take me to the King.' She'd shuffle around the house, saying, 'Take me to King Jesus. He knows my way home.'"

"I used to feel like your grandmother did until Kips's death . . . Meagan, you told me you would never come back up to Buck Mountain, once the property was not for sale. Why did you come?"

"I came to protect you."

He flexed his muscles and chortled. "Since when do I need protection? I'll use my fists against any intruder. My rifles against wild animals. I'm safe. I'm okay. I like it up here."

"Then why do you come down to the Valley so often?"

"You're a good cook. And I like seeing Ryan coming around on his schoolwork—and watching you watching him."

"Please don't come tonight. Stay away for a few days."

"I told you I'd pay for half of the food," he teased.

"Someone is looking for you."

He didn't flinch. "The reporter from the *Washington Post?* I met him years ago, so he looked me up. He's staying at the Boesel Canyon House. I think it suits his personality—it puts him smack up against wildlife and nature. He says he's a friend of yours."

"He was. But what does he want?"

"He wants to interview both of us about friendly fire."

"No. I won't dredge up those memories again."

His strong grip never wavered. "That's what I told him, but you'll never really be happy until you know what happened to Cameron the day he died."

"And Robinson Gilbert has the answers?"

"Hear him out, Meg. Decide for yourself."

"We'll see . . . Tharon, do you see the church steeple down there? I wish I had the money to buy that property."

"I can lend you a FOR SALE sign."

"I want to *buy* that abandoned church, not sell it. If I could afford it, I'd clean it up to keep the environmentalists happy—and turn it into a wayside chapel."

"To keep the old-timers happy?"

"I'd plant flowers and have the building refurbished and get rid of any marmots living there. If I could do that, people might see the cross and find their way home."

"Is that what you've been doing? Finding your way home?" Tharon peeked over her shoulder. "May I?" He didn't wait for approval. He scanned her words. "I thought so. This place does inspire, doesn't it?"

"You love it here, yet Ryan told me this morning you're thinking about going back to Washington. Are you?"

"According to Robinson Gilbert, I have no choice. Others like you are demanding accountability, asking for more reviews on friendly fire deaths. Like you, they feel in limbo. Back in the Vietnam conflict, one mother said her son's death by friendly fire denied him the dignity of being killed. They want the government to do more to prevent such tragic incidents."

Her hand trembled beneath his. "Then you do understand my pain? One of the senators I met with told me Cameron's death was simply a *fait accompli*—nothing but a fact of life . . . This does have something to do with those men from Washington, doesn't it? That's why I came here to warn you. They were at Cragg Realty a couple of hours ago. One of them wanted to speak to you on what he called 'classified business.'"

"So my peace and solitude are about to be shattered?"

"With the younger man it was like one of those *déjà vu* moments. He's with an architect firm. I had the feeling I knew him, but I couldn't place him at first. Then when I realized who he was—all grown up—and mentioned staying in his home in Heidelberg when he was a child, he acted like a stranger."

"Maybe he didn't want you to recognize him."

"Tharon, if you go away with them, will you come back?"

His reply was swift. "Do you want me to?"

Her cheeks burned hot again. "You know how I feel about the Valley and the mountains. This is where I belong."

"You didn't answer my question."

She glanced at her watch and leaped to her feet. "I was due at the office ten minutes ago to meet with a client."

"Meagan, if I go away, will you wait—"

"Can it wait? With any luck I'll make a sale today."

"Try prayer. It might be more effective."

She grabbed her purse and ran. When she reached the car, he called after her, "You didn't put up the FOR SALE sign this time, Meagan."

She glanced back. Smiled. And that made her look different somehow. Not as frazzled. Not as defensive. Her face glowed. Even her eyes smiled. "The property is not mine to sell, Tharon."

He stood watching her truck make the hairpin turns on the rutted road. A trail of dust blocked her from view, leaving him with a tremendous void in his own life.

He picked up the FOR SALE sign, walked it to the back of the property, and dumped it on the wood pile. Without their controversy over the land, would he ever see her again?

CHAPTER 23

SEPTEMBER 11, 2001

In her journal Meagan Juddman marked this day as one that many around the world would remember, few forget. The infamous moment in history when structures of invincible steel became Ground Zero in New York City. When the military strength of America became a target in Washington DC! A day caught in human snapshots—faces of anger and grief, sorrow and silence, finality and fear.

Robinson Gilbert sat in the Winthrop Palace, chewing the fat with the locals when Karl VonHoekle joined them uninvited and ordered a rancher's breakfast.

"What's your next move, Gilbert?" he asked.

Robinson wanted to say, "None of your business." But grudgingly he admitted, "Washington—and with any luck another overseas assignment. I'm itching to report on the Middle East this time."

Robinson would miss this local flavor when he left in the morning and went back to the maddening schedule on the East Coast. He hoped VonHoekle would be moving on too. Robinson couldn't pinpoint it, but there was something about this man he didn't trust. He particularly disliked the man's interest in Meagan Juddman. It conflicted with his own.

He'd already made phone inquiries. The Schmidt and Ludwig Architect Firm was legitimate. A German firm—that fell in with

VonHoekle's background. But why would an established firm specializing in high-rise architecture send their newest designer to the Valley? There wasn't a high rise on the Methow landscape. Yet VonHoekle had come with this cock-and-bull story about the government hiring his firm to lay plans for another war memorial in Washington.

No, there was some other motive. Did he really expect the Methow residents to fund such a project? Once Robinson got back to Washington, he'd do some more checking.

He toyed with his cup of coffee. He'd decided against seeing Meagan again. She didn't need him reminding her that there were still questions regarding Cameron Juddman's death in Iraq. But the more he dug into the past, the more convinced he became that Cameron Juddman had been sent on a solitary mission with no guarantee of a return. The fact that Karl VonHoekle was in town added to the puzzle.

"How long are you staying in the Methow, VonHoekle?"

The German gave Robinson a shifty gaze. "Now that Marsh and the other gentleman have gone back to Washington, I'll be heading out myself. Maybe in a day or two. I'd like to see these plans for the Gulf Memorial pan out."

Would you now? Robinson thought.

VonHoekle's moving on could not be soon enough to suit Robinson. "Meagan Juddman tells me you knew them when they were stationed in Heidelberg."

"They lived in our home when I was a boy. My mother and Mrs. Juddman were good friends once—until my father disappeared."

Robinson didn't bite. "I met the Juddmans in Europe myself. But why this interest in a memorial for American soldiers?"

"As a boy I was drawn to the designs of the ancient buildings in Heidelberg. I studied at the university there and did further studies here in America. When I graduated, the Schmidt and Ludwig Architect Firm hired me to work in their New York office at the World Trade Center."

"But you haven't been with them long?"

"No, but since I suggested the Gulf War memorial, they assigned me to the project." There was a swagger in VonHoekle's body language that irritated Robinson further.

"Have you done other memorials?"

VonHoekle's smile was mocking. "This is the first."

"Surely Meagan told you that her husband died in that war. Is that your interest?"

"It's more personal than that," VonHoekle fired back.

The food turned sour in Robinson's mouth. *What had VonHoekle said? Our families were friends—until. Oh, Meagan, are you safe with this man in town?*

If I smoked, Robinson thought, *I'd be lighting a cigarette this minute, buying time to work it out in my mind.* The puzzle pieces fell together. *VonHoekle. Europe. Cameron. Yes, Cameron Juddman at— the Italian Riviera.*

No wonder the name VonHoekle had stirred Robinson's unease. The scene from the olive grove in the Riviera came crashing back. He remembered Cameron confronting a man named Wolfgang. Wolfgang VonHoekle, a man tied to an ex-Nazi.

Robinson's thoughts spun. *Karl VonHoekle had a father with a questionable past. What about the son?*

Aloud he stated, "Your parents—they're still in Heidelberg?"

"I told you, Gilbert, my father disappeared."

Robinson risked it. "To Argentina?" He didn't wait for Von-Hoekle's answer but challenged, "You know, VonHoekle, you spoke of a longtime friendship with the Juddmans, so what happened to that friendship when your father disappeared?"

VonHoekle's eyes narrowed. "Gone just like that."

"You're angry. I can see it. So why would you want to design a memorial that would honor Cameron Juddman and men just like him?"

"I wondered how long it would take you to ask me that." His eyes blazed. With a twisted, sarcastic smile VonHoekle lifted his second cup of coffee and saluted Robinson.

And then as the television announced the terrorist attack in New York City, the coffee spewed from VonHoekle's mouth.

They stared at the monitor as the North Tower of the World Trade Center burned in front of them.

Robinson pounded the table, rattling his unfinished plate of eggs and bacon. "What kind of an idiot pilot flies off course like that?"

When the second plane flew low, he thought they had another imbecile at the controls. When it nosed into the South Tower, he was on his feet, heading for a phone. "I've got to call SeaTac for a flight back to Washington."

VonHoekle grabbed his arm. "Gilbert, I think you're out of luck. The newscaster just announced that your president has cancelled all commercial flights."

"Then I'll rent a car and drive straight through."

VonHoekle's cockiness had drained from his face. "I need to get back too. The men I worked with—the office I worked in—just went up in that inferno. We can drive back together."

Robinson didn't like the company, but Karl VonHoekle would be someone to spell him at the wheel. He'd take VonHoekle as far as he could—and then be grateful to head south to Washington alone.

In Kansas Conaniah Juddman held the picture of Becky in his hand. "It's happening again, Becky. The world gone mad. Another Anzio beachhead at Ground Zero."

Halfway across the country Robbie Gilbert and Adrienne Winters, his fiancée, were having a quick cup of hot chocolate when the news broke.

Robbie pushed his cup away. "The Pentagon's my beat this week. I can't miss this one."

"Be careful, Robb." A troubled flush crept into her silky complexion.

"Adrienne, go home."

Her luminescent eyes looked worried. "But the traffic will be snarled."

"Go while you still have a chance." He reached across the table and squeezed her fingers. "I'll rest better if you can reach the Winterfest Estates before any more planes fly in over Washington."

In South America, Wolfgang VonHoekle sat in his chair sipping wine as he stared at the TV monitor. He had lived in exile in Argentina ever since he walked out on his family and became a fugitive from the life he longed for, from the country of his birth. He missed his wife. Missed his only son, grown now. He longed for one of those rare visits from Karl, but knew for his son's safety, he must not come back.

Wolfgang had no love for Americans, but he would never wish this destruction on America. He picked up the remote control and turned off his television. But he could not erase the images. His mouth was dry as he dialed Bernhard Grokov.

Grokov answered on the fourth ring.

"Is this your doing, Bernhard?" Wolfgang asked.

The tragedy in New York City found its way to Heidelberg, Germany. Anna VonHoekle stood in her third-floor flat and stared gloomily out the window. She had stood at this same window the day her husband left her. Folding her arms across her bosom, she tried to shed the goose bumps.

The media focused on London, where hundreds of Britains were lined up at the American Embassy to send condolences to America. Even if Heidelberg did the same, Anna would not sign the card.

She held deep resentments against her former renters, so why did she long to reach out to comfort Meagan Juddman? Their warm friendship had ended the day the Juddmans left Heidelberg. Once they were gone, the brazen accusations against Wolfgang followed. For weeks Anna fought the legal attempts of the American military to obtain Wolfgang's private papers.

She wondered now what had become of Cameron Juddman's widow and their son, who would be almost seventeen by now. Anna despaired when she thought of them. America was suffering, and her touch with America had been the Juddmans. Thinking of it now, she was certain that they had betrayed her friendship—perhaps had been influenced to do so by the American military. Anna had not been able to let the resentment go— that nagging belief that the Juddmans had revealed details of Wolfgang's life to the American military . . . details that had led him to forsake his family and disappear.

Anna and Karl had gone on without Wolfgang—without the Juddmans' friendship. But she worried about Karl. Karl was not the kind who would want to put up a memorial for Cameron Juddman. Karl had suffered much, as a teen, because of the Juddmans' betrayal. He had not only lost his father, he had lost the respect of his classmates. So what was he up to now?

As the burning South Tower crumbled, she screamed. "Karl. Karl!" The trembling began in the pit of her stomach. Within seconds the tingling of her nerves consumed her entire body. The New York office of Schmidt and Ludwig Architect Firm had just been lost in the inferno.

Breaking rules had almost lost their appeal. Ryan Juddman jammed his hands in his jean pockets and ambled along the Methow River, kicking stones. He was kicking himself too for skipping school again. When his mom found out, she would want to tear him apart, but he was too tall for her now.

They'd barely talked at all since he'd hitchhiked to Spokane to join up. He crinkled his nose into one of his mom's facial expressions. "Don't you *ever* do that again, young man. I don't want you in the army."

"*You* married a soldier," he had fired back.

"And I lost him."

So what did she want him to do? He'd never aced his grades at school, so college was probably out. And most of the jobs in Twisp or Winthrop went to those with a high school degree. School was not yet a month old, and he was already in over his head. Unless he made up three projects, he'd be doing the school year all over again.

This figuring life out was tough. By the time he got back to school he'd miss the old yellow bus. Maybe he should hike over to the real-estate office and confess that he'd blown it again. His mom would keep her cool in front of her boss.

What good was school anyway? His mom couldn't answer that one without crying and telling him he could do better. He'd rather join the army—be a hero like his dad. And then, maybe, just maybe, he'd make high marks on his mom's approval scale.

He kicked another boulder and groaned when the rock collided with his big toe. *That's what I get for coming out here without my trumpet. Here I am good at something, and Mom doesn't even know it.*

The sky was blue enough, almost as blue as his mood. He saw no rain in the clouds, yet felt the nip of fall in the wind. When he faced his mom she'd accuse him of drugs again. He didn't do drugs. At least not lately. Not since the army recruiter told him that the army checked for things like that. He sauntered along with the weight of the world on his shoulders. This peeing in a bottle shouldn't determine his life's destiny.

He considered his options. Face this misdemeanor head-on. Go talk to his principal and promise to square away. If he could talk the principal into nothing but art and music classes, he'd be an honor student. Or he could beg for help so he could catch up in his classes. He was good with his hands. Good with handling horses.

278

That's what Mrs. Bowers told him.

Maybe he'd go over to old lady Bowers's place. She might hire him again to stack wood for her. Or maybe he could borrow a horse from her field and ride up to Tharon's place. Tharon might be back by now and help him figure a way out of this jam.

Thinking made him move faster. He'd reached the lodging on the river before he knew it. Rustic cabins, picnic tables, and a hammock stretched between trees. He'd like to stretch out in it right now and think away this business of growing up.

The inn was good for a glass of water when he was thirsty. And man, he was thirsty. He ran up on the back steps and entered. The screen door banged behind him.

"Hi."

The owner put her finger to her lips. The television on the wall was a blur of bloody people and black smoke.

"What's up?"

Her finger warned him again. She pointed to a chair meant for her guests. He slouched down, but not before grabbing a handful of chips from the bowl on the coffee table.

She came over and sat down beside him and patted his knee. "It's awful, Ryan. The World Trade Center in New York City is gone and one wing of the Pentagon badly damaged."

A fistful of chips caught in his throat as he realized what was happening. He should get on home to his mom. She would need him. He was the man in the house. But he couldn't budge, not with the way his legs were quaking. This was his country being torn apart and, for the first time in his life, outside of a class assignment, he was glued to the news.

Meagan, I've been trying to reach you for twenty minutes. Quick, turn on your television."

"I can't, Tharon. The electricity is off in part of the Valley. They're here in my neighborhood checking the service right now."

"Trying to find a free phone here in Washington was impossible too. I almost lost my mind trying to find your cell phone number."

"I gave it to you."

"Yes, just before I left Twisp. I shoved it in my jacket pocket. I housecleaned my desk finding it."

"It's good to hear from you."

He grabbed his suit jacket and slipped it on with one hand. "But it's not good news."

"Don't tell me the investigation—the senate committee—is turning against you?"

"No, but the world of terrorism is turning against our country. Right now the senators and congressmen are out on the steps of the Capitol. And the president is somewhere over the Midwest, flying in Air Force One, waiting to get back to Washington."

"Flying over the Midwest? Whatever for?"

"For their safety. Terrorists hijacked some commercial jets and flew them into the World Trade Center in New York City. Both Towers are gone. Hundreds, maybe thousands dead. Meg, are you listening to me?"

"I'm here."

"There's more. The E-ring of the Pentagon is gone too. And rumors of another plane heading for Washington. I'm safe, but there's a lot of smoke and debris and confusion. We've been ordered to evacuate. I just wanted you to know I was all right."

He could hear her teeth chattering over the phone. Knew what she was thinking. *Ryan. Where is Ryan?*

"Meagan, are you all right?" he asked, anxious.

"I have to go find Ryan."

"Meg, he can take care of himself."

"Not if he skipped school again. Who knows where he would be? Last week he hitchhiked into Spokane and tried to join the army."

Tharon stepped from the office and locked his door as he talked. "That crazy rascal. But he knows what he wants, Meg."

"Don't you understand? He lied about his age. The recruiter called me. Ryan was furious when he got home. Told me he'd keep trying."

"I don't think the army wants a kid who hasn't finished high school," Tharon told her. And then, hating to break off the call but knowing he had to, he added, "Meg, I have to go."

"I'm having trouble hearing you. My phone is fading, but I wish you were here. I hate being alone when something like this happens."

He raced for the exit and felt the crush of others trying to escape. "See if you can reach Robinson Gilbert—or go over to your neighbors. This is the kind of day when people need to be with one another."

"Robinson will want to fly back to Washington."

"Won't do him any good. They're grounding all commercial flights. He'll have to rent a car and drive like a maniac."

"Tharon, I can't hear you now."

"I just stepped outside. Oh, Meg, there's nothing but black smoke and fire."

"I'm frightened, Tharon. I keep praying but I'm afraid. I keep telling God Ryan is His—and then I find myself holding out, claiming my own son back. I can't bear the thought of another war—not with Ryan so determined to be a soldier. Oh, Tharon, how can we find peace in a world that's crumbling around us?"

"God is still there, Meg. You know Him now. You met Him up in Buck Mountain. He'll take care of you . . . He'll take care of Ryan . . . I have to go."

"Will you be all right? Oh, come home. Get out of there."

"I'm staying, Meg."

"Will the president call all reservists back to duty?"

Tharon covered his mouth with a handkerchief to smother his cough from all the smoke. "If there's a military buildup I'll be back in uniform." He didn't tell her what he was thinking: *I may be there sooner if they take me.* "I'll come back to Twisp someday."

"So you can finish the house on the mountain?"

"No. This day has changed all that. I know where I need to be

. . . you can put that land back up for sale."

"How can I? It's not mine to sell."

"Ask Bob Cragg to draw up the papers. Send them to me. I'll sign."

"Then you're never coming back."

He heard utter dismay in her words. "Meagan, I have two reasons to come back to the Methow."

"Two?"

"You and Ryan. I love—"

Her cell phone went dead. He stared at his own and thrust it in his pocket as he merged with the crowd. It was best this way. He wanted to ask her to marry him, but who could think of marriage with acrid destruction filling his nostrils and plumes of black smoke rising from the Pentagon?

CHAPTER 24

SEPTEMBER 13, 2001

Robinson Gilbert's mind and body were spent when he reached Washington. His intuition had been right. VonHoekle wasn't the image he presented. Not a man to be trusted.

Robinson dragged his luggage into his apartment and dropped it on the living room floor. His cleaning lady had piled up his morning papers in the corner. He would toss them, but then he'd be tossing out history.

Okay, then, a shower and bed.

But he was fooling himself. Duty demanded that he head to the newspaper office and check in. He'd seen the Pentagon and the gaping hole.

This morning's paper lay open on his coffee table. He grabbed a soda and sat down to scan the names and faces of those who had gone down with the Towers. Some were employees of foreign businesses. Where would they place the blame for this disaster? He ran his finger down the long list again. Schmidt and Ludwig Architect Firm jumped out at him. The names of the known dead were listed. He scanned it again, his eyes settling on one name: KARL VON-HOEKLE, 30, HEIDELBERG, GERMANY.

Dead? No. When the turnoff came for VonHoekle to catch public transportation to New York, he had elected to go on through to Washington with Robinson.

A leech for a companion, Robinson thought. His own credit card had paid for the rental, the gas. He'd even picked up most of the café bills along the way. VonHoekle had a way of heading for the

283

men's room when money was needed.

Unthinkable possibilities played across his mind. What had VonHoekle said in a grubby little café somewhere between Madison, Wisconsin, and Chicago? "Gilbert, the Towers would be a great opportunity for someone to slip into oblivion."

"They did. Several hundred. Perhaps thousands."

"Not that way. Maybe you didn't get to work on time—or didn't intend to be there for your own safety. You could just walk away—take on a new identity."

"The dead can't cash in on their own insurance policy."

"But they could start over again with a new life."

"Only a fool would do that."

"Think about it, Gilbert. What if someone needed to start over? Take me, for instance. The men I worked with are the only ones aware that I was away from the New York office. Our headquarters for Schmidt and Ludwig is in Germany. When they turn over the list of New York employees, my name will be on it."

Robinson had wanted to shut VonHoekle up. "Why don't you take your hand at driving? I'll sleep."

When Robinson woke up, VonHoekle was whistling. The country was falling apart, and VonHoekle was whistling.

"I've decided to go on to Washington with you. There's no point in going back to New York. There's nothing left there for me," VonHoekle claimed.

He's leaving his possessions behind, Robinson thought. "I can't take on a houseguest."

"I'll find my own way. My mother may be informed by now that I am dead. I need to get back to her. Need to report in to my home office in Germany."

VonHoekle left Robinson with that uncanny feeling that he had just left a haunted house with its deceptive mirrors and false exits. Now he couldn't think of enough nasty words to describe the man. He came up with *cunning, clever, scheming, devious*.

He crushed the paper in his fury and tossed it aside. His mind was still on VonHoekle when he finally called his newspaper office.

"I can be there in a couple of hours," he offered.

The voice on the other end argued with him. Robinson sighed and compromised. "Okay. Okay. I'll make it in sixty minutes." He cut his sixty short by dialing Tharon Marsh.

"You're back?"

"Yes." Robinson got right to business. "I want you to turn Karl VonHoekle in to the FBI."

"And what will I use for an excuse? The man has sympathy with our losses in the Gulf War. He wants to build a memorial."

"I doubt that was ever his intention. He would rather destroy us. He's a risk to America right now."

Marsh sighed. "Right now everybody fits that description."

"The obituary list from the Towers includes his name."

"We can have that corrected."

"Not likely. I'm convinced that he's going to board the first international flight he can get and pick up a new identity and lifestyle. Think about it, Marsh," Robinson urged. "He was in Twisp—not the place where you would promote a new memorial. The man had other purposes in the Methow. If you were going to protect someone there, who would it be?"

The major's reply was guarded. "You know my answer to that— Meagan and her son."

"My choice as well. As far as we know, she's the only one in the Methow who lost someone by friendly fire. And she couldn't fund a memorial. No Schmidt and Ludwig would have sent their representative to Washington to propose something like that."

"You don't think he works with them?"

"Of course he worked with them." Robinson thumped the paper. "He's listed as one of the dead. But I don't think VonHoekle's company planned to establish any Gulf War memorial. He told me en route to Washington that it could be decades in coming. I don't think he planned any memorial to honor the casualties of Desert Storm. You need to put the FBI on VonHoekle's trail."

"He's not a known terrorist." Marsh's agitation mounted. "It wasn't the Schmidt and Ludwig Architect Firm that flew into the

Towers or the Pentagon. The hunt now is for al-Qaeda."

At this reminder Robinson's anger cooled. He switched gears. "Have you been in touch with Meagan?"

"I called her." Marsh sounded tight-lipped, irritated. "I asked her to close up my property for me."

"You're not going back, Major Marsh?"

"I'm going back into uniform. I'm not waiting for the next war. America isn't going to sit back and take this kind of destruction. War is inevitable, Gilbert."

"If so, I'll be reporting from the world's next hot spot . . . I wouldn't be surprised if we both end up in Baghdad."

"That would be okay with me," Marsh claimed. "I feel like I tarnished my career there the first time around. I'd like to serve my country there again—this time for glory and my redemption."

"So you won't be debating the issue of death by friendly fire with any senate committee?"

"Not now. My place is back on the frontlines."

"There are some career officers out there who will be glad you're not going to debate the issue. They can save their reputations— keep their battlefield errors under wraps. Only the families will go on suffering."

There was a pause on Marsh's side of the phone. Then his voice picked up again. "No man wants to have his ribbons and promotions taken away."

"Not even Colonel Corbin?"

"Each man has to settle the question of true and honest valor for himself."

"So my research on erroneous battlefield deaths is tabled. Maybe Meagan is right—this friendly fire business is nothing but a cover-up."

"You don't have the whole picture, Gilbert. Or your research was headed in the wrong direction. We don't need more government contracts going out to the highest bidder just to come up with ideas to prevent friendly fire casualties. We need to invest more in training our military, in discovering new technology, and in education. We have to implement changes that will affect the battlefield. Ever since the first Gulf War, every branch of the military has sought for answers and solutions."

Robinson leaned his weary body back against the sofa. "Back when Juddman died, his widow asked me to help her learn the truth. The truth is, we did get blackballed in Washington."

Marsh sounded weary, sorrowful. "I didn't help you any by turning down an interview."

"We can't take away their hurt, but it would help these families if they knew every effort was being made to cut down such casualties." Robinson glanced at his wall clock. "I'm expected at the newspaper office, and I've cut my sixty minutes down to thirty. It's going to be the fastest shower and shave in town. But, Marsh, you need to get VonHoekle's name to the FBI."

"You said he may be leaving the country. Let him go. Right now we're interested in al-Qaeda terrorists still living *here*."

"VonHoekle's father is involved in an old SS organization."

"And you think they are linked with al-Qaeda?"

"They'd have the same goals. I'm telling you, Karl VonHoekle is a risk. The man is shrewd, self-serving."

"And you're short-tempered. Take a shower, Gilbert. Forget VonHoekle. If we get to Baghdad, look me up."

"I'll do that."

Karl VonHoekle was looking to the desert as well. With the architectural firm lying in ashes on Ground Zero, he needed new marching orders. No one knew he was still alive—except for that journalist. He despaired grieving his mother in this way, but he was committed to a greater cause.

Once the commercial jets were cleared for flying again, he'd board the first available international flight to Argentina.

September 26, 2001

Karl VonHoekle paused in the Plaza de Mayo. His fascination with the Argentine way of life and the city of Buenos Aires had grown until his returning now was like coming home.

When he slipped into the meeting room, the old signs of the Third Reich were gone. The photo and flags that once dominated the front of the room had been removed. Bernhard Grokov's massive portrait hung in its place, superimposed against a map of the world. His motto hung beneath it: OURS THE WORLD.

Most of those who had served with Grokov in the *Waffen* SS were gone, including Karl's grandfather, Erich VonHoekle. The old guard were dead. Executed. A few babbled in old folks' homes, still expecting to rule the world. Grokov did not expect success; he manipulated it to his own purposes.

He was a man in his late eighties who still ran every day and existed on juices and vegetables. He planned to go on forever and gave no thought to dying. Karl considered this a good thing. If there was another life on the other side of dying—as Karl's mother insisted—then Grokov was due for a burning. He was fiendish, ruthless, politely barbaric, a token of evil as Anna VonHoekle described him. But he wore a good facade and was well respected as a businessman in his adopted country.

Karl glanced around. His father was there, but most of the men were younger—the sons and grandsons of the old SS, men easily whipped into a frenzy. He ignored his father. He thought him a weakling, not even with the strength of a follower.

But before the meeting began his father made his way to where Karl sat. In soft tones he urged, "Do not get involved, Karl. Go home. Stay safe. Grokov's plans will be disastrous."

Karl's eyes narrowed. "Then why have you served him for so many years?"

Grokov was eyeing them, so his father changed the subject. "How is your mother, Karl?"

"You remember her?" Karl fired back.

Wolfgang produced his wallet and opened it to Anna's picture. "I have carried her close to my heart all these years."

Karl despised his father even more. "Anna threw out your favorite chair and everything that reminded her of you. To protect me, she turned over your files to the American military. How does it feel, *Father?*" He used the word with contempt. "How does it feel to be a wanted man in your own country? Your beloved Heidelberg wants nothing to do with you."

His father ignored the sarcasm and asked again, "Is your mother well, Karl?"

"Old before her time. She leaves the house to shop, to go to church—nothing else."

His father was old too and pathetic in his begging. "Does she ever think of me?"

Loathing welled within Karl. "She still stands in the front window, looking out, waiting for your return."

"Go home to her, Karl."

"No. Grokov promises me great opportunity."

A stranger sat in their midst, his features and mannerisms that of a Middle Easterner, but he wore a tailored suit. The flesh around his jaw and chin did not bear the olive coloring of the man's broad hands. Perhaps, Karl decided, he had recently shaved off a beard.

The man was watching him too. "So you are dead, Mr. Von-Hoekle. That is most helpful to our plans."

The man remained nameless, but during the meeting Karl soon recognized that Grokov was using him. He was associated in some way with al-Qaeda. They would link their efforts, share their intelligence, but never unite. Grokov was not a caveman—not one to live in secret. To have no companion but a rifle. He preferred luxurious living to hiding. Outside of the organization, he was every bit the gentleman, the accepted exporter of wheat from Buenos Aires, of olive oil from the Italian Riveria. He would not exchange his lifestyle for desert living. One day he would rule from Argentina or Brazil or Bolivia. But not from the desert. He had learned from the mistakes of the Third Reich. Power and world domination came slowly, but it would come.

As the stranger stood to leave, Grokov told him, "It is best for you to wage the wars. I'll fund the equipment needed." He turned to Karl. "We have great plans for you."

"*Ja.*"

"An identity change, then a terrorist training camp."

Fear rose in Karl. "I'm a designer, not a terrorist."

"Understandable. You would never have worn the black shirt of our SS officers. But you are still useful to our cause. In our new world order you may be a designer, but for now infiltrate. Learn. Come back to us. You will advance quickly."

His father gripped his wrist. "Have no part of this, Karl."

"He's only testing me."

"No, he is devising a way to be rid of us both."

Karl pulled free. "I have made my choice."

His father pushed himself to his feet. He stared at the retreating form of the stranger. When the door closed behind him, Wolfgang shouted, "I will have no part of this, Bernhard! No more. I have had enough! We have fought the Americans once—"

"Sixty years ago."

"The Americans will fight back. They will not tolerate another 9/11. I want nothing to do with suicide bombers. I want to go home."

"Go then," Grokov told him.

"Come with me, Karl."

"Father, I have made my choice."

With one last look of longing, Karl's father turned his back and shuffled wearily toward the door.

The guard pulled his revolver.

"Not here, Hanz," Grokov ordered. "Let him go." As Wolfgang disappeared from view, he added, "We will not bloody the soil of Argentina with a traitor."

Hanz scowled. "We are to let him leave the country?"

"We will let him go as far as the steps of his home in Heidelberg. But first we must test the son's loyalty."

Karl shot to his feet. Stood at attention. "You have had it since the day I entered the University of Heidelberg."

"We will delay your father's flight until you can board the same plane. He will fly economy. You will board first-class at the last minute. You'll be met and rushed to Heidelberg. When your father reaches the steps of his home, shoot him."

Karl fought for control but could not stop the tick that ran through his jaw, nor the slight flush that crept to his face. "Before he can see my mother?"

"Before he can confess what he knows about our organization. Before he can even suggest that we are linked in any way—however briefly—with al-Qaeda."

Karl tried again. "For my mother's sake, they should at least have a chance to say good-bye."

"He took no time for a good-bye when he left her. There is no need now . . . Your father was never one of us. He had no loyalties to the Third Reich. No stomach when we reorganized. Even your mother has a deep-seated anger with the old SS."

"She was fathered by one of them."

"Perhaps by me. She puts her shame on us, the perfect Aryan race." Grokov spoke with disdain, mockery, yet his cold, steely eyes showed no emotion. "She deserves no mercy, Karl. Your father is not to get beyond the steps of his own home . . . Am I clear?"

"Ja, perfectly."

"A driver will meet you at the Frankfurt airport with a service repair truck with tinted windows. It will create little curiosity when it parks in front of your mother's home." Grokov's eyes gleamed. "Afterward—before the municipal police even come—you are to leave Heidelberg and fly to Munich. You will be met there and told your next move."

"My mother should know the truth."

"She despised her birth into the perfect, pure Aryan race, and that's why she will not be given the satisfaction of knowing the truth. Her husband was here to betray us—to live here with us all these years as a sleeper, for the Americans perhaps. Fool! We suspected him from the beginning. But, Karl, you can prove yourself more honorable, more loyal than your father."

"He was working for the Americans?"

"Possibly. For someone other than us. And what of you, Karl— are you one of us or not? Or is the son like the father?"

Karl, his mind reeling at his father's double betrayal, snapped to attention. "I will serve the cause and do it well—with my life, if I must."

"It may cost you that."

The truck parked catty-corner from his mother's home. Twenty minutes dragged by. Karl fingered the rifle, practiced each move in his mind. He was committed to the cause. Turn back now and they would see him as a coward like his father. He would not bear that shame.

The taxi drew up thirty-six minutes after the truck had parked against the curb. His father stepped out, looked at the home he had deserted, then up at the woman standing in the window. He hesitated for a second.

And just as his mother watched her husband coming home, Karl aimed the rifle and fired. As his father fell, the truck squealed from the curb. Karl was thrown against the backseat. There was no turning back.

CHAPTER 25

SEPTEMBER 23, 2002

A week before Ryan's eighteenth birthday, he defied the house rules and rode to the top of the mountain again. Tharon's unfinished house lay deserted, the shuttered windows barred. A No Trespassing sign was nailed to the door; another sign dangled from the corner post.

I trusted you, Tharon. You promised to come back, but you deserted me too.

Ryan spit on the No Trespassing sign and rode his frightened steed down the narrow rubble of the road, back along the highway into Winthrop and Twisp. The horse perspired, its nostrils flaring.

Ryan stormed into his mother's real-estate office and glared at her. "Tharon is gone for good, isn't he? He said he'd be gone just a week or two. It's been a year already."

"I know. I miss him too."

"All those phone calls. He's just putting us off. He's run out on us like my dad did."

"Your dad didn't run out on us. He was doing what he believed in when he died."

"Then why don't you ever talk about it? Why do Grampa Juddman and Grams shut up like clams when I ask exactly how he died? If he was such a hero, why can't you just tell me what happened?"

"I wanted to protect you."

"From what, Mom? I just want to know about him. You tell me I remind you of him. That's not enough. I'll never know him—

barely remember him—but I just want to know about him." He
slammed his fist on her desk. "Is that too much to ask? I ain't stupid. There's always been something odd about the way he died.
Tharon and I argue about it sometimes. He told me some men die
by friendly fire—"

She gasped. He reached across the desk to steady her. "How did
my dad's tank get blown out of the sand dunes?"

She gripped the edge of the desk. "I wasn't there."

"I'm not buying that."

She licked her upper lip. "At first the army told us he died by
hostile fire."

"But it wasn't true, was it? Americans accidentally killed him.
That's what Mrs. Bowers told me. Said that's what the rumor was
when we came back here to the Valley to live . . . told me she'd
have a hard time forgiving the man who gave that order."

"Your dad, of all people, would forgive the fellow soldiers who
took him down."

Chewing his lower lip, Ryan blurted out, "All that stuff about
honor and valor. You and Tharon both lied to me."

She got up from her desk, her fists clenched. "Don't ever say
that again, Ryan. Your father died a hero. Yes, it was called 'friendly
fire,' but whether it was hostile or friendly, your father died in an
act of heroism."

"Then the Americans did blow him to kingdom come?"

"If . . . if they did, it was an accident."

"That's Tharon's line. The military can do no wrong."

Her anger matched his. "Then why do you want to join the
army?"

Her question hit him in the pit of his stomach. His shoulders
sagged. "Because Grandma Fran tells me he was a hero. And I want
to be like my dad . . . You've always told me he was special."

"Yes, very much so. Your father loved the army. We buried your
father as a hero. You were there—you may not remember it, but
they spoke of his heroism then. They played 'Taps.' They gave him
a twenty-one-gun salute. Fellow soldiers carried him to the grave."

Ryan fisted the tabletop again. "He's still dead."

"He was prepared to die because of his faith. A faith I didn't understand at the time, Ry, but now I do. Dying accidentally happens in wartime."

He watched helplessly as tears rolled down her cheeks.

"I loved your father, Ryan."

"I know. But I never got to know him. I kind of thought if I could be a soldier like him that he'd know how much I loved him too." He paced to the water cooler, then came back. "Don't cry, Mom. I'm sorry. I'm mad at Tharon. At you. At everybody. I got that lousy high school diploma that you and Tharon kept yapping about. And now I don't know what to do with myself. I want to join the army and I'm not even old enough."

He couldn't explain the strange expression on her face. The bewilderment. The relenting. "You will be in a week," she whispered.

Ryan stared back and realized her face looked gray. She gripped her hands, making them knuckle-white, as though she didn't know what else to do with them. "I want to join the army, and you fight me every step of the way. I'm not too good at schoolwork, Mom. But I'd be a good soldier."

The fire in his mom's eyes softened. "I'm so sorry, Ry. I've been wrong. I wanted to protect you. I didn't want to lose you."

"It's funny, Mom. All I've ever wanted to be was a soldier."

She nodded. "You sound like your father."

He grinned sheepishly. "So I look like him and sound like him? Oh, Mom, it's been tough for both of us—him getting killed and all—but he was doing what he wanted to do."

"And died for it."

"Isn't being what you want to be worth dying for?"

"I've never thought of it that way." She took a breath and plunged ahead. "Your dad would be proud to know that you want to be a soldier. Be proud of him too. He loved this country of ours." She crossed the few steps to him and cupped his chin in her hand. "Look at me, Son. Yes, it was a horrible way to die. But your dad was in the Gulf War because he loved this country of ours." Her voice cracked. "He is our hero, Ryan. Someone who loved us both."

"And Tharon? Is he a hero too? He ran out on us—"

"Tharon will be back someday, Ryan." Her anguished face scared him.

"Don't think so, Mom. He's just given us a line of garbage. His place is all closed up. The windows and doors nailed shut. There's a big stone fence around it."

"To keep the intruders out."

"Honest, Mom, I didn't do anything to the place."

"Animal intruders, darling. Uncle Bob had that fence built to protect Tharon's place until he comes back."

"He won't come back. His things are gone, Mom. All his tools. His rifles."

"Uncle Bob packed those away for him."

"Then Tharon has no reason to come back. So where's he hiding out in Washington?"

D*are I tell him the truth?*

Meagan avoided the truth until late that afternoon. She had sought escape in returning to Twisp, but the political war games in Washington and the ripples from the burning rubble of 9/11 had swept them into another year, ensnaring both of them deeper into the war on terrorism. *Patriotism. Terrorism. Al-Qaeda. Afghanistan. Taliban. Iraqi freedom.* These were the words her son knew best.

Ryan watched her, waiting for her to be honest.

She kicked a chair closer to him. He kept standing—his symbol of power over her vulnerability. "Tharon left Washington, Ryan. He's back in the army, back in uniform."

"So why didn't you tell me?"

"I was afraid that it would influence you. At first Tharon was assigned to Afghanistan, where reconstruction is under way. Now they've asked him to go to Kuwait. Honey, he could be sailing up the Persian Gulf right now, or flying in from an air base in Turkey or Saudi Arabia to the command post. I don't know. As soon as he writes again, I'll tell you."

"He didn't even call me to say good-bye."

"But he did send his love."

This time Ryan pounded his fist into the palm of his hand. "Will that God of yours protect him? Or will he get himself killed like my dad did?"

She steered him outside. They leaned against the porch railing. In the distance the river raced through the valley. "You're like the river, Ryan. Angry. Struggling against the rocks and debris, just trying to find your way. But what happens to the river?"

"Anybody with half a mind knows that." Ryan's voice was rich and deep, like Cameron's had been. "The Twisp and the Methow will merge and keep flowing as one."

"We're like the river, Ryan. One day everything will come together for us. Everything will merge. Tharon told me he had a wrong to right in the Middle East. I don't know what he meant, but I have to trust him. As soon as Tharon ties up the loose ends of his life, he'll come back. I promise you, Ryan, he has every reason to come back to us after his year abroad."

"Name one. Just one." He was still defiant.

"You're one reason. You're the son he always wanted. And . . . I think I'm the other reason. He may not know it yet, but he loves us. He'll come back, and we'll be here waiting for him."

"Mom . . . I won't be here. And when I'm eighteen next week, I won't need your signature."

"My *approval*, you mean?"

"I'm going to join the army. I'm not going to let Tharon win this war all by himself."

Meagan took a deep breath. She had brought her son to the Methow Valley, certain that they would find happiness here. But Ryan needed the plains of Kansas. No, he needed more than that. He needed the camaraderie of his own platoon of soldiers.

"Did you hear me, Mom?" He raised his voice. "I'm going to join the army."

"I heard you."

What had happened to her cute little boy? The one who used to hold her hand when they crossed the main street in Winthrop. The one who sat on her lap when she read to him. The one who giggled when she tucked him in bed.

In his last phone call Tharon had reminded her, "Ryan is no longer a child. He'll be eighteen his next birthday."

Meg had caught her breath. Cameron was eighteen when he enlisted. She loathed war. Loathed the terrible pain she felt inside. Feared, more than anything else, enduring that kind of pain again if something happened to Ryan, to Tharon.

"Mom, I hope someday you'll be proud of me. I kind of messed up in school, but I think I'll make a good soldier."

She stared in disbelief, accepting now what she had wanted to deny. He had grown up. He was a man now, but the little-boy defiance—the wounded Ryan—still struggled inside him. He was still her boy who wanted to please her. "You're your father all over again."

"Is that a good thing?" It was clear from his face that he wanted to know . . . had to know.

"Yes. He was a wonderful man—a good soldier . . . Would you like me to drive you to Spokane on your birthday?"

"I'd like you to bake me a chocolate cake, but I want to take the bus to Spokane. I want to do it myself."

"That's the way your father did it. But I'd drive you."

His boyish grin widened. "No, I have it worked out in my head. I've been there. This time they won't turn me down. I'll be eighteen. The bus plaza is just a couple of blocks from West Riverside."

"I assume that's significant."

"Yeah. That's where the Recruiting Liaison Office is. They already told me that chances are good I'd go to Fort Benning for my basic training. I'll put in for mechanized infantry—like Dad did."

"I thought so."

"Promise me you won't cry when I leave, Mom."

He was his father all over again. Handsome. Independent. Wanting nothing else but to be a soldier. "I promise."

Three weeks later, as he left the house for basic training, Meagan broke her promise. He walked away, straight, tall, broad shouldered—the very image of Cameron going away. But at the end of the walkway Ryan, unlike Cameron, turned back and waved at her.

Meagan closed the door and wept.

MAY, 2003

The man who found her son on the battlefield eight months later had borne the heat of the grueling 350-mile march from Kuwait into Baghdad. For him, Operation Iraqi Freedom had taken twenty-one days across the desert sands. Soldiers had died. They would continue to die. But Robbie Gilbert had survived.

Now Robbie was coming home.

On the first of May 2003, Robbie was sleeping in economy class on board a commercial jet when the president of the United States stood on the deck of the USS *Abraham Lincoln* and declared that the major combat operations in Iraq had ended; the reconstruction of the war torn country would begin.

Both men were returning to Washington—the president to the White House on Pennsylvania Avenue, and Robbie to the sprawling luxury of Winterfest Estates and the waiting arms of Adrienne Winters.

CHAPTER 26

Just before midnight, a week later, Robbie Gilbert and Colonel Tharon Marsh were cleared for entry into Andrews Air Force Base. Their special clearance allowed them to be on the field when the C-17 came in for a landing.

They stood beside a silver-haired chaplain, all three of them scanning the night sky. Ambulances were lined up behind them. The glitter of Washington lay in the distance.

A gust of wind from the air traffic blew against them, sending dust particles into Robbie's eyes. He rubbed against the irritant. "Do you think he'll be on board, Colonel?"

"Either tonight or tomorrow night," Tharon replied. "That's as close a call as the Pentagon would give me."

"A friend?" the chaplain asked.

"More than a friend. Ryan Juddman is like a son to me."

"One of the medics?" the chaplain asked again.

"One of the wounded."

The chaplain winced. "How badly, Colonel?"

"Quite serious. Back, legs, head."

"An amputee?"

"We don't know yet. But they almost lost him at Landstuhl."

"They'll take the seriously wounded direct to Walter Reed or in to Bethesda Medical Center," the chaplain advised.

"Ryan is slated for Walter Reed."

"By the way, my name is Wainwright—I'm at Walter Reed, so if I can be of any service . . ."

"That's good of you, Chaplain Wainwright. But the others may need you more. The two of us will be there for Ryan—supporting him, praying with him."

Colonel Marsh nodded toward Robbie. "This is Robbie Gilbert, Chaplain. He was one of the embedded journalists in Iraq. He's a pretty good preacher boy himself."

"Then he's not here for a story?"

Robbie spoke up. "The story is on hold, Chaplain. I just want to make sure Ryan Juddman's okay. You see, I'm the one who found him. We thought he was dead, but when I turned him over to check his dog tags, he moaned. The worst part was seeing his name—I know his family."

Colonel Marsh shrugged against the midnight chill. "Ryan's father was killed in the first Gulf War . . . by friendly fire. So this is a double whammy for the family."

"A lot of those boys in the first Gulf War were killed by friendly fire." Chaplain Wainwright shook his head. "A number of them in this war too. Seems to me that those who kill their own should be made accountable."

Robbie leaped in. "Mistakes happen, Chaplain. Most of the men I rode with across the Iraqi desert never saw combat before. They were scared. And in those sandstorms it's hard to distinguish the enemy from your fellow soldier."

The drone of the first C-17 could be heard now.

The chaplain pursed his lips. "Some of the wounded coming in this evening will be 'mistakes,' as you call it. Hostile fire? Friendly fire?" He groaned. "War is costly. And now too many are being injured with small-arms fire and rocket-propelled grenades."

"Robbie, the chaplain's right. Accountability would push Washington to fund the program more. To find razor-sharp engineers and the best scientific minds to come up with more methods to protect equipment and men on the battlefield."

The chaplain removed his cap to stroke the back of his thinning hair. "I haven't counted, but I daresay these evacuation flights have brought in hundreds and hundreds, perhaps more."

"Thousands before this is over." The colonel's voice was resigned.

"Colonel, I've been here night after night—just in case I was needed. It's always the same. No fanfare. No public notice." There was a look of pain on Wainwright's face.

"They come that often, sir?" Robbie asked.

"Once they're stabilized at Landstuhl in Germany, they board the giant C-17s for evacuation home. No public welcome home for these soldiers. No cheers. No loved ones permitted here. The planes come in the darkness of night—as they're doing now—as though it can hide the tremendous sacrifice that these men and women have paid."

Robbie grew restless as the deafening sound drew closer. It looked like a giant monster looming in the sky, a massive mechanical bird coming in on wings of mercy. A nagging knot built in his stomach. "Chaplain, you said the most seriously wounded will go to Walter Reed and Bethesda. Will there be others?"

"Tomorrow morning the C-130 transports will take the walking wounded and those emotionally burned out closer to their home bases. Fort Hood. Fort Bragg. Fort Irwin. Fort Lewis. Fort Ord. Wherever. What about you, Colonel? Were you over there?"

"Yes, but I had my baptism by fire in the first Gulf War. Before that it was two years on the DMZ line in Korea."

"He did Bosnia and Kosovo too," Robbie added.

The chaplain sighed again. "Then you know what it's like, Colonel."

"So does my friend here. We both just got back with lots of desert sand in our boots."

The first of the C-17s rambled down the runway toward the waiting ambulances. The roar of the plane's engines ceased. The war had just touched down on American soil, hemming them in with an eerie silence.

It looked as though the entire belly of the plane had opened as the cargo ramp and door swung back. Air Force personnel moved forward on the run to direct the unloading. Some of the wounded were motionless. One, with his head and eyes bandaged, clung to the nurse's hand. IV bottles swayed in the evening breeze. A soundless army passing in front of them.

The three waiting men stood at attention. Robbie's own casual stance turned rigid as litter after litter was carried off the plane with nurses and medics accompanying them. He squinted, trying to recognize Ryan.

Colonel Marsh broke the silence. "Juddman. Ryan Juddman?"

A wounded amputee lifted his stub of an arm and pointed back. "He's coming."

Robbie split the somber night with a shout. "There he is!"

Colonel Marsh, with Robbie on his heels, ran to the litter. Robbie watched as the colonel grabbed Ryan's hand—thank God there was a hand.

Robbie heard the colonel whisper, "Ryan, it's Tharon."

Vacant eyes turned toward Colonel Marsh. Slowly they tried to focus in the darkness. "Tharon?" A flicker of recognition followed. "Mom's friend."

"Yes. You're home, son."

"Mom?" Ryan's voice was weak.

"I'll be flying to Twisp tomorrow evening to bring her back to Washington."

"Does she know how badly wounded I am?"

"She doesn't even know you're back yet."

"Tharon, they tell me I might not walk again. I'm not certain how Mom will handle that."

"You'll walk again," the colonel promised. "We'll be with you all the way."

Robbie agreed. "And when you reach the rehab phase, my fiancée wants you to stay at the Winterfest Estates. We'll transport you from there for any outpatient treatment."

Confusion crossed Ryan's face. "I don't know who you are."

"A family friend of long standing. I knew your dad."

"My dad?" Again a veil crossed over Ryan's dark eyes. "I don't know what happened. One minute I was running with my M-16, firing it. After that I don't remember a thing. I don't even know who found me."

Robbie gazed down at him. "That was my privilege, Ryan."

"At Landstuhl, when I came out of my coma, I didn't even know who I was. They keep telling me I'm Cameron Ryan Juddman."

The litter bearers picked up their pace. "Colonel, we have to get this young man to the ambulance."

Colonel Marsh tucked Ryan's hand under the blanket. "You're going to Walter Reed Army Medical Center. We'll see you there. Maybe later this morning once they get you settled."

Ryan glanced around. "Did the others make it okay? There was a kid in the litter beside me . . . Chuck something—"

The nurse smiled at him. "All forty-four accounted for, Private. You're home, back on American soil. All of you."

Tears sprang in Ryan's eyes. "I'm home. If only I could remember what happened."

The nurse checked his IV. "Give yourself time, soldier."

PART 4

Coming Full Circle

At midnight I will hold this hope,
This trust I'll take . . .
It matters not, the worried hours,
Morning will break!

—Agnes Wonson, "Morning Will Break"

CHAPTER 27

SPRING 2003

At midnight in Twisp, Meagan reread Cameron's letter, the letter she'd found in the trumpet case that had shouted Cameron's love to her across the twelve silent years. Her tears stained the pages as she read and reread. But a calm came with each reading. She awakened before dawn and read it again.

> My darling Meagan,
>
> I leave for Saudi Arabia in just a few hours. I love you and Ryan more than anything in this world. I had to tell you that once again—but tonight was not the right time. I sit in this old farmhouse—the place where I grew up as a boy. It has always been a happy place for me, but I realize now that you long to be elsewhere.
>
> When I come home, if you still want to move to Twisp, I promise you I will think seriously about leaving the army. I'm not sure what I could do there, but we both love horses. Maybe we could start a horse ranch. I know we can make a go of it. Please wait for me to come home again.
>
> As I write this you are upstairs showering. Perhaps donning that black lace negligee I gave you this evening. I would like to remember you that way. In a few hours my unit will board the plane for Saudi Arabia. I hate to say good-bye, my darling.
>
> Someday you will wonder what became of the letter from the lawyer. You will wonder whether I took it with me. Or whether Mother confiscated it. Neither happened. I just now came back

from the fireplace, where the embers caught hold of it and turned the threat of a divorce into ashes.

You will always be my wife, no matter what happens. My first love. My companion. The mother of my son. From the day I handed you a glass of punch at your school prom, it's been a wild ride. I would never have made it without you by my side. I didn't need to play the field—from the moment I saw you I knew you were the one for me. Don't leave me. Whatever dizzying serpentine roads lie ahead, we can work it out.

And if not, I pray for a willingness to let you go. I will always remember that ride to the Italian Riviera. Hairpin turns. Unbelievable rocky cliffs dropping down to the Mediterranean. You riding beside me in that borrowed convertible. Your tawny hair windblown. Your face flushed with excitement. You cautioned me to slow down. How could I? I was invincible on those winding curves. I wanted those seven days just with you. Do you remember sitting on the patio of the villa, watching the moon come up and tracing the moonlit path across the shimmering waters?

I just peered out the living room windows. It's still snowing. The sky is black tonight, a stormy darkness hanging over Kansas. The haze is too thick to see the moon or stars. But there were other moonlight walks for us—times when we marveled on the face in the moon being quartered or halved or round with two eyes. But the brilliant orange moon that shone over the Riviera was different. Tranquil. Hidden by clouds. Peeking out again. We were just a couple of silly kids, holding hands, dreaming, counting the stars. I don't think we ever mentioned the army those seven days. And you never found the courage to mention the VonHoekles. Nor did I find it in my heart to tell you that I saw Wolfgang the day before we left—I refused to let him spoil our joy.

I don't know what the moon will be like in Saudi Arabia—or Kuwait or Iraq. Perhaps it will be dimmed by the sandstorms or blacked out by the smoke from bombs and artillery . . . but the same moon will shine down on you and Ryan.

So long ago in Twisp I promised you the moon and the world.

You told me recently that all you had left was a fallen star. I never told you my wish that day. As the star fell I wished that we would spend our lives together. I prayed that we would always be happy.

But it was not the Italian Riviera that came between us. We had left the army behind at Heidelberg and gone together just the two of us—to celebrate each other and to lay plans and dreams for the baby you carried in your womb.

When we lost our other child—when you miscarried there at Fort Hood—I grieved for that little girl who would never be part of our family. I wanted her to live and be like you. To be a beautiful little girl.

Dear, dear Meagan, you have always been the joy of my life. But someday you will find this letter. If you do, you will know what it means . . . I have an odd feeling about this tour. I am not afraid of dying or hearing heaven's reveille. Of giving my life on the battlefield. But I wanted to grow old with you.

When I joined the army, I knew the risks. I knew wars were inevitable. They happen. I didn't like the prospect. But I accepted it. It's been a good life for me. Rich experiences. Travel. Security. The respect of my men. The power I feel at the wheel of the Bradley. But in the military there's always a good chance that we will be asked to go into harm's way. We face that now. I anticipated at least another year at Fort Riley before my next assignment. But the unexpected happens. We suck it up and move on. Nothing is set in stone in this man's army. Everything has an exception.

But if anything happens to me, Meagan, if I fall on the field of battle, know that I was doing what I loved doing. I never wanted to be anything but a soldier. To serve my country. I think it blinded me to your needs. Right now, with all the memories rushing at me, I think the last time we were ecstatically happy was that week we spent on the Italian Riviera. If I survive, will you go back there with me after this bloody war?

And if we cannot go together, will you go back there for both of us? Rent a villa for a week. Listen to the same classical music.

Sit on the beach. Watch the moon cut across the rippling Mediterranean like we did, night after night. And count the stars like we did when we were there. Let Ryan count them with you and tell him how much I cared about him.

If something happens to me, go on with your life. Be happy. If someone else comes along who can love you as much I do, marry him. Take care of my son. Someday, when he is old enough, give him my trumpet. I love you.

> Your lover,
> Cameron

My *lover*. Dear Cameron. She had come full circle. So much of what she had loved and cherished was gone. Her grandmother. Cameron. Perhaps her son. She had stood in this very town when her father took her from Twisp, from the security of her childhood, to places in Kansas and into a world that had been cruel to her dreams.

Only her grandmother's God remained. Cameron's God. Her God ever since that time on Buck Mountain. A God rooted, steady, unmovable—even in the midst of great uncertainty, great pain.

As she looked up into the face of an early dawn, her tears flowed. After those painful silent years, she was free. But in that precious moment of freedom the doorbell rang again.

She went reluctantly to answer it. Two side panels on either side of the front door revealed only shadows. She peeked through the louvers, her eyes downcast.

Spit-shiny black boots!

Not again, Lord. Not again.

The toe of one shiny boot moved. A chaplain? An army officer? She collapsed against the doorjamb. Life in the Valley had been all she ever wanted, but even here the pain of the past had betrayed her again. The same fear. An extension of the same war. The same spit-shined boots on the messenger at the door.

"Open the door, Meagan. Open the door. I know you are there." A familiar voice.

Her hand shook as she turned the knob and threw the door open. Tharon Marsh stood there, spotless and rigid in his spanking new colonel's uniform, his cap in the crook of his arm. The early morning sun caught the ginger freckles on his unsmiling sunburnt face.

"Tharon." The word squeaked out. She glanced from Tharon's handsome, rugged face to the man beside him. A younger man with his jacket tossed casually over his shoulder. Smoky blue eyes. A steady gaze. There was something familiar about him . . .

"Tharon, I thought you were from the chaplain's office."

"They would have dispatched a chaplain from Fort Lewis, but I volunteered to come myself." He nodded to the young man beside him. "This is Robbie Gilbert. Perhaps you remember him?"

The name swam around in her subconscious, but she couldn't make sense of it.

"I asked Robbie to come with me . . . he's the one who found Ryan."

She swayed. Tharon grabbed her. Held her as though he would never let her go.

"Not Ryan too," she whispered.

"We need to sit down, Meagan."

"Oh no," she cried. "He's dead! Not my son. Dead like his father. It's come full circle."

Robbie spoke up. "Ryan was wounded, Mrs. Juddman. He's not dead."

She turned to Robbie Gilbert. "How badly wounded?"

"His legs. And back. But there was a head injury too."

"His head?"

Tharon tightened his grip on Meagan. "He has no memory of being injured."

"That's good, isn't it?"

"There's some memory loss. Temporary perhaps."

"Why wasn't I notified?"

Tharon's probing gaze sought acceptance. "He listed me as next of kin."

She felt lost, confused. "But I'm his *mother*."

"He wanted to spare you the pain of a chaplain at the door."

"So you came yourself."

"They had trouble locating me. And when they told me what happened, I insisted that I be the one to tell you. I talked with Bob at the real-estate office yesterday. I told him we were coming and why."

"Then the call was for me?"

"No. Just to warn Bob what was happening and to enlist his aid."

Her panic grew. "I want to see my son."

"I'm going to take you to him," Tharon promised. "But he may not remember you."

"My son—not remember me?"

Robbie spoke up. "Shock can do that. The noise of war. The pain of injury. We can't give up hope . . ."

There was something about his kind manner, his deep steady voice. A flash of yesterday as she recalled a teenager giving her son a piggyback ride just before Cameron's memorial. A teenager making Ryan giggle. The fog in her head cleared. Robbie Gilbert. She studied his face again. "We know each other, don't we?"

"You know my father better. Robinson Gilbert, the journalist. I followed in his footsteps."

"But you were just a boy when we met. A teenager when I last saw you."

"Boys grow up, Mrs. Juddman. I was at your husband's funeral too. That's the last time I saw you . . . I found your son the day my unit reached Baghdad. We thought he was dead. But when I turned him over to check his dog tags, he stirred. He kept asking for his father."

"He barely knew his father. Ryan was only six when Cameron was killed."

"Meg, listen to me. Cameron has always been alive in Ryan's heart and mind."

"Mrs. Juddman, once we found him, he had the best of care. He was treated at Landstuhl Medical Center in Germany about eight hours from where he was injured."

"That's where he is now? Then take me to him."

"Not so fast, Meg. They're hoping that something familiar—that some*one* familiar—"

"Take me to him," she insisted again.

"Meagan, is there anything else—anyone else—that might bring him back?"

She pointed to the trumpet. "You know he always wanted his father's trumpet."

"We'll take it. Anything else? Anyone?"

"Cameron's grandfather—Ryan's great-grandfather. Conaniah adored Ryan. But we haven't seen him for a long time."

"Where is he?"

"In Kansas. He's not well. Not apt to travel."

"We'll find out."

CHAPTER 28

Walter Reed Army Medical Center was a sprawling campus. Meagan missed the details and saw only trees and green grass and medical and military personnel moving briskly along the walkways. As they drew closer, she wondered which window hid her son from her.

Tharon reached out and squeezed her hand. "I called ahead. We need to speak to one of the doctors before you see Ryan."

"Why?"

"So we don't rush him."

"If anyone is going to stir a memory, I'd be the one, wouldn't I? He's my son." Her words grew heated. "I carried him in my womb. Carried him on my back when he was little. Carried him in my heart every time he got in trouble." She fought the burning behind her eyelids. "I carried him in my heart the whole time he was in Iraq. I've wept for him more than once. Tharon, if my tears were diamonds, I'd be rich."

"The doctor wants to speak to you about this next-of-kin business. Ryan listed me as next of kin. They're not sure what your relationship was with your son—and they don't want to upset him in any way."

"You mean they don't trust me?"

"Before this is all over they will want an accounting. If . . . if we could just say we are engaged, it might not bother them."

"You're asking me to consider marriage at a time like this?" Meagan asked, shocked.

"You always have an excuse."

"Not now, Tharon. Not now."

Inside the massive complex they took an elevator and were ushered into a small office where two men waited for them. The man behind the desk rose, his hospital whites a dead giveaway. As she and Tharon sat down, Meagan eyed the other uniformed man with caution.

"I'm Dr. Michaels—and this is Major Jennings."

"Another doctor?"

"No, Mrs. Juddman. I'm here to investigate—"

Tharon interrupted. "Mrs. Juddman wants to see her son. She's not interested in any military investigation. She's been that route once before."

The doctor shrugged. "We spoke on the phone before you came. You're aware of the severity of your son's injuries."

"Only one thing concerns me—will he get better?"

"The prognosis is guarded. A lot depends on your son. The shrapnel wounds in his back were close to the spine."

Her words were clipped. "Then remove them."

"At this point in time, that's too risky. We have to wait for the swelling to go down. The wounds in his legs are healing nicely. The head injury is still of grave concern."

Tharon leaned closer. "He looks fine, Meg. He's having difficulty remembering things. From what they've told me, a bullet grazed his temple. But no bullets lodged in his skull."

"Colonel Marsh, we know there was trauma to the head," the doctor explained. "Either from the way he fell or something that fell on him. One of the soldiers with him kept talking about a part of the chandelier falling. If so, it would have merely grazed him."

"Amnesia?" Meagan asked.

Dr. Michaels shook his head. "It's not a case of your son forgetting what he once knew. Like his family. His home. His lifestyle. Whatever happened, happened at the point of injury."

Meagan tried to remain calm, but her heart was racing. "What do you expect of me, Doctor?"

"No tears. No emotional display when you see him."

"Mothers cry over their children, Doctor."

Dr. Michaels smiled. "I'm a parent too. But what happened in Baghdad when your son and two other soldiers came under attack is vague. Private Juddman seems to have no memory of that incident whatsoever. And yet . . ."

She waited.

The doctor was cautious. "We have to keep in mind the blow to the head . . ."

"You seem to have another option. What are you not telling me, Doctor?"

Major Jennings broke his silence. "We're not certain why your son and the others were in the palace. Whether they were there on their own—seeking shelter from the skirmish."

She was outraged. "My son is not a coward."

"That's why this incident is under investigation." Jennings stared Tharon down this time. "We're trying to determine whether he was hit by our own people."

"Friendly fire? That's what killed my husband." *The nightmare is happening again—and this time, to my son!*

"We're aware of that, Mrs. Juddman. I believe your husband was infantry too."

She nodded. "Mechanized infantry."

Tharon massaged his temple. "Her husband was killed in a Bradley fighting vehicle." He kept his eyes on the doctor. "Juddman and his men were military decoys, sitting out there in the desert with the moon suddenly beaming on them. Making them a clear target."

Meagan gasped. "Tharon, how could you know that?"

The doctor interrupted. "Iraqis, Colonel?"

"Friendly fire, Doctor."

Dr. Michaels looked puzzled. "You seem quite certain, Colonel. Were you there?"

Tharon lowered his head into his hand. "Dr. Michaels, I gave the order that blew that Bradley out of commission and those men—"

Meagan stared at him. Willing him to look up. As he kept his face hidden, her shock grew. Anger. Betrayal. Tharon Marsh had known all along how Cameron died. "Why didn't you tell me the truth, Tharon? Why did you let me find out this way?"

He sat up at last and faced her. He looked cadaverous, his skin deathly pale. She remembered their first bullish encounter. His grim, spare smile. His metallic voice. His mood as black as a slimy, stagnant mill pond as he ordered her off his property while she attempted to hammer the FOR SALE sign back into the ground. This was not the same man in drab, washed-out jeans defending his land.

This time he was defending his honor.

"Why, Tharon?"

"At first I didn't think it was important. We were fighting over ownership of the land. Confessing my pain over your husband's death would not have settled the property line."

"You gave the order that killed Cameron." Her tone sounded hollow, flat in her ear.

Tharon's eyes misted. She had never seen a man more grieved.

"Are you all right, sir?" Dr. Michaels asked. "And you, Mrs. Juddman?"

Her head snapped in Michaels's direction. "I'll be all right. I just didn't know—"

"I couldn't tell you." Tharon's eyes begged for understanding. "Not after I fell in love with you. All I could do was befriend your son. Be a half-baked father to him. I tried in some crazy way to make it up to Cameron for robbing him of life."

She ignored the army officers again. "Is this why you moved to the Methow Valley, Tharon?"

"Not at first. Maybe subconsciously. I searched for the truth about who you were, where you were. I even wrote to the editor at the *Washington Post* trying to locate you." He sighed. "Ironic, isn't it? I still owned property in the mountain. I didn't remember my great-grandfather's shack being so dilapidated, but I knew I loved the view. No one could reach me there. I'd build a house. Try to forget everything—my wife's death. The friendly fire incident that awakened me night after night . . . And maybe find the courage to face you."

"And then you met my son. So is that what you meant when you said you owed Ryan something—owed Cameron something?"

"Yes." He seemed to strangle on the word, on the memory. "I longed to find a way to ask you to forgive me. But we were at war the minute we met."

She was crying. "I wanted to sell that property."

"It wasn't for sale, Meg."

She touched his hand. "I never realized how painful Cameron's death could be for the one who gave the order to fire. I always thought of that man as a monster. As someone who got off the hook after killing one of his own men. I hated that man so much I couldn't even put a human face to him. And now I find out that man is you."

"Can you ever forgive me?"

Meagan avoided his eyes. "I don't know." She turned back to the doctor. He was writing in the chart in front of him. "I want to see my son, Doctor."

Dr. Michaels looked smug. "What happened here may be the very link that we need to help your son."

"What do you mean? He was young when his father died."

The doctor flipped through the chart. "He's been an interesting case."

Meagan frowned. "He's not a case, Doctor. He's my son."

He nodded, apologetic. "When the colonel mentioned the Bradley, something triggered in my own mind. Perhaps it will trigger in the patient's—in your son's—memory as well."

Major Jennings thumbed through some notes of his own and looked up. "Your son made it through the desert march to Baghdad unscathed. He did well in the first ambush. Proved himself a real soldier. They considered a battlefield promotion to corporal. The men in his unit respected him."

She sat immobile, her hands folded on her lap.

"Shall I continue, Mrs. Juddman?"

"Yes. I want to know what happened."

"He reached Baghdad and was on one of the street-to-street sweeps when he and two other soldiers ended up in the ruins of Saddam's palace. As they took cover behind some of the ruins, they heard the rumble of a vehicle charging in through the crumbled wall. It came in with its crew firing because snipers were rumored to be there."

"How would you know all of this, sir?" Meagan asked.

"One of the soldiers injured along with Private Juddman returned to the States on board an evacuation flight."

"May I talk to him?"

Major Jennings shook his head. "He was flown on to a medical facility closer to home. He was hurt physically, but not badly."

"His emotions?" Tharon asked.

"Yes. He fell apart. But he did tell us that they were hemmed down by enemy fire when the Bradley broke through and came in firing. He thought they were all going to be crushed. He said your son tried to stop them. Used his own body as a shield."

She worried lest they hear her teeth chattering, the way they did when she was in crisis. "They were obviously fired upon from both directions. By hostile fire or friendly fire, Major Jennings?"

"Both." The major drummed on the desktop. "That's why the incident is being investigated. Mrs. Juddman, would you care for some coffee?"

"No, thank you. Please go on with what you were saying."

"Your son's wounds were more severe than the others. When we found him, he was deployed to a tactical surgical unit where he lapsed into unconsciousness. They suspected a head injury and transported him to Landstuhl, Germany, immediately. When Private Juddman came out of his coma at Landstuhl, he kept asking for his father."

"But he barely knew his father."

"And that's my fault." Tharon turned his ashen face to her. "I told you before that Cameron lives in the heart of his son more than you know. He asked poignant questions—had his father suffered?

What made him a hero? If his father died in the Bradley and why? He asked about the tank." He shuddered. "All of this took place over a matter of days. And then he came up with the bombshells when he told me, 'My Grandma Fran thinks my dad was on a special mission. That he didn't need to die. That maybe our own men killed him.'"

Meagan closed her eyes, fighting back the tears. "Did he know you were involved, Tharon?"

"He may have guessed who gave the order to fire. I couldn't bring myself to tell him."

Her body tensed. "But you wanted him to know the truth. You wanted to shed your own pain. Wasn't it enough that he lost his father? You allowed yourself to become so important to my son that he wouldn't dare ask for the truth."

Tharon straightened his back. Slumped forward again. "Ryan told me once that accidents happen. That he'd run into a lot of them himself. That you and Mrs. Bowers were always forgiving him for his foolish stunts . . . And one day, when we walked out of church together, he talked about the pastor's sermon. Asked me whether that meant he had to forgive his enemies. And then he asked me whether his father was still a hero if he didn't die by hostile fire."

Meagan couldn't take her eyes off Tharon's troubled face. For a moment she pitied him.

"We had just reached the car," Tharon explained, "when Ryan told me he wanted to forgive the man who killed his father. And then he just took off."

"You put so much on his young shoulders."

"And you didn't trust him with enough. All he ever wanted was to know more about his father—so he could be proud of him. Maybe be more like him."

She curled her long necklace chain around her fingers. "Tharon, maybe after this is over, it would be best if we don't see each other again . . . Now, Doctor, take me to my son."

The men stood.

"We'd like Colonel Marsh to go with you," Dr. Michaels suggested. "He knows the way to your son's room. He met him at Andrews. For a very few moments your son recognized Colonel Marsh as a friend. Since then he vacillates back and forth. At times he doesn't remember arriving at Andrews. Then hours later it's clear for him again."

"Has he lost his mind, Doctor?"

"No. Just some facets of his memory. Something traumatic happened. If we go slowly—give him time—I think he will have a good recovery."

"And his physical wounds, Doctor?" Tharon asked.

The doctor met Tharon's gaze. "It will be a slow recovery. A long rehab. If he walks—"

"He will walk again, Doctor." There was a resolve in Tharon's voice.

The doctor took Meagan's hand as they reached the door. "Where are you staying, Mrs. Juddman?"

"Tharon has his own apartment. I'm staying at the Fisher House."

"Then you're in close proximity."

"It's lovely. Every amenity I could think of. A room to myself. There are other families staying there. They've come to support their wounded too."

"When you see him, let Private Juddman set the pace. Don't smother him," the doctor warned. "Don't force his memory. Let him reach out."

Meagan felt an amazing calm walking down the hospital corridor. Other parents were pushing their loved ones in wheelchairs. One soldier made his way down the long corridor on crutches—on one leg.

Her heart twisted with sympathy. "Hello there."

He paused. "Hi. You coming to see your boy?"

"Yes."

"Was hoping it was someone coming to see me."

She touched his arm. "Your family hasn't come yet?"

"Not coming. They hate hospitals and invalids."

Her stomach curled. "Tell me your name and room number. When I come tomorrow, I'll bring some flowers. Or a book, if you'd like."

"I'm Buck Lawson. I'd settle for French fries or candy."

"I'll see what I can do, Buck."

"You might have to sneak it past a metal detector. Or some nurse."

"Thanks for warning me."

As they neared Ryan's room, Tharon reassured her. "You'll do okay." He held out his hand. "Here, let me carry the trumpet for you."

Ryan was in a semiprivate room, asleep on his back. The other bed lay empty. But for how long?

Meagan could barely stomach her pain as she looked at her son. The tips of her fingers were like chips of ice as she touched his pale cheek. His emaciated body was wedged into a partial cast: one leg swathed in bandages, the exposed foot bruised and swollen. Her hand moved gently to the two-inch wound on his temple—it was still puffy and red, but healing. The IVs and heart monitor alarmed her, but she swallowed her fears and sat in a chair by his hospital bed. Her hand rested on his. Hers was cold, his flushed with fever.

When he awakened, he turned her way. For a moment he looked puzzled, and then his sleepy eyes brightened. "Hi. I wondered when you'd come."

"I flew in early this morning." *Does he know me? He hasn't called me by name yet. Perhaps I am just a friendly face.*

"Mom, did they tell you I might not walk again?"

Tharon shook the end of the bed. "You'll walk."

"Yes, sir." Ryan grinned. "I'm not always sure who he is, but he's a great guy. We've got to keep him around. He's been to Twisp and Winthrop. Did you know that?"

"Yes, that's where we met him."

Ryan pointed to his head. "Something in here keeps telling me we were all friends once. It's coming back slowly. Don't be upset, Mom, if I forget things. They tell me that it takes time."

She nodded. "We have plenty of time—now that you're home. I'll be here for you."

He glanced at the empty bed. "Do you have a place to stay?"

"Yes, at the Fisher House. It's just a walk away from the hospital."

If it weren't so sad, she would laugh. He was trying so hard to be hospitable, to bring up the social graces that he lacked in his boyhood. Even his grammar had seemed to improve. Had the army even stripped *ain't* out of his vocabulary?

"You're comfortable there? It's not a cheesy old hotel?" Ryan asked.

"It's a lovely place provided for the families of the military. I have an air-conditioned room to myself with rose walls and pretty draperies and two big poster beds and a desk all to myself."

"You won't go hungry."

"No, there's a community kitchen and once a week officers' wives bring in casseroles. It's all state of the art, sweetheart—and all of that for ten dollars a night. And they gave me a free phone card so I can call your grandparents and tell them how you're doing."

He frowned again—that puzzled look veiling his memory.

"Your great-grandfather is coming to visit you, Ry."

"Conaniah?"

You remembered. You remembered.

"But it's not Christmas."

Meagan grinned. "He doesn't want to wait that long."

"Will he stay with you at the Fisher House?"

"No. Robbie Gilbert, the young man who found you in Baghdad, has invited Conaniah to stay at the Winterfest Estates. Your grandfather will be treated royally."

"Mom." Ryan twirled the word around on his tongue. "I forgot how beautiful you were. How much I missed you. You're not angry with me for joining up?"

"No. I'm proud of you." And she meant it.

He ran his finger along her cheek—the way Cameron had done so long ago. "Don't cry. I know my memory will come back. But something keeps blocking the way."

Was it the armored vehicle rumbling into the palace that reminded you of your father?

"It's okay, son. We'll talk about it later. Don't upset yourself."

"I gave those Iraqis the devil for killing Dad."

Iraqis? Does he know for certain? Is he just coming to terms with the truth and needing to blame someone else? "Your dad wouldn't want revenge. He loved God too much for that."

"Maybe that's why killing them didn't make me feel any better." Ryan looked puzzled. "I made it into Baghdad. That's when I got hit—and while we were hunkered down this big thing came at us—" He was getting excited.

So was she. "An armored vehicle?"

He shuddered. "It wasn't an Abrams, Mom. It was a Bradley."

The room turned silent. The minutes ticked away. They had warned her not to prod his memory. To give him space. And she had rushed ahead.

He tapped his head. "I've been sorting the details. And this morning, I asked Dr. Michaels—I think he's a shrink—how my dad died. He told me that my dad was on a special mission—that Americans accidentally fired on him. That he was killed in his Bradley."

She nodded. "That was a long time ago."

"Not yesterday?"

Sweat dotted his forehead. The EKG monitor went erratic. He stirred restlessly in the bed. The nurse was there moments later with a reprimand scowl for the visitors and a kind smile and a sedative for Ryan. She adjusted the IV. "That should help you rest, soldier."

His fingers grew cold in Meagan's hand, his bruised hand limp.

While they waited for Ryan to awaken again, Tharon sat beside her—neither of them speaking.

When Ryan came to this time, he studied them both. "You've been promoted, Tharon."

"Yes. They're talking about a promotion for you too, Ryan." Tharon moved to the foot of the bed.

"I'd have to sew a stripe on."

"I'd do it for you, son. I'm sure I could do it. I've had a lot of experience at the quilting club."

Tharon smiled. A proud fatherly smile. "And there may be some medals to pin on you too, Ry."

Ryan turned to Meagan. "You won't hide them this time, Mom?"

"No. I took your father's medals out of hiding just before we came here. And I brought something for you." She lifted the trumpet case.

His eyes went wide.

"I thought they were going to confiscate it at the front desk. When they put it through the metal detectors, it almost played itself." She placed the case on his lap and unsnapped the lid.

"My dad's trumpet."

"It's yours now."

He fingered it, his face bathed in a smile. "That's better than any medal, Mom."

"This one is for valor too."

CHAPTER 29

On the seventh day Ryan seemed more alert. More clearheaded. The cardiac monitor and IVs had been removed, the head of his bed elevated. His father's trumpet was pressed to his lips and the sweet notes of "Out of the Ivory Palaces" filled the room.

Meagan gazed at her son and saw Cameron as he looked that first time she heard him play his trumpet at the school prom. "You're playing your father's favorite song."

He grinned—Cameron's grin. "Yeah."

She felt lightheaded, faint.

Ryan's grin spread from ear to ear as he looked at her. "My lungs may split my cast, but otherwise, it's good exercise. Maybe it's sending oxygen to my brain. They're threatening to move me to another room unless I quit making so much noise."

Tharon nodded his approval. "You really make that instrument talk. And you pulled one on me, didn't you? You never even mentioned—"

"I didn't think I played well enough to tell you. I kept practicing. It was my secret. Mine and Mrs. Bowers." A frown knit between his brows. "We lived with Mrs. Bowers, didn't we?"

"Yes, she sent her love. She's baking cookies to mail to you."

"Can she still see to read the recipe?"

"Not well, but, Ryan darling, how did you learn to play so well?"

"I learned at school, Mom. I didn't learn much else." He patted the trumpet. "This is a great instrument. I did so well that my music teacher got me a loaner from the hand-me-downs at school.

I knew you frowned on me playing the trumpet, so a couple of those times when I ditched school, I practiced down by the river. I timed it so I'd be back at school in time to catch the school bus home."

"Your father would be so pleased."

"That I ditched school?"

"No, that you play so well."

"My music teacher said I was a natural. Then I figured I needed my own instrument . . . Mom, do you remember the time I borrowed money from old lady Bowers?"

"Stole, you mean? And it's Mrs. Bowers to you, dear."

"Yeah."

The old familiar *yeah*. It made her smile.

"I was too big for you to tan, but you piled on the time-outs and took away my privileges."

"The game you wanted to play in that Saturday, for one."

"It's okay. You tried so hard to get me to tell you where the money was. You ended up bailing me out that time too. You see, Mom, I spent money on a beat-up old trumpet of my own. When she found out why I needed the money, Mrs. Bowers let me keep my trumpet at her place." His eyes shone as he held up his father's shiny trumpet. "This makes me feel close to my dad. That's why I can play it so well."

"You've grown up, Ryan."

"No, I just started figuring things out for myself." He nodded at Tharon, the puzzled look on his face returning. "I lie here in this stupid hospital bed, trying to figure out why the colonel here was so important to me. I realize now he wanted me to take responsibility. One of the first things he did was drag me back to old lady Bowers."

"Mrs. Bowers to you, sweetheart."

"I told her I'd taken her horse more than once. You know what she said? She told me the old nag needed riding. She'd known the truth all along, but she loved me too much to tell on me. As far as she was concerned, I'd square away one day. But Tharon made me work out the wrong. She was pretty quick to come up with a lot of projects, but Tharon here worked right beside me. It was his way of bailing me out."

There was so much Meagan hadn't known . . . about how much Tharon Marsh had cared for Ryan.

"My way of helping you to take on responsibility," Tharon added. "And I liked working side by side with you."

The fog lifted from Ryan's eyes again. "And do you remember that time, Mom, when I came home with a black eye and bloody nose and told you I'd run into a school prop?"

"Tharon didn't . . ." Meagan glared at Tharon.

"No, Mom. Tharon made me face up to a bully—the leader of the gang. He made us fight it out. Bare fists. I didn't win. It was a draw. But after that—even though you never believed me—I didn't need to sneak behind the school to smoke pot or sip beer."

Her voice was soft. "You grew up in spite of me."

"No, I grew up loved by you. I always wanted you to be proud of me. In fact, yesterday I got my first invitation to play Dad's trumpet in public."

"Where? When? At the hospital chapel?"

"No, Mom. For Robbie Gilbert's wedding. He's the guy who found me—probably the one who saved my life."

"That will be at the Winterfest Estates. That's where your grandfather will stay."

"When I get my first pass from this lockdown, Robbie asked me to spend it there."

She kept glancing at her watch. Robbie was scheduled to pick Conaniah up at the airport and drive him to Walter Reed. Maybe he had missed the plane. Maybe he was too tired to come for a visit.

"Are you anxious to leave, Mom?"

"No, I was expecting company."

"Can't be Tharon. He's already here." Ryan lifted the trumpet and played again.

She closed her eyes to hide the tears. How long she had

deprived him of this moment. Cameron was right. Their son would love music—just as his father had.

On the tenth day of Ryan's stay at Walter Reed, Meagan dozed in her chair and awakened to the silence of the trumpet and the sound of the television news station in Ryan's room. "This is Robinson Gilbert, reporting for the last time from Baghdad, where freedom is never free."

She sat up. "Ryan, that's Robbie's father."

"I know. Robbie's proud of that guy."

Robinson's voice remained steady. He looked older, weary. The colored television highlighted the silver in his hair, the blue of his eyes. His voice seemed deeper, baritone.

The war is officially over, but the battle is not won. Normalcy cannot be restored as long as the war on terrorism is ongoing. Victory comes village by village. Street by street. Inch by inch. The winning of one Iraqi at a time.

"Water and electricity are still out in parts of Baghdad. People are hungry, but the coalition forces cannot guarantee the safety of the supply lines. As long as our men and women are stationed in this country, they face danger.

"Last night my cameraman and I went on patrol with a platoon of Army Rangers. Thirty-two of America's finest. These men had slept during the day in 109 degree heat. Walked in 130 degrees, in full dress.

"It was unbearable inside the Bradley with my Kevlar helmet on. Yet these men patrol night after night. We rode in the Bradley, forging ahead in the dark, searching for our objective. The officers read maps with dirt flying in their faces. The soldiers waited with their rifles ready.

"America, the men are tired. Longing for home. Yet there's bravery here. Soldiers committed to a task. They believe in what they're doing. These men carried their M-16s; I carried my water canteen and a laptop.

"I will not show the footage my cameraman took today. Our men came under fire. One of them died. Freedom is never free.

"When we got back, a chaplain met us. Eight of our platoon joined him in a circle there on the desert sands of Iraq and prayed. How ironic. Here, in Iraq, no one tried to stop them.

"As they settle down to sleep in the heat of the day, they talk of home as they ease their bloody, blistered feet out of their boots. They dream of home and taking showers more than once a week. I look for the last time at this platoon and know that some of them will never go home.

"They argue about football scores. Talk of homemade cooking. They joke about sending out for pizza. They talk about campfires in Yellowstone. Of being home for an anniversary or a kid's birthday or a sister's wedding or the birth of a first child. They boast of the children left behind, of the wives waiting for them. They joke about tent mice and the sand. They speak of the schoolroom that they were able to ready for the children in a village north of Baghdad. They talk about the Iraqi home they helped to clear so the family could move back in. They talk of home, always of home, but the only way home is by defending Baghdad or going on another night patrol.

"We do not say good-bye. But I will carry the memory of their faces home with me. We shake hands and I set out for my more comfortable hotel room, confident that I will have enough water for a shower.

"On the way back to the hotel, I took my last walk on the streets of Baghdad. A soldier was kneeling by the door of an Iraqi home—one hand on his M-16, the other soothing the fur of a little kitten. At mail call, a soldier from last night's patrol lifted the letter to his nose and smiled. He was wearing a wedding band and that perfumed touch of home had reached him deep inside. Just before I reached my hotel to pack, another soldier leaned down to a young Iraqi child. He must have said, 'Give me five,' for the two clasped palms together. The friend beside him cradled another Iraqi child and cried.

"Are we winning? Not yet. Perhaps not tomorrow. The journey

will be long. But I am among the fortunate. I'm going home. I'm heading home for my son's wedding.

"This is the way I see it across the world from you. This is Robinson Gilbert, reporting for the last time from Baghdad. While I am gone, I will miss the companionship and camaraderie and courage of our men and women in uniform."

It was after lunchtime when Robbie Gilbert and Chaplain Wainwright joined them.

Relieved, Meagan stood up. "Robbie, I thought—"

There was no need to finish her question. Roberto, the young Italian caretaker, was already pushing the old man into Robbie's room. Without any sense of safety, Roberto did wheelies with Conaniah's wheelchair. Meagan blew Conaniah a kiss, feeling both joy and sadness at the sight of him.

He wore the gauntness of the aged and the familiar tweed jacket, shirt, and tie. His face was more wrinkled, his cheeks hollow. Yet his presence commanded attention. Ryan turned his head at the commotion.

Would he recognize Conaniah?

Conaniah leaned forward. The veins on the back of his hands bulged as he gripped the arms of the wheelchair and squinted at his great-grandson. Were those tears in his eyes? No, they were red-rimmed rheumy eyes, another onslaught of his aging.

The nurse was at Ryan's bedside at once. "Private Juddman. You must not overexert yourself."

Ryan rubbed his head. "Mom, I'm not sure how I got here."

"You're at Walter Reed hospital." The nurse fussed over him. "You were wounded, Private. You arrived here ten days ago."

"Did my friends get out?"

"I'm not certain." She pointed to Robbie. "This young man found you."

Conaniah coughed. "Don't fuss over him, Nurse. I might not

331

live long enough to shake his hand if you don't leave us alone."

As she walked away frowning, the old man wheeled himself closer to Ryan. "Well, you old scalawag. You wouldn't come to see me, so I came to see you." Conaniah's words were gruff, but there was a twinkle in his frosty blue eyes.

Ryan tried to sit up. The partial body cast restrained him. "Gramps."

"One and the same. I'm still alive."

A crooked grin spread over Ryan's face. "So am I."

"Your grandparents sent their love."

"Which ones?"

"All four of them. They're anxious to come as soon as you're better. I couldn't risk waiting—I'm getting too old."

"I've been to war and back, Gramps."

"So have I, Ryan. At long last I am really home from the Anzio beachhead."

Ryan nodded toward Conaniah. "Chaplain, this is my great-grandfather. Lieutenant Conaniah Xavier Juddman," he added with a twinkle. "I used to visit him when I was a boy. He's a soldier too. Just about my favorite warrior."

The chaplain reached out his hand to Conaniah. "Welcome back, soldier."

Chaplain Wainwright had thought to excuse himself, but there was something special going on in this room. A young soldier was being drawn from his mental abyss. He took note of the old man—the old soldier in the wheelchair—and saw a clear resemblance to the young patient in the hospital bed.

Conaniah met the chaplain's glance. "Chaplain, could I have a word with you?"

"Of course."

"Not here, sir. Privately." The old man's voice was a low growl.

Roberto reached out to push Conaniah from the room. "No, Roberto, I want to be alone with the chaplain . . . I'll be back, Ryan. Don't send out for pizza without me."

"Will we talk about the Anzio beachhead when you come back, Gramps?"

"No, son. We'll talk about you getting well."

The chaplain pushed Conaniah to the hospital chapel. He arranged the wheelchair so he could face him. "Now what is it that I can do for you, Mr. Juddman?"

"I'm an old man."

"Are you?"

"If you have to ask that, you're as blind as I am. But the last few days—before I knew that Ryan made it out safely, I told God I'd do anything if Ryan lived to come home again."

The chaplain had heard it many times. Promises in a desperate moment. He nodded.

"I'm . . . I'm an old reprobate. I lied to God when I almost drowned at the Rapido River. And then I lied to Him again back in the foxhole in Anzio."

The chaplain held his breath. *So this was one of the men who'd suffered, yet survived, the Italian campaign. And he was still carrying the burden of Anzio and the Rapido.*

"But I want to keep my word to Him this time," Conaniah went on. "I just don't know how to do it."

The chaplain leaned closer. "Could you be more specific?"

"You won't let me off easy, will you?"

"Not if your soul is at stake. And I daresay I think that's why we're sitting here together."

Conaniah's knuckles blanched as he gripped the chaplain's hand. "I promised Him I'd serve Him the rest of my life—if . . ." The old man's voice trailed. The vessels in his neck bulged.

"If your great-grandson came home safely?" the chaplain prodded.

"Sounds foolish now. There's not much life left in me."

"You're wrong, Mr. Juddman. All God wants is all of you now."

Tears reached the rheumy eyes. The proud old codger sat ramrod-straight, twisting the sleeve of his tweed jacket with gnarled fingers. "I'm not certain how to do that, sir."

Chaplain Wainwright had come to Walter Reed to serve the wounded. In the last few days it had been overwhelming. Young soldiers without limbs, with long-term injuries. Some angry at God. The man in front of him had also been wounded—a long time ago, on the Anzio beachhead.

Go gently, Wainwright. Go gently. This old man is sitting in the vestibule of heaven.

The chaplain flipped open his Bible. "There was another man once who wanted to know how to find peace." He pointed to a page. "Here, Mr. Juddman. I want you to read this out loud. This is about that man."

Conaniah squinted. "Nicodemus? That Pharisee?!" He spat out the name.

The chaplain drew back. He didn't want to lose this man. Time for Conaniah Juddman was running out. "Then you are familiar with the story?"

"I read that Book through more than once—just to please my grandson Cameron. Had a bit of trouble sorting out the prophets and apostles. But I could name the judges, good and bad. Spent plenty of time reading that Book. It never took. It was literary in places. Kind of gruesome in others."

"This is neither literary or gruesome, Mr. Juddman. Would you read it please?"

The old man pushed the Bible away. "The eyes aren't that good, Chaplain. Could you do the honors?"

"Of course. It says, 'For God so loved the world . . .'"

The old man's shoulders shook. Parkinson's? No, this was not a physical defect. It was a spiritual turning.

The chaplain rather imagined that Conaniah Juddman was about to make peace with God. He read on, his voice stronger, bolder. "'. . . that He gave His one and only Son.'"

"Cut to the quick, Chaplain. Read that part about me."

The chaplain controlled his smile. "That whoever believes in Him shall not perish."

"That's it. My grandson Cameron—Ryan's daddy—used to tell me that I was part of that whoever." The tremor moved to the old man's voice. "Was he telling me the truth, Chaplain?"

Their eyes locked.

"Yes, he was telling you the truth."

"Does it include old reprobates?"

"Everyone."

"Does it include old soldiers who hated war?"

"Everyone."

"Does it include a lieutenant who couldn't keep his men alive at the Rapido crossing?"

"Everyone."

"I've been bitter against the Creator."

"That's between you and Him."

"Can He make me clean, Chaplain?"

Chaplain Wainwright patted the old man's arm. "Whiter than snow, Conaniah. Whiter than snow." He paused, smiled. "Conaniah, God has stilled your storm to a whisper. I can see it in your eyes. And He will take you into a safe harbor."

"Heaven?"

"When the time comes, Lieutenant."

"Haven't been called that for sixty years, Chaplain."

Conaniah bowed his head, silent for a moment. The chaplain watched him move his lips, as if in prayer. Then the old man looked up and brushed a tear from his eyes. "Oh, how I wish the trumpeter could know that the old reprobate is almost Home."

"The trumpeter, Mr. Juddman?"

"My grandson, Cameron. Ryan's daddy. The one who kept talking to me about God. He died in the last Gulf War."

"Then he's safely Home."

"I know he is! He may even be blowing a trumpet up there." Conaniah shouted the words. "Now I know for certain I will see him again. But does Cameron know I'm coming?"

"I don't know heaven's intricacies or quite how things happen there, but if your grandson doesn't know at this moment, he will know one day."

The wrinkled face glowed. "All these years I grieved that I would never see Cameron again and now I will."

As joy registered on the old man's face, Chaplain Wainwright's own faith mushroomed. He had just witnessed a modern-day Nicodemus finding his way to peace.

His beeper interrupted. He checked it and stood. "They've just admitted some more of our boys from Iraq. Shall I wheel you back to your family before I see them?"

"Will you, kind sir? I must tell them what happened to me."

CHAPTER 30

On day thirteen, no one had to tell Robbie that something good had happened to Conaniah Juddman. He saw it in the old man's face and smiled to himself. Good things were coming thick and fast. Whatever happened in Ryan's long time of healing would have God's stamp of approval on it.

He gripped Conaniah's hand and noted that the old man's grip felt stronger. "I have to leave, Conaniah. I'm meeting my dad."

"Then he's back from Baghdad?"

"Yes, and safely. I have an appointment at the newspaper office, so Dad's going with me. But you'll meet him at dinner when we get back to Winterfest."

Conaniah nodded toward the young Italian by the window. "Roberto is crazy about Winterfest. He thinks your Adrienne is beautiful—like his Teresa."

"And I'm looking forward to going to Winterfest to get away from these four hospital walls," Ryan announced. "I get my first pass out of here in a month."

The nurse cocked her head. "*If* you continue to make progress in physical therapy."

O'Sullivan's newspaper conglomerate was worldwide, but this local display of power was larger than Robbie expected. It stretched a full city block and a half, with several impressive buildings and the warehouses in the rear.

"You're sure you don't want to go in with me, Dad?"

His father smirked. "Let's just say O'Sullivan and I are not the best of friends. Been known to cut you down with a smile."

"Thanks for warning me. O'Sullivan put off seeing me until today. Kind of a control freak, I think, although the paper seemed pleased with my work."

"I reserve judgment. Just hold your own."

"If you've had run-ins, I'd better not admit I'm your son."

"You're your own man all right. I'll just pace the sidewalk until you get back. I'd chew on a cigar except I don't smoke." He pointed toward the main building.

Robbie ran up the dozen steps with diminishing confidence. *O'Sullivan has to be a definite media heavyweight*. He stopped at the reception desk. "I'm Robbie Gilbert. I have an appointment with O'Sullivan."

The receptionist lifted one brow. "I wouldn't call her that when you see her. But go on up. She's waiting for you."

"*Her*? She?"

"Yes, *Catherine* O'Sullivan."

He tried to swallow his surprise. "A woman runs this paper? The masthead says C. R. O'Sullivan."

"C. R., yes, but a capable woman. Don't cross her. She could blackball your career in several countries. We tread lightly around here." She looked amused now, eyes twinkling. "I've been around for fifteen years and, Mr. Gilbert, we liked your work in Baghdad."

"Did *she*?"

"She'll soon let you know."

"Could you direct me?"

"I just did." She grinned. "But go to the next floor. At the far end of the building. I'll let her know you're here."

He made his way down the wide corridor, peering in the rooms as he went. A swank paneled boardroom, empty at the moment. An employee lounge with comfortable sofas and chairs. The other

cubicles were crammed with reporters—answering phones, screaming orders, clacking away on their computers. The newsroom
sounded like a madhouse as well, a massive room cluttered with
computers and desks. He found O'Sullivan's plush office at the end
of the hall and almost collided with a dark-haired young man with
a camera slung over one shoulder.

"*Mi dispiace.*"

Robbie took a second to regain his composure, then peered in
through the open door. O'Sullivan was sitting on the edge of her
mahogany desk, scanning the headliner, pink-rimmed glasses in
her hand. She appeared well into her fifties—and powerful, confident, and attractive in a mature way. Yet her cheeks were flushed,
as though the man who had left her office had angered her, robbed
her momentarily of self-control.

For a second Robbie couldn't remember what her first name
was. Well, small matter. Taking his clue from the man who had just
made his exodus, Robbie knew this woman was to be handled with
kid gloves and demanded respect. "Mrs. O'Sullivan."

"Robbie Gilbert."

He heard the catch in her voice. A flicker—of pain, despair—
seemed to engulf her as her eyes misted. Then she lowered her
lashes and glanced down at the diamond watch on her narrow
wrist. "Right on time. I like that."

There was a strange scent in the room—not papers or must.
Nothing to do with the smell of newsprint, but a tantalizing aroma
like the scent of a Hawaiian lei after the rain.

Her clothes were tasteful, professional, and yet the long sleeves
of her silk blouse were folded back above her wrists. Her skin was
weathered from too much sun. Her eyes, framed in skin creases,
were dark, impressive—and watching him.

He did a quick survey of the room and its occupant. Her desk
was covered with paperwork in organized piles. A box of nutritional bars—looking less appealing than his MRE rations—and an
open can of Slim-Fast sat on the blotter. Several phone directories
and dictionaries were stacked by her desk, the top one readily

available. She seemed calm, unperturbed by the phones ringing or voices in the corridor. Her hair was short and graying, but not a strand out of place as she sized him up.

He did the same. She was a woman of average height, but he was only guessing, since she didn't stand to greet him. Again he caught the floral scent and tried to place it. Lilacs? Carnations? No, plumeria. A scent of perfume. It stirred a childhood memory—a woman leaning over his bed, tucking him in. A woman dressed for the evening out—dabbing perfume behind her ear.

"Do I pass your inspection, Mr. Gilbert?"

"Do I pass yours?" he fired back.

"You're taller than I expected. Thinner."

"I lost fifteen pounds crossing the desert."

"Were you ill?"

He glanced at her nutritional bars. "No, hungry for a decent meal."

"You mentioned a project on the phone." Again she checked her watch. "We have about fifteen minutes."

He wasn't certain how a woman would respond to his project. "I've been working on some articles on the boys coming home from Iraq—some who didn't come home. I was wondering if—"

"If I would publish them? They'd have to be good."

"I am good, O'Sullivan."

"I don't like being called by my last name. My competitors do so. My friends do not. So you can call me Catherine—my close friends do and those few employees who feel comfortable doing so. But I agree with you. Your work from Iraq was commendable. I rather imagine you've learned the trade from your father."

"He said you knew each other."

She laughed, a deep amused chuckle. "I suppose you could call it that. You're tall like your father. It was difficult to tell when you aired the evening news. Sometimes you were sitting. And always in camouflage dress with your helmet on. It ruined the perspective."

He was blunt. "It saved my life."

"Thank you for your good work in Iraq."

"Thank you for sending me."

"I like your work, Gilbert. I'm prepared to offer you a perma-nent job as a reporter on my paper."

"At the bottom rung?"

"All of my reporters start at the bottom rung."

"Not this journalist. I've worked my way up the ladder already as an investigative reporter."

"I know. I've seen some of your work."

If he was expecting another compliment, it was not forthcom-ing. "I want to go back to my post in Washington."

"If you ever change your mind—you did a good job for us."

"I still can't figure out how you knew about me."

She allowed a slight smile. "Rumors get around."

"I rather imagine it is something more specific than that." Still, he was puzzled.

"Let's just say I owe you one . . ." She snatched up the jangling phone. "Catherine O'Sullivan," she snapped, "and this better be important." She covered the mouthpiece and, with a quick wave of her slender jeweled hand, dismissed him. "Leave your portfolio with me, Gilbert. I'll get back to you on those articles."

"When?"

She raised her pencil-thin brows. "After I read them."

His dad was waiting for Robbie when he reached the curbside. "How did it go, Son? What did you think of her?" his father asked.

Robbie opened the car door and got in. "You didn't tell me O'Sullivan was a woman. She's tough, but under it all she's very attractive. Ladylike. Efficient."

"My exact description. But how could you tell that on such a brief visit?"

"It's all the time she allowed me. Dad, I think I just met that photographer friend of yours from Baghdad."

"Don't tell me. Let me guess. De Nuccio. Friend? Hardly."

Robbie rubbed his shoulder. "Yeah, Ricardo de Nuccio. He was leaving as I arrived. Almost knocked me over."

"I questioned his credentials, so don't tell me he works for O'Sullivan."

"I'll pass on that one. But it was clear they'd met before. He strutted out with a brash smile on his face. Confident. Arrogant. She was flushed when I walked in, but I don't think she plans to put him on the guest list for her next Washington bash."

"Will you make the party, Robbie?"

"Not likely. But, Dad, O'Sullivan offered me a job."

"Did she now?" He reached up and adjusted his hearing aid. "You did say she offered you a job?"

"She said she owed me one."

A tick started at the corner of his father's mouth and worked its way up his jaw. "She did."

"So, Dad, did you beg her to send me to Iraq as an embed?"

His answer came out in a baritone whisper. "No one tells O'Sullivan what to do. But this time she came through for me."

"Dad—she's my mother, isn't she?"

Robinson ran both hands through his silver hair. "I should have told you long ago."

"But her last name—it's different."

"It's her maiden name. *Gilbert* wasn't good enough for her. Her father was a powerhouse newspaperman. She rode to success on his coattail—but she's good."

"I asked you in Baghdad, but I'll ask you again. What happened between you and O'Sullivan, Dad?"

Silence. Finally Robinson explained, "Her fiancé was in Vietnam with me just before the war ended. She loved him. Planned to marry him. He never came home again."

"You were second fiddle?"

"I was a shoulder to cry on. But, Son, Catherine and I cared about each other very much."

"Not enough to stay together."

"Our ambitions drove us apart. It was difficult for me to settle down. Impossible for Catherine."

"A long time ago I decided that if I ever met her, I'd tell her what I thought of her. But she commands respect. She's graceful. Feminine."

"Did you ask her how high to jump, Robbie? I used to."

"She never raised her voice once. I laid out my plans on her desk. She gave me fifteen minutes to convince her I was good. Then her phone rang and she dismissed me."

"You'll hear from her again."

"But it's unlikely I'll work for her again. Hey, Dad, we're going to get a parking ticket if we don't get going."

His father stopped tapping the steering wheel, turned the key in the ignition, and drove off toward Winterfest.

"For a year after she left us, you used to wake up crying for her."

"I don't remember."

"I'm glad. I wanted to be enough for you."

"You've been everything I ever needed."

They sped along the expressway, heading for the Virginia side.

"What did she think of your articles?" his father asked.

"She said she'd get back to me on them."

"When?"

"After she reads them."

His father sighed. "I hated that about her—always having the final round."

"If O'Sullivan turns them down, I'll try someone else—but tell me, what would you think if I invited her to my wedding?"

"Your call, Son."

"Do you think she'd come?"

"You can never outguess Catherine—all you can do is live in her shadow."

AUGUST 2003

Spring had slipped into summer. And summer into the glorious days of August. Tharon Marsh sat on the balcony at Winterfest overlooking the wooded hills, a frosty glass of lemonade in his hand. He stole a favorable glance at his hostess sitting beside him and knew why Robbie had fallen in love with Adrienne Winters.

Adrienne was twenty-eight, a beautiful woman as stylish and gracious as the fashion world in which she worked. She had been born into wealth and position and was mistress of this vast Winterfest estates since her father's death, and yet seemingly unaffected by the power and privileges that wealth had brought her. When she spoke her voice was soft and Southern, and her smile was full of charm and gentleness.

"Adrienne, I want to thank you for all you and Robbie have done for Meg's son. For *all* of us, for that matter."

"We've enjoyed being part of your lives . . . Robbie says it's going better between you and Meagan."

Tharon took a long swallow of lemonade, then placed the frosty glass against his cheek. "We've spent considerable time together at Ryan's bedside. Ryan is quite subtle, but I think he's trying to match us up. Meg has mellowed with his efforts."

"And will anything come of your relationship—before you go back overseas?"

"If I have my way, it will. Meg said last evening that God is helping her get over the hurdle of who I am. I never planned to fall in love with her, Adrienne. It just happened. The more important she became to me, the harder it was to tell her that I was on the battlefield when her husband died. That I gave the order to fire."

"And Robbie told me you gave the order to stop firing."

Tharon sighed. "It was too late by then."

Adrienne's mahogany eyes were compassionate. "I hope it's not too late for you and Meagan. You seem so right for each other."

"You've done your best—inviting Meg and me to do things with you and Robbie. I think we'll take you up on that invitation to go horseback riding on those trails of yours. Meagan and I can come over early. She'll want a docile animal. She's actually an excellent rider, but she's exhausted these days. It's hard to pry her away from Ryan's bedside."

"Quite understandable. I can't guarantee a docile mount, but we'll saddle the Tennessee Walkers for you. But, Tharon, make certain you come to my wedding. That might put ideas of marriage into Meagan's head. I have a feeling they are already on your mind."

Embarrassed, Tharon lowered his eyes. "We've been grateful that you put Conaniah and Roberto up while they were here."

"Roberto has been a help to the gardeners, and Conaniah has been a treasure to have around. Mother—Mara—understands him. They sit out there in the gardens in their wheelchairs, solving the world's problems like they're doing right now. But he insists on leaving and going back to Kansas soon."

"He's happier in his own place. Once Robbie is well he plans to visit Conaniah—if the old man lives that long."

"I've liked having the old soldier around. He talked about Anzio and Becky the whole time. Why didn't he marry her?"

"She died on the Anzio beachhead."

"I didn't know. War does crazy things, doesn't it? The battle for Iraqi freedom—the war on terrorism—has captured my attention. My heart. I can't turn a blind eye to what's happening and hide in my fashion world. Oh, I love fashion—love what I'm doing but . . ."

He waited.

Her attention never wavered. "Just seeing how much being at Winterfest meant to Conaniah set me to thinking about the future. We're working out plans now to make Winterfest available to others. Always before it was our secluded haven from the pressures outside our perimeter. But walking into Walter Reed . . . Getting acquainted with Ryan and watching his slow progress, his determination to walk again. His groping to remember everything . . . And Robb, who put his whole life on the line, our wedding even, to accompany a unit of soldiers into Baghdad. These things are changing me, Tharon."

She turned her pretty face away from him, but not before he saw the tears in her eyes. "One of the young men in the unit Robb traveled with never made it to Baghdad. He was killed en route, leaving behind a pregnant widow. Robb told me he had to find that soldier's widow and asked me to go with him. We drove to West Virginia one weekend to meet her."

He laid his hand on hers. "You don't have to tell me."

"Oh, but I do, so you'll understand the plans I have for Winter-fest. When Jared's widow opened the door, Robb explained very quietly, respectfully, 'I'm Robbie Gilbert—and this is my fiancée. I was with your husband when he died.'"

Tears fell afresh from Adrienne's gorgeous eyes. "He opened his arms and with that big belly of hers she collapsed into them. And I knew that somehow we would be there with her when the baby came."

"You're a remarkable woman, Adrienne."

"No, a wealthy woman. My grandfather Harrison invested wisely—not just a thick portfolio, but he bought up land in Virginia and Maryland and in upstate New York. Winterfest was his home, but his land investments were legendary. But more than that, Tharon, for some reason God in His great kindness saw fit to bless this family with worldly goods . . . It was always my grandfather's wish to keep possession of the land on the Winters' side of the family. But Mother is well provided for. Always will be. And Robbie loves the land as much as I do."

"Robbie is a lucky man."

She shook her head. "No, Tharon, I'm the lucky one. I've learned so much from Robbie. He's so steadfast in everything he does, particularly in his pursuit of God's pleasure. Watching him, learning from him, sharing with him, I'm just beginning to under-stand that 'to whom much is given, much is required.'"

"I still say you're remarkable."

"Then you don't really know me. I was a spoiled child. Never lacked for a thing. Robbie was casual, content with what life sent his way. When I first met him in Paris, he was carting his Bible around in his school rucksack. It embarrassed me back then. But now I know where he was coming from. His great strengths. Robb is good for me, Tharon."

"Then why didn't you elope the minute he got back from Iraq?"

"Robbie needed time to rest. It was Rolf and my mother who insisted that he close out his apartment and move to Winterfest. For the last two months we've spent the evenings playing Scrabble or waltzing in our stocking feet. Sometimes we sat like a couple of old fogies in Mara and Rolf's easy chairs, just listening to classical music or sitting by the fireplace reading."

"You had a fire going on those hot summer months?"

"Yes, it seemed to comfort Robbie. Tell me, Tharon. Have you asked Meagan to marry you?"

"No, not yet."

"I see. But, foolish man, you need each other," she advised. "Are you going to let what happened back in the Gulf War keep you apart forever?"

"It's friendly fire that keeps us apart."

"No, it's how Cameron died that keeps troubling you. I think Meagan has a greater capacity for love and forgiveness than you give her credit for."

"She'll be going back to Twisp—to her quiet life there."

"Not if you propose. Not if you get married."

"You have more confidence in our relationship than I do."

Adrienne smiled. "Since I've known Robbie, I've become more of a romantic. Promise me, Tharon, you won't let her go back to Twisp until you have talked this out."

He covered his doubts with an argument. "It's unlikely Meagan would give up her career and move here to Washington."

"You mean it's unlikely that she would want to be a soldier's wife again. If she stayed on here in Washington, she could help me with the Winterfest projects."

"She's not a gardener."

"But she has a heart for people," Adrienne insisted. "I've watched her there at Walter Reed befriending some of the families. Encouraging them. That's what we'd be doing here at Winterfest. We are in touch with Chaplain Wainwright at the hospital. We want to set up day outings and miniconcerts for the families."

"At Winterfest?"

"Yes. Lunch in the gardens and music for some of those families who are not certain their loved one will ever be well again. Classical or jazz concerts. Or sacred music."

"And when winter comes?" Tharon asked.

"We'd move inside the estate. It would just be a family or two at a time. Never more than fifteen or twenty. Rolf wants to extend it to cover some of the walking wounded who could get all-day passes from Walter Reed or Bethesda."

"Meagan would love to be part of something like that."

"It's still in the planning stages, but we've had positive responses at the hospital. We've already had families here twice, and Rolf and Mara will continue while Robbie and I are on our honeymoon."

"You'll run out of funds."

"Not likely."

"But some publicity on your endeavor might be helpful."

"Yes, but we're not set up like a Fisher House for housing accommodations. It would just be a brief reprieve for the men and women and their families who have given so much in Iraq."

"You are a remarkable woman," Tharon murmured again.

"No, just a woman 'of whom much is required.'" She glanced at her watch, and they stood at the same time. "I guess I won't see you until the wedding Saturday. Robbie is eager for you and Meagan to be there."

Tharon gave Adrienne a quick, spontaneous hug, then stood back. "We'll see you then."

EPILOGUE

It was a glorious Saturday, with billowy clouds skipping and dancing in a sky of peacock blue. August at Winterfest—at least this particular August morning—broke with a brilliant sun sweeping the haze and dew away.

Tharon Marsh surveyed the Winterfest Estates in much the same way as Harrison Winters must have done on the day he took possession of this sprawling acreage with its wooded hills and riding trails. The lawn sloped down to a meandering river at the foot of the bank. The pride and love of this land—an isolated world in the shadow of Washington—had passed to Harrison's heirs. Tharon hoped that when Meagan married him—*if* she married him—that it would be this kind of day, this kind of celebration with fragrant flowers blooming on the hillsides.

His gaze strayed to the gazebo in the center of the gardens that would serve as the altar for Robbie and Adrienne. Two Tennessee Walkers grazed undisturbed near the riding stables. The white stucco mansion lay spotless and polished, readied for its two hundred wedding guests—Adrienne's friends and the elite of Washington.

His gaze swept the land in the opposite direction, where caterers buzzed about setting the tables and filling the punch bowls. Tharon would give anything for a glass of punch right now to quench his thirst. He imagined that Robbie Gilbert would gladly forego all of this fuss and extravagance, and yet there was a simplicity to it all—a strange blending of Adrienne Winter's fashion world and the marvelous landscape that God had created.

349

A man could envy the owners of Winterfest. Instead, Tharon felt grateful for their friendship and marveled that he had been included in Robbie Gilbert's wedding day.

He would have ordered the two hundred folding chairs arranged closer to the fountain, so they blocked out the two head-stones that honored the former owners of Winterfest. This was Mara's arrangement, no doubt. She proved a powerful woman, but no less than her attractive daughter.

His brows arched in surprise as Adrienne stepped outside, dressed in a casual summer frock. This was the woman who worked in the fashion industry, wasn't it?

"I thought you'd be in a long white bridal gown—one you designed yourself."

"I will be." She seemed calm, unhurried. "And I did design the gown."

"I thought brides were supposed to be nervous and fluttery. You seem completely at ease."

"Wait until the ceremony. I may become the wreck Mara pre-dicts. Otherwise I'll disappoint my mother."

"I always laugh when I hear you call your mother 'Mara.'"

Adrienne's eyes grew wide with merriment. "Her preference. She's never taken to the thought of growing old. We're comfort-able with it."

"In another hour they'll be playing 'The Wedding March' as you walk down that aisle."

"No, Colonel. It will be to the tune of 'Unforgettable'—the way Nat King Cole used to sing it."

"That slid past your mother?"

"She settled for the guest list and controlling the menu for the sit-down luncheon. Robbie and I didn't care as long as we had a few special friends. That was enough." Her laughter rippled in the air. "Mother even invited the president and his wife. But if it makes her happy—" She smiled without rancor. "Bring Meagan early. The string quartet will be playing for an hour before the ceremony."

Tharon enjoyed teasing her. "Love songs?"

"Robb insists on 'Unchained Melody' and Gershwin's 'Rhapsody in Blue.'" Then she added, tongue-in-cheek, "I voted on the 'Unfinished Symphony.'"

"Schubert."

"And Strauss's 'Blue Danube.' We agreed on 'One Night in Venice.' There won't be time to play them in their entirety, but it will be such beautiful music wafting over Winterfest. Like the old days when my mother had her teas and concerts."

She shaded her eyes and looked out over the land. "It's peaceful here, isn't it? I wanted to walk through the memorial garden one more time. Would you care to walk with me, Colonel?"

"I'd be honored." Tharon offered her his arm.

"You probably don't know too much about us."

"A little. I know that your grandfather Harrison was the original owner. And then your father."

"And did you know Rolf oversaw the property for both of them? Rolf's the one who planted the gardens in memory of my brother."

"You had a brother?"

"Yes . . ." Her word dangled, trailed. Shadows crossed those brilliant eyes. "My brother's name is on the Memorial Wall at Central Intelligence."

The brother was dead, but the gardens very much alive with magnificent colors—bright vermilion, rich cadmium red, canary and sunflower yellows—all playing against the lush emerald lawn. "I've been admiring the flowers for the last half-hour. They're beautiful."

"They're vibrant like Jon was. I was out here early this morning picking a fresh bouquet for Mother's room."

"She should be picking flowers for you. You're the bride."

"But my mother needs the attention. She used to be the belle of the ball, but now she only has Winterfest. That's why we've asked the string quartet to play 'Belle of the Ball' when she's seated."

"She's ill, Robbie tells me."

"Yes, Parkinson's. She spends much of her time in the wheelchair, but every day Rolf forces her to walk with him in the garden. We're both committed to taking care of her. But don't feel sorry for us, Colonel. Mother has Rolf. I have Robbie—and the land." She bent down, plucked a rose and lifted it to his nostrils. "Tharon, my whole life is scented like this."

Tharon laughed. "When I first visited, I had the impression that Rolf was the butler."

"He was, and he has difficulty breaking away from the image. Rolf is tall and proud like my father was. Dad would be pleased to know that Rolf is still here overseeing the land. Caring for Mother . . . They haven't been married long, did you know that, Colonel?"

"Robbie mentioned it."

"Mara is happier now. I didn't think she would ever be happy, but Rolf is good for her. Sometimes he seems as old as the land. He moved here with my grandfather as confidant and helper, and he lived with us in Paris when Dad worked for the State Department."

"Will Rolf be giving you away this afternoon?"

"We planned that at first—because he's dear to me—but a friend from Paris will do the honors. Rolf needs to be with Mother during the wedding. She loves excitement, but it's not good for her."

A friend from Paris. It sounded like someone closer than a friend. There was something behind her words, something he would never know, but he accepted what she wanted to tell him and let the rest slide by. "That man with the cane and those two boys over there in tuxedos—sneaking peppermints from the reception table—who are they?"

He was sure she caught her breath before answering. "That's Jacques, the family friend I told you about, and two of his children. They'll be going back to Paris after the wedding. They can never stay long."

Something about Adrienne Winters radiated joy, mystery. "Robbie and I will join them there next week and then we'll all be together for a whole month. Jon—Jacques—and his wife want to adopt Gavin."

Jon—Jacques. Strange, Tharon thought. Adrienne had made the name change quickly, a slight flush to her cheeks. Had she spoken the words accidentally? Or was there a tie-in between Gavin and her brother?

But she went on calmly. "Gavin's the impish-looking one. Mother and Rolf have been taking care of Gavin for some time now. They will miss him dreadfully when he moves to Paris, but he'll at last have a home and family of his own."

"Is Gavin an orphan?"

"His mother is dead, his father incarcerated, his beloved grandmother, Nell, gone. That's tough for any youngster. But Jacques has five- and seven-year-olds of his own. It will be wonderful for Gavin to have a brother and sister."

She stood on her tiptoe and kissed Tharon on the cheek. "I must run and dress, or I'll be late for my own wedding . . . Thanks for being Robbie's friend, Tharon. He's never had a home of his own. Oh, condos and apartments and the rich experience of traveling with his father in several countries—but never a place of his own." Her face glowed as she looked up at him. "I've had it all my life, and now I get to share it all with Robbie."

"You're going to be a beautiful bride."

"I'm a fortunate woman, Tharon. I have always loved this land. And I love Robbie."

Rolf beckoned Tharon from the doorway. "Robinson Gilbert needs help with his bow tie and boutonnière. Right now he's kicking things about in his room. Can you help him?"

"Where?"

"Second floor, third door on the right. Approach cautiously."

Tharon took the palatial carved stairs two steps at a time and heard Robinson Gilbert swearing as he pushed the door open.

"Need help?"

"This . . . this miserable tie," Gilbert growled.

Tharon butted the door closed behind him. "I wanted to talk to you, Gilbert—"

"I'd rather go for a drive and forget this wedding. I didn't know what I was getting into when my son asked me to be his best man. Tuxedo. Didn't have one when I married Katy-did."

"Who else would Robbie ask? You're his dad, his best friend. Now stand still."

Gilbert bent his head back.

"What are your plans after the wedding?" Tharon asked as he adjusted Gilbert's tie.

"After I rest up, I'd like to go back to Iraq. This war isn't over yet, and I want to be there reporting on it."

"Would you consider a side trip first?"

"Try me."

"I can't guarantee when you could publish your findings."

Gilbert inspected himself in the mirror. "Couldn't have done better myself. So what's the scoop, Marsh?"

"You were on the right track nineteen years ago when you met Bernhard Grokov on the Italian Riviera."

"Little good it did me. Could never prove my suspicions. He can't still be alive."

"He's alive. That's as much as we know from Karl VonHoekle. The Americans are detaining VonHoekle at an unknown location. I've been asked to fly over and interview him. I'm willing to see whether I can take you along."

Interest sparked in Gilbert's eyes. "Interrogate, you mean? When do we leave?"

"The coalition is holding him as long as they can. But Germany is fighting any accusations that he's involved in terrorism or linked in any way with al-Qaeda."

Gilbert frowned. "I don't buy that one either. Grokov and his organization would still want world domination, but under a perfect, pure Aryan race. That would negate any partnership with al-Qaeda and its Islamic ties."

"Agreed. The Germans were opposed to America's intervention

in Iraq. But they don't approve of murder. If the military is forced to release him to German authorities, they'll turn him over to the Heidelberg police. At least we can get him on murder. There's evidence that VonHoekle killed his father."

"His own father?"

"They wouldn't listen to you before, Gilbert, but the FBI is far more willing to track down the source of Karl's funding. We know now that Karl VonHoekle worked with Bernard Grokov."

"I tried to warn you on 9/11, Colonel Marsh. The original dream was for the Third Reich to be in power again. Most of the SS men died off, so that never worked out. But Grokov has long led a splinter group. There might be times when they'd work with al-Qaeda, but they'd never unite with them."

"That's why we need to interrogate VonHoekle. Learn what we can. We'll only be gone two or three weeks. Then, of course, you can head back to Baghdad—unless you want a side trip to Argentina. We're certain the group that Grokov masterminded may still be there."

Gilbert raised an eyebrow. "Or maybe tucked away in an olive grove on the Riviera. I'll find them."

Tharon clapped Gilbert on the shoulder. "Brace up. We'll talk more later. We've a wedding to attend."

Tharon and Meagan were escorted to front seats where they could watch Ryan when he played the trumpet. Tharon leaned over and squeezed Meg's hand. "He's going to be fine, Meg."

"I'm not worried about Ryan. He's his father all over again. He's turned into such a fine young man." Pride in her son softened her features.

He rested his arm on the back of her chair. Touched her tawny hair. Longed for the right words to say. "Meagan, are you aware that your son has forgiven me for my involvement in his father's death?"

Tears brimmed on her lashes. "Yes. And I've forgiven you too, Tharon. It took me longer than my son, but how can I hold a grudge like that when God has been so good to me?"

"Then it's okay between us? My record is clear?"

"The memory is still there—the way Cameron died. But I do forgive you."

He leaned forward and turned her face so she was looking at him. "Meg, would you ever consider being an army wife again?"

"Me?"

"Yes, you."

"Do you mean marry you, Tharon?"

His hopes dwindled at the sound of her indignation. "I guess that's what I had in mind."

The violinists and the cellist lifted their instruments. In perfect harmony their bows touched the strings with "Unchained Melody."

"How soon would you want my answer?" she whispered.

"Take whatever time you need. I know it would be a tough decision, but I love you, Meg."

The music grew sweeter. She slipped her hand in his. "Would it be soon enough if I gave you my answer at the reception?"

"You mean today?"

"Yes, today." There was a twinkle in her eyes.

"That would be wonderful."

Her only response was a gentle squeeze of his hand, but its warmth told him her answer . . .

As the full rich notes of a trumpet echoed in the air over Winterfest, Robbie gave a thumbs-up to his friend. Ryan sat propped up in the white lawn chair with a pass from Walter Reed in his pocket and a shiny golden trumpet to his lips as he played the clear clarion call of "Savior Like a Shepherd Lead Us."

Robbie turned and winked at his dad, standing so proudly

beside him. "Thanks for everything, Dad." Then he faced his guests, waiting for his bride to come down the aisle. For just an instant his attention was diverted as his mother, the regal Catherine O'Sullivan, slipped into the last row with a young woman beside her. Now every chair was filled but two. Mara had insisted on saving chairs for President and Mrs. Bush. The thought appalled him. But glancing around again he realized that the *guests* had come. He let his gaze sweep the property. That had to be Secret Service men mingling with the caterers and sitting on the rows close to George and Laura. It would be a wedding that he and Adrienne would remember forever. One day they would tell their grandchildren that the president and his wife had attended their wedding!

At last his beautiful bride started down the aisle to the sweet strains of "Unforgettable." And she truly was unforgettable. The sun caught the radiance of her hair, the softness of her smile, as she moved with a graceful cadence on the arm of Jacques d'Hiver. As she reached the gazebo, her wide mahogany eyes sought Robbie's. His heart swelled. No one else mattered. His beloved Adrienne was *unforgettable—in every way*.

His bride—his Southern beauty—was coming to him with the faint scent of Shalimar, her complexion soft like the petal of a rose. She stirred whispers among the guests, but she was his. Even before the preacher asked him to repeat his vows, Robbie was already promising to comfort Adrienne, to cherish her with all of his heart, to love her forever.

WANT MORE SUSPENSE?

WANT MORE ROMANCE?

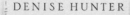

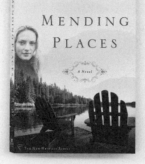

Hanna Landin's past holds her captive, but Micah Gallagher, the rugged mountain guide she hires to help the family's floundering mountain lodge, makes her wish she could move beyond it. Together Hanna and Micah face the past. But it's more horrifying than either of them feared, and Hanna faces the ultimate challenge.
ISBN:1-58229-358-9   www.denisehunterbooks.com

Welcome to Oak Plantation, an expansive rice plantation in the Old South. When the overseer's daughter, Camellia York, accidentally causes the death of the plantation owner, she is haunted by guilt. But when she finally tells the truth about what really happened in the cookhouse, she discovers a startling truth about her family's past.
ISBN: 1-58229-359-7

WANT MORE MYSTERY?

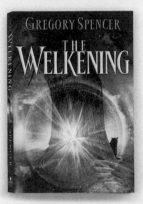

Lizbeth, Bennu, Len, and Angie are misfits who are often overlooked and ostracized. When bullies attack them, the four friends find themselves suddenly thrust into an alternative dimension—the realm of Welken. Several mysterious adventures reveal that weaknesses in their own world are powerful weapons in Welken. Unless the misfits find the courage to wield their weapons and turn the battle, Welken will fall.
ISBN: 1-58229-355-4

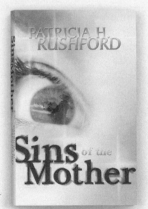

Fame has created a glimmering facade in Shanna O'Brian's world, but when the spotlight fades, even her success fails to penetrate the darkness of reality. With Shanna's ex-husband now in control of her record label, Shanna's life careens out of control. Shanna's need to reclaim possession of a life she's too often surrendered to others leads her down a path of self-discovery that is cruelly threatened by unseen forces.
ISBN: 1-58229-342-2

www.howardfiction.com

WANT MORE INTRIGUE?

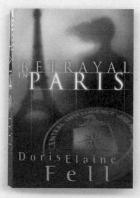

Amid the trauma of the September 11 Pentagon tragedy, twenty-seven-year-old Adrienne Winters fights to clear the names of her brother and father, who were victims of a double betrayal on foreign soil. As she pursues her quest, Adrienne discovers a gentle romance as she sorts out her family's history and her faith in God.
ISBN: 1-58229-314-7

ENJOYMENT GUARANTEE

www.howardfiction.com

About the Author

DORIS ELAINE FELL holds a BA in education, a BS in nursing, has pursued graduate studies in education, and has studied Bible and journalism at Multnomah Bible College. Christy Award finalist, 2003 SPU Medallion Award winner, 2004 Silver Angel Award, Excellence in Media (EIM), she is the author of seventeen novels, two nonfiction books, and articles in mainstream and inspirational publications. Her multifaceted career has taken her across the world and has inspired a six-book Seasons of Intrigue series, as well as *Blue Mist on the Danube* and *Willows on the Windrush*. She now lives in Southern California.